Slip from Sight

Maggie Sloan Thriller, Book 6

Judith A. Barrett

Slip from Sight

Maggie Sloan Thriller, Book 6

Published in the United States of America by Wobbly Creek, LLC

2023 Georgia

wobblycreek.com

Cover by Wobbly Creek, LLC

ISBN 978-1-953-87030-8

Slip from Sight is dedicated to the colors gray and brown and especially old, brown dogs with gray muzzles like Lucy.

PREVIOUSLY...

My name is Maggie Sloan Ewing; my tall, blue-eyed husband is Larry Ewing; his original name was Kevin, but he's become so accustomed to being called Larry that he claims Kevin is his undercover name.

Larry; Lucy, our sweet, old, brown German short-haired pointer; the imaginary men, Palace Guard and Spike; and I are in Tennessee while Larry attends crime scene specialist training for his new position with the Georgia Bureau of Investigation. I am excited that we're here because Larry has always wanted to investigate the technical aspect of crime scenes.

You might have noticed I mentioned "imaginary men." There's a long story behind that, but the short version is I was severely injured several years ago by a massive explosion in the library where I worked as I hurried to tell my boss to get out of the building; the force of the blast tossed me across the lawn, almost to the parking lot.

Palace Guard and Spike helped me when I struggled with physical therapy then stayed with me after I left the hospital. Palace Guard ran with me to build up my strength and taught me how to throw a knife; Spike toughened me up and taught me how to cheat.

Lucy originally lived with Kate Coyle, my best friend who taught me how to cook, shoot, and fight. Her parents, Jennifer and Glenn, have become my safety net.

My severe injury days weren't quite behind me, though; after I caught a custo-
dian at a senior center in the act of replacing valuable jewelry with fake, the jewel
thief sprayed my face with a powerful alkaline cleaning solution. The surgeon
couldn't save my left eye but has hopes my right eye will eventually heal enough
that I'll have at least partial sight which will be an improvement over the blurriness
I have now. One positive side effect of my loss of vision is that my sense of hearing
has become extremely sensitive, probably to compensate for my sight limitations,
but that's enough about dreary medical stuff.

I don't know why it didn't occur to a serial killer that a young, petite woman
with only one eye and limited sight, at best, in the other eye would stop him from
killing her and her friend, but with Palace Guard's help to guide my aim, I did.

CHAPTER ONE

Larry burst into the apartment and snatched me off the ground. He nuzzled my neck and whispered, "Don't hurt me when I set you down."

When I laughed, he kissed my open mouth and kicked the door closed behind him. After an incredibly passionate kiss, he said, "Let's celebrate by going out to dinner. Wear something fancy, like your sparkly eye patch."

I covered my mouth with my hand as a barrier to another ambush kiss when I giggled. "Sounds great; do I have a sparkly eye patch? What are we celebrating?"

"I've finished the ten weeks of training, but I have two more weeks of school; most importantly, there isn't another bad guy around here to kidnap, wound, maim, or kill you."

Palace Guard smacked his own forehead, Spike put his hands around his own neck and pretended to strangle himself, and Lucy growled in her sleep.

Larry frowned. "Yeah, that was a rookie mistake: I shouldn't taunt any possible killers."

"Why are we celebrating two more weeks of school? Are you taking classes for a certification?"

"Exactly; I'll have chemistry certification after the two drug classes. My advisor told me my degrees in chemistry and biology and the chemistry and firearms certifications will give me more options with my career."

"I've always been impressed by my super-smart cop." I kissed him lightly on his chin as he set me back down, so we could change.

Larry chuckled. "Sweetie, I've been in awe of you since the first time I saw you right after you started working at the library. I happen to know you have not always been impressed by me, but you can keep telling me that anyway."

While Larry changed out of his uniform, I changed to clean jeans then stood in front of my shirts. *Today's Friday: the fifth day of the week, so I'll wear the fifth shirt.*

After I put on the fifth shirt, Larry said, "You haven't worn your hot pink shirt in a while. It looks good on you."

I peered down at my shirt and frowned. *I thought it was a grayish-lavender.* "I thought it might be nice to bust out of the Gray Lady mold; does it match my sparkly eyepatch that Jennifer made?"

"Not exactly, but do you really care?" He kissed my forehead.

"No." I smiled and grabbed my jo, my cane that was actually a martial arts staff with built-in audio and video recorders, courtesy of Heather, an undercover police detective in Georgia, who had access to awesome surveillance equipment that she liked me to test.

When we headed to the front door, I asked, "Who's going with us?"

Spike pointed to the sleeping Lucy and shook his head; Palace Guard joined us as we climbed into the truck.

After we were on our way to town, I asked. "Where are we going?"

"What's your favorite? That's where we'll go."

"Cassandra's café, but they're not open."

Larry parked and fake-coughed into his fist.

"Did you forget that everybody except you, Palace Guard, Spike, and Lucy are blobs to me? I see your face; are you smirking? What are you so pleased about?"

He climbed out of the truck, opened my door, and helped me step out. "I'll show you."

When I stepped onto the sidewalk, I squealed. "It's the café. Why are they open?"

"I'll let Cassandra tell you the entire story."

Larry opened the door, and Cassandra said, "Gray Lady's here, Anna; tell Chef."

Cassandra hugged me. "You're looking hot tonight; that pink looks good on you."

"Why are you open?" I asked.

Palace Guard nudged me, and Larry snickered.

I cleared my throat and added, "Thank you."

"I won't reveal any names," Cassandra whispered, "but some certain decision makers from a nearby training center came into the shop for lunch earlier this week and didn't realize that a private conversation in a corner is easily overheard by the staff, and papers spread out on a table aren't as private as they seem. When I learned that a small group of talented individuals would be attending additional classes for the next two weeks, Chef and I decided we'd open Friday and Saturday evenings as a special treat."

She led us to our table near the kitchen.

"There's more to your story," I said.

"I can't pull the wool over your eye." Cassandra's chuckle was musical. "Tonya asked Justin to call us while she was in the hospital because she knew Chef would be worried about her, so I had his number. I called Justin and asked him to tell your brilliant husband that we'd be open for dinner tonight."

"Larry didn't tell me we were coming here or that you were open. It was a wonderful surprise."

"See how brilliant he is? We're thrilled that you are here. I'd offer y'all menus, but Chef has already decided what she will prepare for you. You're having wine with your dinner, Gray Lady; Mr. Ewing, I assumed you would want sweet tea, but if not, Anna will bring you whatever you would prefer."

"Sweet tea is perfect; please call me Larry."

After Cassandra-blob hurried to the host stand, Anna brought our drinks. "I brought you ice water, Gray Lady, but I can bring you sweet tea if you like; I knew

Chef would plan wine with your dinner. Sweet tea for you, Mr. Larry." She placed our drinks on the table.

"Ice water is perfect. Thank you. You can read upside down, can't you?" I asked.

"Yes, ma'am. I learned to read upside down when I was little because I sat on the floor in front of my older sister while she read to me and my four brothers, who crowded around her. I read upside down in school instead of right side up, but nobody noticed."

After our server left, Larry asked, "How did you know?"

"I've watched her and decided she must be an avid reader; I think reading whatever happens to be on a table is her entertainment. My entertainment has been watching her as she puts herself in a position to read without being obvious because she moves around so much that she gives the appearance of being hyperactive."

Larry chuckled. "You see more with one eye than anyone else does with two eyes."

While we sipped on our drinks, Larry told me about his day until Cassandra and Anna brought our plates from the kitchen.

"Your fine dining experience this evening is brought to you by the traditions of the Volunteer State: country ham with red eye gravy, macaroni and cheese, turnip greens, and biscuits with a side of fresh-churned butter," Cassandra said. "Enjoy."

After Cassandra and Anna left our table, Larry whispered, "Where's the tofu?"

I smiled when Anna-blob, who was across the room at the drink station, giggled.

Larry glanced at her then leaned forward and said in a quiet voice, "You heard me, didn't you, Anna?"

"Anna nodded, sweetie." Larry chuckled.

"Anna has amazing hearing, doesn't she?" Cassandra asked as she breezed past us toward the kitchen.

"We have no complaints about the entertainment, and the food is wonderful." Larry glanced at the ceiling then grinned. "Sweetie, the ceiling is a parabola. Anna, is the drink station the focal listening point?"

Anna strode to our table with a pitcher of tea. "I heard you were smart, Mr. Larry. More tea?" She refilled his glass then headed to the other tables with her pitcher.

After Larry cleaned his plate, and I ate what I could, Cassandra asked, "Would you like to relax a bit before dessert? Coffee, Larry?"

"I'll wait and have coffee with my dessert," he said.

Anna walked past our table with two plates of fried chicken and macaroni and cheese. "Your friends just came in, Mr. Larry."

Larry glanced at the door. "She's right, sweetie. They'll be taking the drug classes too."

"Would you like to visit with Chef, Gray Lady?" Cassandra asked as she carried a large platter of cornbread past us.

"You can visit your friends if you like; I'd like to see Chef," I said.

Larry smiled then strode to his classmates' table.

Cassandra stopped on her way back to the kitchen, and I rose from my seat then walked alongside her with Palace Guard's guidance. "That was pretty slick, Cassandra. What's up?"

"We'll talk in the kitchen."

Palace Guard led me to the barstool at the counter in the kitchen, and I climbed up on it with his help. I pushed on the middle pearl on the back of my jo to record. *I have no idea if Heather will hear this or even why I think this is important to record, but I have a feeling.*

"Chef can't hear us, but she knows what I'm telling you. She'll watch our faces and let me know if she has anything to add or any questions. Keep your hands away from your mouth, so she can read your lips."

Cassandra exhaled then pulled out the stool at the end of the bar, so she could see me and Chef. "A large number of girls from town have run away from home in the past month. I heard it was at least five, and some are saying twelve, so I'm guessing it's between five and eight, which is quite high because our normal number of runaways is one or two every other month. All the parents reported that their home life was perfect; I'm certain they meant perfectly normal: their moody teenager slammed doors and screamed, and the parents yelled and argued with each other and their offspring."

Anna came into the kitchen. "Cassandra, I'm sorry to interrupt, but the folks at table two would like to talk to tell you how much they love Chef's food."

Cassandra sighed. "I just gave Gray Lady the background. Tell her what you heard."

After Cassandra left, Anna sat on the stool at the end of the bar. "It was lunchtime on Wednesday, and two men came in that I haven't seen before. The first one was cute, young, and wore a nice shirt, jeans, and brown loafers, which is a little dressy for around here. The second guy was a little older, looked rougher, and swore a lot. They were talking about the runaways, and I didn't pay much attention until the tough guy complained about the grooming and how much effort it took; he asked when they could leave this jerkwater town. That's derogatory, right?"

"Yes, let me know when you want a full explanation of where the term originated."

Chef chuckled and spoke in her loud, flat tone. "Once a librarian, always a librarian."

Anna nodded. "I thought it wasn't very complimentary, Gray Lady. At first, I thought the young guy was in charge; he tensed up and glanced around then told the other guy in a voice that could be heard two tables away that it was not easy to run a cheerleading camp. I continued taking and delivering orders, and they glared at each other and didn't talk until the tough guy told the other guy that even though they'd met their quota, one more would be a bonus, and the drink girl would be great because she could be easily convinced to cooperate. The cute guy told the tough guy he was being greedy, and that would get him into trouble. The tough guy asked if they would be taking the cheerleaders to Atlanta or somewhere else because he'd heard Atlanta was too hot right now, so he hoped it was Charleston because he has a girlfriend there."

"We're sure Anna is the drink girl," Chef added.

Anna nodded and continued, "I kept serving my customers, but I didn't miss a word of their discussion. The tough guy said the caretaker gave him the creeps, and the cute guy laughed at him and told him that being creepy was the guy's job, then the tough guy mentioned a high school track runner and a lonely girl who was always in the library by herself. The cute guy got pretty agitated and said it would take too long to go through another round of grooming and mentioned several people in town that would be great followers. The tough guy said he had another possibility for a bonus, and the younger guy told him their priority was to identify a few potential followers for the big boss who would be here next week to recruit them. The tough guy grumbled that he had two jobs and said he wasn't interested in a third; the younger man told him he would quit complaining when he saw his bonus. I don't understand any of this, but Cassandra wants me to leave for my brother's ranch in Texas right away."

"I have some good friends that might have some suggestions for what would be the best course to take. Can you give me until tomorrow, and I'll get back to you?" I asked.

Anna nodded. "Will you help me with Cassandra, Chef?"

"Yes," Chef said.

"Good. Anything else?" I asked.

Palace Guard smirked.

I know I stole that from Larry. He won't mind.

"I took a photo of them. Should I send it to you?" Anna asked.

"Please do."

"Hold out your phone." Anna tapped my phone with hers.

"That's it?" I shook my head. "I'm an old codger."

"Yes, you are." Anna giggled as she left.

I exhaled and rose. After Chef turned back to her stove, I said, "I'll make a phone call tomorrow if I don't get one tonight."

I pressed the bottom pearl on my jo and turned off the recording. When my phone buzzed a text, I said, "Before I return to my table, I'll go to the restroom."

After I left the kitchen, Anna hesitated as she breezed past me, and I quickly pressed the record pearl before she said, "Cassandra reminded me to tell you the drink girl would cooperate because of a threat to Chef."

I turned off the recording then glanced at Palace Guard, and he glowered then guided me to the women's restroom.

After I checked to be certain I was the only one in the room, I lowered the volume on my phone then tapped to listen to the text. "From Paul. Got it."

Heather must be working undercover somewhere. Paul Vargas from the Coyle Detective Agency must have volunteered to cover any recordings from my jo for her.

I quietly spoke to my phone. "Reply to Paul. Thanks. I sent a follow up. Talk tomorrow."

When I stepped out of the restroom, Palace Guard waited in the hallway with his arms crossed. After he guided me to our table, I relaxed and listened to the excitement in Larry's voice as he and his two classmates discussed their plans for their two drug classes.

Cassandra brought two small bowls with large scoops of ice cream melting on hot cherry cobbler and giggled as she set them on the table. "Shall I tell Larry his dessert is here, or do you think you could eat both of them before he notices?"

Anna bumped Larry on his shoulder with her elbow as she passed him; he rose from his friends' table then sauntered to join me.

"No way could you eat two desserts, Gray Lady, and that's not a dare." Anna poured Larry a cup of coffee before he made it to our table.

After Larry polished off his dessert, he sipped his coffee and told me the study plans for the drug classes. I continued eating but didn't mention I'd heard everything they'd said because his perspective was much more interesting.

On our way home, Larry continued talking about his upcoming classes and what he and the guys expected. He was so excited that he didn't notice when my phone buzzed a text. After we were home, he took Lucy out back, and I listened to my text.

"From Paul. Tell drink girl to never be alone and to stay inside at all times. Send me the photo."

"Send a reply to Paul: Will do."

I sent the photo to Paul then called Cassandra; Palace Guard stood close to my phone to listen. When she answered I said, "This has to be quick. Tell Anna to never be alone and to stay inside at all times."

"Consider it done. Chef told me that Anna forgot to tell you one more thing: the tough guy said he thought the one-eyed girl would be another quick bonus because she was married and would be easy to manage into cooperating by threatening to hurt the husband, but then they changed the subject, so Anna must have forgotten about it."

"Thanks." *I'm glad Paul didn't hear that; he'd have told Larry.*

Palace Guard's face reminded me of the expression on Larry's face when he was really mad.

I flipped my hair back. "If Larry knew about that one-eyed girl comment, I'm afraid he'd cancel his classes. I won't be alone, so we'll be following Paul's advice."

Palace Guard marched to the front door and left. *Maybe he's going for a walk to cool off.*

I sent the photo of the two men to Paul then sat on the sofa and put up my feet before Larry, Lucy, and Spike came inside with Palace Guard following them. When I raised my eyebrows, Palace Guard smiled and shrugged.

Oh, good. He's not mad at me anymore.

"I haven't given you a chance to talk all night." Larry rinsed Lucy's water bowl and refilled it with fresh water. "Tell me about your day."

"It hasn't been very exciting..."

"I love it already." Larry smiled as he joined me on the sofa. "Sorry, I interrupted you."

"Lucy, Spike, Palace Guard, and I walked around campus this morning; after lunch, I took a nap, then we called Tonya to see how she is doing with her recuperation at her mom's. Tonya told us her mother is hovering, and she misses Justin who has one additional week of advanced training for his specialty."

Spike raised his eyebrows at me then Palace Guard, who rolled his eyes. Lucy nudged my hand, and I rubbed her face and shrugged. *Maybe the nap part was a bit much.*

"That's the kind of day you deserve: taking a walk and catching up with a close friend. Justin and I talked about having coffee early tomorrow morning. Would you like to go?"

"Not really; I'd like to call Jennifer in the morning, and if you aren't here, I won't feel guilty about a gab fest. We're still going to your graduation tomorrow, aren't we?"

"If you feel up to it, but everyone will understand if we can't make it," Larry said.

"I wouldn't miss it for the world." When he hugged me, I mumbled into his chest, "You've really worked hard to get this far."

⸻

I woke to the sounds of Larry cheerfully singing in the shower and smiled at his off-key tune.

When he tiptoed into the bedroom, I smiled. "I'm awake."

"I'll get the coffee going; what would you like for breakfast?"

I headed to the door for the shower. "If you'll pour me a cup of coffee, I'll have yogurt later."

"Are you sure you don't mind if I have coffee with Justin and the guys?" Larry asked while he dressed.

I smirked as I turned on the shower. *I caught that little slip, honey; you went from only Justin to Justin and the guys. Your class is getting together one last time before all the families arrive for graduation.*

After I showered, I dressed then hurried to the kitchen.

"Your cup is on the table, sweetie. As soon as Lucy eats her breakfast, she and Spike are going outside. I poured a carafe of coffee for you, and I'll start a load of laundry; is there anything else I can do before I leave?"

"Thanks for the coffee; I'll be fine."

After Larry left, I ate my cup of yogurt, then while I made our bed, my phone buzzed a text.

"From Paul. Is it too early to call?"

I called him. "I have the morning to myself."

"Maggie, I've listened to that recording a dozen times. I researched recent runaway stats, and there are a disproportionate number in south Georgia and north Florida in comparison to the Georgia and Florida urban areas and the surrounding states. Heather is scheduled to resurface from her assignment by Monday. I have some ideas of what might be going on, but she's the expert. The smooth, attractive, young man and the tough young man seem to have stereo-typical roles: nice guy and bad boy, especially with their reference to grooming. I'll have to talk to Heather before I go too far off the deep end though. Don't go wandering off anywhere by yourself; their reference to the girl who ran track and the one in the library definitely points to young women as their target. What does Larry think?"

"Larry's excited about his classes in drugs the next two weeks that will give him the chemistry certification in addition to the firearms certification."

Paul laughed. "You haven't told him a thing, as usual."

"I'd feel awful if he was this close to what he wanted then let it go because of me."

"I'll keep my mouth shut until I have a chance to talk to Heather. If she tells me to blow the whistle, I will."

"I just need two weeks," I said.

"I'll let Heather know. We'll do what we can to help you. Call Jennifer Coyle when you have a chance. She would fire me from the Coyle Detective Agency if she found out I've talked to you and won't tell her what you said, and Glenn would back her up on it."

After Paul hung up, I called Jennifer. *Can't blow my cover story.*

When Jennifer answered she said, "I'm so glad you called. Glenn and I miss you, Larry, Lucy, and the imaginary men. Are you okay? Doesn't Larry graduate this weekend? Do you know yet where you'll be going?"

"His graduation ceremony is this evening, then he has two weeks of additional training for the chemistry certification; we're hoping to find out soon where his assignment will be."

Jennifer caught me up on all the news: the Coyle Detective Agency had gained quite a reputation, so Glenn and Paul were busy, almost to the point of being overloaded.

"Ella is enrolled in classes to become a detective, and she and Moe, I mean police detective Lester Ross, can't agree on a date to get married. You've been a terrible influence on me. I still have trouble calling Moe 'Les,' but Ella doesn't speak to me the rest of the day when I slip up; Glenn says that's not all bad."

I snickered.

"Ella and I decided to hire someone to replace her in the office, so after Ella gets her certification, she'll be able to start working with Glenn right away. Kate's working; we never know where. Glenn said as long as no law enforcement shows up on our doorstep, we'll know our FBI daughter is okay. How is your sight?"

"I haven't noticed any improvement; people are still blobs, except for Larry, Lucy, and the men."

Jennifer chuckled. "Your self-preservation kicked in."

"I hadn't thought about that, but you're right. Larry knows I see him clearly, but he forgets, and I've caught a few things I wouldn't have when I saw him as a blob."

We talked for another hour before we reluctantly hung up.

I moved the laundry from the washer to the dryer then called Tonya.

"How did you know?" she asked. "Mom, Kiki, and I are coming to graduation to surprise Justin, but don't tell him. We'll be there in ten minutes."

I chuckled. "I called to tell you we talked for a long time yesterday on the phone, so you have to cover me."

She giggled. "I've missed you. See you before you see me."

I grinned as we hung up. "Tonya and Kiki will be here in ten minutes to surprise Justin. I'm waiting outside for them."

When I put on my warm coat, Palace Guard blocked the front door.

"I planned to wait in the backyard." I tossed my hair, and Spike mocked me by pretending to toss his hair with his hand. When he sashayed to the back door, I snort-laughed.

"I do not walk like that," I growled and sashayed to the front door then whirled and sashayed to the back door. Lucy howled, Palace Guard rolled his eyes, and Spike did his wacky dance as Larry came in the front door.

"What is going on in here?" Larry asked.

When I turned to glare at Larry, a blob stood in the doorway with him.

"Looks like the normal Ewing shenanigans if you ask me," Justin said.

"I recognize your voice, Justin; thank goodness it's only you," I said.

"She meant it exactly the way it sounded, didn't she?" Justin asked.

Larry laughed.

An SUV pulled in front of our apartment; when the driver honked, Justin dashed to the SUV and opened the passenger's door.

"I saw you first," Tonya said as she came into the apartment. "What do you see?"

"A Tonya-blob. Where's Kiki?"

Tonya laughed as she hugged me. "Our tiny dragon, Kiki, has abandoned both of us for an older woman; she stays close to Mom. Come to our apartment; Mom wants to put up her feet."

"We'll be there after lunch to give you a chance to get settled. Are you staying or going back to your Mom's?"

"I'd rather stay, but I hate for Mom to make that long drive by herself. We're leaving on Monday."

After Tonya and Justin left, Larry asked, "What was going on when I opened the door?"

"Spike started it. I was on my way to the back door to go outside, and Spike mocked me by doing a really prissy walk, so I copied him."

"All I caught was your walk and Lucy howling, and I knew it had to be something, but I sure am sorry I missed the rest of it." Larry chuckled.

"How was the get together?" I asked as we sat on the sofa.

"It was great. Everyone is pleased with their assignments so far. One of our instructors dropped by, and he told us we'd hear officially at graduation, and there might be a few last-minute changes. After he left, one of the guys said he heard they rarely make any changes, but we'll see. Did you know Tonya would be here? Did she say anything when you talked to her yesterday?"

"Not a peep; she really wanted to surprise Justin."

"Ready for lunch? What would you like? Half a sandwich and some yogurt?"

"Just half a sandwich, but I can make it myself."

"Okay, but I'll hover."

CHAPTER TWO

I glanced at Palace Guard, and he nodded.

"So will Palace Guard, but I'm used to you two, so I'd like to give it a try. I'll make a folded over ham and cheese sandwich."

I spread mayonnaise on a slice of bread then squirted some mustard on it.

"Sweetie, you missed the bread. Your mustard's on the counter. Do you want to skip it?"

"Yes," I grumbled and placed a slice of ham and a slice of cheese on the bread then folded it.

Larry finished making his sandwich. "I'll pour our tea."

After we sat at the table, Larry asked, "Did you talk to Jennifer this morning?"

I smiled. "We talked almost the entire morning." I told him about Ella and Moe, Ella's classes, and how busy Glenn and Paul were.

"I heard from Mom this morning. She decided they're coming to the graduation and took an early flight this morning; they're on their way here in a rental car, and she made reservations at a nearby hotel. Mom wanted to take us out to dinner, but I declined, mostly because I know both of them will be tired from the traveling. Mom actually sounded relieved. She wants to bring lunch tomorrow and eat at the apartment before they leave town. I told her I didn't know what our plans were. What do you think?"

"I think it's a much better idea except I'm not sure when Tonya will be leaving. I'd like to spend time with your parents but with Tonya too."

"Why don't we invite Mom and Dad here for dessert after graduation this evening, then they can leave tomorrow anytime they like," Larry said.

"I'll call Cassandra and see if she has something we can pick up."

Larry nodded. "I'll call Mom."

After we made our calls, Larry said, "Do you want to visit with Tonya? I could pick up the dessert for us."

"Why don't we both go? Cassandra offered to bring the desserts out to the curb when we drive up to save time." *Or she will when I ask her. It's not safe for Larry to go into the café. Somebody might slip.*

"That's a good idea."

After we finished eating, Larry and Spike took Lucy out back while I called Cassandra. After she laughed, she agreed to bring out the dessert if I'd give her a call when we left the apartment.

"I'll be the courier, like in a spy movie. What's my code name?"

"Coriander."

"I like it; how did you come up with that?"

"The short answer is that it popped into my head. The long answer is I considered all the possibilities for the best code name for you, and it popped into my head."

Cassandra chuckled. "I asked for that one, didn't I? I'll have dessert for four waiting for you. Just give me a five-minute warning."

Larry came inside. "Lucy wasn't ready to come back in, so Spike is staying with her."

Palace Guard joined us in the truck.

"I'm glad you're sticking close to Maggie, Palace Guard. I have a feeling that things aren't as quiet as they seem," Larry said.

Palace Guard nodded then peered at me.

I wrinkled my nose at Palace Guard. *No need to gloat. I heard what Larry said.*

On the way to the café, I called Cassandra. "We'll be there in five minutes."

"I'll be ready. Chef made a raspberry cheesecake earlier, in case Larry asks you what the dessert is, and I'll be watching for you."

When Larry double-parked in front of the café, Cassandra-blob dashed out and handed me a sack. "Here you go; nice to see you, Larry."

She ran back inside, and Larry pulled away and headed toward home. I caught Larry peering at the tightly closed sack as he drove.

When we reached our apartment, Larry asked, "Do I put the dessert in the refrigerator or the freezer?"

"You're so subtle," I giggled. "It's raspberry cheesecake; put it in the refrigerator."

While I climbed out of the truck with Larry's help, Palace Guard strolled to the corner and slowly scanned the neighborhood and the streets then returned.

When we went inside, Larry asked Palace Guard quietly, "Anybody following us?"

I glanced at Palace Guard as he shook his head, and I frowned. I wonder if Paul talked to Larry. I'll have to ask him.

"I'm ready to go to spend some time with Tonya. Are you going with me, sweetie?" I asked.

"I'll be there in a few minutes; I have a couple of things to do first. Palace Guard will go with you."

Spike and Lucy came inside. "I'm going to visit Tonya. Anybody coming along?"

Spike shook his head, but Lucy trotted to the front door.

When the three of us reached Tonya and Justin's apartment, I tapped on the door, and Justin opened the door and asked, "Where's Larry?"

"He'll be along soon. He said he had a couple of things to do."

Justin nodded then headed toward our apartment as we went inside, and Tonya hugged me.

"Hello, sweet Lucy. How are you, Palace Guard? Come on in, everybody."

Palace Guard smiled.

"Maggie, this is my Mom; Mom, we call Maggie Gray Lady. It's a great story: I'll tell you later."

Tonya's mom hugged me. "Call me Martha, Gray Lady. I'd shake your hand, but hugs are quicker. It's nice to meet you."

After we talked for almost an hour, Tonya yawned. "I'm sorry; I woke up at four yesterday because I was so excited to be coming here. I know Mom's exhausted."

"You have two choices: take a nap now or fall off your chair during the graduation ceremony." I faced Tonya and spoke in a loud voice.

Tonya giggled. "That sounded like the voice of experience to me."

"Maggie, you are brilliant." Martha's blob-hands moved as she spoke. "If you'll take a nap, honey, I will too."

She's signing to Tonya, but she's saying it aloud for me.

Tonya said, "I'm pretty sure that's blackmail, Mom, but I know you must be as worn out as I am."

On our way home, we met Larry and Justin.

"Sorry that I took longer than I expected," Larry said. "Justin and I were given an open case to research; we'll go to the library for a few minutes after Justin checks in with Tonya. Do you want to go to the library with us?"

"Tonya and her mother plan to nap. Lucy and I thought we should relax too."

Palace Guard side-glanced me as Larry said, "That's an excellent idea. I'll be home soon."

"I'll check in really quick then meet you at the library, Larry." Justin hurried to his apartment.

Lucy, Palace Guard, and I strolled to the apartment. When I reached the door, I glanced back, and Larry still stood where we'd left him. I waved, then the three of us went inside.

"That man certainly can hover." I picked up a book out of habit then sat on the sofa and put up my feet while Lucy flopped down next to me. I sighed as I looked at the book in my hand. *Sorry, book; maybe I'll be able to read after my eye sees a little better.*

I closed my eye and relaxed.

I woke when Lucy whined and nudged my elbow, and I sat up before the front door opened. "Thanks, girl," I whispered and picked up my book from the floor then set it on the table as Larry came inside.

"Sorry, sweetie. I didn't mean to be so long, but Justin and I had to dig to find any information that was related to our assigned case. I'll take a quick shower, then we can leave for graduation. I need to be there early. You don't mind going early with me, do you?"

"I'll need a quick shower too, and I'll need you to help me get out the tangles in my hair."

"You go first, sweetie," he said. "I'll set up the coffee to have with our dessert."

After my shower, and while Larry showered, I sent a text to Jennifer. "What do I wear to Larry's graduation ceremony?"

She replied: "Your green shirt and gray slacks. Palace Guard can show you."

Palace Guard nodded, then he followed me to the closet and pointed out a shirt then a pair of pants.

After I dressed, I called Palace Guard back to the bedroom. "Which pair of boots do I wear?"

He shrugged then pointed.

"Ready for me to brush your hair?" Larry stood in the doorway.

I smiled. "You are dashing in your dress uniform."

"Thank you. Your green shirt matches your eye, and the gray pants are for the Gray Lady, aren't they? Your wardrobe selection for the evening is courtesy of Jennifer, I take it."

"You would be correct. Could I get by without brushing my hair?"

"No, I'll give it a quick brush then deal with any tangles later."

After we reached the large hall, Larry hurried to the front to join the few that had arrived before we had, and Palace Guard selected a seat for me near the wall and close to the back. I held my backpack on my lap as I listened to the conversations up front. When the blobs of people drifted in, I enjoyed their comments as they discussed then selected their seats.

I smiled when two blobs beelined to join me. After Tonya and Martha sat next to me, I felt tiny talons on my shoulder, and I giggled when Kiki tickled my neck with a dragon kiss.

"Thank you, Kiki."

"We napped, and I feel much better," Martha said. "What about you, Maggie?"

"I thought I'd read a book, but Lucy woke me up when Larry came to the door."

I heard two familiar voices mention Kevin then my name; I jumped up and hugged Larry's parents when they came to my seat. "I'm so glad you could be here."

I introduced them to Tonya, who introduced them to her mother, then we shifted over two seats, so we could all sit together. Lauren sat next to me, and Sean sat at the end of our row.

"You look stunning, Maggie," Lauren said. "How are you feeling?"

"I feel great; my eyesight hasn't improved, but I'm certain it will over time."

When the microphone squealed, I covered my ears and shuddered then pulled out my earplugs from my backpack. Tonya's blob-hands moved. *Tonya must have told Martha about my sensitive hearing.*

Lauren leaned close and whispered, "Your hearing must still be very sensitive; that screech was grating."

The speaker blew on the microphone and said, "Test, test," before he began with his welcome speech. I glanced at Tonya then pulled out my small notebook and a pen and wrote as well as I could without being able to see. "U missed nothing."

"Thanks," Tonya said.

The sound volume was too loud for me to understand the words, so I sat back and imagined the layout of the room. When everyone rose and applauded, Tonya tugged on my elbow, and I rose with her.

Tonya whispered, "Didn't hear a thing, did you?"

I turned to Tonya and put my hands on my cheeks in my best shocked face, and she snorted. Martha shushed us.

Sean chuckled.

My face warmed. *I forgot that Sean is just like Glenn and doesn't miss a thing.*

After the speaker sat down, everyone applauded, then another man approached the microphone, and the graduates lined up. As the man at the microphone announced each graduate, another man handed the graduate a slim box.

"The graduates are receiving framed certificates for them to hang at their offices. That's a nice touch," Lauren whispered.

When Larry received his certificate, I wanted to dance Spike's wacky dance. I glanced at Palace Guard, who stood behind me, and he smiled.

Palace Guard knows exactly what I'm thinking.

Lauren squeezed my hand as she whispered, "He's always wanted this."

I nodded, and Sean stepped past Lauren and hugged me then whispered, "I'm proud of both of you."

They're really proud of him; so am I.

When the announcer called Justin's name, Kiki squealed, Tonya hugged her mother then me, and her mother sniffled.

After everyone in line received a certificate, there was a loud shout from one of the graduates, and I smiled. *That's my Larry.*

His shout was answered by the rest of the graduates, and the entire audience rose to their feet, applauded, whistled, and cheered.

Tanya started a chant, "Proud of you," and I joined her, then the rest of the wives chimed in. The parents, family members, friends, and faculty jumped in, and even though the sound shook the windows, and I thought my eardrums would burst, it was wonderful to hear the joy in the voices.

When the chant disintegrated into laughter, I wrote on the notebook then handed it to Tonya. "Awesome. Thanks."

She elbowed me. "Thank you, partner in crime. Wonder who started it?"

We giggled, then our husbands joined us.

Larry lifted me off my feet and hugged me. "We did it, Sexy Maggie."

"We sure did, Mr. Sexy Pants."

Larry set me down then showed me a white envelope and grinned as he tapped it. "Our assignment is in here. Shall I open it?"

"I suppose, but only if you don't want to be tossed to the floor by your one-eyed wife."

Larry chuckled. "You'd do it too. You open it, and I'll read it." He handed me the envelope.

My hands shook. "I'm too excited. You open it."

Larry pulled out his pocketknife and slit open the envelope. "Statesboro, sweet thing."

I squealed then hugged him. *I thought he wanted to go to Savannah.*

"Statesboro?"

"Savannah is in the largest county of the region where the Statesboro office is. We call it Savannah because hardly anyone knows where Statesboro is. It's just simpler. We have to find out where Justin is going. Where are they?" I asked.

"Did you say Savannah?" Sean asked.

"I hoped that was where we'd go," Larry said. "There's a senior investigator there that is brilliant; I'll learn a lot from him in the field."

"I've never been to Savannah," Lauren said.

"Guess that might change," Sean said.

"Where are you going, Justin?" Larry asked.

"Going home to Savannah," he said.

"I'll be there a week after you," Larry said. "You owe me a cup of coffee."

I snickered. *Larry bet Justin both of them would be going to Savannah.*

After all the congratulations and hugs, the celebration moved toward the large room where the buffet was set up. Lauren and Sean stopped to talk to old friends in the hall, two graduates stopped Larry to talk, and Palace Guard and I followed Tonya, her mother, and Justin to the buffet. When two caterers rolled in carts with food, Palace Guard tapped my shoulder to indicate where I should aim.

"Video?" I asked, and he nodded.

I pressed the button on my jo to turn on the video then pointed it as Palace Guard tapped my shoulder to indicate changes in direction. *We're taking a video of the caterers. Hope Paul understands this because I'm lost.*

When Palace Guard tapped stop, I pressed the button to stop the video and waited for Larry. *There are so many blobs.* I shuddered. *It's almost overwhelming.*

One of the graduates joined me, "Gray Lady, would you do me the honor of allowing me to bring you a plate of food?"

Palace Guard poked me, and I said, "Thank you."

"I'll find you," he said.

I smiled, then when I turned, I jumped as a blob touched my arm.

Martha said, "Sorry, I didn't mean to startle you; we snagged a table. Care to join us? It's big enough for all of us."

"I'd love it."

The young man brought me a plate and a cup and set it on the table.

"This is wonderful; thank you very much," I said before Palace Guard could poke me again.

"That warmed my heart; these young men look after each other and their families, don't they?" Martha said.

"Makes it hard to get into mischief, though," I sighed dramatically.

Martha chuckled then signed.

"I can see how that would cramp your style; you are the master mischief maker, Gray Lady." Tonya giggled.

Palace Guard nodded.

"Are you and Larry really coming to Savannah?" Tonya asked. "That is awesome. We'll get into so much trouble, won't we?"

"Please don't," Martha said.

Justin brought plates for Tonya and her mother. "Oh good; you already have food, Maggie. I hoped someone would bring you a plate because this room isn't quite big enough for all these people, and the buffet table is almost a free-for-all. I'll be right back with the drinks, sweetheart."

I peered at my plate. "I'll be adventuresome and eat what's here."

"Everything on your plate is finger food," Martha said. "You have a napkin next to your plate on the right and a brownie and a pastry on your plate at two o'clock, so you have the choice to eat your dessert last or first."

Tonya giggled. "Mom, you never let me eat dessert first."

"Shortcoming in your childhood. Save it for your therapist," Martha said, and I giggled.

I frowned when my phone in my backpack buzzed. *I wish I could read it or listen to it without anyone else hearing it.*

Tonya tapped my arm then leaned close and whispered, "What's wrong?"

I forgot how closely Tonya watches me.

I mouthed, "Nothing. My phone buzzed a text."

She continued whispering, "Is it important? Do you want me to read it to you?"

"Don't know." I mouthed then shrugged and pulled out my phone from my backpack and unlocked the screen.

Tonya whispered, "From Paul. Same two as café. Do you understand?"

I smiled and nodded; after she handed back my phone, I slipped it into my backpack then squeezed her hand and signed, thank you.

Martha leaned, so I could hear her, and Tonya could read her lips. "I could teach you a few basic signs tomorrow, so you can sign to Tonya, but I realized you can't see my hands."

"Good idea, Mom," Tonya said. "We might be able to work that out, right?"

Palace Guard smiled and nodded.

"More imaginary dragons?" Martha asked.

"Something like that," Tonya giggled.

"What's funny?" Larry asked as he kissed me then sat next to me. "I heard one of the guys brought you a plate. Do you have enough?"

"Plenty," I said.

"How did y'all get a table large enough for all of us? Are you as excited as we are that Larry and Justin will be in Savannah? Isn't that where you live, Martha?" Lauren asked as she sat across from me, and Sean sat next to Larry.

"I am thrilled, and as far as the table is concerned, this is not my first buffet rodeo." Martha chuckled. "I beat everyone into the room and planted my flag, also known as my oversized red purse, on the table. Not knowing anyone here that might want to chat was a huge advantage."

When Justin arrived with their drinks and his food, Martha moved to sit next to Lauren, and Justin sat next to Tonya. While everyone chatted, I smiled and nodded but paid extra attention to Larry and Sean, who whispered to each other.

I ate a little over half of the food on my plate then put my hands in my lap.

"Are you full?" Tonya whispered. "You didn't touch your dessert."

I mouthed. "We have dessert at home for the parents."

"I'll put it in a napkin for my midnight snack that I have at nine o'clock."

I grinned and nodded. *That is so Tonya.*

"Martha, can you tell who the caterers are?" I asked. "The food was really good, and it seemed to me that they did a great job of keeping the buffet full and the line moving."

"That's a good question; I won't rest until I find out."

Martha rose from our table, then I lost sight of her as she blended in with the other blobs.

Tonya tapped my arm and whispered, "Are you interested in what Mom's doing?"

I nodded then pushed the pearl on the left side of my jo to start the audio recording.

"Mom is on a mission. She picked up a plate and put a few items on it," Tonya said quietly. "She wandered over to a woman who has an official air about her, and they are chatting. They are pointing and smiling; I think they are talking about the food. The woman just walked away, but Mom's still smiling like she knows the woman will be right back."

I'm getting a running commentary. This is awesome.

"The woman's back, and she handed Mom a business card. They just hugged. I guess they are BFFs now." Tonya snickered. "Mom stopped to talk to Roxanne. Do you know her? Mom and I met her when we came to check out the housing, and she and Mom hit it off. Actually, Mom makes friends wherever she goes. Dad used to say that she'd be easy to kidnap, but he stopped saying that after I started dating Justin because Justin took Dad seriously and asked if he should hire a guard for Mom."

I chuckled and mouthed carefully, "Larry would have said the same thing. They have no sense of humor at all."

"Isn't that the truth? Mom told me she appreciated finding someone here she could ask to check on me, and I was highly insulted; Mom's headed back."

"That was an interesting conversation," Martha said. "The caterers are new, but the event coordinator is pleased with the feedback. I have their business card. Their main office is in Atlanta; isn't that interesting?"

"Could I take a photo of the business card?" I asked. "Mother's friends throw fancy parties and love to outdo each other; I know several of them that would be very interested in trying a new caterer before anyone else has heard of them."

"Why don't I just give you the card?" Martha said. "My version of a party is pizza and wings."

I giggled as she handed me the card. "Sounds like my kind of party."

I held the card in front of me and my jo and pretended to read it. "I can't read it, but it looks pretty," I said.

"You just like the gray border." Tonya giggled.

I grinned. "That must be it." I stopped the recording and stuck the card into my backpack.

As the conversations at our table started to wind down, and people from other tables returned to the buffet, Tonya whispered, "It's almost eight o'clock. Don't yawn."

I tried to hold it back, but I yawned, and Tonya giggled.

"Would it be rude for us to leave?" Martha asked. "Tonya and I had a long drive, and I know both of our young women must be worn out."

"What a good idea," Lauren said. "I need to kick off these shoes and put up my feet after our all-day travel too."

"Come on, sweetie," Larry put his arm around me. "We'll go to the apartment while everyone else says their polite goodbyes."

Larry, Palace Guard, and I headed toward the door, and everyone at our table slipped out behind us.

When Larry opened the front door, Lucy trotted to me, and I leaned down and hugged her. "It was a nice ceremony, and Larry officially graduated, and we're going to Savannah. You were smart to stay here, Lucy, because it was noisy and crowded."

After we went inside, Larry said, "That was the slickest exit I've ever seen. I was glad no one else in the room noticed us and felt obligated to leave too. Whose idea was it?"

"Tonya must have been ready to leave because she told me not to yawn." I giggled.

"You two are a mess." Larry snorted as Lauren and Sean came into the apartment.

"Thank you." I kicked off my boots and sat on the sofa.

"We have dessert and drinks. I'll start the coffee. What would you like to drink, Mom?" Larry asked.

"Coffee in the evening is not my friend; I'd rather have a cup of hot tea." I nodded.

Sean said, "I'll take coffee when it's ready."

Lauren sat on the chair that was opposite the sofa and sighed. "It feels good to relax."

"Can I help?" Sean strolled into the kitchen.

"Neither one of you can be trusted with the dessert." Lauren rose from the chair and rushed to the kitchen. "I'll plate it."

While Larry and Lauren waited for the coffee to perk and the water to boil for tea, Sean sat next to me.

"Larry's worried that all this is too much for you. How are you holding up?"

"Better than he is," I said. "I don't have any deadlines, looming tests, or spouse with minimal sight to worry about."

"What's your biggest worry, Maggie?"

"It bothers me that I cause extra work for Larry, but that's kind of where we are for now."

"Love your attitude," Sean squeezed my hand. "Let me know if you think of any way that we could help ease the burden. Have you thought about hiring a cleaning service or a personal chef after you move to wherever you're going?"

"Good idea; I'll think about it because both of those will ease the work that Larry takes on when he gets home."

"Let me know because I'll be happy to foot the bill," Sean said.

"Thank you; we can afford a cleaning service and a personal chef; I just never thought of it before."

CHAPTER THREE

"I have a suggestion: you might want to ask Jennifer to interview potential candidates by phone then spend a few days with you and help you interview in person. You have good insight, but Jennifer is formidable."

I nodded and smiled. "Another good idea; I'll talk to her, and I know Larry will be happy that I'll have help interviewing, and I'll be happy that he won't feel obligated to help."

Lauren joined us in the living room with two plates. "We have raspberry cheesecake, and the portions are generous." She handed one to me, and Larry brought our hot tea.

Sean joined Larry in the kitchen, then they returned with their dessert and coffee.

The room was quiet while we ate, except for a few mmms.

While Larry collected plates and forks after everyone had eaten, Lauren asked, "Where did you find that cheesecake? Did it come from a bakery?"

Larry had stacked the dishes on the counter and loaded the dishwasher, but he stopped and smiled. "No, the chef at a café in town bakes fresh desserts every day, and Maggie has become close friends with the owner and the chef."

"The chef must be very talented," Lauren said.

"She is," I said.

"We have a long day tomorrow, honey," Sean said.

Lauren sighed. "I know, and we're all tired."

After a flurry of hugs and good-byes, Lauren and Sean left, and Larry sat on the sofa with me.

When he put his arm around me, I leaned against him. "It was a good day."

Larry took my hand in his and kissed it. "Sure was; thanks for suggesting Mom and Dad come here for dessert; I know they appreciate being able to leave early in the morning."

"What are your plans for tomorrow?" I asked.

"It kind of depends on you. Justin and the guys and I thought we'd help those that are leaving load up, or if you like, we could relax or go on a hike on an easy trail."

"I'd like to spend time with Tonya and her mother tomorrow. Martha offered to teach me some sign language so it would be easier for Tonya and me to communicate; I thought I could learn by watching Palace Guard while he mimicked Martha."

"That sounds great; what do you want for breakfast?"

"Something light; I'll need to save room for the morning snack that I'm certain Martha will have prepared for us."

Larry smiled. "Would you like to take Lucy for a walk? We have a little time before the mosquitos are out."

"That would be great, and I know Lucy would enjoy it too."

I put on my sweatshirt to thwart any early-bird mosquitos, then the five of us took a long walk.

"What were you and your dad talking about when we were in the buffet room?" I asked.

"Dad asked me what was bothering me, and we talked about what we could do to make your life easier. I've been wondering if there isn't some new technology that would make managing your phone, for example, easier for you, but I don't know what that might be. I'll ask Heather. One thing I thought of was that if we bought you a single cup coffee maker, you won't have to wait for me to make coffee, and if it doubled by providing hot water for your tea, that would be a bonus."

"The coffee maker is a great idea. I'll ask Jennifer tomorrow what she'd recommend."

When we returned to the apartment, I said, "I'd like to take my shower tonight, so I can get an early start with Martha and Tonya."

"Good idea," Larry said.

After my shower, I dressed for bed then slipped under the covers while Larry took a shower.

I woke to the beckoning aroma of coffee and listened while Larry whistled softly under his breath. I quickly dressed then hurried to the kitchen.

Larry kissed me, and I tasted coffee. "Good morning, sweetie. I've already poured your coffee. I'll scramble eggs for both of us then pop the bread into the toaster."

"I'd like to talk more about Savannah before you leave for the day. I'll ask Martha where we should look for a place to live, but what do I tell her we'd like? What would you want in a house? Something like we've had, or do we want to go a little larger, so people can visit us?" I sat at the table and sipped my coffee.

"I like the idea of an extra bedroom or two, and two bathrooms sounds good too. I trust your judgment on everything else."

"I'm excited about being there with Tonya and Justin. Will anyone else we know be going to Savannah?"

"I'm not sure if there are any others going that you know; I'll be sure to ask this morning when we all get together."

After breakfast, Larry left, and I relaxed with my coffee.

My phone announced, "Call from Paul."

I answered.

"I should have texted you, Maggie. I didn't realize how early it is. Call me back later."

"We've already had breakfast, and Larry left to help the guys who are leaving today pack and load up."

Paul exhaled. "I've been up most of the night because this is bothering me; the catering company has been in business over fifteen years and is completely legit. They do like to hire locals, though, to work their contracts, but they always have one of their regional managers oversee the operation. Their regional managers are in Georgia and South Carolina, but I haven't found any region that includes Tennessee. One thought I had was that someone may be using the catering company's name as a front for some reason. I'll call the main office tomorrow to see if they had a contractor provide the banquet because it could be a test to see if they should expand to a new territory. So far, we keep uncovering more questions with no answers. I keep meaning to ask: do you know yet where Larry will be assigned?"

"We heard last night; we're going to Savannah in two weeks."

"What does Larry think? Be sure to have enough bedrooms for Jennifer and Ella to visit because they've already announced we'll have to cover the office."

"He's really happy about Savannah. It sounds like they have a good team, and he's excited to work with them."

"Let me know after you've talked to Jennifer, so I know it's common knowledge."

"Good point. I'll call her as soon as we hang up."

"If you come across anything else, let me know."

After we hung up, I realized my coffee cup was empty.

"I should have asked Larry for another cup of coffee before he left."

Palace Guard poked me then pointed to the counter. After I reached the counter, I found the insulated cup that Larry had filled, so I would have an extra-large cup for the morning.

"Thanks, Palace Guard. I should have realized that Larry would have thought of more coffee for me."

I sat at the table with my large cup and called Jennifer.

When she answered, she asked, "Where's Larry going? We've been waiting to hear. Do you know yet?"

"Savannah in two weeks."

"You're happy, and he's happy, right?" Jennifer asked.

"Yes."

"Good, then I'm happy too. Larry's assignment is Savannah, Glenn."

I giggled when Glenn whooped.

"Don't pay any attention to him. He won't admit it, but he and Moe and a few others had a pool going. I think he and Paul did a little research. Here, he wants to talk to you."

"Tell Larry congratulations from us. This can go public, right? How's Lucy?"

"Lucy's doing great. We have a backyard for her and a nearby park, so she can clear the grounds of squirrels."

"Is she reminding you to relax? When I was recuperating with that leg injury, she mastered the fine art of napping in front of me, so I couldn't get up without disturbing her."

"She does that to me too, but I thought it was a coincidence."

Jennifer took back the phone. "What can I do for you to help you?"

"Larry suggested we get a single cup coffee maker; he's fussy and won't let me use the stove."

"Easy. I'll order you one. I assume you want one that has an automatic turnoff and simple buttons on top that you push to turn on and select small, medium, and large sizes, so you can make a large cup of coffee and a medium cup of hot tea, if you want."

"If you'll send me the link for the one I should get, I can order it."

"Too late. I've already ordered it."

"Thank you." I shook my head. *She carefully explained the operation of the coffee maker to stall me, so she could order it.*

"I've been worried about Larry because of all the time-consuming tasks he has taken on at home: cleaning and cooking, in particular. Sean suggested that I ask you to help me find a cleaning service and a personal chef. He thought you could start the search and conduct phone interviews, then after we move, you could help me interview the top candidates in person."

"That is a marvelous idea. I'll need to know your requirements for both of the services; I'll write something up and email it to you, then you can send me back your comments. I love a good project, and this is right up my alley. Can I pull in Ella as a consultant?"

"Absolutely, if it won't overload her."

Jennifer chuckled. "I don't think it's possible to overload Ella, but I'm happy to try. Don't forget to call your mother."

"On my list," I said.

"Of course, it is; watch for my email." Jennifer hung up.

I guess I should call Mother.

Mother's voice was loud when she answered the phone, so I turned down the volume as far as I could and held the phone away from my ear.

"Margaret, what a surprise to get a call from you. Is Larry okay? I lost my hearing aids; I'm doing well without them and decided I didn't need to replace them after all. Big D told me they would be good for backup, but I'm not sure what that means. We're in North Dakota, but Big D said it's time to head back to Georgia. I thought we should have left two weeks ago, so I was glad to start packing up. We'll leave in the morning."

Mother took a breath, and I jumped in and spoke as loudly as I could. "Larry graduated from his crime scene investigator training last night, and we'll leave for his new position in Savannah in two weeks."

"Havana, but isn't that in Florida? I thought he'd be assigned somewhere in Georgia. I'll tell Big D Larry has his assignment; he'll call Larry for the details."

I shouted as loudly as I could, "Get new hearing aids, Mother."

Mother continued, "Tell Larry congratulations from both of us. It was nice to talk to you, Margaret, and I'll tell Big D you agree with me."

Mother hung up, and I sighed. "Mother's hearing is worse than it was before she got the hearing aids. I'll talk to Tonya; she might have some ideas. I need to warn Larry that Mother thinks I agree with her about not needing hearing aids, though, so when Sarge calls him, he'll know what I really said."

Palace Guard nodded.

I sent Paul a text: "Told Jennifer."

He replied immediately, "K."

I wonder if he has been hiding until he heard from me; glad I told him right away.

I dictated a text to Larry: "Talked to Mother. She lost her hearing aids and thinks we're going to Havana, Florida. Sarge will call you; tell him I said she needs new hearing aids."

Larry replied, "Will do. Thanks."

My phone rang then announced, "Call from Martha."

"Come to Tonya's apartment. Tonya said Kiki wants you to bring the men and Lucy."

"We'll be right there," I said.

"That's great." She chuckled. "You realize if either of these phones was under surveillance, they would never crack our imaginary code."

I giggled as she hung up, then I opened the back door, and in the spirit of our imaginary code, I called out, "We're going to Tonya's, and Kiki would like to see you."

Spike and Lucy dashed inside; Lucy stopped at her water bowl for a long drink while I put on my jacket and picked up my backpack.

Tonya opened her door as we hurried down the sidewalk. "Kiki wanted to wait outside, but it was too chilly for me."

After we were inside, Martha said, "We assumed you've already had breakfast, so I made a coffee cake. Do you want coffee or hot tea?"

"Coffee, please."

Tonya hugged me, then I took off my jacket.

Kiki chirped hello to me from Martha's shoulder then chittered where Lucy relaxed on the area rug in the living room.

"Is Kiki saying hello to Lucy?" I asked.

"Exactly; I love how well you hear." Tonya pulled me to sit on the sofa with her. "I'm going home with Mom. Justin is kicking me out..."

Martha burst out laughing then said, "Poor, kind-hearted Justin would be horrified to hear you say that, honey, but it was really funny."

"Thanks, Mom." Tonya continued, "Gray Lady, I don't want Mom to drive home alone, and it's only a week until Justin joins us."

"We decided there was no reason to disrupt Justin's first day in a new class by leaving at the same time as he had to leave for his class," Martha added.

Tonya giggled. "Not even Justin could argue it wasn't logical. Mom and I hope to find a place for us to live before the end of next week; I'm really excited he was assigned to the regional office near Savannah after we've been practically across the state from our families."

"I think leaving today is smart," I said.

Palace Guard nodded.

"Mom, Palace Guard agrees with Maggie." Tonya giggled.

Martha smiled. "Maggie, we've loaded the car with all of Tonya's clothes and books; Justin will bring whatever we've forgotten. Tonya wanted to tell you in person."

"I appreciate it. Martha, I wanted to ask you if you could suggest the best place for us to live too? We think we'd like to have a two- or three-bedroom house with two bathrooms because we know we'll be having out of town guests regularly; most importantly, it has to have a big backyard that is fenced for Lucy."

"I have some ideas; do you want a list, or shall Tonya and I scout some out for you? Tonya wants a smaller place, so it's not like the two of you will be in competition."

"Thank you, a list would be perfect."

"I'll text you my email address, so you can send me your must-haves and nice-to-haves. I'll send you the links of what is available that might be acceptable, and you and Larry can discuss."

"That would be great. I can get you our list this evening after Larry and I work on it together."

The three of us sat at the table with our coffee and coffee cake.

"Is there anything else I can do for you?" Martha asked.

"You're already doing a lot." I took another bite of my coffee cake.

"Kiki said there is," Tonya said.

"Don't feel bad, Maggie. Kiki reads me all the time too," Martha said.

"She's right; Sean and I had a long talk last night, and I told him I felt guilty because Larry had to take care of all the cooking and cleaning. Sean suggested that one of our friends that he knows could help me find a personal chef and a cleaning service. I talked to our friend this morning, and she was excited to have a project she could work on. Would you have any suggestions?"

"I have a few ideas, but I definitely have friends who have contacts. Tell your friend to get in touch with me."

"That's great. Her name is Jennifer Coyle; she's the mother of my best friend, Kate Coyle, who is an FBI agent. After I talk to Jennifer, I'll give her your number and text you hers, so y'all can communicate directly, but if you have any questions, call me."

After we finished our coffee cake, Martha wrapped the individual servings and gave two to me then put the remaining four into the freezer.

"Thank you for the coffee cake; Larry will really appreciate having a treat with his breakfast tomorrow. Are you ready to leave? Can I do anything for you?"

"We're ready. If I think of anything, Mom will call you," Tonya said. "We'll start your lessons after you move into your new house, and I'm so excited you'll be in the Savannah region with us."

Lucy, the men, and I walked with them to Martha's car, and I waved until Palace Guard tapped my shoulder, then we returned to our apartment. Lucy flopped down on the rug, and I called Jennifer and told her about Martha.

"That's great to have someone local who can recommend the best area for a home for you that is also close to Larry's new office; it's fantastic that she also has the contacts who can recommend cleaning services and personal chefs. It would be ideal if the personal chefs have a description of their business model, so you can get an idea of what your options are."

"Larry and I will talk about what would work best for us."

After we hung up, I sent the texts with phone numbers to Marth and Jennifer then put on my coat and went out back with Lucy, Spike, and Palace Guard. "Wind's not blowing, so it's not too bad. I miss being outside and running. Maybe Larry wouldn't mind going for a run later."

We went inside, and I turned on my computer and dictated a list for the house: no more than a thirty-minute commute for Larry, three bedrooms, two baths, fenced back yard, and a utility as must-haves, then I included a gas stove, fireplace, walk-in closet, and a large lot as nice-to-haves. I stopped the dictation and saved my document.

When Larry came into the apartment, he kissed me. "It took longer than I expected because it's almost eleven, but everyone who planned to leave today is loaded and on the road. Tell me about your morning; Justin told me Tonya and Martha were planning to leave after they talked to you."

"Do you suppose we could go running, shooting, or both today? I can run with Palace Guard's help if you want to run faster than I do."

"I know where a track is that we can run; do you want to go now?"

"After we run and have lunch, can we go shooting?"

"Up to you. The range will be crowded."

"I don't like that I can't glare at anyone who stares at me. Can we go tomorrow?"

"No one will stare at you," Larry growled. "I can't glare as well as you can, so I'll talk to the range manager. She won't tolerate rudeness."

"I'll need a long-sleeved T-shirt and pants for running."

"I can help you pick out what you can wear to be warm enough but not too warm."

After we dressed for the track, Palace Guard met us at the door in his running shorts and shirt. Lucy rolled onto her back, and Spike rubbed her belly and waved to us as we left.

"I think I'll run with my jo," I said. "It will be good practice."

I crammed on my Texas Tech ball cap and grabbed my jo and my backpack.

On the way to the track, Larry said, "I'm not sure I would have thought of your backpack."

I shrugged. "I can't stick my carry piece into my waist band because it would drag down my pants as I ran. I'll run with my jo for balance and defense and my backpack for the weight and defense because I learned it's important to train the same as I would be any time I'm running with or without you, especially on a track."

"Kate trained you well."

"I'm not sure if she actually told me that, or if I figured it out from all the times she ambushed me before I started ambushing her first."

Larry chuckled. "I'm sorry I didn't think about how much you missed your training. Running is a good place to start, but I'm still not convinced starting with the weight of the backpack is a good idea."

When Larry parked the truck at the track, I said, "The backpack might slow me down, but if I have it, you and Palace Guard can race a few laps around the track after I turn back."

Palace Guard patted my back. "Thanks, Palace Guard."

"That's true; I wouldn't leave you if you didn't have your backpack," Larry said.

After we stretched, I began running, but Palace Guard put his arm in front of me to slow me down. *He's right; I started out too fast.*

I slowed my pace and ran almost halfway around the track then waved Larry and Palace Guard on ahead while I turned back.

"Are you sure?" Larry asked.

"Positive," I called back and kept going.

As I ran, I heard a runner coming up behind me; I maintained my pace.

"On your right," he called out then kept going.

I watched the blob as he ran in front of me. A few minutes later, I heard the sound of an idling car engine. When I neared the parking lot, the idling car pulled away and left.

I cooled down with a walk past the bench then returned and waited for Larry and Palace Guard. *I'm glad Tonya went home with her mom; she wouldn't have heard anyone coming up behind her on one of her walks, and I don't know if Kiki could have warned her in time.*

"Are you doing okay?" Larry asked as he and Palace Guard ran past the bench.

"Doing great."

I snorted as Larry stepped up his pace, and Palace Guard sped up to be a half-step in front.

After their fourth lap, they slowed then walked to join me.

"That was brutal, Palace Guard," Larry said. "Thanks."

Palace Guard saluted him.

Larry completed his cool down. "Are you ready to go, sweetie?"

"Ready when you are."

Larry wrapped his arm around my shoulder as we headed toward the truck. "I'll have to take a shower before lunch; I'm dreading pulling off my shirt over my head, though. Did that guy say anything when he ran past you?"

"Nothing other than warning me he was coming up on my right, but I wasn't surprised because I heard his footsteps long before he was close."

"I was hoping you would; that's at least one advantage of your super-hearing."

When we went into the apartment, Spike waved his hand in front of his nose and fake-gagged, and I giggled.

"Very funny, Spike," Larry growled and hurried to take his shower. While he dressed, I jumped into the shower.

After lunch, we went to the range, and I wore my earplugs and a headset that Larry bought at the range store. Larry corrected my stance, and Palace Guard tapped my shoulder to adjust my aim, and just as Larry said, no one bothered me.

On our way home, Larry said, "You did very well."

"Thanks, I'll clean our guns when we get home."

"I'll gather your supplies for you then stay out of your way," Larry said.

Later in the afternoon, we took Lucy to the park and walked a trail in the woods before supper.

While I cleared the dishes and Larry loaded the dishwasher, I said, "This has been the best day in ages; I've really missed being outside."

"It's been a while since I've run; I didn't even know how much I missed it until Palace Guard ran my legs off. I'll have to keep it up because otherwise, it wouldn't be long until you're running faster than me with your backpack."

I shook my head. "Not likely to happen, but now it's my goal."

Larry grinned and palm-smacked his forehead, and I laughed.

"Why don't we sit on the back porch where the security cameras can't see us and toss down a couple of beers for old times' sake, Sexy Maggie?"

"That sounds great," I giggled. "That was one of the sneakiest stunts you've ever pulled."

He shrugged as he opened the refrigerator and pulled out two beers. "It worked; you were so busy disabling cameras and writing notes that you didn't even notice that you were safe for one night."

"I was so mad the next morning, I would have gladly pushed you and Kate off the balcony."

"That might have worked too," Larry said as we sat in our chairs on the porch. "I would have been hurt, so you would have had to take care of me, and you would still have been safe."

"I forgot to put a dishwasher on my must-have list."

"What?" Larry stared at me.

I tossed my hair. "I changed the subject because I would have lost whichever way it went. Martha will send me links to houses in the areas she recommends, and I made a list of our must-haves; I need to know what you want too before I send her our list. That shouldn't take us long, but then we also need to talk about a personal chef and a cleaning service." I smacked a mosquito.

"Let's go inside, and you can show me your house list."

Larry read my list. "You're right about the dishwasher; you could add a washer, dryer, garage, and blinds on the windows to the nice-to-have list. Where would a back porch be on our list? I think it's a must-have."

"I think so too; put all that on the list." I pointed to the keyboard. "Anything else?"

"Not that I can think of; you could tell Martha to let you know if she sees anything we should have added."

I dictated the email, then Larry added the list as an attachment and sent it to Martha.

"I'd like the cleaning service to clean every other Friday, so the house will be clean for the weekend," I said. "I don't think we'd need anyone more often than that, but we can see how it goes."

"I agree; now the personal chef. What were you thinking?"

After our long discussion, I said, "I think our idea of having a personal chef come to our house every Monday to prepare five days' worth of meals would work the best for us, so we can have the weekends to go out or cook together. I'll see what Jennifer suggests."

Larry leaned down for a kiss, but I moved to the side and quickly jumped to my feet then tossed him to the floor.

He laughed as he rose. "No fair, Crazy Lady; I wasn't ready for an ambush."

"Fine, then I'll race you to the bedroom."

He grabbed me up in his arms, and I giggled and nibbled on his neck as he carried me toward the bedroom; when he reached the doorway, he backed into the room. "I win."

CHAPTER FOUR

After Larry left the next morning, I called Jennifer.

"Good morning; I've been waiting for you to call. Do you have coffee?"

"Yes, Larry filled the insulated tumbler with coffee, so I can make it through the morning."

"Good. What did you come up with?"

I told her our cleaning service plan and what we decided for the personal chef.

"That's great. I'll get with Martha. I'll ask for sample menus for you to review too when I interview the chefs."

After we hung up, I went out back with Lucy, Spike, and Palace Guard. While I listened to a mockingbird, I heard a hawk call as it circled overhead until it screeched and flew away. *I wonder if a gang of smaller birds attacked it from behind and drove it away.*

"Be small and attack in force when they aren't looking; there's a lot to learn from birds," I said.

Palace Guard nodded.

The mockingbird trilled through its songs even louder until a garbage truck rumbled by, then Lucy barked, and all the neighborhood dogs joined in and drowned out the trills.

"I guess everyone in the neighborhood is awake now; we can go inside."

My phone buzzed a text from Larry. "Basic chemistry first two days. Please toss me off the balcony."

"Will do. That's brutal."

"Yes."

An hour later, my phone buzzed another text from Larry. "I looked ahead. Deep dive day three into organic chemistry. We'll lose people."

"Not good."

"Another chem major and I will lead a study group this evening and maybe tomorrow too. Crash course in organic. OK with you?"

"Absolutely."

I glanced at Palace Guard; he put his right hand on his heart and patted his chest.

"He's a very kind man, isn't he? I'm so proud of him."

Palace Guard nodded.

It was close to lunchtime when Tonya texted me. "Mom and Jennifer are talking. BFFs."

I replied, "I'm not surprised."

While I was eating the sandwich that Larry had made for me, my phone announced, "Call from Paul."

"How do you do it, Gray Lady? A few girls in a small town in Tennessee run away, and Kate Coyle calls me and tells me to back off."

"What? That doesn't make any sense."

"I know; just a few simple searches seemed innocuous enough to me. The officers of the company are legit, but when I started digging into the Board of Directors, I get the call from Kate, who claimed her call was unofficial, but that's like a tiger licking its lips and saying, 'let's do lunch'."

I giggled. "I didn't expect you to get a call, unofficial or otherwise, from the FBI. What do you think triggered it?"

"You. Kate assumes anything I do is for you, and therefore, requires her immediate intervention. I pulled Securities Exchange records that are public information; anyone can access them online, so I didn't think a thing about it. I found five board members listed, but with a little more digging, I found all five are listed as the executive officers in an offshore supply chain company based in the Cayman Islands."

"A foreign corporation? Doesn't the SEC require board directors of US companies to list any foreign interests?"

"I'm sure there are people who have read and can interpret the SEC's rules and regulations, but since I haven't any inclination to even tackle the SEC language, my uneducated ignorance says probably."

"Is that when Kate called you?"

"No, it was after I found the obituaries for all five of them. They all died ten to fifteen years ago. If the youngest of them was still alive, he'd be ninety-eight years old."

"Holy cow. Does that mean they're zombies or something?"

"I think they'd be vampires, but I'm as knowledgeable about undead or whatever folklore as I am on SEC rules and regs. I think they are just dead, and someone decided to use their names and reputations. All of them were highly respected businessmen and served on several boards of directors."

"What will you do now?"

"For starters, I'll carry a sharp stake with me at all times in case they are vampires, then I'll tackle this from a slightly different angle."

I need to read up on zombies. "I'll bet you'll focus on the supply company: their product and their customers."

"I planned to do something else like eat a half gallon of ice cream by myself, but that sounds like a much better idea, so yes, that's exactly what I planned to do. What's so amazing to me is that I've spent only a few hours this morning on a few runaway girls in Tennessee, and Boom! Kate calls. That's a new personal record for me."

I giggled. "You're the best."

"Maybe not: there's more. Kate called her dad and told him to pull me off any further investigations into whatever I was doing, so Glenn wanted to know what's going on; he's onboard now. I'll get back to you when we have more; meanwhile, keep the bail money handy."

After we hung up, I finished eating then sat on the sofa and flipped through two books.

"I don't want to listen to a book; I want to read a book," I grumbled and set the books on the table.

I exhaled then paced in front of the front door. "I need to run."

Palace Guard pointed to the backyard.

I glared at him, but he crossed his arms and blocked the front door. I put on my running shoes and slipped on my backpack then went out back and ran the perimeter of the fence as fast as I could. I kept going until I was dizzy from running in such a tight circle. I sat on the grass to keep from falling, and Lucy licked my face.

"Thanks, girl. Running helped clear my head, and nothing tops off a good run like one of your kisses."

I brushed off the grass before Palace Guard and I went inside; Lucy and Spike stayed on the porch.

My phone announced, "Call from Cassandra."

"We'd like for you to have lunch with us tomorrow, and I have someone who can give you a ride unless you want to come with a friend."

"Tonya left yesterday, but I'm sure I can find someone else. What's going on?"

"I could tell you that Chef and I would like to see you, but this is a job for the Gray Lady: one of our regulars might be in trouble and not know it. We need your expert ears to see what you think." Cassandra sighed. "I'm sorry; that didn't come out right, did it?"

I smiled. "I understood what you meant. What's going on?"

"Patty is recently widowed and middle-aged. One of the nicest people you could ever meet. Today she was gushing to her friends about a new special friend she met in the grocery store yesterday that completely understands her. After they chatted for a while at the store, she invited him to go home with her for a nice supper."

"That sets off a few alarm bells," I said.

"No kidding; she is not an impetuous person. Patty's whole conversation the entire time she was here was 'Rodney this' and 'Rodney that.' She invited him to join them for lunch today, but Rodney is a busy man, according to him. Two of her friends rolled their eyes while she talked, but her third friend stayed back after Patty and the other two left and told me she was afraid Patty might be getting into a situation that might not be safe; she asked me to see if you could come here tomorrow for lunch to listen to Patty and tell us what you think. Poor Rodney could be a really nice guy, the two of them had instant chemistry, and we're all busybodies, but I don't believe it. When she talked, it was like she was in a trance or something; it was surreal. Patty's friend told me she would be honored to buy you lunch, and if you needed a ride, she'd come get you."

"I'll see who is still around this week. It will be fun to check, but if no one I know is still here, I'll let you know."

After we hung up, I picked up my phone. "I wonder if Lori or Jessie are still around?"

Palace Guard shook his head and waved his arms. "You have a different idea? Who?"

He frowned then pointed to the print on the wall that was here when we arrived.

"I don't understand. It's just a print of a ranch."

He shook his head then strode to the print and waved his hand in front of it like he was writing on it.

"Are you painting? Art?"

He nodded.

"Oh, I get it. Our retired FBI art expert, Della. She did say she'd be back in a couple of weeks."

I sent Della a text. "When will you be in Tennessee?"

"Why? Are you out of gumbo?"

Palace Guard smiled.

"I know. That is so Della, isn't it?"

I answered my phone before it finished the first ring.

"Whatcha got, kid? I know you didn't just get lonesome for Grandma D."

"Something might be going on here." I told her about the runaways, Anna and the two young men, and Patty.

"Only the Gray Lady could take three seemingly unrelated, completely innocent events and discover an ominous cloud of mystery. I'll be right there, or at least in time to pick you up for lunch tomorrow. We'll go to the café and spy on Patty, right? Maybe I can finagle an invitation to meet good ole Rodney. Meanwhile, call Cassandra and ask if Patty described him. You might be twice as smart as I am, but I'm a tad sneakier than you are."

I called Cassandra. "Grandma D will be here tomorrow, and she's looking forward to coming to the café for lunch, so I won't need a ride. I've been wondering, did Patty happen to say what Rodney looked like?"

"Oh, yes, and this is when her friends started rolling their eyes. I won't use all of the glowing adjectives that Patty did. He has a muscular build and is medium height with no belly fat. His eyes and hair are brown. His face is rugged looking, but I'm not sure what that means; he has two days' beard growth because he decided he liked the scruffy look. He must use a distinctive men's cologne because Patty was all wound up, and the entire café heard a detailed explanation of how manly he smelled."

"Thanks, and I'm glad I missed it."

"I'm sure there will be more tomorrow; don't say I didn't warn you." Cassandra giggled.

I texted Della. "I have a detailed, gag-worthy description."

"Good."

Palace Guard grinned.

My phone rang and announced, "Larry."

When I answered, he said, "The guys want to stay after class and dive into the study session right away. The plan is to order pizza. One of the guys asked his wife to plan something, so she's hosting a get together at their place. I can come get you and take you there."

Spike poked me then waved his hand toward the door. I shuddered and shook my head.

"We have food here I can eat; I'm too tired to go anywhere."

"I'll come home and fix us something, so we can eat together," Larry said.

"No. I'll be fine. Palace Guard and I can go out back, and I'll shoot a bear then pop it into the oven."

Larry laughed. "How do you come up with stuff like that?"

"I had to remind you that I'm not helpless," I said.

Spike rolled his eyes.

After we hung up, I headed to the sofa. "I have plenty of time to decide whether to make a ham and cheese sandwich with or without toasting the bread; I'll rest my eye for a few minutes."

My phone buzzed a text and startled me awake. I stretched and when I looked for the phone, Palace Guard pointed to it.

"Are Lucy and Spike outside? I didn't hear them leave; I must have been tired."

Palace Guard nodded.

My text was from Jessie. "Call me."

When I called, she said, "I thought you weren't here, then Lori heard Kevin was leading a study session tonight. There's a big soiree being planned by the wife of one of the students. Did you hear about that? Are you going?"

"Was that a rhetorical question?" I asked.

Jessie chuckled. "It was my attempt to open a polite conversation. We knew you wouldn't want to go, and we don't blame you a bit. Lori is planning an equally big party, except it's for the three of us. We decided it was your turn to be host, so we'll be there at five thirty with food and gossip. Lori wants to know if you have wine."

"Probably."

"We'll bring some just in case you decide to hide yours before we get there."

After we hung up, I said, "I'll have half a toasted ham and cheese, but you'll have to help me with the toaster and the mustard. I can pour a glass of water at the sink; I want to save room for food this evening."

While I ate lunch, Palace Guard made a throwing motion.

"That's an excellent idea. I do need to practice my knife skills, and today's weather is perfect for being outside."

After I rinsed off my plate, I strapped my knife holster onto my lower leg, then Palace Guard, Spike, and I went out back and left Lucy sleeping on her favorite rug.

I exhaled to relax. "Okay, ready."

Palace Guard tossed a small rock that hit the grass in front of me three yards away, and I tossed my knife at the sound. Spike held his arms out to indicate three feet.

"That's a big miss, but I guess I have to start somewhere."

Spike waved his hand in a circular motion to indicate, "Again."

After I hit close to the nearby rocks that fell in front of me, Palace Guard went to the next level: random throws in random directions at irregular intervals. I was feeling confident in my skills when Palace Guard tossed a rock ten feet behind me. I whirled and threw my knife, and Spike broke into his panda grin as he pulled out a large handkerchief and wiped his brow.

"I guess it is time to quit; I am really sweaty and should probably drink a big glass of water. Thanks, I definitely needed the knife training: my skills needed work, and I needed the morale boost." I held up my hand, and Palace Guard and Spike smacked it, then we went inside.

When I went inside, Spike pointed to my phone.

"Did I miss a text?"

Palace Guard nodded, then he, Spike, and I listened to the text. "From Jessie: spicy or not spicy chicken."

I responded, "Spicy."

"Good because that's what I made."

Spike elbowed me and grinned as I hung up.

"I expected Jessie to go with spicy whatever I said too."

Spike waved his hand in front of his face then held his nose.

I curled my lip to sneer, but Palace Guard and Spike laughed, and I sighed. "You weren't supposed to laugh; I was trying to snarl. I'll take a shower, but first I need to drink some water and cool down a bit."

After my shower, I towel-dried my hair before I dressed. I tried to brush my hair, but I couldn't get through the knots. I pulled it away from my face with my fingertips; when I went into the living room, Palace Guard's eyes widened, and he shook his head.

I shrugged. "It seemed like a good idea to wash my hair, but my plan to dry it with a towel didn't quite work out. Maybe Lori or Jessie will attack the tangles for me, so I won't look so scary."

Spike pointed to my ball cap, but Palace Guard rolled his eyes.

I went to the bathroom and returned with my hairbrush. When Lucy yipped, I opened the front door with my hairbrush in my hand.

Lori-blob said, "We have a hair emergency, Jessie."

"I've never met a tangle I couldn't tame," Jessie said as she breezed past me then placed a large, covered platter on the kitchen table. "Come sit, Gray Lady, and we'll get your feral hair tamed."

I breathed in the blended fragrances of amber, orange flowers, and sandalwood that whirled around Jessie while she gently separated my hair into sections then paused before she began brushing. "Have you ever thought about going red? I'll bet you'd be stunning with red hair."

I snorted. "Before Larry and I were married, he had to go undercover after the bad guys rammed his car and thought they'd killed him. He might have thought I planned to dye his hair darker, but I dyed it red because that was more of a change. He was surprised, but it looked nice."

"Surprised? Really?" Lori chuckled.

"Surprised not in a good way, I'm guessing," Jessie added.

"Maybe, but I'm sure it was because he was so badly injured," I said.

"Keep going; there's more to this story," Jessie said.

"Later, Larry decided I needed to be less recognizable too and made a hair appointment for me. I thought maybe a haircut would be the best way to go, but he sabotaged me and arranged for the hairdresser to dye my hair red. It absolutely ruined my Gray Lady image."

Jessie guffawed, and Lori snort-laughed.

"Y'all are a mess," Lori said after she caught her breath.

"And this was before you were married?" Jessie giggled. "I'll bet you two are still as competitive as ever." Jessie finished removing tangles and braided my hair into one long braid.

"We can eat whenever we like, but I brought hors d'oeuvres if we'd like to nosh with a glass of wine. Gray Lady, I invited someone to join us. I don't know if you've met Dana. She's only been here a few weeks because she was completing a contract before she left home. I ran into Dana at the library last week. She's going to the big get together because she wants to meet more wives and thought that would be a great place to start. I told her if she decided to leave, to come here because we were having a quiet evening with our suffering, injured friend to support her in her last hours."

Jessie snorted. "What did you really say?"

"I told her the large group had a tendency to prefer uniformity, and we were beyond hope." Lori sighed. "I liked the melodramatic mood of my first version better."

"The second version is sufficiently dreary, though," I said. "Did you put the back of your hand on your forehead?"

"Dang, I didn't think of it," Lori said. "Let's have snacks."

Jessie opened the refrigerator. "There's a ton of food here, Lori. Let's sit at the table."

"I'll pour wine. Red okay? Don't answer because that's all I brought."

While we drank our wine and nibbled on cheese, olives, tortilla chips, guacamole, and crab dip, Jessie said, "I think I told you I grew up in Haiti, and my grandma was a highly respected Mambo, a healer and leader of Vodou. She spoke only Haitian Creole to me, and I spent most of my time with her. Part of her mystique was because only a few people were as fluent in Haitian Creole as she was, so her words must have sounded exotic to many. I always thought part of her success as a healer came from her attention to detail. She watched people carefully: their facial expressions and body language, particularly when they interacted with others or thought no one was watching them. She always said a person's spirit and body told her things the person wouldn't share or didn't know about themselves. I've tried to be a good observer, but I get too distracted, so I never notice things she did."

"I never catch details either," Lori said. "I'm always scanning the room for what might need corrected; it must come from organizing large events. What about you, Gray Lady?"

"I miss the minute details that I used to see about people; Larry's not a blob anymore, so I'm hopeful that my eye will continue to heal, and according to the surgeon, it will."

"You're still amazing; your sense of hearing has really kicked in for you, hasn't it?" Lori leaned past me to clear the appetizers from the table, and I caught a whiff of her peach and vanilla bath soap.

I nodded. *My sense of smell has heightened too. Is that a good thing or a bad thing?*

When she opened the refrigerator, the tantalizing aromas of Jessie's spicy chicken and Lori's homemade potato salad made my mouth water.

I smiled. *A keen sense of smell is a good thing.*

Lori poured sweet tea while Jessie served potato salad on our plates.

While we passed the chicken around the table to serve ourselves, Lucy yipped, and I rose. "Someone's at the door."

"I'll get it; it's probably Dana." Lori rose from her seat and beat me to the door.

When she opened the door, Dana said, "I brought wine as a peace offering for crashing your exclusive party."

Lori chuckled. "'I brought wine' is the secret password. Come on in. Gray Lady is short, and Jessie is tall; at least that's how I tell them apart."

Jessie and I laughed, then Dana joined in.

"Gray Lady, short; Jessie, tall. Glad you gave me that hint," Dana chuckled.

Jessie put the dips, chips, olives, cheese, and a plate and fork for Dana on the table. "What would you like to drink, Dana? Wine, iced tea, or water?"

"I'd like iced tea if it's sweet; otherwise, water is fine."

Jessie poured sweet tea into a glass of ice; Dana sat at the empty chair across from Lori, and we resumed eating.

"Mmm, this is really good," Dana said. "I didn't know I was starving for something that wasn't full of preservatives. I got the impression the wives who were at the large meeting were skilled at opening cans and boxes, which is fine, but they're really missing out on the satisfaction of creating great meals."

"People who also work a full-time job get a pass," Jessie said.

"Right, and mothers with children," Dana said.

"And people with one eye," I added.

When Lori burst out laughing, I held my hand up for a high-five, and she and Jessie smacked it, then Palace Guard and Spike did too.

Dana choked on her tea, then chuckled. "Y'all are a mess, and I'm finally with my tribe."

While we ate, Dana said, "I wondered why you invited me here if I left the wives' group, but it didn't take me long to figure it out. Was there a spouses' meeting at the beginning of the session that you first became acquainted with the lovelies?"

"Sure was, although the instigator of the group you met with earlier today is no longer here," Jessie said. "If this were high school, they'd be the mean girls."

"Exactly," Dana said. "Evidently, a wife of one of the instructors was friends, in a very loose sense, with two of them who were at the meeting. According to the mean girls, the instructor's wife has a new so-called friend who is a young guy that is a hunk, and the wife goes on and on about her new friend, Rodney, and how charming he is. It was clear to me that the mean girls have been goading her on and laughing behind her back. I left."

"I'd like to talk to the instructor's wife," I said. "Did you catch her name?"

"No, but I can ask," Dana said.

"If you're thinking about going back to the meeting, I'll go with you after we eat," Lori said. "We can pop in and pop out then come back to Gray Lady's for a glass of wine to clear our heads of the trashy talk."

"That would be perfect," Dana said. "Gray Lady, did you really take down that killer that hurt Tonya? I didn't know Tonya, but I hated hearing how badly she was injured."

"It was a team effort."

"That makes sense," Dana said.

After we finished eating, Lori said, "Wish us luck."

"I wished we could have gone too," Jessie said, "but neither one of us blends in around here. We could have stood at the door, but you would have to tell me what you heard because I would miss something, then I would have had a snappy response that came out a little louder than it should have..."

"We'd be a disaster as a spy team."

"You are so right," Jessie said. "I'll put the food in the refrigerator, then we can have a glass of wine without them. I want to try that wine that Dana brought."

"I can clear the dishes and put them in the dishwasher," I said.

Palace Guard corrected me as I set the dishes in the racks then guided me as I started the dishwasher.

"I thought your husband's name was Kevin. Why do you call him Larry? Is that his middle name?" Jessie asked while she covered the food.

"Lawrence is an old family name; I started calling him Larry long before we were married, and everyone we know calls him Larry now."

"So, he wouldn't mind if I call him Larry too? It would be a lot less confusing, and he definitely looks like a Larry, not a Kevin to me, except I'll probably forget."

I nodded. *Exactly what I thought too, but please don't tell him that.*

Jessie sighed then closed the refrigerator. "We forgot to ask for permission to eat dessert while they were gone, but if they take too long, we'll go lurk in the doorway and whistle until they notice us."

I giggled. "That will work; tell me another story about your grandma."

"I have another idea; would you be more comfortable sitting on your sofa or chair?" Jessie asked.

"Good idea."

After I sat on the sofa, Jessie sat on the soft chair, and Lucy jumped up next to me.

"When we first met you, you said your mother taught you a few fairy songs. I'd like to hear one, if you're up to it."

"It's interesting that you mentioned whistling because I only know how to whistle a fairy song." While I whistled, Jessie-blob leaned back in her chair.

When I finished she said quietly, "That was beautiful. What are the words?"

I whistled the words then said, "I don't know how to say them any other way, and they don't translate very well because they are feelings more than what we call words, but they kind of mean we are here; be brave and kind."

"That is so sweet," Jessie said. "Are fairies always so nice?"

"No, sometimes they are kind of bratty and even hateful."

Lori and Dana knocked on the door, and Jessie let them in.

"We need wine," Lori said.

CHAPTER FIVE

"I opened the bottle Dana brought, so it could breathe, and we could drink it if you didn't get here soon." Jessie hurried to the kitchen and poured four glasses. "What about dessert?"

"I forgot about dessert. Wine's on hold for now. We should eat at the table because I made it today, so it's very moist. I made it with Meemaw's recipe, and I'm not talking cooking instructions and ingredients, that Mom brought me in a canning jar when she came to the graduation ceremony," Lori said. "We'll have a glass of water instead of wine to go with the cake because Meemaw's moonshine has quite a kick."

While she sliced the cake into small pieces, Lori continued, "Meemaw always said never serve coffee with one of her recipe cakes because everyone will not only be tipsy, but wide awake and tipsy."

"Worst kind of tipsy there is," Dana said, and I nodded.

Jessie opened the cupboard where we keep the glasses. "We'll have to skip water unless anyone wants a coffee mug of water. We went through all the glasses, and the dishwasher is still running."

"Do we have a clean wine glass for Dana?" I asked.

"Sure do," Jessie said.

"We'll survive then," Lori plated the cake while Dana set out the forks Lori had set on the counter.

"This cake is really good," I said after my first bite. "I'm really glad I eat slowly, so it will last longer."

Jessie exhaled. "If I exhale on a candle, will my breath look like dragon fire?"

When we all laughed, Jessie-blob rose and bowed.

After I ate half my cake, I said, "I'll save my other half for tomorrow. Tell us what happened at the meeting."

Dana put down her fork. "Lori was awesome. Our plan was to go into the meeting and split up, but we didn't have any plan after that other than to freelance it. Lori joined a group then started a big argument, so I slid a little closer in case I needed to snatch her away from the mob and run."

Lori smiled. "First thing someone said to me when I joined what looked like a core group was that a wife of one of the instructors was having an affair, so I asked them who. The one who seemed to be the leader said she didn't know, but wasn't it awful, and I lit into her for spreading rumors. She and her friends got huffy and one of them asked if I was calling her a liar, and I used my grandma's favorite line: 'If the shoe fits.'"

"Lori had the entire room engaged, but not in a way that I would have expected." Dana giggled. "I noticed a woman standing in the doorway who looked ready to bolt. I joined her and asked her what was going on, and she told me she just dropped by to say hello on her way home and was surprised to hear the group gossiping about an unnamed wife of one of the instructors who was having an affair with some young guy. She told me that her close friend Macy did have a new friend who was nice, but he wasn't her boyfriend by any means. I tried to make small talk, so I asked the woman, her name is Roxanne, if she was a trainee or faculty wife like her friend, and she told me she was faculty, and Macy was too. I thought I would die of embarrassment and apologized for being so presumptuous. She assured me that she wasn't offended, and we laughed at my awkwardness and naivety at believing a rumor then had a nice chat about the campus. We're meeting tomorrow morning for coffee in the campus coffee shop at nine; she'd like to meet the Gray Lady if you're available. I invited her to come here to meet a small group of nice women, and she might drop by."

"I don't remember ever riling up a group so quickly before, but they were more than willing to battle me for challenging them." Lori chuckled. "I glanced at Dana periodically, and when she flashed a thumbs up, I quietly disengaged and left the group arguing with each other. That's about it."

"Lori definitely stirred them up; it was amazing to see. Lori was in the middle of what looked like a foray that was about to explode into a fist fight, but after I signaled a thumbs up, she slipped out of the middle without disturbing any of the combatants and practically glided across the floor to my side, and we left."

"I think I can make the coffee tomorrow at nine. My Grandma D will probably be here by then, so she'll come with me, if that's okay," I said.

"That's perfectly fine," Dana said. "I'll send you a text before I leave tonight, so you'll have my number. I got the impression Roxanne might bring Macy with her."

I smiled. *That will get Grandma D here for sure.*

"Anyone care for wine?" Jessie asked.

"No takers? Lori asked. "I'm ready to call it a night: a wonderful, glorious night. Gray Lady, can we leave our wine here for our next get-together? I'll leave the tiny piece that's in the fridge and wrap four large pieces of cake, so the four of us can enjoy cake all this week. I'll take the chicken, potato salad, and appetizer leftovers and send the food with Bud in the morning for the class to have for lunch. I'll spread the word tonight that no one should pack a lunch."

"We'll need extra chicken for them," Jessie said. "I'll send more with John tomorrow."

"I'll send a little something with Jerry too," Dana said.

"Before you go, Dana, I'll show you my phone for Gray Lady's phone number," Lori said.

"Okay, got it and sent," Dana said.

My phone buzzed a new text and cheerfully announced, "Text from new caller."

"Did you hear how happy my phone is that I finally made a new friend?" I asked.

When Jessie laughed, everyone joined her, then after hugs and good-byes, they left.

Palace Guard exhaled and dropped onto the sofa while Spike did his wacky dance.

"It wasn't that bad. Next time, you can join Larry if it was too much for you."

When Larry came home, he kissed me. "Yum, cake and alcohol. Successful evening?"

"Very much so, and I had a wonderful time. It's nice knowing that after the two weeks are over, my new friends and I will still get together when we can because all our husbands are with GBI."

Larry hugged me. "It does feel like we're putting down roots of sorts, doesn't it?"

"Sarge would say we're finding our tribe. How did your study session go?"

Larry pulled out a beer and opened it. "It was a rough start: the other instructor and I agreed that we would assume a basic knowledge of chemistry then quickly move on because the classes today were so watered down. After an hour, a few of the guys started catching on, and by the end of the session, everyone was with us. It was a gutsy way to go, but we had to get them used to a faster pace if they were going to survive after the third day. We'll probably go with another full speed session tomorrow; is that okay with you? We need to get everyone ready for day four."

I giggled. "I may have to schedule you on my calendar. I'm meeting a few of the wives for coffee tomorrow morning at nine; if Della's here by then, she'll go with me. Della and I have plans to go to lunch at the café. Chef loves Grandma D, and our group tonight talked about another get together this week for appetizers. Our appetizers ended up being a full course meal with wine and dessert. We had cake, and I have the leftovers for us, but I'm warning you it has a nice kick. Lori soaked it in her MeeMaw's moonshine."

"I've been worried you'd be lonely because I'm gone so much. Now, I'm worried you'll have more friends than I do."

"You're too competitive, but just for the record, I have more friends this week than I did last week."

"Ouch. I need cake, so I can think of a snappy comeback for that." Larry hurried to the refrigerator then opened the door. "Whew, I can smell the moonshine in that cake. There's half of a piece in here. Is that yours? Do you want it?"

"I'll have it tomorrow; turns out my limit is half a piece of Meemaw cake."

"I'll start with a half too."

While Larry put his cake on a plate, I sent a text to Della. "Coffee with friends at nine."

She replied, "I'll be there."

Larry returned to the sofa with his plate. "Our wine collection suddenly grew."

"It's for our next get together here this week."

"There are some great wines there. You and your tribe take a sip of wine seriously."

After he ate his first bite of cake, Larry exhaled. "This is really good: it took my breath away; it's definitely soaked in moonshine, not store-bought whiskey."

"How can you tell?" I asked.

Larry chuckled. "The summer I was fifteen, a couple of guys and I had a friendly chemistry competition, and I won, or I would have if Dad hadn't found my end product and dumped it."

I snickered. "You made moonshine?"

"All in the interest of science."

I shook my head. "You are full of surprises."

While Larry talked about the class and the study topics for Tuesday and Wednesday nights, I smiled. *I don't understand half of what he's talking about, but I love how excited he is.*

"Sweetheart," Larry said, and I jumped.

"I didn't mean to startle you, but you fell asleep; let's go to bed."

I listened to the soft sound of running water in the shower and Larry as he hummed a tune quietly and slightly off key.

I smiled. *Best wake up sounds in the world.*

When he tiptoed into the bedroom, I said, "I'm awake, honey. I almost forgot to tell you not to make your lunch today because your class is getting the leftovers from our party last night, minus chemistry cake."

"There was that much left over?"

"Jessie said she was making extra chicken because we ate most of it, and there may be an extra side dish or two. The wives here are great cooks and are excited to have an outlet for their skills. I can't wait until my eyesight clears, so I can join them. I know everyone would love Chef Daryl's recipes."

"I'll help you with gumbo when cold weather rolls in," Larry said.

"That's a great idea, and your schedule may be a little less demanding, so you'll have time to do a little sous chef work in the evenings."

"I'm leaving early. I have a breakfast taco for you in the oven, but I'll put it on a plate when you get out of the shower. I don't think it will be too messy for you."

When I stepped out of the shower, Larry opened the bathroom door and whistled long and low. "Naked Maggie, you are looking as good as ever."

He kissed me then patted my bare bottom. "See you later, cutie."

I smiled as I dressed. *He always brightens my mornings.*

I peered at the blob in the mirror. *I wonder how my braid is doing?*

After I dressed, I hurried to the kitchen as Spike and Lucy came inside. "Did Larry feed Lucy?"

Spike nodded.

After I drank half of my coffee, I glanced around the room. "Where's Palace Guard?"

Spike held up his forefinger and thumb in the shape of a gun and blew on his finger.

He hasn't used his sign for Larry in a long time.

"He went to class with Larry? Any idea why?"

Spike shook his head.

"Is it because Della will be here?"

Spike shook his head.

I picked up my breakfast taco then took a bite. "Larry did a great job of wrapping my taco like a small burrito, so it wouldn't fall apart while I'm eating it."

While I loaded my plate into the dishwasher, my phone rang and announced, "Call from Glenn."

"Are you okay, Maggie?"

"I'm fine. Why?"

"Just checking. Paul and I expect to have news for you today, but I wanted to check your schedule. Will you have some alone time later this afternoon to talk?"

"I can make time; Lucy and I can always go to the backyard for some fresh air."

"I'm not supposed to tell you that I'm snooping for Kate, so I won't, but if I were, it would be because Kate wanted me to find out if anyone will be visiting you this week; she thinks you have something going on that she needs to stop."

"Wasn't Heather due back from her assignment yesterday? Will Kate be aware of what jo records when Paul hands over monitoring jo to Heather?"

"Jo is Paul's permanent assignment; we'll let you know if that changes," Glenn said.

"Even though you aren't interested and didn't ask, nobody's coming to see me this week. I'd be lonely if it weren't for Lucy, the imaginary men, and the wives' group."

"I'm glad you didn't tell me about the wives' group because Jennifer would grill me on details."

"Since we never had this conversation, you're fine."

Glenn chuckled as he hung up.

"Sometimes I have the most bizarre phone conversations, especially with Glenn; have you noticed that?"

Spike broke into his wacky dance, and I laughed.

When I heard a car pull up in front of the apartment, I hurried to the door, but Spike blocked it.

"Fine; you can check to see who it is," I grumbled. "You're as bad as Palace Guard."

I snickered while Spike strutted to the window.

When he stopped but watched me closely instead of looking out the window, I said, "I won't touch the doorknob; is it Della?"

He peered out then nodded, and I waited for the knock before I opened the door.

"Sorry I'm slow. I had to pull into a grocery store parking lot to answer my phone. Ms. Kate Coyle wanted to know where I was. She should have known this is the week I go to Tallahassee."

I snorted. "Do we have time to talk? The coffee shop is a short walk."

"I went into the store and bought a few things after I talked to Kate; I'll bring in the groceries from my car, then you can talk while I put them away."

When Della came inside, I said, "It's almost too early for the details about Patty's new friend, but here's what I have."

After I told Della about Rodney, she said, "That is definitely a gag-worthy description. I may have to dump you, so I can meet ole Rodney. We need to see him in action, and I'm sure you're too young for him."

I continued with the gossip at the meeting last night, Roxanne, and what I knew about Macy.

"The similarities and differences between Patty and Macy are interesting. I'm looking forward to meeting both of them. I'm ready to leave when you are." Della closed the refrigerator, and I grabbed my jo and backpack before we left the apartment.

When we reached the coffee shop, Dana met us at the door and hugged me.

"I'm glad you are here," Dana said. "Roxanne brought Macy with her. Both of them knew about the Gray Lady."

I smiled. "Grandma D, this is my friend Dana."

"Call me Grandma D, Dana. It's nice to meet you."

"You too, Grandma D. I'll introduce you to Roxanne and Macy."

On the way, Dana said, "We have a large carafe of coffee that we can refill and pastries. My grandmother would have my hide if we didn't have a little something to eat with our coffee."

"Your grandmother raised you right, hon," Della said.

After Dana introduced all of us, she said, "Gray Lady, sit here next to Macy and across from Roxanne. Grandma D, I thought you might like to sit next to Gray Lady, so you can keep an eye on the door."

Dana's brilliant. I know where Macy and Roxanne are sitting, so I'll know who's talking.

Della poured coffee for me then herself.

"Gray Lady, it is such a treat to meet you; I'm sure you've been told more than once that you don't look formidable at all, and I mean that in the nicest way possible," Roxanne said.

Della chuckled. "My petite granddaughter has surprised more than one killer, as I'm sure you know."

"I feel like I've known you forever, Gray Lady," Macy said. "Roxanne and I were just comparing notes on which of your cases are our favorites, but that's the past, isn't it? What's going on now?"

"I have a question for you. What would you think if the number of runaways in a small town suddenly increased in a short amount of time?" I asked.

Della choked then coughed. "Excuse me; the pollen gets me every fall."

"The pollen does get bad this time of year," Dana said.

"Gray Lady, are you talking about here? My first thought would be that all the girls are partying somewhere at their parents' lake house," Roxanne said.

"Aren't you assuming the girls know each other and are close enough friends to do something like that as a group?" Macy asked. "Do we know anything about the girls?"

"Not really except all the parents were adamant that their daughter did not run away." I bit into my scone that Dana had put on a plate for me then continued, "Two young men, not from around here, were talking about runaways in a local café; one of them mentioned that grooming took a lot of work, and the other young man loudly announced that running a cheerleader camp wasn't easy. The grumbler asked if they were taking the cheerleaders to Atlanta or Savannah, then their conversation turned to a quota, and they discussed taking the young woman who served drinks at the café because it would be easy to convince her to cooperate."

"Are you thinking our runaways are the cheerleaders? The men could have been having a completely unrelated conversation, or the runaways were kidnapped or enticed. I realize that there may be one or two that ran away, but is there any difference between kidnapped and enticed?" Macy asked.

"What about ransom?" Roxanne asked.

"None of the parents admitted to any ransom requests." I sipped my coffee.

Macy chuckled. "Do you have any more zingers, Gray Lady?"

"Of course, she does," Roxanne said. "She's the Gray Lady."

Macy cleared her throat. "The first year I was here, I taught in a classroom that was next to a brilliant instructor. When I asked her if she would be back the next semester, she said her specialty was crime, not teaching. You have your knowledgeable specialists right here, Gray Lady, and you have our full attention. How can we help?"

"I have one more seemingly unrelated piece. A middle-aged widow in town has a new friend who pays her compliments, gives her gifts, and is essentially showering her with attention; Patty has been talking about him incessantly to her friends. She met him in the grocery store only a few days ago. Grandma D and I are having lunch today at the café where she goes regularly."

"Do you know what this awesome friend looks like?" Macy asked.

Grandma D snorted. "Remember, you asked."

I gave Macy, Roxanne, and Dana Rodney's full description.

"Why do I feel like we need to hire a security guard for Ms. Patty?" Dana asked.

"I need a shower or a flame-thrower," Macy said.

"The two young men talking about grooming, then Rodney's sudden, intense attention on Ms. Patty that borders on love-bombing set my criminal psychologist's teeth on edge," Roxanne said.

"Ms. Patty's Rodney isn't the man I met yesterday, who introduced himself as Walt. He has a military air about him: straight back, chest out, close-cropped hair cut, slender waist, muscular torso, and medium height. He wanted to meet me for coffee this morning, but when I told him I already had plans, he said he would call me later today to see if we can meet at a coffee shop tomorrow morning," Macy said.

"You're inviting your Grandma D to go with you, aren't you?" Della asked.

"What a wonderful idea; of course, I am, Grandma D." Macy's voice lilted with her delight in Della's offer. "Gray Lady, I guess that makes us cousins."

"Do you expect Patty and Rodney to go for coffee tomorrow, Gray Lady? Dana, are you available? I don't have any classes," Roxanne said.

"That's a great idea," I said. "Can I get back to you? If Patty and Rodney are meeting for coffee tomorrow, we can show up."

"I'm definitely available," Dana said. "I have a feeling they will meet at one of the two fancy, touristy coffee shops downtown, so even if they don't say anything today, we might want to check both shops in the morning."

"Perfect," Roxanne said.

"Back to the runaways," Della said. "Won't it be easier to find them while they are still here? How long do you think it will be until they are moved?"

I told them about the caterers.

"There's a faculty appreciation recognition next Tuesday," Roxanne said. "I know the event organizer; she's swamped and probably hasn't made any arrangements for the dinner yet. I'll see if I can convince her a catered dinner would be best. I can help her by contacting the caterer to set up a meeting toward the end of the week."

"Better you than me." Macy snorted. "My ex-husband is the vice president of operations for the catering company; Flint Turner is a snake. I have a little snake repellent potion that I'll give you to counter the snake oil he sells."

"You're so helpful," Dana said; Roxanne, Della, and I laughed.

Before we left, Macy said, "Gray Lady, I can't thank you enough for bringing us into your latest. I've needed to exercise my investigator's chops and didn't realize it."

Grandma D asked, "Do you know Kate Coyle?"

"Of course, and all of this is just hypothetical conversation," Macy said.

"Right," Roxanne said. "I'm too busy with managing my classes to mingle with the new people, but I would enjoy meeting the Gray Lady."

On our way back to the apartment, Della said, "You shocked me at first when you brought up the runaways, then I realized there are too many possibilities and too little time for you and me to cover everything."

"Were you the brilliant instructor that Macy mentioned?" I asked.

"Whatever gave you that idea? What's our next step?"

Nice deflection, Grandma D.

"Would you like to go for a ride around town and in the country?" I asked. "It's a long shot, but I'd like to see how many abandoned buildings and vacant, large homes there are."

"That sounds like a pleasant way to spend the morning. What do you have in mind?"

"I was thinking we could do a grid search, starting with the core downtown, then if we have time this morning before lunch, I'd like to focus on the industrial area and collect addresses of possible places to house the cheerleaders. Paul Vargas can check the names of the owners of the buildings."

"We're looking for a building owned or rented by the catering company, aren't we?" Della asked.

"That would be the best case, but we'll have to see what we can find."

"I know the town fairly well, and I have an old map of the town, so I can mark off the sections as we cover them; we can leave whenever you're ready."

"I'll take Lucy out for a quick break, then we can leave."

After we went inside, I asked, "Ready to go out back with me, Lucy?"

Spike shook his head as Lucy rose from sleeping on her favorite rug then lumbered to the back door. When we were outside, Lucy and Spike stayed on the small porch while I walked to the fence and back three times.

Lucy watched me then nosed the back door. "Okay, we can go back in now. Thank you for humoring me; I didn't want Della to think I neglect my dog."

When we went back into the apartment, Lucy trotted to her rug and flopped down then closed her eyes.

"Lucy had the right idea, but we have buildings to stalk," Della said after she turned toward downtown.

"All these small shops are new, and there is very little parking left on this block. We'll have to pick a nice day to stroll a block or two." She chuckled. "We've got two weeks before you leave; surely we can catch a few dozen bad guys and still have time for a cup of tea and a scone at that little tea shop we just passed."

When she turned toward the commercial and industrial buildings on the edge of town, she said, "I see a large building with no cars in the parking lot. Can we assume it's abandoned?"

"Pull into the parking lot. How do I lower my window?"

"It's a button, but I can do it for you. Do you want it all the way down?"

"Yes, then stop the car."

When she stopped, I listened. "It's completely silent; I don't hear an air conditioner, heat pump, or any type of motor. It's not in use."

As Della headed to the next building, she said, "This one has four or five cars in the lot, but two of them have flat tires. Do we check?"

I nodded. "I smell something garlicky like spaghetti sauce or pizza."

"The doors and windows have been boarded up."

"That's interesting. I hear an air conditioner running. Don't pull into the parking lot. What's the address?"

Della slowed the car as she read the numeric to me, then I pushed the record button on my jo and repeated the full address. "Do you think you could pull into the parking lot across the road, so I can take a video of the building?"

"Sure can."

After Della parked near a dozen other cars in the lot, I stepped out then pressed the record button on top of my jo for the video.

After I climbed back into the car, Della left the parking lot, and I pulled out my phone from my backpack and dictated a text to Paul: "The building is boarded up, but I heard an air conditioner running and smelled cooking. Please search for owner and type of business."

Paul replied. "Got it."

"Tell me what magic you used to send him the address and take a video of the building."

I giggled. "Heather magic."

"I should have realized our technology wizard had a hand in it. How does it work?"

"I don't know the details of how it works because all I do is push the right buttons on my jo. Heather would normally be monitoring the transmissions, but she's on assignment, so Paul Vargas has taken on the task."

"How does he know when you're sending something? Is there an alert?"

"There must be, or else he's listening night and day."

"I know Paul; he's listening night and day because he wouldn't trust an alert," Della said.

CHAPTER SIX

"Our next building has a three-quarters full parking lot, There are several people going into and out of the main building. One guy is in a suit and is carrying a large briefcase. Looks like a salesperson to me," Della said.

"We can keep going," I said.

After another block, Della said, "That's it for the industrial and commercial crowd, and we don't have any possibilities except for that one boarded up building. It went faster than I expected. We have a little more time before we'll need to be at the café unless you want to go early."

"Do you know of an area of town with older houses that aren't very close together?" I asked.

"All the older houses in town have either been demolished or restored. I think we would have to go out into the surrounding rural areas."

"If we were in Harperville, I could ask our brilliant real estate agent, Harriet, for some leads," I said.

"Aren't you just the smartest little thing? One of my oldest friends is a real estate agent here; she'd disown me if she knew I didn't think of her. Shall we go to the café? You can go inside or sit in the car with me while I talk to her; I'll probably be on the phone for a while because she loves to chat."

I snickered. "I wouldn't mind having a little extra time to visit with Cassandra and Chef before the lunch rush starts."

While Della parked, my phone buzzed a text. "From Macy: Coffee confirmed in am for nine. Will pick up Grandma D from your apartment at eight thirty."

"I'll be at your place by eight," Della said.

I replied, "Ok."

When I tapped on the locked café door, Cassandra opened it and hugged me.

"My regulars try to sneak in if I leave the door unlocked before we open, so they can grab their favorite table. I have great news for you: I've given away your table," she said as we strolled toward the back of the café.

"You sound very proud of yourself."

"I am. Patty called and asked me to reserve a private table for her and a special guest for lunch today, so I gave her yours, but I saved the most undesirable table for you."

I giggled. "Right next to the drink machine, right?"

"Absolutely. You and Grandma D will have full benefit of the entire Patty and Rodney conversation while they are here."

"You are absolutely brilliant, Cassandra."

"I know, except the table switch was Chef's idea. My theory is her head isn't bombarded by all the chatter around here, so she can think without constant interruptions and in peace, not that I have any idea of what that might be like."

"Grandma D's on the phone and might be a while; do you suppose I could interrupt Chef?"

"She'd have my hide if you didn't," Cassandra said. When we went into the kitchen, Chef said, "Nice to see you, Gray Lady."

I faced Chef-blob, so she could read my lips. "Nice to hear you, Chef."

Chef chuckled, and I grinned.

"I have things to do to be ready for our customers," Cassandra said.

After she left, I asked, "What's your theory about Rodney?"

"He's playing a role," Chef said. "He was here several times last week before he approached Patty. He watched the different groups of our regulars, then I think he selected the most vulnerable woman to manipulate."

"I didn't know he had been here before he met Patty."

"He didn't call attention to himself at all. It will be interesting to see whether Anna recognizes him if he comes in with Patty. Where's Grandma D?"

"She's on the phone in her car."

"Want a snack of sweet plantains?"

"I love sweet plantains, but I don't want to fill up before lunch."

"They're part of your lunch; you'll just be pacing yourself. I've cut them into pieces for you, and I'll give you a fork. I'll let you know when you have eaten all of them."

I ate my sweet plantains slowly as I relished each bite. *Chef certainly knew how to shut me up.*

"Last bite," she said.

Cassandra hurried into the kitchen. "Anna's here, and she's pretty upset. Remember the young woman in the library that the two men mentioned? Her grandmother reported that she didn't come home last night. Her grandmother found a note on her bed that said, 'I love you. You'll be safe.' I have a friend who works in the same city building as the police department; I'm going to give her a call to see if the young woman was added to their list of runaways."

After Cassandra left, I muttered, "They met their quota."

"Yes," Chef whispered.

"Did you read my mind or my lips?" I mouthed.

Chef giggled then whispered, "It's our secret."

Chef hugged me. "Be safe, Gray Lady."

After I sat at my new table, Anna said, "I put your sweet tea in a to-go cup with a lid and a straw in the lid. Grandma D's glass of tea is on the table for her. I see you've been promoted to my favorite table."

I smiled. "I should have realized that's why Cassandra reserves this table for trusted friends."

"Cassandra went outside to talk to Grandma D. Do you think they are planning a big going away party? Cassandra was very secretive."

"No one has mentioned anything to me, but thanks for the heads-up."

Cassandra led Della to our new table when they came inside.

While Della sipped her tea, she said, "This is definitely the catbird seat, isn't it? The two women that just came in are whispering about how fancy the café is. Can anyone hear us?"

"No one except someone who is standing next to us and the drinks." I sipped my tea.

"When Patty comes in, we'll be able to hear what she says without being obvious. How do we sort out all the other voices?"

"I don't know, but I'm interested in learning. We could ask Anna, but that somehow feels like cheating, which makes it perfectly okay. I'll ask her."

When Anna came to the drink counter for drinks, I said, "I have a question when you have a minute."

"Be right back." Anna hurried to deliver the drinks then returned. "You have a question about the menu?"

I smiled. "Yes, how do you keep the different dishes straight?"

"Pick one at a time; you'll catch on." She giggled as she hurried to take the next drink order.

"What does that mean?" Della asked. "I mean, I heard what she said, but I'm still not sure how to pick one."

"It makes sense to me: don't listen to all the voices; listen to one at a time."

"I'll have to try it, but I suspect you'll be better at it than I am. What are we having for lunch? Did you already order?"

"We're having whatever Chef..." I paused and listened. "Patty just walked in the door."

"How do you know that?" Della asked.

I snickered. "A woman said, 'Hi, Patty.'"

"Cassandra led a woman and a man to our old table near the kitchen. I'll let you listen; I'll watch Patty and her gentleman friend," Della said.

"This is a nice restaurant, Patty; it's quite a surprise for such a small town. This is something you'd expect only in a hidden side street in Paris. You definitely have a discerning eye for quality," Rodney said.

Patty gushed. "Thank you, Rodney; you are so kind. I thought you would like it, and I'm really relieved that you do."

"She patted his hand, and now he's taking her hand in his hands. I'm glad I can't hear what they are saying," Della said.

"Their conversation is at the same level as the hand touching," I said.

After they ordered, Patty said, "I've been thinking about what you suggested for my nerves, and a week at a quiet resort does sound nice."

"I think the seclusion will grow on you," Rodney said. "You don't mind leaving all your friends?"

"I don't really have any close friends here. Everyone is so shallow, not like you at all. Are you sure we'll be properly chaperoned?" she tittered.

"I'm positive, and you'll meet new friends and finally find your purpose in life, like we've talked about. You have a real gift in wanting to encourage and help people adjust to whatever the circumstances are. Are you sure you aren't a trained psychologist?"

"He squeezed her hand, and she blushed. This is like a bad movie," Della said. "No, it's more like a train wreck that I don't want to see, but I can't stop watching."

Cassandra set our plates on the table. "I have your lunch. Gray Lady, Chef grilled a small smoked pork chop and baby carrots then cut them into bite-sized pieces and prepared sour cream mashed potatoes for you. Della, you have a pressed Cuban sandwich with sweet plantains as your side dish."

Cassandra refilled Della's glass and my cup then said, "Those two will go on like this for a while, then I suspect Rodney will go in for the kill. Any bets?"

"I'm not handing you any of my money; I think you're right," Della said.

While we ate, Rodney said, "This will be a great test of our relationship."

"Patty's face went beet red; what did he say?" Della asked.

"He used the word, 'relationship'; I think he's testing her to see if he can go to the next level of control," I said.

"Whatever do you mean, dear?" Patty asked.

"She called him, 'dear'. That's a green light," I said.

"I could have guessed that. He has a very self-satisfied look on his face," Della said.

"Let's enjoy our lunch, then we can talk more while we eat dessert," Rodney said.

"He's going to let her sweat until dessert," I said.

"Thank you, Rodney. I was afraid I wouldn't be able to eat my sandwich without gagging," Della said.

After they finished their lunch and while I was still eating, Rodney said, "I've been afraid to bring this up, but sometimes you act like you don't want to make me happy and do things deliberately to annoy me."

"He went straight for the throat," I said. "He's accusing her of deliberately annoying him."

"I am so sorry. I would never do anything that would annoy you. All I want is for you to be happy," Patty said. "Please forgive me."

"She just apologized. Can I shoot him?" I asked.

Della snorted. "I get the first shot."

Rodney sniffed. "I don't know; we'll have to see how things go at the resort. I may have to leave for a day or two on business, and I don't want to hear that you were complaining while I was gone."

"He told her he'll leave her at the resort for a few days and doesn't want to hear she complained."

"What do we do?" Della asked.

"This is really touchy. We need to undermine him somehow in her eyes. Let's ask our crime specialists because I have no clue."

I took a video of Rodney and Patty while I said quietly, "Need to know who this man is. Talks like a con artist. More later."

"Think about it, and we can talk in the morning. Is there a nice place we can meet for breakfast?" Rodney asked.

"Of course. I'll text you the address and make reservations. What time do you want to meet? Is eight o'clock too late?"

"Is that as early as you can get up?" He sighed. "I suppose eight would be fine. I could finish up quite a few things before breakfast and meet you there."

"Thank you so much for giving me another chance. I'm so sorry I've displeased you. I won't do it again."

"I have to go; can you pick up the check? I'll reimburse you."

"Oh no, it's my honor to pay for lunch. Thank you so much for the chance to make things right." Patty's voice became shrill.

"Don't act hysterical. It's unbecoming in a woman of your age," Rodney said.

"Sorry, I won't do it again," Patty said softly.

"See that you don't." Rodney walked out.

"Patty has tears running down her face. I heard the entire exchange; I was shocked at how rapidly he escalated, but it must have worked because she's hooked," Della said. "We need an emergency meeting of the crime experts because he has her off balance and won't give her any time to recover. The good news is that they won't leave before tomorrow morning. I'll send texts to Roxanne and Macy."

After Della sent the texts, she said, "Patty left money on the table and is walking out. She looks totally defeated."

Della's phone buzzed, and she read her texts. "Roxanne and Macy can meet us at your apartment at four. We've got plenty of time for our dessert then check out the four properties my friend recommended. I told her a friend of a friend was thinking about opening a bed and breakfast and didn't mind a house that needed work, as long as it had electricity and running water and wasn't infested with vermin."

"Here's your dessert," Cassandra said. "Chef made a strawberry cake topped with whipped cream and fresh strawberries. She calls it strawberry long cake instead of shortcake because it's a cake that's long in the strawberry department."

I chuckled, and Della laughed. "Chef is a genius. I'll need to see her before I leave."

After Della and I went into the kitchen, Della and Chef began a silent, animated conversation. *I didn't realize Della was so adept at signing.*

Cassandra tugged on my arm; I followed her back to my table, and she sat with me. "Patty's behavior reminded me of a high school friend who got involved with a gang that bordered on a cult. The more her parents and friends tried to talk to her, the more she dug in her heels. One of our friends had a cousin who was kind of high on the gang ladder. Her cousin did us a favor and spoke out about how unfit our high school friend was for the gang because she was so unstable; they dropped our friend, who was brokenhearted but moved on and became a GBI agent. We think she's undercover and busting up gangs from the inside. I don't know how to do it, but Rodney needs to believe that Patty isn't the right person after all."

"I'll talk to Grandma D. We'll need to move fast. We need to find the cheerleaders and rescue Patty and probably need to wrap it up in a day or so."

"That about sums it up. Let me know how I can help. Here's Grandma D," Cassandra said.

When I rose to leave, Cassandra hugged me. "Be safe, Gray Lady."

After we were in the car, Della said, "My real estate agent gave me the best route to cover all four in the least amount of time. They're all at least four bedrooms, two-story, old mansions or maybe I should say mansion-wannabes. The first one is only ten minutes from here."

When we reached the address, Della pulled onto the side of the road. "There's a long driveway to the house; I didn't think about how we could check it out without being blatantly conspicuous when we drive down the long, gravely driveway and pull in front of the house. We would need to walk in, wouldn't we?"

"Can you pull up an aerial view of the house? Maybe there's better access behind the house," I said.

"That's smart. Give me a few minutes."

While Della pulled up the address then switched the view, I pushed buttons and locked and unlocked my door then finally lowered my window and listened.

"It's faint, but I hear an air conditioner running, except I just now realized that only means the owners don't want the house to grow mold."

"The house sits on the back of the property, and there is a small field behind it; hopefully, we'll be able to at least see the house."

We need Spike or Palace Guard to do an initial check for us.

"I have a brilliant idea, but it will sound a little strange to you."

"Does it have anything to do with your imaginary men?" she asked.

I jerked my head and tried to peer at her, but she was still Della-blob.

She laughed. "Kate told me about the imaginary men ages ago when she asked me to pick up the art from you, but you never mentioned them, so I didn't either. What's your idea?"

"We can go back to the apartment and pick up Lucy and Spike. Lucy will be our reason to stand alongside the road while Spike checks out the house." I sighed. "This would be a better job for Palace Guard because he's much more efficient and will focus on the task, but he's with Larry today. Spike is easily distracted, especially by young women. If Spike returns right away, there are no girls; if he takes forever before he shows up, we've found the girls."

"Good. I was not crazy about the idea of fighting my way through high grass with ticks sucking away every drop of blood I have. I am not a fan of ticks or rats."

On our way to the apartment, Della asked, "What are the plans for dinner?"

"We're having leftovers from last night plus a portion of whatever else anyone makes for tonight's study session that Larry and one of his friends are leading. The course jumps from three days of basic chemistry to advanced topics on the last two days; the purpose of the study session is to fill in the intermediate topics before Thursday."

"That has always been a problem with that class. I had hoped they would have corrected it by now, but the gossip was they'd change the class as soon as a certain faculty member retired," Della said.

After Della parked in front of my apartment, she said, "I'll go in with you and start a batch of chili in a slow cooker before we leave. It won't take me long."

When we went inside, Lucy and Spike came in from the backyard, and Lucy stopped for a drink.

Della browned the meat and chopped vegetables then tossed all her ingredients into the large slow cooker before she put on the lid and turned the setting to 'high.'

"Spike, we need you and Lucy to go with us, so you can check out old houses in the country for us before we drive up to the house," I said. "We need to know whether the house is occupied because we're trying to find a group of girls who supposedly ran away. Della, Lucy, and I will wait on the side of the road while you see if anyone is there."

Spike grinned and held up a thumb, and I added a bowl and two bottles of water for Lucy to my backpack, then we joined Della in her car.

When Della approached the driveway of the first house, she pulled onto the shoulder, then the four of us climbed out.

"The grass isn't too high for Lucy here, but we'll still want to check her for ticks and burrs when we're back at the apartment," I said as Spike headed down the driveway.

Lucy investigated the grass alongside the road. When she found a hole, she sniffed all around it then snorted and walked away.

When Spike returned, he shook his head.

"Nobody is there," I said, and the four of us climbed back into Della's car and headed to the next house.

As we neared the next house, Lucy was ready for our new game of exploring a place she'd never seen before. When I opened her door, she yipped and bounded out, and Spike jogged to the driveway.

"Is Spike enjoying this as much as Lucy?" Della asked. "Does it sound strange that I just asked you if an imaginary man is enjoying exploring old houses?"

"Yes, he is, and it definitely sounded strange." I giggled.

When Spike returned, he held up two fingers then pointed to Della and smirked.

I coughed to keep from giggling. "An older couple is in the house, but no one else; did I get that right, Spike?"

Spike grinned, and we all climbed back into the car.

When we came to the third house, I pulled out the bowl and water I'd packed for Lucy, and Della opened a bottle of water and poured it into the bowl while Spike hurried to the driveway.

Lucy drank down half of the water then wandered around the field for the best place to relieve herself. She finally found the right spot, and I whispered, "Success."

When Spike returned, he scowled as he held up three fingers then motioned flipping hair and mimed rubbing his eyes with his fists.

"Three girls, and they're crying? Do we know why?" I asked.

He nodded then held up five fingers then repeated his hair and eyes motions.

"Five girls crying?"

He nodded then waved good-bye followed by a shoving motion with both hands.

"The five girls were forced to leave? How many guards are there?"

He nodded then held up two fingers then pointed his index finger with his thumb upright.

"Two armed guards. We need the professionals to take over. How do we do that?"

"Now you're in my territory. Give me a minute, then we can leave." Della pulled out her phone.

"It's Della. What do you know about the eight or so runaways here?"

She paused, and I listened to the man on the other end of the line as he spoke. "I haven't been involved, but I suspect this might not be a simple case of runaways. Do you have something for me?"

"Three of them are in an old, abandoned house and are being guarded by two armed men," Della said. "Five of them have been removed from the house, but I don't know where they were taken. I'll text you the address."

"Don't be anywhere close to the house in ten minutes. We'll get them out safely."

Della hung up then sent the text with the address. "Now, we clear out. It will be handled."

"Spike, do the girls know where the other girls were taken or why the three of them are still there?"

Spike shook his head, and I shook my head.

"We have to beat feet," Della said, and we all hurried to the car.

After we were on the road, Della said, "Sweet girl, you and Spike were amazing. If we had blindly gone in there, the results would have been disastrous. Spike, you're my new hero."

I glanced at Spike's red face. "Spike's flattered. Thank you."

As Della parked in front of the apartment, I said, "I need to call Paul."

"I'll refill the tank and be back before Roxanne and Macy show up," Della said.

After Lucy, Spike, and I went inside, Lucy hopped up on the sofa, and Spike sat next to her and checked her coat before she spread out.

When Paul answered, I said, "We checked abandoned rural houses, and Spike found three of the girls. Della called it in, and they may have already been safely rescued."

"Only three?" he asked.

"That's it. Spike said the girls talked about five others that had been forced to leave earlier, but he didn't have any other details."

"That's not great, but at least Spike found the three before they were gone too. What's our next step?" Paul asked.

"Della and I may tackle the Rodney and Patty angle, and we have a new charmer on the scene, Walt, but his intended victim is Macy."

"Macy? Isn't she an instructor for the more technical crime scene classes? Does old Walt know what he's walking into?"

"Evidently not; Macy intends to learn more about his organization, but that could be risky. What do you have?"

"I found one of my old contacts, so we have a little information about the offshore supply chain company. It's a conglomerate that distributes food and supplies to restaurants, hotels, and hospitals; they have a major interest in commercial real estate investments, are actively purchasing residential properties in Florida, and own several gym franchises. They recently purchased the building at the address you sent me. It was on the market for several years, so they probably bought it at a rock bottom price. I'll bet there are squatters, which would explain why you smelled cooking."

"Do you think it's a dead end?" I asked.

"Yes, but I would like the address of the house where Spike found the girls. It sounds like a property the offshore company might have been interested in. That's an easy check," Paul said.

"I'll text you the address."

"We've identified the nice guy and the tough guy; both of them have arrests for shoplifting, robbery, and car theft. Sounds like they've worked together as a team since high school, but we're still digging. The uncle of the nice guy is the local catering manager. I have a friend who is in the catering business checking for more information. I'll text you their names and their parents' addresses."

"Della and Macy have local contacts; maybe we can locate the two guys."

Paul continued, "We haven't been able to identify your Rodney guy yet. I might put Ella on that one; she'll turn it into a project for credit in the class she's taking; if you can, get me a photo of the new guy, Walt. I'd love to have a sliver of evidence that there is one organization behind Rodney, Walt, and the kidnapping of the runaways. See if Della can find out the names of the two guards with the three girls. My money is on the nice guy and the tough guy, although nothing on either of their records indicates that they've ever been armed before."

After I hung up, Della asked. "What did Paul say?"

"He'd like to know the names of the two guards. He's identified the nice guy and the tough guy that were at the café and will send me their names and their parents' addresses."

"I'll get the names for him."

CHAPTER SEVEN

When Della lifted the crockpot lid, I inhaled the distinctive aroma of spicy chili. "Mmm, smells good."

"I hope it's not too spicy," she said.

"It won't be too spicy for Larry and me. We burned our tastebuds on delicious, spicy chili when we were in Galveston."

"If we have leftovers, we'll freeze them in meal-sized portions for you and Larry," Della said.

While my phone buzzed to notify me of a text, Della answered the knock at the door.

Macy carried in a large sack and set it on the dining room table. "Roxanne and I picked up snacks for the study session."

Roxanne hurried to the kitchen. "What a day."

She opened the sack she had brought with her and removed a bottle of wine then uncorked it. "This is for emergencies: I'll start. I didn't know the event co-ordinator had a bad case of stomach flu and couldn't leave home, but I somehow became the event coordinator for the faculty dinner next week. The good news is that I have a team: I corralled Lori into helping me. After a heated discussion, Lori and I decided to meet with the caterer on Thursday to review menus and discuss prices. I tried to convince Lori to take the event coordinator title too, but she laughed at me and dared me to fire her, so I'm cutting her pay in half for insubordination. We are meeting with the head of finance tomorrow because the event coordinator didn't know what her budget was. I would have strangled the so-called event coordinator on the spot when she told me money was a detail and she is a big picture person, but she was at home and probably would have thrown up on me."

"I'll pour you a generous glass of wine right now, honey," Della said. "You've earned it."

"Pour one for me too, Grandma D," Macy said. "Walt called me, but I didn't answer because I didn't feel like it, and twenty minutes later he knocked on my door. That is probably the creepiest thing I've ever had happen in my life. I didn't open the door; he yelled that he was sure something was wrong with me or my phone because I didn't answer when he called. I almost told him to shove off, then I remembered I'm supposed to get information from him. I told him it was my meditation time, and I would see him in the morning. I still hadn't opened the door, and he talked loudly through the door about how good meditation was for the mind and blah, blah, blah. When I saw him at the window, trying to peep inside, I lay down behind the sofa."

Roxanne and I giggled, and Della shushed us, which made us giggle even louder.

"You're supposed to be feeling sorry for me," Macy grumbled. "I have no earthly idea why I did that, but he finally left. I realized later my feet were sticking out, and he could have easily seen them through the window."

Even Della laughed at the telltale feet.

"What the heck, Grandma D, pour me a glass too," I said. "We had lunch at the café, and Patty and Rodney were there. Rodney upped the ante and went from adoring suitor to demanding narcissist. Patty apologized for disappointing him, although he never did tell her what she had done, and she fell all over herself to pay their bill. Her voice squeaked when she became excited, and he told her never to do that again because it was unbecoming for a woman of her age, but the worst part is that Grandma D wouldn't let me shoot him because she wanted the first shot."

"I'm having a glass too because if I had let my sweet, frail granddaughter have the first shot, there would have been nothing left of his sorry carcass for me to aim at," Della said.

While we sipped our wine, I said, "Rodney has Patty totally hooked, and there's nothing anyone could say that could change her mind. I'm worried they may leave tomorrow for what he called a resort. Cassandra suggested rather than trying to stop Patty from going, we could make her undesirable to Rodney's organization to the point that it would ruin his standing if he took her to the resort. Cassandra and some of her friends did something like that in high school when one of the more naïve girls in their class planned to join a tough gang."

"I have an idea that I totally hate," Macy said. "I could call Walt this evening, apologize for not being available when he showed up unannounced at my house, be all chatty, and share in confidence that Patty's son, who is an undercover FBI agent, has a team investigating Rodney because of Patty. Of course, I would assure him that I don't have any family members who would do anything like that."

"I don't know." I frowned. "We'd have to assume that Walt isn't a weasel and would tell Rodney rather than let Rodney get into trouble with the organization."

"Walt could easily be a weasel, and we don't know how fierce the competition is in the organization, do we?" Macy asked.

"We know Patty and Rodney are having breakfast in the morning. Could we sit at a table and gossip about the undercover FBI agent that has a team investigating something or other? What could we say they are investigating?" Roxanne asked.

"Well, we don't really know," Della said, "but I heard someone's friends were worried about their friend, so one of them talked to her son, the undercover FBI agent, to see if he'd look into it, and doting son that he is, he assigned his entire team of gung-ho investigators. The investigating team arrived in town yesterday morning and have already interviewed all of the friends and may even have a warrant for an arrest."

"I like this much better than talking to Walt," Macy said.

"Do we know anyone that knows Patty?" Roxanne asked. "We could tell one of her friends what we heard, and it would spread like wildfire."

"I know just the person. I'll give her a call," Della said.

She's going to enlist her real estate friend as another member of the team to take down Rodney.

Della stirred her pot of chili then went out back to make her call; Lucy and Spike went outside with her.

When Della returned, she said, "The gossip wagon is on the roll. My friend knew exactly who to call."

"I'd say congratulations to us, but is there any way we can find out where the five girls went?" Macy asked.

"They would need at least a van for a driver and six passengers," Roxanne said.

"Or an RV," Della said. "While I was filling the tank at the gas station, an RV pulled in at the pump next to me. The driver was obviously inexperienced because he almost clipped the pump when he cut his turn too tight like he was driving a car. He was a middle-aged male, and so was the passenger, and they looked more like city guys straight out of a CPA office in their suits; there was nothing casual about them that you'd expect from a typical RV camper. The passenger had a bulge on his right side near his waist, which didn't go with his CPA persona. The driver complained about the terrible wind that made keeping the RV on the road so difficult as the two of them went into the store. I wanted to snap a quick picture of their license plate, but it was a temporary one and had faded."

"There wasn't any wind today," Roxanne said.

"Exactly; I can only imagine how much he'd freak if a crosswind caught him."

"The timing isn't right," I said. "The five girls were gone when we checked the house where the other three were. You were at the gas station after that. Could there have been five girls in the RV?"

"I suppose, but it's not very likely. Did all five girls leave at once?" Della asked. Spike shook his head, and I copied him.

"They could have been moved in two small groups to another location to wait for the RV," I said.

Spike nodded then held up three fingers then two fingers, and I nodded.

"We have two possibilities: the fourth house or the commercial building; all we need to see is the RV, then I can call it in," Della said.

Spike shook his head, and I frowned. *Something isn't right.*

"I'll go with you, Grandma D," Macy said. "I'm a good wingman and a great shot."

"Let's go, wing-girl." Della grabbed her keys. "That chili is ready whenever you want to dish it up for the study session, Roxanne."

After they left, Roxanne asked, "You aren't convinced they'll find anyone, are you, Gray Lady?"

Spike shook his head.

"Not really; even though all the pieces seem to fit, something feels off." I frowned. "It doesn't make sense to take the girls away from the house at two different times unless there were two different transport vehicles, and the timing of the RV doesn't really fit."

"How long would it take to get to Savannah or Charleston?" Roxanne asked. "Give me a second, and I'll answer my own question."

I continued, "It doesn't make sense for the kidnappers to move the girls to a location to wait for another vehicle to take them to their destination. I don't see any benefit to taking the risk. Why not just whisk them out of town?"

"It's between six and seven hours from here to Savannah or Charleston," Roxanne said.

"Maybe the girls were being held here until the vehicles could arrive from Savannah or Charleston with drivers and passengers from the resort group."

"That makes sense, in a criminal sort of way," Roxanne said. "Hired thugs to kidnap the girls and hold them until someone from the resort group picked them up."

"We still don't have anything to go on, but this theory makes more sense to me. I have a couple of names and addresses." I showed Paul's text to Roxanne. "Do you know these people?"

"I don't know them very well; a friend of mine teaches at the high school. It seems like she's fairly close friends with them. What do we want to know?"

"I'd like to know where their sons are; they were working for the catering company, but I'm not sure if they are still around town or left."

"My friend would know," Roxanne said.

While she looked for a large container for the chili, Dana joined us.

"Lori and Jessie are taking food to the meeting room to set up the buffet. Do you have anything for me to take there for you?" Dana asked.

"I'm dishing up some of the chili that Grandma D made," Roxanne said. "I'll go with you and carry the snacks from Macy and me."

After they were gone, Jennifer called me.

"Martha and I have found three reasonable personal chefs that her friends highly recommend. All of them will prepare a week's worth of meals at your house; I'll send you their sample menus after we hang up. Martha and I decided on four homes that are for sale in the area she recommends and that look like good possibilities for you, but she's going to check them out first. She and I also considered rentals, and we found five rentals that might work for you, but Martha did a drive-by and vetoed all of them. Martha said sometimes properties look good on the internet but fall short in person. It looks like buying a house is your best option since this is Larry's permanent assignment."

"I don't know how we could have managed without your help; thank you so much."

Jennifer chuckled. "You know any house we find for you will have two guest bedrooms for me and Ella, right? Martha found a hotel with a nice dog park that specializes in two to three-month rentals, so you'll have a place to stay until your housing purchase is final. It sounds like it might be very similar to your fancy apartment here. She's going to check it out to make sure they have ground level suites available."

I giggled. "As long as Lucy doesn't have to wear a bow on her head, she'll love it."

"Glenn said to tell you that Lucy can always stay here until you get your house," Jennifer said.

"Thanks for the offer, but I don't think that will really work for any of us."

"Glenn knew you'd say that, but we wanted you to know the offer is always open. Kate called and wanted to know how we were doing. She's never done that before, so I was instantly suspicious. When she asked how you were doing, I almost shouted, 'Bingo.' I told her your eyesight was about the same, then I launched into a long discussion about Martha and me finding a personal chef and a house for you. While I was in the middle of a detailed description of the process we used in our rent versus buy decision, she asked me if you had any visitors. I told her you didn't, but if she planned a surprise visit, she had better let me know, so I could be there when she showed up at your apartment."

"Do you think she's suspicious?" I asked.

"She's always suspicious," Jennifer said. "I'm not going to ask what's going on because I'm certain Glenn and Paul are in the middle of it, and I've got plenty to do. Just don't tell Glenn and Paul that I covered for them; they're more fun to watch when they're trying to be surreptitious."

After Della and Macy returned, Della said, "The RV was at the abandoned building; they were loading the RV with boxes and doing a lot of furtive glancing around, so we decided I should call in an anonymous tip about smugglers loading contraband into an RV at the warehouse."

"On the way back, we decided that was pretty lame, but it felt good at the time. I'm not sure where that leaves us, though," Macy added.

Roxanne, Dana, Lori, and Jessie joined us.

"Any luck?" Roxanne asked.

"Nothing," Macy said.

"The five girls are probably on the road somewhere, but at least three girls are safe," Della said. "I normally wouldn't have rushed off like that with such slim odds that we'd find anything, but I'm glad we checked because I would have stewed about it all night."

Lori pulled out the leftovers, Jessie set the table, and Dana dished up bowls of chili while Della fed Lucy. After Lucy ate, Della opened the back door, and Spike went outside with Lucy.

"You and Grandma D sit at the table, Gray Lady," Lori said. "Macy and Roxanne, we'll let you be guests, so you can sit with them; the rest of us will sit at the bar."

After we ate, I went outside to check on Lucy and Spike while the other women tackled the dishes and put away leftovers.

While I sat on the porch, Palace Guard joined us in the backyard and saluted me.

Before I had a chance to say anything, my phone rang.

Larry said, "Palace Guard just left; he'll probably be there soon. He was a huge help. We were worried that some of the guys were trying to fake their way through some of the exercises, so I asked Palace Guard to stroll around to keep an eye on everyone's progress. He found three guys that were really struggling, so we were able to give them extra help without drawing any attention to them. The guys think I'm psychic or something now. Palace Guard really made a difference. I'll probably be home in an hour or so; if Palace Guard hadn't been here today, our session tonight would have gone another three hours, at least. We really had a feast for supper; being able to take a break and eat rather than leave and come back later really cut the amount of time for us to be away from home too. I finally feel confident with what we've been doing. Gotta go; loved you first." He chuckled as he hung up before I could say anything.

"Larry's really happy that you were able to help him with the guys at the study session that were having trouble keeping up, Palace Guard, but I'm glad you're back. Do you think you'll be going to class again tomorrow?"

Palace Guard nodded, and I smiled. *He's really proud that he could help Larry.*

Macy opened the back door and leaned out. "Grandma D is heating water to make hot tea to go with our Meemaw cake. Would you like some hot tea? Lori said we can't have coffee, but we can have wine later or tomorrow."

I chuckled. "Hot tea sounds good. Meemaw's cake really has a kick, but it is so good."

"Jessie insisted that Lori cut each piece into quarters, and I understood why after I accidentally breathed in while I was standing next to it."

While we ate our cake and sipped our tea, Della's phone buzzed a text.

She said, "We're at least partially vindicated. I'll read my text to you: 'We got a tip about an RV. Was that you? Cargo was stolen electronics, jewelry, and gold. Quite a haul.'"

"We're awesome," Macy said. "Is it the cake, or am I a crimefighter now?"

Della chuckled. "You're a crimefighter until Meemaw's cake wears off, then you'll revert to your everyday, stellar crime investigator professor self."

"Speaking of stellar," Jessie said, "Johnny told me that Kevin is a patient, outstanding instructor. He had planned to skip the study sessions because he thought he'd be fine, but when everyone else decided to go, he did too. He told me last night that he would have been over his head on Thursday and Friday and would have failed the class. He would have been crushed because this is what he really wants to do."

"I'm going to talk to Kevin tomorrow to see if he would mind if I sat in on their last session," Macy said. "I'd love to take over this class when Professor Bailey retires."

"This may be the cake talking, but I think I can arrange a nice retirement party for Lori to run," Della said.

"Can you arrange it to fit in with the Faculty Appreciation dinner next Tuesday?" Roxanne asked.

"Bless your heart, girl. You set the bar high, don't you?" Della asked. "Fine; I'll take on the challenge. Give me another quarter piece of that cake, Lori, so I can come up with a hairbrained scheme that will work."

"Tell me what you need me to do," Macy said.

"How well do you know the old coot?" Della asked.

"I don't think he knows my name, but that might not be all bad," Macy said.

"He taught high school chemistry, and my mom was in his class. She told me he's always been a stinker; she'd be happy to help," Roxanne said.

"Ask her to call me. I suspect she'll be perfect," Della said.

Roxanne sent the text and received a reply almost immediately. "Mom would be thrilled to help, and she can bring in more people, if you need them, Grandma D."

"Send her my number and ask her to call me," Della said.

"She'll call you immediately," Roxanne said. "Do you want me to tell her to call you tomorrow?"

"Nope; we'll get the ball rolling." Della strolled to the back door with her coffee. As she closed the door behind her, I heard her phone ring.

When Della came back inside, she said, "The steamroller is moving. We'll have a retirement party next Tuesday, and we'll all dress up fancy. I'll wear my dress western boots and clean jeans."

"Way to raise the bar, Grandma D." Macy chortled. "I need a tiara, and I think I'll call an old buddy of mine with the FBI, Kate Coyle, and ask her if anyone has considered investigating Professor Norman Bailey. I have the feeling he's on the payroll of someone whose best interests are served by limiting the number of crime scene investigators."

I listened to the chatter and smiled when I thought one of the blobs might be looking my way. *I need to talk to Paul; I was distracted and a little scattered today.*

A phone buzzed a text. "The study group is finishing up. Our hubbies will be home in ten minutes, so it's time for me to go. Thanks for a great evening; same time, same place tomorrow?" Dana asked.

"Sounds good to me," I said.

Everyone else prepared to leave as Dana hurried out the door.

Macy was the last one to leave. "Grandma D, I really appreciate what you're doing for our training program and our trainees."

Macy-blob hugged Della-blob. *I thought those two were hard-core. Guess I was wrong. Everybody has a soft side.* I furrowed my brow. *A vulnerable spot: that's what I need to focus on.*

A half hour after everyone left, including Della, Larry rushed into the apartment and grabbed me up then whirled me around. "We had some real break-throughs this evening, thanks to Palace Guard."

I glanced at Palace Guard, who had replaced his usually stoic facial expression with pink cheeks and a small smile.

Larry's opinion means a lot to him.

Larry set me on my feet then strode to the refrigerator and pulled out a beer. He opened his beer and took a long drink. "Ah, that's good."

When we sat on the sofa, Larry put his arm around me while he talked about the night's study session and the problems that stumped some of the trainees. I leaned against him and relaxed in the warmth of his intensity to help others to be successful.

"Thanks for listening, sweetie." Larry hugged me tight. "Let's call it a night." ***

After we ate breakfast, Larry refilled my coffee then loaded the dishwasher. "Do you and Della have anything special going on today?"

Other than exposing whoever is behind the kidnapping?

"Della's having coffee with a friend this morning, so I can catch up with phone calls; we may go to the café for lunch."

"Justin, three guys that Justin and I have gotten to know pretty well, and I may pick up sandwiches and find a quiet place to eat. Only Justin and I will be going to the office near Savannah, and the other three are leaving at the end of the week for other offices. Jerry, one of the three guys, mentioned having a potluck dinner at his place before they leave. You might know his wife; her name is Dana." He kissed me, then he and Palace Guard left.

"I wonder if Dana knows she's hosting a potluck later this week."

Spike shrugged then he and Lucy went out back, and I called Paul.

"What's up, Maggie?" he asked when he answered.

"Too much." I told him about the three girls at the house, the five girls who were taken at two different times, and the diversions of the RV and the soon-to-be retired professor, Norman Bailey.

"I should hear from Della today about the names of the two guys that were arrested at the house. I showed Roxanne, one of the faculty here, the text you sent me about the parents, and she has a good friend who is a high school teacher who may know where the two young men are."

"Sounds overwhelming. How can I help?"

"I really can't decide what I should focus on."

"I'll make a call or two and see whether the three girls had any additional information that might find the others; it seems like our best path is to find out where Rodney's resort is and who is behind it."

"Maybe we should work backwards and check for large organizations or groups in Savannah and Charleston," I said. "Seems like it would need to be a large compound or something."

"I like how you think, Gray Lady. I have a good friend in Savannah who could tell me by the end of the day if there are any possibilities there."

"If there are, I could go to Savannah and check it out. Remember Tonya? She's from Savannah and her mother, Martha, has found some houses for us. Martha and Jennifer have been working together to find a cleaning service and a personal chef for us too."

"If you can get a ride to Savannah, Julie and I can meet you there."

"I'll see if Della can take the time to take me there. Another possibility is that I can catch a ride with Tonya's husband because he'll be leaving here as soon as the first chemistry class is over at the end of this week. Thanks, Paul. I feel much better."

"Good; I'll talk to you later."

I stared at my phone. *Dana and Roxanne are looking for Patty and Rodney.*

I sent Dana a text. "Where is the resort?"

She replied, "I'll make it a point to listen for that."

Not long after I sent the text, my phone rang.

When I answered, Dana spoke so quickly that I couldn't understand her. "What? Are you okay?"

"Sorry, I'll start over. I'm fine. Have you talked to Kevin this morning?".

"No, but that's not unusual. Is something wrong?"

"I just heard from Jerry. That old scumbag of an instructor, Professor Bailey, decided that tomorrow is the last day of the month, so he announced he's retired as of noon tomorrow. The jerk-face is fast-forwarding them through the two days of the advanced section today and will administer the test in the morning. The class is ready to lynch him, but there's nothing anyone can do."

"That is absolutely terrible. Does the head of the department know?"

"The old stinkpot is the head of the department. Kevin is planning a session at lunch then as long as it takes tonight to get everyone ready for the test. I called Macy to let her know. She plans to catch Kevin on their break to tell him she can help target the material on the test."

"Wow. I can just imagine how crushing the stress is for everyone."

"I know. Macy told me she'd meet with the class at lunch with copies of a lesson plan to help them to calm down, so they can focus and pass the test in the morning. Della might help her with the class too. I'll talk to you later. I think I may have spotted Patty, but she's by herself; I'll sit at the table next to her then start up a conversation; it shouldn't be too hard: you know, two solo women in a restaurant sitting at tables next to each other. I'm going to smile and be nice. Wish me luck with the being nice part." Dana chuckled as she hung up.

I frowned. *I thought Roxanne was going with Dana.*

My phone rang again, and announced, "Lori."

"Did you hear about the class?" she asked.

"I just did."

"I'm canceling the retirement dinner and cutting back to hors d'oeuvres for the faculty appreciation meeting after I talk to the caterer on Friday; I'll report that the caterer reluctantly turned down the engagement because of the short notice."

"Give Cassandra a heads-up; she and Chef may be able to cater the hors d'oeuvres."

"Brilliant idea; thanks."

After we hung up, I joined Spike and Lucy in the backyard. "We may be going to Savannah early, so I can look at some houses. Paul and his wife will meet us there. I'll call Martha."

My phone rang before I called Martha and announced, "Call from Paul."

CHAPTER EIGHT

"What's up?" I asked when I answered the phone.

"There are two possibilities for Rodney's resort in the Savannah area, and both of them are in remote areas," Paul said. "Julie has packed our things for two weeks; she decided we're leaving here after lunch to pick you up and take you to Savannah tomorrow. I wasn't going to argue. We'll let you buy us dinner in Savannah." He chuckled as he hung up.

I called Martha. "Have you heard about the class?"

"We just did. Even though Justin isn't in that class, it was quite upsetting to hear, but Tonya told me Justin is confident that Larry will get everyone up to speed for the test tomorrow."

"One of my good friends reminded me that Larry will be ready to move in a week, and if I get the ball rolling on housing and the personal chef, it will be less stress on him when he arrives. She and her husband will be here tonight. We'll leave for Savannah tomorrow, so they can help me look at houses."

"That's an excellent idea. I'll confirm the apartment rental for you. I think I can persuade them to offer you a one-month rental to see if you like it well enough to stay for a few months. Do I need to find an apartment for them too?"

"They're planning on staying for two weeks, so a hotel close to the apartment would be ideal. I'll be bringing Lucy, so Spike will come along too. Palace Guard has been helping Larry with the study sessions, so he'll probably stay here. I'll tell

Larry the plan later, probably after the test because I don't want to add to his stress, so please don't say anything to Justin. One of the professors here is going to give the class a study guide at lunch today to help them with the material," I said.

After I hung up, Spike stood in front of me with his arms crossed and a scowl on his face.

"What's wrong with you? I'll tell Larry tomorrow after the test. I don't want to add to his stress."

Spike rolled his eyes then nodded.

"Thanks."

I went inside and exhaled. *After all these elaborate plans, I hope the resort is in Savannah. I'm not sure I could come up with a reason to go to Charleston, South Carolina.*

Spike and Lucy came inside, and Lucy stopped at her water bowl.

"I'll need to pack, but maybe Julie can help me tomorrow. I'm excited that I can finally do something besides come up with ideas for things for other people to do."

Della was going to check on the men who were arrested.

I called the library and asked for Lily, my librarian friend.

When Lily answered, she sounded out of breath. "I hurried to my office to answer in case you had something that was hush-hush. How are you doing, Maggie?"

I smiled. "I still see blobs, but I'm actually doing pretty well. Did you hear about the two men that were arrested yesterday?"

"You mean the thugs who kidnapped those sweet girls? I certainly did. How can I help?"

"I have a friend who is investigating a similar crime, and he asked me what their names are. Normally, I would have looked it up in the arrest record for yesterday, but my sight isn't quite good enough for me to read yet."

"I'll look them up for you; it won't take me long. Would your friend be interested in the investigation for the five others?"

I blinked. *Am I ever!* "He probably would."

"That won't take long either. I found the names of the two men arrested yesterday with Gavin's help. He's our new volunteer and a computer whiz with searches; he has shown me some slick shortcuts that have really saved me time. I didn't recognize the names of the two men, so they aren't local. Shall I text you the names?"

"That would be perfect. My phone will read the text to me, and I can forward it to my friend."

Lily continued, "The current investigation is focused on identifying a gang that kidnaps and moves their victims to an out-of-state location to hold them for ransom. The parents all deny having heard from anyone, but that's the norm, isn't it? I think the investigators are too focused on the precedence of recent crimes and assume this is a copycat."

"What do you think?"

"I think they are making a big mistake and wasting time on waiting for the ransom calls. I would be more interested in what one of the girls reported to her mother as being rewarded when they were 'good' girls by being quiet and doing exactly as they were told. I thought her story was a little strange because they were told to sit on the floor or crawl from one end of the room to the other, for example. Those who immediately followed the instructions without question earned a small piece of chocolate. According to the girl, it became almost a competition."

I shuddered. "That is so creepy."

"It is, isn't it?" Lily sighed. "Unfortunately, no one took much note of it other than the mother who called me and asked for a book on calming fears, so she could help her daughter deal with the anxiety she has now. I set aside several books for her, and she picked them up this morning. How else can I help you?"

"I have an address for a house out in the country, and I was curious who owns it."

"Another easy one. What's the address?"

I told her then smiled as she hummed and tapped on her keyboard.

"A conglomerate owns it. They may intend to build luxury condos there. People like to live where they think they're out in the country if they don't have to mow the fields, don't they? I'll text you the business name."

"I really appreciate the help," I said.

"I'll keep it under wraps. Talk to you later."

After Lily hung up, I giggled. *I love a good coconspirator.*

Della called. "Macy canceled the meeting with Walt, who whined about the last-minute notice and tried to get her to commit to lunch. After she hung up, Macy said at least she was keeping him occupied. I'll review Macy's study outline for the meeting at lunch while she goes through her old notes. Did you know she wrote the test when she was a graduate student? I'm going to help her with the meeting then again with the evening session. There is no way the personal betrayal of that old fool to his class will cause any of them to fail. Macy convinced him that she and I will be happy to proctor the test tomorrow if he wants to prepare for his big speech next Tuesday. If nothing else, we'll write the answers on the board. Macy has the material to develop an on-line class for the trainees they can complete in eight hours after this debacle is over, so they will have the background to operate efficiently in their new positions. I'm not leaving you in the lurch, am I? I'll be back on the job tomorrow afternoon or Friday morning at the latest."

"I'll be fine; the class is definitely the highest priority," I said.

After I hung up, Spike rolled his eyes.

"It's been good for me not to have Della to lean on. I'd forgotten I'm perfectly capable of taking the initiative and finding answers in my own way."

Spike raised his eyebrows, and I laughed. "I don't believe me either, but wasn't it an outstanding pep talk?"

Spike did his wacky dance, and Lucy howled.

My phone rang and announced, "Call from Paul."

When I answered, Julie said, "Paul is taking care of a few issues here, Gray Lady, so we'll probably be leaving not long after lunch. We know you haven't told Larry you're leaving for Savannah tomorrow. Paul wants to know what your thoughts are. I'll put you on speakerphone, so I don't misinterpret."

"There's been a complication." I told them about the sudden shift in the course that totally sabotaged the trainees and the plans to make certain all of them pass the test.

"Should we wait until Friday to leave?" Paul asked.

"I have a feeling it's urgent for us to find the resort, but I can't explain it."

"I guess your only option is to treat it like an adhesive bandage and rip that sucker right off," Julie said. "Could Spike take you to the lunch meeting? Tell Larry you have to talk to him, and let him know the urgency, then tell him everything and take the heat because he's going to blow a gasket either way."

"I know Larry; he already knows something's up, and that's eating at him worse than if he knew what was going on. It's what he does," Paul said.

"He's been with you since forever, hasn't he? He knows," Julie said.

"I've been telling myself that I didn't want to add to his stress, but I realize I already have. The lunch meeting is probably the only chance I'll have to talk to him until after the test and tomorrow feels too late."

After we hung up, I received a text from Larry. "Be home in a second."

Spike elbowed me.

"I know this is my chance to talk to him, but what if he has only a few minutes?"

Spike glowered, then he and Lucy went out back as Larry burst into the apartment with Palace Guard following him.

"You've already heard, haven't you?" He rushed to sit next to me on the sofa. "It will work out, though. Macy pulled me out of class, and she's going to talk to the group at our lunch meeting. She showed me the draft of an outline to prepare everyone for the test, and she'll share it at lunch. Macy said she'd pick up sub sandwiches at the grocery store for us and charge them to the department. I'm not sure I would have thought of that."

Larry chuckled before he continued, "She says we'll have everyone ready for the test by nine o'clock this evening, so all of us can get a good night's sleep. Macy wrote the test, so she knows exactly what to hone in on. Della has taught the class too, so she's helping Macy with our session this evening."

"Good; my phone has been on fire all morning."

"What's going on with you?"

"Martha has some houses she'd like for me to look at before someone puts a contract on them. I thought I might get a ride with Justin when he goes home, so I could look at the houses."

"I'm not crazy about the idea, but it does make sense; do what you think is best."

Palace Guard narrowed his eyes as Larry kissed me lightly on the forehead then left.

"That was a set-up to throw me into a false sense of security; wait for it..." I counted down on my fingers while I chanted, "Five, four, three, two, one."

Larry stormed back into the apartment, slammed the door behind him, and shouted, "Why won't you ever just tell me what's really going on? Why, when, and how are you going to Savannah?"

I should have put in my earplugs.

"There's a resort..." I began.

Larry narrowed his eyes and growled, "I don't have time for you to make up a long, convoluted story; I want the short answer, so I can get back to class."

"I think the kidnappers took the five girls from here to Savannah."

"It's not your job to rescue them. You have to turn over what you have to the GBI team in Savannah." He frowned. "You don't have anything, do you?"

"I have a feeling." I jutted out my chin.

Larry sat next to me. "If it was anyone else except you, Maggie, I'd say that's nice and move on. How are you going?"

"Paul and Julie are going to pick me up early tomorrow, and I really do have to look at the houses; Julie's going to help me."

"How long have you been working on going to Savannah?" He growled.

"All morning. Paul and Julie are taking a two-week vacation in Savannah, so I won't be alone."

"You've been working one morning on something that would have taken a normal person a week to pull together? At least Julie will be there to bail you and

Paul out of jail, and Justin will be there on Friday, so maybe he can keep me posted on how much your bail is. Where are you staying?"

"In a short-term condo that's close to the GBI office. It's where we'll stay until we close the deal on a house."

"I'm supposed to believe you pulled all this together in one morning, and it's not even lunchtime." Larry shook his head and exhaled. "Dang it, Maggie, I believe you because it's too far-fetched, even for you, to be anything but the truth."

When I opened my mouth to protest his lack of trust in me, Larry kissed me with passion. After he released me, he said, "See you tonight, Gray Lady, and you can give me the long version over a glass of wine, then I'll show you what I know about anatomy."

When Larry winked, I giggled, then he and Palace Guard left.

"That went better than I hoped. At least he wasn't yelling when he left."

Five minutes later my phone announced, "Text from Larry: Tell Paul we'll meet them in Savannah tomorrow evening. We'll leave tomorrow as soon as the last person turns in their test."

I whooped, and Spike wacky-danced while I called Paul.

When he answered, I said, "We have a change in plans. Larry and I will leave for Savannah in the morning and will meet you there tomorrow evening."

"Good. Let me know where Martha recommends for us to stay, and Julie will make our reservations."

After I called Martha, she gave me the information for the hotel; I told her Larry was coming with me.

I called Paul, and Julie answered.

"I have the name of a hotel for you that is close to our extended stay condo. Martha put a hold on a room in Paul's name: it's a suite on the second floor and overlooks the pool."

After I told Julie the name of the hotel, she said, "Thank you so much; I'm really looking forward to a vacation and house hunting, and Paul's excited about working with you again. Did Larry meet your expectations and hit the ceiling?"

"He sure did; in fact, he tried to catch me off balance." I told her about nice Larry telling me to have a wonderful time and leaving the apartment then roaring back in as monster Larry.

"Did you freak over the nice Larry?"

"He definitely wasn't himself, so I knew something was up, but I didn't quite expect the full blast he delivered after he acted so understanding; he was really angry, but I love that he's going to look at houses with us and check out the two resorts."

"We'll see you in Savannah. Last one there buys dinner," she said.

I frowned. "Y'all are still leaving today, aren't you?"

"Yes, we are." Julie tittered as she hung up.

I put up my feet and breathed out in relief. "It's been a busy morning."

Spike nodded and put his finger over his mouth to shush me. I smiled at the sleeping Lucy stretched out on her favorite rug. I closed my eye to relax.

When Lucy snorted a light 'boof,' her version of a semi-bark, I woke.

"I didn't even realize I'd fallen asleep. Is someone coming to the door?"

Spike nodded, and I stretched and as I rose, our visitor knocked on the door. Spike peered out the window then flipped his hair and put his hand on his hip in a prissy stance.

"One of my friends?" I giggled.

Spike grinned.

When I answered the door, Jessie said, "I know you've heard the news. What are we doing for lunch? Would you like to go to the café?"

"That sounds great. I was supposed to have lunch with Della today, but I think she's helping with the study session, and I'd love to see Cassandra and Chef."

"Are you ready?"

I grabbed my backpack and my jo. "Ready."

Spike waved as I headed to the door, and I said, "See you later."

"I always talk to my cat too. She's ten and a gorgeous white Persian cat with a wonderfully disapproving, grumpy face. My honey said she keeps him grounded," Jessie said as we walked to her car.

On the way to the café, Jessie asked, "I love how many eye patches you have. Are they custom made?"

"I guess you could say they are. A close friend of mine made them for me. She initially had them matched to outfits for me, but I lost track and didn't want to ask for help, so now I just grab one and slap it on."

"They really are beautiful."

"Here we are."

When we walked inside, Cassandra asked, "How are you? We've got a full house, so if your table isn't satisfactory, we'll have another one available in thirty minutes, if you'd like to wait. Would you like to take my arm, Miss?"

"Thank you. We'll be fine wherever you can seat us." I put out my hand, and Cassandra placed it on the crook of her arm then led us to the table near the drink station. She put the braille menu in front of me, and a regular menu in front of Jessie.

While I rubbed my fingers across the braille on the menu, I said, "Someone's here that Cassandra wants me to listen to."

When Anna came to the table, she asked, "Are you ready to order?"

I pointed at the menu. "I'll have this, please."

"Good choice; you, miss?"

"The same."

After Anna left, Jessie giggled. "We each just ordered an umbrella for lunch."

"My Rodney just texted me and told me he needs some money. I was afraid it was over between us because he said I couldn't go with him to the resort."

Patty.

"I'm sure he'll change his mind after I give him my bank account ID and password. He gave me the instructions on how to send him the money directly from my bank account, but I'm not all that technical and couldn't figure it out. I don't want him to think I'm not smart enough for him, but I finally told him I was having trouble maneuvering the bank website. He was very understanding and told me to give him my user ID and password, and he'd take care of it for me;

I told him I'd send him my information right after lunch. That means he still likes me, right? It's the local bank, so I'm sure it will be easy for him."

"Bingo," I said. "Jessie, go to the kitchen and tell Cassandra that Rodney plans to empty Patty's local bank account. She'll know who to call."

"You're awesome; I caught only snippets of her whining."

Jessie-blob headed toward the women's restroom then diverted to the kitchen.

After a few minutes that seemed like an hour, I groaned inside as I listened to Patty drone on about Rodney, Rodney, and Rodney.

Jessie returned. "Cassandra's on it. Do you think Patty might be superstitious? I'm wearing my favorite fancy Haitian skirt and the blouse that my grandmother embroidered for me; do you think I could approach her and offer to read her palm or something?"

"I like it. What are you going to do?" I asked.

"Wing it."

I nodded. "My favorite plan. What do you need me to do?"

"Wing it."

I sagely nodded. "You got it, boss."

Jessie-blob hummed as she strolled through the café then stopped at a table.

"Oh my, your energy." Jessie's voice was sultry. "May I sit with you a moment? Your energy speaks to me."

Patty giggled. "Thank you, yes, please join us."

Anna-blob stopped at their table and refilled their glasses with the pitcher she carried. "What an honor to have Miz J. select you, Ms. Patty. This is your special day, isn't it?"

Anna whispered, "Miz J. is a world-famous mystic."

Cassandra joined me at the table. "I wouldn't miss this for anything. What's going on?"

"Jessica is winging it."

"May I see your hand?" Jessica asked.

Patty tittered. "Of course."

"Hmm. Has anyone told you how much strength you have? You can break men's hearts with a glance."

"Really?" Patty asked.

"Your hand doesn't lie." Jessie whispered words that weren't in English.

"What language is Jessie speaking?" Cassandra asked. "It's so captivating."

"It must be Haitian Creole. It's all she and her grandmother spoke when she was growing up," I said.

Jessie gasped. "There's a man."

"Yes, yes, there is," Patty said breathlessly.

"Ohhh," Jessie moaned. "There is something in your heart, but he is blocking it."

"Blocking what?" Patty asked.

Jessie grumbled, "I can't see; he's in the way." She softened her voice. "What is really in your heart?"

"Well, Rodney..."

She paused, and Jessie stayed silent.

Anna joined us at the table and whispered, "The entire room is entranced by Jessie. Have you noticed how quiet the café is? No one is eating or even drinking; they're watching Jessie and listening."

Cassandra whispered, "Jessie is awesome. She's even pulled me in. I can't wait to hear what Patty has to say, and I never thought I'd hear those words come out of my mouth."

I chuckled and nodded.

Patty continued, "My sister and I bought a pottery shop a few years ago, and my husband and I always planned that as soon as he retired, we would move to North Carolina and take over the retail side of the shop, so my sister could focus on teaching and creating her own pieces for us to sell. She's very talented."

Jessie quietly hummed a haunting tune, then Patty spoke.

Patty sighed. "My sister is overloaded because our shop has become so popular; she regularly stays up all night to finish her work. If I go with Rodney, she'll have to sell the shop, and that will break both our hearts."

Cassandra, Anna, and I jumped at the sound of a hand slamming down on the table.

"I can't do that to my sister or to myself," Patty said in a firm voice. "You're right, Miz J; Rodney has no business blocking my heart, but what do I tell him?"

"Tell old Rodney to bring a pile of cash to buy pottery if he comes to see you in North Carolina," a man called out from a front table.

The entire café burst into applause and cheering, and Jessie-blob breezed past us and went into the kitchen.

"That was wonderful." Anna rose, picked up the tea pitcher, then bustled from table to table.

"Be right back," Cassandra said.

I waited for Cassandra, but she didn't return.

Anna stopped by my table. "The party's in the kitchen; follow me. I told them you were lonely from being abandoned."

Before I went into the kitchen, Anna said, "Look pitiful when you go in."

I nodded; after I walked in, I sighed, long and loud.

"Oh my gosh, I told you I'd be right back, then I got super-involved with telling Chef about Patty and Jessie," Cassandra said. "Will you forgive me?"

I sighed again. *This is fun.*

Jessie laughed, and I giggled.

"Dang it, Jessie; you broke my sorrowful mood."

"I seriously am sorry," Cassandra said.

"I seriously am pitiful," I said. "I'd sigh again, but I don't want to be overly dramatic."

"Jessie is amazing," Chef said.

"You're right; it was definitely a magnificent performance."

I knew Cassandra-blob was signing for Chef.

"Thank you, Gray Lady," Jessie said. "It was a blast; my grandmother would have been proud."

"Chef said I should have passed a basket for tips for Miz J. Jessie, you would have had a nice bonus to help you after you move," Cassandra said.

"I wouldn't have been able to accept it. Grandmother never took money; she accepted only fresh fruits and vegetables, fine wines, freshly-caught fish, and laying hens. I don't remember Grandmother ever buying food from a store, and we had a feast every evening."

"Here's your lunch: enchiladas verdes de pollo." Chef placed our plates in front of us then pointed to my plate. "I cut your enchilada into small pieces, Gray Lady. Cassandra can put it into a bowl if it won't behave for you."

"That's perfect. I can use a tortilla chip as a food pusher if I have any trouble," I said.

"Your enchiladas are made with freshly roasted peppers, so your lunches are on us," Cassandra said.

After we ate, I said, "Larry and I are leaving tomorrow for Savannah, so I can check out some houses for us. I'll be back for his graduation next week."

"Come here for dinner Friday night. Will you be riding back with Tonya and Martha for Justin's graduation? I'll have a large table for you next to the drink station."

"That would be wonderful," I said.

"I just heard about another missing girl," Anna said when she came into the kitchen with a pitcher.

As she refilled our glasses, I asked, "Do you know any details?"

"It's a girl I know; she's been talking about her new online friend for a month or so, then she has suddenly become standoffish lately. Her mom called me to ask if I'd seen her. She texted her mom just a few minutes ago that she was walking to her friend's house who lived three blocks away. Her mom was worried because of all the runaways, so she immediately called her daughter, but the girl didn't answer her phone. After her mom texted the friend and found out the friend is out of town, she called me. I haven't seen the girl in weeks, so the mom said she'd call several more of her daughter's friends to see if anyone knew anything."

"Tell her mom to go to the bus station immediately," Jessie said.

CHAPTER NINE

"I'll call right now." Anna hurried out the back door to make the call then rushed back inside. "Her mom can't get away from work for at least forty-five minutes. Is it okay if I go to the bus station, Cassandra?"

"Go," Cassandra said.

After Anna left, Cassandra asked, "Why the bus station?"

"Because Jessie is brilliant," I said. "This missing girl doesn't match the pattern of any of the so-called runaways. It has all the classic markers of an online predator: the girl obsessed with a new online friend, then removing herself from her old friends before suddenly disappearing. It's only logical that she'd be on the next bus to meet her friend."

"I'm checking the bus schedule; maybe I can guess where she's going," Jessie said. "Interesting; the next bus to leave the station departs in thirty minutes and goes to Cleveland, Ohio, with a short stop in Atlanta. It's almost a twenty-four-hour trip."

"That would be exhausting," Cassandra said.

While we sipped our tea, Cassandra said, "This waiting is killing me. I'll refill drinks, clean tables, and chat with the customers."

After she left the kitchen with the pitcher, Chef said, "I wish I could have gone with Anna."

I nodded and spoke clearly, so Chef could read my lips. "I would love to hear how Anna convinces the girl to stay."

Cassandra rushed into the kitchen and grinned. "Success. Don't go anywhere; Anna will be here soon, and we'll have details with our dessert."

"My life was so ordinary until I met you, Gray Lady," Jessie said.

Anna came in the back door then rushed to the café without saying anything. "She better be going to help Cassandra catch up with the customers then come back as quickly as she flew through here," Jessie grumbled.

Chef sliced four pieces of pie and put the slices on plates.

"What kind of pie is it?" I asked.

"Tart cherry," Chef said.

'Yum," Jessie said. "My favorite."

A few minutes later, Anna returned with a large tub of dirty dishes, and Cassandra followed her.

"Tell us what happened first, then I'll take care of loading the dishwasher," Cassandra said.

After the three of us sat on the stools at the counter, Anna stood where Chef had a clear view of her face.

"Her bus to Cleveland hadn't loaded yet, but everyone was lined up. I asked her to go to the restroom with me." Anna shrugged. "It was the first thing that crossed my mind that I could say in a crowd as a reasonable excuse to pull her out of the line. She stared at me like I'd lost my mind, then she laughed, and we went to the restroom."

"I never would have thought of it," Cassandra said. "What would you have said, Gray Lady?"

"Nothing nearly as brilliant as Anna," I said.

"On the way to the restroom, I told her I had something highly confidential to tell her, and I needed her help. We went into the restroom, and I went into a stall a few minutes while I tried to figure out what I was going to say, then I came out and washed my hands,"

"She was still there?" Cassandra asked. "Did you tell her you were pregnant?"

"I seriously thought about it, but I didn't."

"So, what did you tell her?" Chef asked.

"I told her I wanted to go back to school, but I couldn't because we would need someone to cover part of my shifts at the café, so I could go to class. I asked her if she'd help me find someone that was a hard-worker that I could trust to do a good job."

"Didn't she think it was strange that you showed up at the bus station and pulled her out of the line to ask her to help you find someone who could work for you?" Jessie asked.

"Of course, she didn't. Anna is very eccentric, aren't you?" Cassandra asked.

"I must be because she didn't indicate it was a strange request at all." Anna continued, "We discussed a few people and swapped stories, then she realized her bus had left. She told me she could catch the next bus then told me about a wonderful art instructor she had found online who wanted her to take his advanced class on art. He said her talent was unbelievable and offered the two-week long class for free, which also included her lodging at a nice hotel. She showed me his picture and his website, and I told her I recognized him."

"Did you tell her he was a predator or an ax murderer?" Jessie asked. "Sorry, didn't mean to interrupt."

"I told her he was well-known for stealing his students' work and selling it as his own. In fact, several of his former students are suing him for theft, and he's been banned by all the art dealers. She was very indignant that he'd done that to his students. I offered her a ride home, so we could continue talking about someone to take my shifts. She told me she'd get back to me if she thought of anyone and thanked me for telling her about the art instructor."

"Was any of that true?" Jessie asked.

Anna shrugged. "Could be."

Jessie laughed; I held up my hand, and Anna-blob smacked a high-five.

"Do you really want to take some classes?" Cassandra asked.

"Not at all. I promised myself a year off school and classes, so you're stuck with me." Anna picked up a clean pitcher and left.

"That was exciting," Chef said. "Enjoy your dessert."

On our way back to my apartment, Jessie asked, "Is this what your life is like, Maggie? One adventure after another?"

"I guess; it all seemed normal to me."

Jessie snorted. "It isn't, honey, but I loved it."

"You did a magnificent job of helping Patty realize what she really wanted to do," I said.

"Seemed normal to me," Jessie snickered, and I laughed.

After we reached my apartment, Jessie asked, "What are your plans for this afternoon? Need an accomplice?"

"I have to put up my feet and read a book."

Jessie snickered. "Enjoy your nap; you deserve it."

When I went into the apartment, Lucy was stretched across the sofa and was sound asleep. Spike sat on the floor next to her and put his index finger over his pursed mouth. I tiptoed to the bedroom and closed the door then removed my boots and lay down on my bed and flopped from one side to the other.

I sighed then padded to the window.

I can't read; I can't enjoy looking out of the window. I'm really tired of not being able to see clearly.

I sat on the floor and hugged my knees. Spike joined me and patted my hand, and a tear slipped down my face, then I sobbed and rocked while I clutched my knees. After I had no more tears to cry, I leaned against the wall and peered at my outstretched legs.

"Even my legs are blobs," I said.

Spike elbowed me; when I glowered, he pointed to my legs and grinned.

"Blobby legs are not funny," I grumbled.

Spike rose to his feet and staggered across the room as he feigned unsteady legs.

"At least my legs aren't wobbly, and no one else can see the bobbly, I mean blobby." I giggled. "That was hard to say, and you've completely ruined my pity party."

Spike did his wacky dance, and I rose to my feet and joined him. When Lucy nosed open the door, she barked her approval, then the three of us went out back.

My phone rang and announced, "Larry."

"I'm sorry if I woke you, sweetie," Larry said when I answered. "We're on a short break, but I have great news. Our illustrious Professor Bailey asked Macy to take over the rest of the day at our lunch break, so we've got a good five-hour jump on our study session. She and Della dove right in. They're going fast, but Palace Guard is watching to be sure no one gets behind. I've asked Macy to repeat a section a couple of times when Palace Guard alerted me that someone was struggling. What have you done today?"

I smiled. "Are you fishing for a confession? Jessie invited me to lunch, and we went to the café. I was very grateful to see Cassandra and Chef before we leave tomorrow."

"At least I can trust Jessie because she's no-nonsense from what I've seen. You didn't shoot anyone then, I take it."

"Nope; no shots fired today."

"So far," he muttered.

I wrinkled my nose at the phone, and Spike grinned.

Larry continued, "I'll let you know whether we'll be able to have supper together; Della said if the class continues, and we eat here, she'll eat with you."

"I'll check with Jessie; she and I may do something," I said.

"That would be good; if the class ends in time, we could invite John and Jessie to go with us somewhere to dinner; I know Macy and Della wouldn't mind getting together before tomorrow, but if Della's available, I'll invite her to go with us."

"That sounds good; I'll let Jessie know."

After we hung up, I called Jessie.

"Did you hear Professor Bailey turned the class over to Macy?"

"I just got a text from Johnny. Isn't that exciting?"

"Exciting and surprising. Larry called to tell me, but I think he really called to check up on me. He was happy that I had lunch with you because, according to him, you are 'no-nonsense,' and he can trust you to keep me out of trouble."

Jessie chortled. "You're kidding me; I hope he doesn't tell Johnny because my husband may be too polite to argue with Kevin, but he'll rib me about my no-nonsense side for years."

"The study session may wrap up in time for our husbands to eat dinner with us," I said. "If they're available, the four of us could relax this evening with a quiet dinner together."

"I'm right there with you. I'll find a soothing restaurant that all of us would enjoy, since I'm the trustworthy one."

I laughed with Jessie.

"Larry plans on inviting Grandma D, but I think she and Macy will use the additional time to plan how they'll manage the test tomorrow," I said.

After we hung up, Spike smirked.

"You're right: I'm happy; leave me alone." I flounced into the house.

"I can do laundry if you'll help by telling me if I miss any dirty clothes or drop them before I get to the washer," I said when Spike and Lucy came inside.

Spike followed me as I gathered up clothes from the bedroom and bathroom. Before I headed toward the washer, he pointed to the bedroom, and I followed him. He pointed at the floor, and I reached down and picked up the errant sock.

"Thanks, Spike. Maybe I can even fold the clothes after they're dry, if you'll supervise."

Spike grinned.

"I'm not sure how smart it was to invite you to be bossy," I snickered.

After the clothes were in the washer, my phone rang and announced, "Call from Martha."

"Gray Lady, I have appointments for two houses for you and Larry to look at on Friday afternoon, and one on Saturday morning. Is that okay, or do you want me to cancel, and you can reschedule at a better time for you?" Martha asked.

"Don't cancel the appointments; Larry will be excited that he's there to look at the houses with me."

"I'll email you the times and listings, so you and Larry can go over them together; shall I forward the listings to Julie and Paul too?"

"Absolutely; I'm sure Julie will be excited to dig into the details."

"That's how I would feel too," Martha chuckled. "We're planning on having you, Larry, Paul, and Julie at our house on Friday night for a barbecue to welcome Justin home. I'll invite Julie and Paul when I send the email."

Martha paused then said, "Just a second, Tonya wants to talk to you. We're synching her newfangled hearing aids that we love to my phone."

"What's going on?" Tonya asked.

I chuckled. "I'll save the long version for later, but the short version of the best news is that the cranky Professor Bailey turned over his class to Macy right after lunch. She and Grandma D have already begun the study session, so the class won't be going late tonight as they had originally thought."

"That is great news; I've been worried about them being stressed by the test and short on sleep. They might still be stressed but not nearly as much with the confidence I'm sure Macy and Grandma D are giving them."

"Anything going on with you?" I asked.

"Nothing except I'm ready for Justin to be home," she said.

"I'll be at that same point next week, I'm sure," I said.

"Safe travels, and I'll see you before you see me." Tonya giggled as she hung up before I could reply.

"I'll hear you before you hear me." I smiled. *It never gets old.*

When someone knocked at the door, Spike peered out the window then flipped his girl-hair and held his arms straight up.

"Somebody tall? Jessie?"

He nodded and grinned as I hurried to the door. "Come on in. Are you as bored as I am?"

"You got it. Do you feel like a walk? It's a little cool, but a sweatshirt feels good. We can walk down to the track, and I'll describe all the runners and tell you stories about them, then we can return."

"That's a great idea. I'll put on my sweatshirt then grab my backpack and my jo."

Spike waved good-bye.

"See you later, Lucy."

When we were outside, Jessie asked, "Do you want to take my elbow? How do you want to walk?"

"If you walk on my right side at your pace, I'll walk alongside you."

"I'll have to remember you can't see any obstacles, or uneven cracks, right?"

"Yes; it would work better for me if we walk in the street because there are fewer uneven surfaces to trip me."

"Let's do this, girlfriend," Jessie said.

At first, she walked at a slow pace.

"Is that the best you can do?" I asked.

"No, I can leave you in the dust," she said.

"Try it." I grinned and stayed next to her as she widened her stride and quickened her pace.

When she reached the track, she gasped, "You win. Let's sit on the bench for a bit. You can't ever tell anyone that you ran me to the ground."

"Are you kidding? You're the best walking partner I've ever had. I'd never give you away."

"I'll outdo you yet, Gray Lady, but maybe not today."

After Jessie caught her breath, she said, "There are five runners on the track. Did you ever run?"

"I did until my second surgery. My energy has been super low since then. I'm hoping that Larry and I can run together again after we move."

"You'll be ready because you weren't even breathing hard when we got here, and I thought I was going to pass out. I've never walked with anyone who could keep up with me before, much less push me like you did."

"I wasn't pushing you," I said.

Jessie snorted. "Then why were you always a half step in front of me?"

"I didn't even know I was. Larry complains about my competitive side, but he's much more competitive than I am."

"That's really hard to believe." Jessie described each runner's style and their clothing as they ran past us.

"Evidently, there's a runner's dress code on the track," she said after the fifth runner went by. "I wonder if any of them has noticed."

"Do we fit in?" I asked.

Jessie laughed. "No, honey, but if we were on the track regularly, they'd all be dressed like us. By the way, did you know you're wearing a dark purple patch with a black long-sleeved T-shirt? The color combination makes you look mysterious, but you're still short, in case you forgot."

"Dang, I did forget; thanks for the reminder." I giggled. "All of my eyepatches match a shirt that I have, so maybe sometime I'll wear a dark purple shirt with a black patch. Larry used to comment on my color choices, but since he's been in class, he's been too busy to complain."

"He's smart enough to know he would have taken on a new task of putting together your patches with their shirts."

"Correct, and who has time for that?"

"My dress code is extremely colorful, so I love your choices," Jessie said. "Are you ready to head back?"

On our way back, Jessie strolled, and I strolled with her.

"I found a restaurant for us; it's fairly new, but its reviews are good except for one curmudgeon who went to the restaurant on Easter Sunday and complained because the restaurant was closed. Their website clearly says they are closed every Sunday, so I cannot fathom why the reviewer thought they might make an exception for Easter Sunday."

When we reached my apartment, Jessie said, "Gray Lady, you're incorrigible. You even stroll competitively; did you know that? I'm going to take a shower before we go anywhere. You didn't break a sweat, but I did."

"If I take a shower, will you untangle my hair before we leave?"

"I'd love to," Jessie said. "We'll have plenty of time because if Johnny's going with us, he'll want to shower first, and if we're going alone, we're still not on a schedule."

After I went into the apartment, Spike raised his eyebrows.

"It was a great walk; we walked really fast, and it felt good."

Spike held out his hand, and I smacked it.

"Is it time to feed Lucy?" I asked.

Spike nodded, so I measured then served her food. "Here you go, girl."

While Lucy ate, I said, "I'm taking a victory shower."

Spike grinned then waited for Lucy at the back door. After my shower, I towel dried my hair and peered in the mirror. *Still a blob.*

I selected a shirt that Jennifer called a blouse because it buttoned down the front and an eye patch. I put on a clean pair of jeans and my shirt that I buttoned from the bottom up, so I'd know it wasn't cockeyed before I put on my eyepatch.

Clean clothes feel good. Oops, laundry.

I hurried to the washer and moved everything to the dryer and started it. *I'll ask Jessie to check the setting, so the clothes will actually dry.*

My phone rang.

"Do you have breakfast plans tomorrow?" Lori asked.

"No, tomorrow's the big test day, so Larry will probably dash out of here without eating anything unless he grabs something from the refrigerator."

"I'm planning a light breakfast for the class: egg and biscuit sandwiches, fruit, and coffee; Dana and Jessie will help me with the food. We're planning on having a breakfast for us too, maybe not quite as light, and you're invited to join us, since we're meeting at your apartment."

I giggled. "One of these days, you're going to invite me to a big party that will be held at my house, won't you?"

"You know I will; it may or may not already be in the works, but I'll let you know before we show up."

Not long after Lori hung up, Jessie came to the apartment and began working on my hair. "I love your hair. It's almost a shame to take a comb to these curls. I'll show you how to finger-comb your hair, so you don't have to depend on someone else to comb or brush it every day. Your hair has loose curls, so it will be easy for you once you get the hang of it. I'll do a section and explain what I'm doing, then I'll talk you through the rest while you ease out the tangles."

When we finished my lesson, Jessie said, "Your hair looks like you spent all morning with a hair stylist. If you finger comb your hair after you shower and before you put on your cream rinse, you will have fewer tangles."

I felt my hair. "It feels soft. Thank you, Jessie."

"You're welcome; I'm glad I could help. You're far too independent to depend on others for your personal care."

"I didn't even realize I was dreading next week without Larry to brush my hair for me; that's a lousy reason to miss my favorite man."

"We should be hearing from one of them in the next half hour or so. Did Lori call you about breakfast tomorrow?" Jessie asked.

I nodded. "I would like for you to check the dryer to make sure I have it on a setting that will actually dry the clothes."

When she returned she said, "Proud of you; your clothes will be dry."

My phone announced a text: "From Larry. We'll eat here. See you later this evening."

"That's our cue: I'm ready to leave when you are, Gray Lady."

As Jessie backed out of the parking slot, she asked, "Do I know why you're Gray Lady?"

On our way to the restaurant, I told Jessie about my childhood and wearing black because that was what spies wore, and the fits Mother threw because it was so hard to find black clothes for a tiny girl.

Jessie laughed. "You were definitely the Gray Lady-in-training."

I nodded and continued. "After I graduated from high school, I learned about the Gray Man."

"You mean like a spy who blends in is called a Gray Man?"

"Yes, except according to Larry, I am frequently quite literal."

"No, don't tell me: you dyed your hair gray and wore all gray."

I smiled.

"The famous Gray Lady emerged from her cocoon." Jessie chuckled. "How long were you the all-gray Gray Lady?"

"For a few years until I went undercover and that stinker, Larry, had the hairdresser in Galveston dye my hair red."

"Did you have any idea what color your hair was?"

"Before I dyed it black, Mother always said I had beautiful blonde curls. I think it was brown before I lost my eye, but I was never that great at subtle colors."

Jessie snort-laughed. "Gray is not a subtle color?"

I shrugged. "I didn't think it was a color at all."

"I get it. It's not a color because it's a blend thing like a shadow. What color is a shadow? The answer is it depends. Hmm. You could have been the Shadow Lady."

"No because there isn't a Shadow Man, only a Gray Man."

"Of course, silly me."

When we reached the restaurant, Jessie said, "I'll deny saying this, but your husband is right: you are literal."

After we were seated, Jessie asked, "I didn't even think about the menu. Do you want me to read it to you?"

"Give me two or three choices, so I don't have to remember everything. I don't want an appetizer with my meal."

When the server approached our table, he said, "Gray Lady, Ms. Cassandra called and ordered both your dinners for you as a surprise."

After the server left, I asked, "How on earth did Cassandra know we were having dinner here, and how did our server know I'm the Gray Lady?"

"Who do you think gave me the recommendation? She probably told them the famous Gray Lady was the short one too," Jessie chuckled. "I don't know anything about the restaurants around here, so I called the expert. Cassandra told me she'd order your dinner for you, but she didn't mention she would order mine too. She actually got both of us."

I nodded.

While Jessie told me about some of her grandmother's favorite clients and their antics, a familiar voice at the bar across the room caught my attention. *Rodney.*

I smiled and tapped Jessie-blob's arm. When she paused, I whispered, "Rodney's at the bar."

She said quietly, "Can you hear his conversation clearly?"

I nodded.

The server came to our table. "Ms. Cassandra ordered a small appetizer for the two of you to share."

"What is it?" I asked after the server left.

"I'm not very American food savvy, but I think we each have a piece of sushi and a fluffy pastry thing."

I smiled and nodded. *I'll taste the fluffy pastry thing first to see what it is.*

"Walt, my client didn't work out. I'm leaving for Atlanta in the morning; I have to check in with HQ, and maybe I'll find another prospect there," Rodney said.

"Mine's being pretty elusive too, but I think I can close the deal next week; if not, I have another one in the wings that I'm priming. It's all about patience."

"Patience wouldn't have worked with mine; my client turned from hot to cold overnight. I think I was underbid."

"It happens, doesn't it? Takes a little finesse, sometimes; the heavy hand technique doesn't always work, especially if you don't have a backup in place."

"I'm not going to defend my methods to you," Rodney hissed. "Let me know when you need a friend."

Rodney left.

"Will your friend be back?" the bartender asked.

"It doesn't look like it, does it?" Walt asked in a bored tone.

"He was running a bar tab. Here you go."

Walt growled, "That sorry sack of..."

"Sir?" the bartender asked.

Walt mumbled.

"A little falling out," I said. "We'll talk over wine back at my apartment."

I took another bite of my appetizer. "The tiny shrimp are delicious. I've never had a pinwheel like this," I said.

"It's really different; I love it. I'm guessing this is puff pastry that the pastry chef rolled out, but who cares about details when it's this yummy?"

After our delicious dinner of crab cakes, coleslaw, and sweet potato fries, we had a small serving of apple crisp.

On our way to our apartment complex, Jessie said, "I'll park at my apartment if you promise you'll walk with me to your apartment and not leave me behind."

After Jessie parked, she asked, "Would you like for me to help pack your clothes? We can pack and sip wine."

"That would be outstanding. Friends of mine were going to pick me up in the morning, and she was going to help me pack when they got here, but now, they are going to meet us in Savannah. Walt would chastise me for not having a backup plan."

Jessie chuckled. "He won't hear it from me."

As I climbed out of the car, I saw a blob standing at the corner, and I paused. *Do I tell Jessie to get back into the car?*

"I thought I saw someone standing at the corner when you were parking," I said after Jessie locked her car.

"I saw him when I turned; it's just Gavin, the new volunteer at the library. He's an old guy and really helpful."

I exhaled. I need to stop seeing bad guys on every corner.

CHAPTER TEN

Jessie poured wine into my cup and into a wine glass then snapped the lid onto my cup and inserted the straw. "We're packing all your clothes, right? Should we pack anything else?"

"Maybe we can pack part of the kitchen. Larry will want to cook his breakfast next week. I think he could use the same frying pan for his supper, and we should leave at least one saucepan and two days' worth of dishes because he'll run the dishwasher every other night or hand-wash his dishes."

"Let's start with your clothes, then we can pack up the kitchen. What about the bathroom?"

"We can pack it too except for Larry's shaving stuff and what he'll need for his shower."

"Yay, I can do something productive while I worry about Johnny," Jessie said.

Jessie-blob stepped into the closet. "There's a large suitcase in here. Can we commandeer it?"

"Sure can. What can I do?"

"Pick out your clothes for tomorrow and Friday, so you don't have to unpack tomorrow night. I found an empty backpack. Can we use that for your Friday clothes?"

"I'd rather pack my Friday clothes in my backpack; I have room." I selected three T-shirts, three eye patches, and two pairs of jeans then enough underwear and socks for four days, so I would have spares.

"This won't take me long," Jessie said. "What about an extra pair of boots?"

"They're too bulky for my backpack; boots can go into the suitcase," I said.

"I can get everything in the suitcase and still have room for your things from the bathroom that you won't need tomorrow or Friday."

After a few minutes, Jessie said, "Your clothes are packed."

"Ready for a wine sipping break?" I asked.

"I'd rather get everything packed that we can then totally chill with our wine."

We went to the bathroom. "I'm not sure I see anything here I can pack tonight except for a few extra towels."

"Let's pack at least two, so I'll have my own towels if I want them."

"You're staying at one of those extended stay hotels, right? They'll probably have the basics in their kitchen and bathroom, but it won't hurt to have your own."

When we moved to the kitchen, I said, "Let's pack what Larry and I will need for the weekend, then Larry will still have pots, pans, cooking utensils, and dishes here."

It wasn't long before Jessie said, "That's it. I put the kitchen items in one of the empty medium-sized cardboard boxes I found in your closet."

"Good because I've just been carrying my cup around but haven't had a sip yet."

Jessie chuckled. "Same for me."

After we sat in the living room, I kicked off my boots. "I don't remember where you are going, Jessie. Is it Atlanta?"

"Yes, it is, and Johnny's family is ecstatic. It's actually Conyers, but you know all about using the closest large town thing, right?"

"Not until last week." I smiled. "When Larry told me he was assigned to Statesboro, he was happy. I was confused because I thought he wanted to go to Savannah. It's like a secret handshake, isn't it?"

"Something like that; in a way, it's a layer of protection for the families if it's common knowledge that we're going to Atlanta, for example, and you're going to Savannah."

"I hadn't thought of that, but it's actually brilliant."

"What are you going to do after you're settled in Savannah?"

"I hadn't even thought about it; what about you?"

"I think I might like to pursue a career in art but not necessarily as an artist. I thought I'd take some design classes to see what areas really speak to me."

"That's smart; I've spent my entire life studying to be a spy. Maybe there is something I can do with all that training and study."

"Become a spy?"

"I don't know; Larry might object if I fly to Paris or Argentina to shoot an international criminal."

"Surely there are plenty of criminals for you to shoot in Georgia. How do you do that? Do you shoot, and they rush to step in front of your bullet?" Jessie snickered.

I giggled. "Can you imagine trying to choreograph a bad guy?"

Jessie laughed. "Bad guy ballet. We are so hilarious; just ask us." Jessie yawned. "I need to go home and collapse. It's been a long day."

I tried to stifle my yawn, but my mouth didn't cooperate. "You're right. Text me the second you get home, or I'll come in with guns ablazing."

"You got it, girlfriend." Jessie rose, then after she rinsed her glass, she hugged me.

Jessie-blob strode to the front door. "You always have a friend in Atlanta, Gray Lady. Just holler."

"You too; we never know when we might need a friend to cover our backs, do we?"

After Jessie left, I put up my feet and relaxed while I waited for Larry.

Jessie texted me. "Safe at home."

I exhaled. *I don't know why I have a feeling that something bad is about to happen.* I closed my eye and focused on breathing slowly to calm my nerves.

Spike poked my arm, and Lucy nudged my hand to wake me, then I heard the key in the door and smiled.

Larry and Palace Guard grinned as they came inside, and Lucy danced.

After Larry scratched behind Lucy's ears, he said, "We're all pumped and ready. Everyone feels up to speed and is confident about the test."

Larry joined me on the sofa and put his arm around me. "Macy is a whiz; she told us she'd send us the link to the online class tomorrow after lunch at the latest. Having Della coteach helped because Macy worked on the online class while Della reviewed sections of the material, then when Macy taught, Della reviewed the online class. The unit really wasn't hard after all; at least it wasn't the way that they taught it. Palace Guard was the real star, though; he strolled past each trainee then would stop next to anyone who was struggling. I sat in the back and would hold up my hands to indicate row and seat for Macy or Della to stop and probe for questions. It was slick."

Larry gave me a sloppy kiss and grinned. "I can have a beer; would you care for one?"

Larry hurried to the refrigerator.

"A beer with you sounds wonderful," I said.

Larry popped the caps on our beer bottles. "Too bad we don't have a balcony; you could write imaginary notes, and I could pretend I believed you when you told me what they said."

I giggled. "Just like old times."

Larry handed me my beer then sat close with his arm around me. "Snuggling on the sofa beats the balcony. How was your day?"

"Everyone was busy today, so Jessie and I went to the café for lunch then to a fancy restaurant for dinner tonight, and the food was delicious. After we returned to the apartment, Jessie packed my clothes for me."

"I wondered why your suitcase was close to the front door; does that box go with us tomorrow too?"

I nodded. "We put in a few things from the kitchen that you might use this weekend. Martha said the hotel suite included the kitchen basics, but if they don't have a good frying pan, we'll have one there for eggs."

"I'm sure Paul and Julie will make sure you don't starve next week; that was my biggest concern other than worried about how you would get around while you were there without me for a week."

"Are you saying I don't have enough body fat to stay alive for a week?" I asked in feigned surprise.

"I do not respond to trick questions." Larry snorted.

I smiled. "Martha is hosting a barbecue Friday night to welcome Justin home; we're invited, and she said she was inviting Julie and Paul too. Martha and the real estate agent scheduled appointments for us to see two houses on Friday afternoon and one on Saturday. She and Jennifer selected these three for us to tour after they examined the longer list from Nell, the agent; Martha said if we don't really care for any of them, the agent assured her there are more that will be on the market sometime next week. I'm sure Julie and Paul will want to go with us to look at the houses, so Julie can report back to Jennifer. I love to talk to Jennifer, but I can't give her the details that Julie can."

I smiled while Larry talked about the study session, Macy, Della, and the guys.

"I'll leave early in the morning, but I'll fix you breakfast before I leave. We're all having breakfast together before the test," Larry said.

"After y'all start the test, Lori and Dana will bring breakfast here, and our small group of wives will have breakfast together."

"We've met some really nice folks, haven't we?" Larry asked. "How are you doing on that beer?"

"I drank part of it; I'm done." I covered my yawn.

Larry took my bottle. "It's bedtime for my sweetie."

I woke when Larry turned off the water from his shower then listened as he tiptoed toward the kitchen.

"You sure tiptoe loud," I said. "Were you going to sneak out of here without a good luck kiss?"

He grinned as he stood in the doorway. "Pretend you're asleep; I haven't made coffee yet."

"I'll pretend I'm asleep in the shower."

I pulled back my hair into my version of a ponytail then took a quick shower and dressed before I carefully detangled and combed my hair with my fingers. When I went into the kitchen, Larry was pouring two cups of coffee.

"You smell purdy, sweetie; here's your coffee. I recommend letting it cool while I get my first good luck kiss."

"You got it, Mr. Sexy Pants." I kissed him then kept my arms around him while I snuggled against his chest. "Why the first?"

"Because I plan to steal at least one more before I leave."

"Interesting choice of words, Agent Ewing."

"It was, wasn't it?" He leaned in for another kiss, and I pulled him close for more than just a little smooch.

When I released him, he grinned. "I have to go, or I'll miss the test, and I'll have to explain to Macy, Della, and the entire class that Sexy Maggie took advantage of my fragile state."

"I am so sorry I can't roll my eye; go."

Palace Guard left with Larry.

While I dished up Lucy's food, I said, "Spike, I'll bet Palace Guard knows the material as well as Larry does. He'll alert Larry if anyone is struggling."

Spike nodded then tapped his nose with his index finger.

I smiled. *On the nose.*

We went out back after Lucy finished her breakfast, and I listened to the morning traffic on the nearby highway and a trash truck as it rumbled on the nearby street.

"If we strip the bed and wash the sheets, Larry can come back to the apartment with clean sheets Sunday night. I think I can strip the bed, but let me know if I drop any pillowcases. I could even throw in our clothes from yesterday and catch up with all the laundry."

Spike and Lucy stayed outside while I stripped the bed, then they came in, so Spike could check behind me before I started the washer; Lucy padded to the sofa and jumped up for her morning nap.

I answered the knock at the door after Spike checked and gave me a thumbs-up.

When Dana and Jessie came into the apartment, Dana said, "Bossy Lori kicked us out of the room because she said we were disruptive, so I stole three of the venison sausage biscuits that I took for the study group's breakfast, so we could have some too. Do you have coffee?"

I pointed to the pot on the stove.

"I snagged a carafe of orange juice," Jessie said. "Johnny covered for me."

I smiled. "He's a keeper. How were you being disruptive?"

"I was not disruptive; I was supportive and caring," Dana said. "I merely asked Jerry if he was nervous yet because he's been so calm. Lori was cranky and told me it was time to leave."

"I asked Lori who died and made her queen, and she told me I could leave too," Jessie said.

"I thought you were hilarious, but did you notice how red her face turned when I laughed?" Dana asked.

I giggled. "You two are the best, and I love that you stole some sausage biscuits and orange juice on your way out."

Dana poured three small glasses of orange juice. "Your glass of orange juice is half full, Gray Lady. I thought that might work for you."

After Jessie poured two cups of coffee then refilled my cup, she started another pot while we ate our sausage biscuits.

I reached for my glass of orange juice, and Spike shook his head then tapped his finger on the table a little farther to my right. I adjusted, and he nodded, and I smiled as I picked up my glass. After I put it to my mouth, I tipped it. I intended to take a sip, but I misjudged my angle and got a good gulp of orange juice instead. Spike smiled then tapped on the table, and I set the glass down where he tapped and exhaled.

Jessie and Dana exhaled with me.

"You did great, girlfriend," Jessie said.

"Not that we were watching and holding our breath along with you," Dana added.

"It was a major accomplishment for me; thank you."

Spike pointed outside the window, and I said, "Lori's on her way. Someone want to open the door for her?"

"I've got it." Jessie strode to the door and opened it; Lori-blob carried in a large box and set it on the table. "Here's the rest of our breakfast and probably our mid-morning snack."

Dana poured Lori a cup of coffee.

Lori sat next to me while Jessie unpacked the box and set food on the table.

"I want you two clowns to know that Macy congratulated me for setting up the entire scenario to give the study group a pre-test laugh to relieve their stress, so I took full credit," Lori said.

While we laughed, Spike flipped his imaginary hair and did his wacky dance, and I laughed at him too.

"Well done," I said, and Spike took a bow.

Dana whispered to Jessie, "Lori will always win, won't she?"

Jessie whispered, "We'll keep trying; she'll drop her guard eventually."

"There's fruit, Gray Lady; care for some strawberries? Unfortunately, they aren't dipped in chocolate, but I did hull them," Lori said. "I bought strawberries and blackberries from a local farm yesterday."

"Sounds good; I've eaten apple slices and grapes as finger food since I lost my vision but not strawberries, and I don't know why."

After we ate, Lori said, "Does anyone know how long the test will take?"

"I know the previous class took at least three hours to complete the test," Dana said, "but I suspect that was because there were many questions that hadn't been addressed by Professor Bailey. I can't help but wonder whether he is that absentminded or has a more sinister ulterior motive. I'm not one of his fans, so my judgment may be a bit jaded."

"We can expect everyone to finish the test by lunchtime then," Jessie said. "Want to walk to the track, Gray Lady?"

"Y'all go on without me. I have to do my nails," Lori said.

"I'll go too; it's a nice day for a stroll," Dana said.

"I'm going to pack up my dishes and leave; is everyone going to be here next week for the graduation?" Lori asked.

"We won't," Jessie said. "This was the last course for Johnny's specialty, but we won't be leaving until tomorrow."

"We won't be here next week either. Bud's planning a potluck behind my back for tonight," Dana said. "Plan on bringing something because I have no idea what their plan for food is. I envision six or so different types of pizza along with giant bags of chips. We'll probably have enough beer, though."

"I'll spread the word," Lori said. "I hadn't heard anything either, but all of them have been through a lot with this class, so I can't really blame them. I'll bring a large pan of lasagna, and dessert."

"I'll make a huge salad and spicy chicken wings," Jessie said.

"I soaked pinto beans overnight and have them in my slow cooker and bought bread at the store yesterday for garlic bread," Dana said.

"I think we're in fine shape," Lori said.

"I appreciate the help; Bud's going to be pleased by his potluck."

Lori waved as the three of us headed toward the track.

"Do I set the pace, Gray Lady?" Jessie asked.

"You set the pace. Dana, we might walk faster than is comfortable for you. Take your time," I said.

Dana snorted. "I can keep up with you two. I ran track in high school."

"We'll do a little warm up first, then I want to match our pace from our last walk," Jessie said.

"Whatever you want, Jessie; I'm with you."

After half a block, Jessie lengthened her stride, and I stayed half a step in front of her as Dana walked then jogged behind us to keep up.

When we reached the track, Jessie put her hands on her hips then bent over to catch her breath. I glanced at the path leading to the track and saw a blob in the distance that was walking toward us.

"Good pace," Jessie said. "I'm ready to show Johnny I can keep up with him. I'll tell him how I got started, but he won't believe me."

"I don't blame him." I stretched. "Want to take a lap around the track?"

"After Dana joins us, and I catch my breath; did Kevin train you to run or did you start running first?"

"I started running first, but I'm out of practice, so I couldn't beat him now."

"Yet," Jessie said.

"I should have told Martha I need a track within walking distance of our house."

When Dana joined us, she said, "You're a ringer, Maggie; why didn't you tell me, Jessie?"

"I heard Gray Lady warn you; she's serious about getting up to speed."

"I thought I was going to die; there was no way I could have kept up, but it was still good for me. What's next?"

"You're invited to sit on the bench and cool down while I show Gray Lady how to run." Jessie laughed, and I smiled.

I smiled. "Dana, be my spotter: tell me to go left or right if I'm about to run off the track or into anybody."

"I can do that." Dana walked with us to the gate then Jessie-blob ran while I jogged a few feet then picked up my pace to a good run.

"Right," Dana shouted, and I moved right.

"You just passed me," Jessie said, and I nodded then sped up.

"One lap completed," Dana said.

I held up two fingers.

"Two more laps?" she asked.

I nodded then ran the second lap at full speed.

"Second lap; that was fast," Dana called out.

I continued full speed, then Dana said, "You completed the third lap; take it slow for your fourth lap to cool down."

I nodded as I slowed my pace and ran the last lap at an easy speed.

"Slow to a walk for the remaining of the lap for a cooldown," Dana said.

When I reached the gate, Dana and Jessie applauded, and I heard shouts and whistles from the track.

"Did I have an audience?" I asked when I reached Dana.

"Yes, ma'am. After your first lap, all the runners stepped off the track to watch."

"Well, it felt good; let's head back."

"Can we walk?" Dana asked.

"Heck no; let's go, Gray Lady. I've got my wind," Jessie said.

Jessie-blob took off, and I caught up with her and continued to run half a step ahead of her.

When we reached the apartment, Jessie slowed. "I had hoped I could beat you because you should have been worn out from that show-off run around the track, but noooo."

I giggled as we went inside the apartment. "Too bad."

"Whatever. I have to cook for tonight, but I'll wait here for Dana because she will be sympathetic."

"Do you want water or sweet tea? You need to hydrate," Jessie said.

"Water, please." I sat then patted the sofa, and Lucy jumped up next to me.

Jessie dropped ice into my cup and into a glass then filled them with water.

"Here you are." Jessie handed my cup with its lid and straw to me. "Tell me about you and running."

"My best friend in high school was short like me, and we ran together. The track coach accused us of pacing each other because we always tied for first place in every race we ran. What she didn't know is that both of us were trying to outdo the other, which is why the only way I know how to run with someone else is by staying half a step ahead."

"So, if I challenge you to a race, we'd tie?"

"Not unless you can run half a step in front of me because if we're racing, I'll leave you."

Jessie sighed. "I don't think I'll ever be ready to race you, but I'm going to work on it."

Dana came into the apartment. "Excuse me for not knocking, but I need water." She flopped down on the soft chair; Jessie poured her a glass of water and handed it to her.

"Thanks, Jessie. How did you survive running with Gray Lady?"

"I used to run, but use to doesn't cut it, does it?"

After she downed her glass of water, Dana said, "I'm going home to stir my pot of beans and slice bread. I'll see you later, Jessie, whenever you're supposed to be there."

Dana hugged me before she put her glass in the dishwasher. "I am thrilled you're my friend, Gray Lady. Thank you for everything except my lesson in humility." Dana chuckled as she left.

"Anything else I can do for you, Gray Lady?" Jessie asked.

I shook my head.

"Next time I see you, Gray Lady, I want to run with you again, but not a race," Jessie said. "That's my goal, though: to run half a step in front of you."

After Jessie left, I rose, and Spike backed away and waved his hand in front of his face.

I growled, "You really should give me a chance to take a shower before you insinuate that I'm smelly."

I flounced to the bathroom then showered. After I dressed and detangled my hair with my fingers, I said, "Let's go out back. My hair will dry quickly with the light breeze."

While Lucy wandered the yard, I said, "It was totally energizing to run again. Dana stood near the gate and told me if I needed to move right or left if there were any obstacles in front of me, so I felt totally independent. I think I've needed that."

Spike held up his thumb and his index finger then blew on his index finger.

"Larry's here already?"

He grinned and nodded, and I hurried into the house as Larry rushed inside and Palace Guard beamed as he followed Larry.

I smiled. *All of the trainees passed. Palace Guard is as proud as a new dad.*

Larry grabbed me off my feet and hugged me tight. "We all stayed while Della finished grading tests, and everybody passed! Can you believe it? Every single one of us; I can't tell you how exciting that is. Macy sent each one of us the link to her online class to keep us from pestering Della, and we all signed in and started the first lesson."

"I'm not surprised that Macy wanted to be certain that no one had trouble accessing her online class," I said.

"We didn't have much time with the lesson because Della graded the tests as they were handed in. There's a potluck tonight at Bud's; is it okay if we skip?"

"They aren't expecting us, so it's okay to skip."

"All the wives already know about it? It was supposed to be a surprise."

"What was the plan for food for the potluck?" I asked.

Larry gaped at me. "I'm not sure any of us took the time to think that through. I'm certain Bud didn't. Who busted us?"

"I don't know, but it may have been someone who wanted home cooking tonight to celebrate."

"Besides frozen pizza and chips from the grocery store?" Larry chuckled. "I'm going to jump into the shower and change then pack. Are you ready to go? Is there anything I can do for you?"

"I'd like to take the beer in the refrigerator with us."

"I'll grab our small cooler and do it now, so I don't forget."

After Larry put the beer and ice into the small cooler, he asked, "Anything else?"

"Take your shower; I'm ready when you are."

While Larry showered, Spike and I took Lucy out back, then after we came inside, I put her water and food bowls and her treats into a tote bag.

Larry came out of the bedroom dressed and with his backpack.

"Martha texted me the address of the hotel where she made reservations for us." I handed him my phone, and he put the address into his phone.

He scanned the living room then the kitchen. "We're taking the cooler, your computer bag, Lucy's tote bag, and her food. We'll have our backpacks and your jo in the front with us. I'll shift the suitcase and the box to the truck bed then add the cooler and Lucy's food next to them before I load the computer bag and Lucy's tote bag on the back floorboard; Lucy, Palace Guard and Spike should still have plenty of room. Am I missing anything?"

"No, that's it. Do we expect any rain?"

"Doesn't matter; I have a tarp, and I'll cover the suitcase, Lucy's food, and the box with it."

After we were in the truck, Larry said, "The best way for us to go is on the interstate. One of the guys told me about a great sandwich shop at a truck stop a little more than an hour south of here; we can pick up sandwiches and drinks, and Lucy can take a break, then we can eat on the road."

"That sounds good," I said.

"Tell me what you didn't mention to me because I was so stressed over the class."

"The most interesting event of the week was Patty," I said.

"Do I know Patty?" he frowned.

"No, and you're glad you don't."

"Who all is involved in this adventure of yours?"

"Della, Macy, Roxanne, Jessie, Lori, Dana, Cassandra, Anna, Chef, and me. I don't think I left anybody out."

Larry side-glanced me then shook his head. "I can't imagine who you could possibly have left out."

I bit my lip. *Paul, Julie, my favorite librarian Lily, Lily's volunteer Gavin, Della's real estate friend, but I don't know her name, and I think that's it.*

CHAPTER ELEVEN

After I explained who naïve Patty and slimy Rodney were, I said, "Della called a friend who was kind enough to spread our rumor about Patty's bigshot GBI son, who doesn't exist, launching his team on a major investigation against Rodney; Rodney heard the rumor and dumped Patty."

"You all are devious, sweetie."

I smiled. "Thank you. Unfortunately, Rodney wasn't content with dumping her; he reached out to dangle Patty with puppet strings to feed his ego, as far as I could tell, and Patty was falling for it."

"Tell me one thing before you continue: did you shoot Rodney?"

"No, but Della and I did briefly discuss it."

"But you didn't."

"I didn't; so back to Patty: Jessie and I went to lunch at the café."

"What? Am I missing something? What does that have to do with Patty?"

"Do you want to hear this or not? I had to give you at least part of the background because it's an important part of the entire story."

"Sorry; did you shoot Patty?"

"No; forget about shooting. You had Palace Guard with you, and I can't aim without him."

"That's right; go ahead then."

"You make it really hard to tell a story. Patty was certain Rodney was going to take her to the resort, and before you ask, we don't know where the resort is, but we think it's a creepy place; maybe mind control or something like that, and we fully expected Rodney to empty Patty's bank account because he bullied her into giving him her account password."

"What? That's..."

"Della reported him, but we wanted to cure Patty of her obsession with Rodney, so Jessie channeled her grandmother's Vodou skills and told Patty that a man was blocking her heart. Patty told Miz J, which is what Anna called Jessie when Jessie was mystical, that she wanted to join her sister in North Carolina and manage their pottery business."

"Jessie is mystical and has vodou skills? My head is going to explode; can we jump to the happy ending?"

"Okay, Patty and her sister are happy. The End."

"Thank you. I appreciate that you didn't say anything this week while I was so focused on the class and helping everyone to pass the test, but this is absolutely the last time you ever keep anything from me; okay?"

"Is that nonnegotiable?"

"Yes," he growled.

"Okay." *My new rule: agreement doesn't count when it's nonnegotiable.*

Larry's smile was particularly smug; when I glanced back at Palace Guard, he rolled his eyes.

I leaned back and closed my eye. *No sense in watching the blurry concrete highway roll by, even if it is my favorite color.*

As Larry slowed for an exit, he said, "Looks like a typical truck stop, doesn't it?"

I tried to see what he meant then gave up. "Sure does; is this where we're picking up lunch?"

"While I refuel, would you and Spike like to take Lucy for a break? We'll put a leash on her, so she doesn't panic and step in front of a truck."

After he stopped at the pump and opened his door, I cringed at the truck noise, and Palace Guard patted my back.

Larry stayed in the truck as he quickly closed his door. "Sorry, sweetie; I wasn't thinking. I'll refuel then park near the grass; you can stay in the truck while Spike and I take Lucy for a stroll, then I'll dash inside for sandwiches and drinks."

"Thank you. It is extra loud, and I didn't think about putting in my earplugs before we left."

When Larry returned with our lunch, he said, "I went with our old standby: ham and Swiss cheese sandwiches and sweet tea. They bake their cookies here, so we have fresh chocolate chip cookies for our snack."

Larry left the truck stop then pulled into a wayside park before we reached the interstate. "We can brave the bugs here or eat in the truck."

I snorted. "It will be faster if we eat in the truck."

After we ate, Larry tossed my leftovers that I couldn't eat and our trash into the dumpster then continued to the interstate.

"Do you know Roxanne? She and Macy are friends, so I thought you might. Anyway, she taught the profile of a psychopathic killer class this past semester. It was intended to be a short introduction for us, but I learned a lot from her. I heard one of the guys ask Macy about her after the test was over, and I realized how heads down we've all been because Macy couldn't remember the last time she saw her." Larry chuckled. "I thought it was just me who dove into my own world this week to get past that test."

I frowned. *I saw her on Tuesday; she was going to ask her friend where those two guys went, but she could have followed Rodney or taken over Walt for Macy, so Macy could concentrate on the class. Roxanne could have quietly left for Atlanta or the resort.*

I picked up my phone. "Send a text to Roxanne: Sorry I missed you. Happy belated birthday."

"Happy belated birthday? What's that all about?" Larry asked.

"I was going to say I was sorry I missed her, but I felt like I should add something, and that was the most innocuous thing I could think of."

"You outdid yourself," Larry chuckled.

My phone buzzed then announced, "Reply from Roxanne: Ha. Waiting for my special cake. Spinach maybe?"

"Is that a joke? I don't get it," I said. "I'll have to research spinach in a cake."

"I don't think she literally meant spinach cake. I think she was referring to spinach because it makes you strong. Didn't you watch cartoons when you were a kid?"

"No. Mother probably watched television, but I don't remember it. I was focused on my training to be a spy. You knew that."

Larry, Palace Guard, and Spike nodded.

Larry continued, "I thought maybe when you took a break...okay bad assumption, but there was a cartoon character that loved spinach because it made him strong."

Larry's mouth quivered as he fought a smile. "His name was Popeye; he was a sailor and had one eye."

"Are you insinuating that I'm a one-eyed sailor named Popeye? Does that mean Roxanne is waiting for me in Savannah?"

"It wasn't me that called you Popeye; Roxanne did. Maybe, but why would she be in Savannah? You probably know Roxanne better than I do; what do you think?"

"I would have thought she'd have followed Rodney to Atlanta, but maybe she opted to go after the two guys that were grooming the cheerleaders if her friend told her they'd gone to Savannah."

"I know about Rodney, but do I know about the cheerleaders?"

"I'm sure you do. They were the girls that were kidnapped; the two guys that were in charge of their grooming were at the café and discussed what a pain the cheerleaders' whining was."

"Why are you always in the middle of every crime in the state? I've never been in a café or anywhere else and heard bad guys complain about what prima donnas kidnap victims were. How can I keep you safe if you're having lunch with thugs and killers without me?"

I don't think thugs and killers would want to have lunch with a GBI agent.

Larry slammed the steering wheel, and Lucy and I jumped.

"Sorry, sweetie; sorry, Lucy." Larry sighed. "What else don't I know?"

I almost answered but decided that might have been a rhetorical question, so I gazed out my side window and watched the writhing and twisting gray concrete ribbon as the lane on the right suddenly narrowed to a shoulder then abruptly widened to another lane.

I sighed. *I wasn't actually having lunch with them, but Larry probably isn't interested in hearing an important correction to the details right now.*

As we neared the address, I said, "I thought the traffic would be heavier here."

"We're about an hour away from Savannah, so we have the rush hour traffic woes of a small town here that I fully expect to be complaining about in a month." Larry chuckled, and I smiled.

After Larry turned down a small street, he said, "It looks like a nice facility; it's not as fancy as your condo complex was in Harperville, but it has trees, grass, and a trail around a large pond. I'll go into the office for our keys and find out where I can park."

While Larry was gone, I lowered my window. "Will we be able to run the trail around the pond?"

Palace Guard nodded, and I sighed in relief as I leaned back and closed my eye.

A man's voice drifted from the direction of the far end of the parking lot. "Excuse me, could you point me to the office?"

I sat up straight then whispered, "I know that man's voice. He was running on the track in Tennessee when we were, Palace Guard. Can you see him? It sounded like he's at the other end of the parking lot."

When I glanced at Palace Guard, he shook his head. A few minutes later, Palace Guard stood outside the truck near my window. He shook his head again.

"Thanks for trying to find him. I must be more tense than I realized. I must have dozed off and dreamed it."

Palace Guard crossed his arms and scowled; he stayed close to my door until Larry approached the truck.

"We're around the back." Larry climbed into his seat. "I like the privacy and security of not being the first rooms and suites someone sees when they drive in."

When Larry parked, I asked, "How far are we from the pond?"

"It's just around the corner. I knew you'd be interested in the trail. I asked if it was a good running trail, and the desk clerk told me that it was, but very few people use it. I didn't tell her that was perfect, but isn't it? She also told me there are several restaurants that have great meals that are nearby and deliver here; she gave me four or five menus to see what we thought. Maybe we would rather have something delivered this evening instead of going anywhere."

"I'd love that. I want to kick off my boots, put up my feet, and listen to you pop the cork on a wine bottle or pop the tops off a couple of beers. It is sad that we don't have a balcony, except being on the ground floor is better for Lucy."

After I climbed out of the truck, I breathed in a sweet aroma. "Is that magnolia?"

"Sure is. The desk clerk said we missed the magnolias in full bloom for this year, but we may still catch a whiff."

"I can hear the traffic noise from the interstate. Are we close to it?"

"We're maybe two or three miles away, so I'm not surprised you can hear it. I can't; maybe I could if I was very still and focused."

When we went inside, I said, "It smells clean. After you bring in the cooler, my suitcase, and the box, would you give me a tour?"

"Love to, sweetie."

Lucy trotted past me to begin her own tour, and Spike followed her. Palace Guard stayed close to me until Larry returned.

"Your grand tour begins, milady," he said, and I giggled.

"The sitting area is carpeted and has a large sofa, two soft recliners, and a TV. The dining area has a small, square table and four chairs, and the kitchenette has an electric stove, dishwasher, and a large refrigerator. The kitchen and dining floors are tile. The back door is a sliding glass door that opens to a grassy area and may have a privacy fence around the small yard. I'm sure Lucy will be ready to check it out."

"Can we get Popeye on the TV?" I asked.

Larry chuckled. "We may; the desk clerk gave me a listing of all the stations and three of them were what she called classic cartoons."

"Do we have wi-fi?"

"Yes, our wi-fi is supposed to have excellent reception."

"The bathroom is a little larger than most hotel room bathrooms," Larry said. "There are two sinks, a nice-sized countertop, and a tub with a shower. The small linen closet has extra towels and supplies."

"Where's the bedroom?"

"It's next to the bathroom; it has a door that closes, a queen-size bed and two soft chairs next to the window. It's almost like a suite itself. We have a walk-in closet, but it's fairly small, and that's it."

"No washer and dryer?"

"No. Each group of four suites has a shared laundry room, but the desk clerk told me they are rarely used. We'll see."

"If we hate it, I'll see if Martha minds if we take clothes to her house to wash."

"That's a good option. Let's check out the back yard."

Larry opened the sliding glass door. "The patio is nice and larger than I thought. We have a bench seat, a small patio table, and two chairs, but that door is heavy. I'd rather have had a regular door."

"We're not going to be here that long; I'm sure we'll find a house for us soon," I said.

While Lucy investigated the yard, Larry and I went inside, and Larry emptied the cooler into the refrigerator before he picked up the menus.

"We're close to the ocean; do we want fish?" Larry asked.

"Only if it's local."

We sat at the dining table while Larry pored over the menus.

"If we want local, we should order the low country boil," Larry said.

"What's that?" I asked.

"Crab, potato, shrimp, corn on the cob, sausage, and hush puppies. It's spicy; probably not as spicy as we're used to, but we'll get by." Larry smiled. "I'll order a single serving; that'll feed both of us, and we'll probably have leftovers. Beer is a perfect match with low country boil. I don't think we'll have any room for dessert, but if we do, we still have our cookies from lunch."

After Larry ordered our meal, he said, "We can expect the delivery van to be here in about forty-five minutes."

My phone rang and announced, "Call from Paul."

"I'll bet it's Julie."

"No bet," Larry said.

I snickered as I answered.

"You probably guessed it was me," Julie said. "Where are you? What are you doing for supper tonight?"

"We're at our extended-stay hotel; Larry ordered low country boil to be delivered from one of the restaurants the desk clerk here recommended."

"Can we invite ourselves over? Paul wants to talk to you before you're distracted by house hunting."

"That sounds like a great idea; I'll hand the phone to Larry, so I'm not caught in the middle and lead you astray."

Julie chuckled while I handed the phone to Larry.

"The desk clerk here warned me that the low country boil one-person meal is more than enough for two; the way Maggie eats, we'll have leftovers for lunch. If that sounds interesting, I'll place your order, so it will be included with ours. The food will be here in a little over thirty minutes."

After Larry listened to Julie, he hung up then gave me back my phone. "I'll add a second low country boil to our order; their hotel is only ten minutes away, and Julie's bringing a bottle of wine because she doesn't care for beer, and they'll stop for dessert at a bakery they found earlier that is close to their hotel."

"We have sweet tea, right? Paul doesn't drink alcohol."

"I'm not sure I knew that, but thanks. I don't drink alcohol if I'm going to be driving, and none of the guys do either, so it isn't unusual as far as I'm concerned."

When Paul and Julie came into the apartment, Paul put a small sack into the refrigerator while Larry took the bottle from Julie and popped the cork for us. "When shall I pour your wine?" he asked.

"With dinner would be perfect," Julie said.

Paul sat across from me in the recliner. "I have news for you. When I checked with the county assessor's office, I wasn't surprised to find that there were two different owners for the two different resort properties, but Julie checked with the Georgia Corporations Division and found three businesses near Savannah that are part of the catering conglomerate in Atlanta. Two of them are the resorts, but the third business is an exclusive private wellness camp and conference center, and it's as vague as it sounds. I missed that third one because I had limited my initial search to only resorts, then I confirmed my faulty data by checking the assessor's office in only one county; the wellness camp is in a nearby county."

"That's what a team does: cover for each other," I said.

Larry smiled. "I can vouch for that. Can we drive by all three in the morning, or will we have to save one for Saturday afternoon or early Sunday before I leave?"

"I've mapped out a route for us; it looks like we'll have time to talk to someone in their office if we can get past their gates," Paul said.

"It would be ideal if we could pick up some brochures and drive around their grounds," Julie added.

"If not, we'll take pictures; I need a drone," I said.

"That's not a bad idea; we'll look into how much an aerial photographer costs," Paul said.

I cleared my throat, and Larry glanced at me then said, "If you can find someone, it would be worth the cost. We have a small monthly allowance that we rarely touch."

"Isn't that your money you've been saving to buy a house?" Julie asked.

"No, this is our separate egg money: you know, just a little extra we set aside that we don't need to include in our budget," I said.

"A drone is a great backup plan if we can't get onto the grounds," Larry said.

"I'll take care of drinks: sweet tea or wine?" Julie asked.

"Sweet tea for me," Larry said.

"Same," Paul said.

"Wine for you and me, Gray Lady?" Julie asked.

"Absolutely; we're not driving, and we're not on call." I giggled.

"I wish," Larry mumbled; Palace Guard and Spike nodded.

"You got that right," Paul added.

"Do you want a glass or your cup with the lid and straw?" Julie asked.

"I'd love a wine glass, but it's safer if you put the wine into my cup," I said.

Spike pointed to the front door as Lucy whined.

"I think I heard a car." Larry rose and opened the door before the delivery-blob rang the doorbell.

After Larry set the large bag of food, a roll of paper towels, and silverware on the table, he said, "Dinner is served."

He escorted me to the table, then we all sat.

After Larry laid the sacks with the low country boil on their sides then tore them lengthwise in half, he said, "Sweetie, this is a lot of food. What do you want to start with?"

"I'd like a small taste of everything."

"You got it. The corn on the cob is already buttered and seasoned. That's handy, but it's going to be messy."

I inhaled the heavenly blend of the bouquet of spices that reminded me of Chef Daryl's Cajun seasoning and the mouthwatering seafood aroma of shrimp and crab.

"I don't care; it smells delicious," I said.

Paul chuckled. "I'm going to need an entire roll of paper towels."

No one talked while we ate until Larry rose and opened the refrigerator. "More tea?" he asked as he pulled out the pitcher.

After he refilled his own and Paul's glasses, he hurried back to his meal.

I tried to roll my eye, but I don't think I managed the look I was going for because it felt more like I was trying to see my nose. "Were you worried I'd scarf down your food if you stayed away from the table too long?"

"Yeah," he mumbled with his mouth full of food.

"Smart man," Paul said between bites.

After I ate a small piece of potato, most of my corn on the cob, a few bites of sausage, my hushpuppies, and all the shrimp and crab that Larry served me, I wiped my fingers with two paper towels then sipped my wine while everyone else continued eating.

"This is really good, but I can't keep up with these men," Julie said.

"Would you like to sit on the patio for a while?" I asked.

"That sounds nice," Julie said.

Julie slid back the sliding glass door. "This is heavy, but I suppose that's good; I'm sure Larry will come up with a trick you can use to open it."

Spike and Lucy slipped out before Julie closed the door; Lucy stood on the patio, and her nose twitched as she checked all the new smells. After Julie and I sat at the small table, Lucy investigated the yard.

"I'm not going to last out here very long," Julie said. "I didn't see any gnats when we sat down, but these little guys are trying to drown themselves in my wine; I'm holding my hand over my glass to keep them out, but I can't sip any wine with my hand guarding it, and my damp hair is sticking to the back of my neck. If that sounded like a whiny complaint, it was."

"It's muggy for me too, especially after Larry and I spent five months in the cooler mountains of Tennessee; it may take a while for me to get acclimated. We can go inside whenever you like," I said.

"I'll wait until the starving men finish eating, then we can go inside for dessert. I do like your eight-foot privacy fence. The wood is nicely stained, and no one can walk by and peer inside your backyard."

I smiled. *Palace Guard and I will have somewhere to work on my knife skills.*

Lucy trotted past us and scratched on the door frame.

Larry hurried to open the patio door. "How can y'all sit out here? It's stifling."

Lucy dashed inside.

"We're tough," I said, and Julie snorted.

"Come on in; we finished off the shrimp, crab, hush puppies, and sausage, and we're ready for dessert," Larry said.

"Thank goodness for Lucy," Julie whispered as we went inside.

"What do you want to do with the leftovers?" Larry asked.

Julie pulled out small plates and forks for our desserts. "We're having barbecue at Martha's house tomorrow; the potatoes and corn will make a generous side dish for two nights."

"We could pick up some fried chicken at the grocery store on Saturday for the four of us after we look at the last house," Larry said.

"Fried chicken sounds good; we'll have a chance to relax and talk about the pros and cons of the houses," I said.

"We have a perfect plan because Jennifer will expect a complete report on the houses." Julie pulled out the bakery sack from the refrigerator. "We bought a small key lime cheesecake mostly because it's so pretty. The edges are piped with fresh whipped cream then topped with fresh strawberries. The strawberries on desserts traditionally have the green tops left on for color, but I asked them to cut off the tops on ours. The baker told us that many people cut the cheesecake into six pieces, but he recommends eight because it's so rich."

"When the baker said, 'so rich,' I knew what we would have for dessert," Paul added.

After Julie placed each slice of cheesecake on a dessert plate, Larry set the plate and a fork at each of our places at the table. Julie covered the cheesecake and returned it to the refrigerator, then we all dug in.

"Mmm, this is really creamy," I said.

After I finished my cheesecake, I sighed. "We'll have to run the trail early in the morning after our coffee. I'm too stuffed tonight, and it's too hot and humid to run."

"I'll set the pace," Larry said. "You'd run as hard as you could until you dropped."

"I can run slower than you can," I smirked.

Julie laughed. "I know that was a challenge; you two are hilarious. We need to go back to our hotel, so I can put up my feet and be ready for tomorrow's house hunting competition."

"It's not a competition," I said.

"Of course, it isn't, but you'll come up with a way to make it one, Maggie." Paul chuckled.

After they left, Larry and I sat on the sofa together.

Larry asked, "Where are you on the personal chef?"

"Martha and I narrowed it down to three."

"Talk to Martha, but you might want to have each chef come here and prepare a meal this next week for you, Julie, and Paul. Julie will give you a good critique, and Paul and I tend to like the same food, so he's a good fill-in for me."

"That's a great idea; I'll call Martha in the morning, but should we check with Julie and Paul first?"

"Yes, are you tired? Your eye is drooping; we've had a long, busy day."

I yawned. "I wasn't tired until you asked."

While Larry took Lucy out for one last break, I plodded to bed.

When I woke the next morning, the room didn't smell like our bedroom, and I shuddered. I tried to roll over, but I was trapped. I grabbed for the pillow next to me and inhaled. *Ahh. Larry's pillow.*

After I untangled the sheet I had wrapped around myself in my sleep, Lucy padded into the bedroom as I swung my feet over the edge of the bed.

Larry said, "Did you get all tangled up in the sheet? We've been up for a while; are you ready for some coffee?"

"I'll be right there." I dressed in my running shorts, a patch that I decided was my running patch for the day, and a T-shirt that probably was not my running T-shirt, but it was soft.

When I made my way to the kitchen with my jo, Larry said, "Your coffee is at your place at the table. Would you rather drink it on the patio? It's nice outside."

"I'll give it a try. It was a little buggy last night."

CHAPTER TWELVE

We carried our coffee to the patio then sat on the bench. Larry put his arm around me, and I snuggled against him.

He pulled me closer then asked in a poignant tone, "Are you happy, sweetie?"

I tilted my head to see him better. *Where did that come from?*

"I couldn't be happier; I love you, honey."

Larry sighed. "Sometimes I worry..."

I sat up and examined his face. "Worry about what?"

Larry shrugged.

All the stress has brought back his old insecurities.

"Nothing could have kept us apart, you know," I said. "We've always been a team: just the two of us, every single time we've been together. Tell me that's not true."

Larry chuckled. "It wasn't always clear that we were on the same team, but you're right."

"Of course, I am. Would you say that again, so I can record it with my phone?"

Larry rolled his eyes. "I loved you first."

I smiled. "I love you more, and I'll take that as a maybe. Let's go for our run."

Lucy and Spike stayed in the air conditioning; Palace Guard went with us.

"I'll set the pace," Larry said when we reached the trail.

"You'll try to run at a pace that you think I should be running, and it will be frustratingly slow. Palace Guard won't let me run too fast. We'll be better off if I set the pace."

Larry glanced at Palace Guard, who nodded.

"Okay, let's go."

I started off at a slow pace to warm up then increased my speed with Palace Guard next to me and Larry behind me.

After our first loop around, I said, "I can go two more."

"Why don't you sit it out, and I'll run the trail a couple of times with Palace Guard."

Palace Guard shook his head, and Larry peered at him then glared at me.

"What don't I know?"

"Palace Guard is being cautious; he doesn't want me to sit here alone. Take me back to our suite, then you and Palace Guard can run."

Larry narrowed his eyes. "Is that right, Palace Guard?"

Palace Guard side-glanced me then nodded.

Technically, there might have been more, but overall, it was right.

"Let's run back to our suite, so I can make my phone calls while you're running," I said.

After I returned, I called Paul's phone to talk to Julie.

When Julie answered, she said, "Don't tell me you're ready to go."

"No, Larry's gone for a run. I called you because of a brilliant idea Larry came up with last night."

"I'd be worried if it was your brilliant idea," Paul said.

"Hush, or I won't turn on the speaker on your phone next time," Julie said. "Go ahead, Gray Lady."

"Martha and Jennifer narrowed down the personal chefs to three. Larry suggested I ask Martha to arrange for each chef to come here and prepare a meal, and I'd appreciate it if you could be here too for the prep and the meals. Larry trusts our judgment, Julie, but he said he and Paul like the same kind of food, so Paul may have a view we didn't think of."

"We'd love it," Julie said. "It will be our private supper club."

"Eww. That sounds like sissy food," Paul said.

"You have veto rights over sissy food, Paul. If we have to send you for burgers after a chef leaves, that is not the chef for us," I said.

Paul grunted, and Julie chuckled. "I think he's up for the task."

"Good; I'll give Martha a call and see what she can arrange."

"When should we be at your place this morning?"

"Give us thirty minutes. Larry will be back soon from his run, then he'll want a quick shower."

After we hung up, I called Martha, and Tonya answered.

"Good morning, Gray Lady. Mom lets me answer her phone when you call, so I can use my new hearing aids; I've turned on the speaker, so she can hear you too."

"Larry suggested we schedule the three chefs to prepare sample menus this next week for Paul, Julie, and me. Larry was specific about Paul because he's afraid Julie and I might not have the right perspective for his tastes."

"Like tofu instead of elk?" Tonya giggled. "At least, that's what Justin would worry about."

"Exactly. What do you think?"

Martha said, "I think it's a great idea, and I'll call them this morning. I will ask for sample menus, so you can pick one, and I'll check on their availability, but I'll try to schedule them on Monday, Wednesday, or Friday to kind of spread them out. I'll ask for a rate sheet for their proposed menus, and I suggest we pay them their rates for one meal, so you'll have a good comparison of what you can expect. If one chef's food is superior, but their price is three times the other two chefs, you might want to go for the excellent meal instead."

"I agree completely; it's only fair to pay them for their time, skills, and food."

"Do you think y'all could be here at five? You are bringing Lucy and the imaginary men, right?" Tonya asked. "Justin says he'll be here by four or four thirty. He packed and loaded his truck last night, so he'll be on the road as soon as his test is over. He said this is the one time he was excited to have taken a class that met at eight o'clock on Fridays. I'd like some time to catch up on your news before we eat."

"It might be closer to five thirty, but we can shoot for five o'clock, and all of us will be there."

"Good. Kiki wanted to know. Wait; Mom has one more thing."

"Jennifer ordered your coffeemaker and had it shipped to my house, so you'd have when you got here. You can pick it up this evening."

After we hung up, I showered, finger-combed my hair, and dressed. With Spike's guidance, I opened the sliding glass door then closed it.

"I'm not sure if this humidity will help my hair dry at all." I sat at the small patio table while Lucy roamed to discover her favorite spot. I heard Larry running full speed to our place. *Maybe a blink will have to do for my version of rolling my eye.* I blinked. *That works.*

"Larry and Palace Guard must be racing back," I said.

Spike stood close to the sliding glass door then grinned.

"Did Palace Guard come inside first?" I asked.

Spike nodded as the front door opened. "If I could disappear then show up inside, freshly showered, and ready to go somewhere, I would still wait for you," Larry grumbled.

Spike elbowed me, and I snickered then leaned back to use my weight like Spike showed me to open the sliding door.

"Wow, sweetie. Good job." Larry closed the slider behind us then hurried to take his shower.

After he dressed, he asked, "Do we want to follow them in our truck, so all of us can go?"

Spike shook his head.

"Are you going, Palace Guard?" Larry asked.

Palace Guard nodded.

"Their rental car should be large enough for five. The three of us could ride in the backseat comfortably. I think Paul knows about Palace Guard and Spike, but I'm not sure, and I don't know about Julie," I said.

"It's an easy check, just tell them that Spike is staying with Lucy," Larry said.

When Paul and Julie arrived, Paul carried in a grocery sack; he handed it to Julie, and she placed it in the refrigerator.

"We think our best travel arrangement is for Paul to drive; our car isn't one of the new-style cramped models, so there's plenty of room for all of us," Julie said. "Larry, you can ride in the front with Paul because the front seat has a little more legroom."

"Makes sense to me," Larry said.

"Spike is staying here with Lucy," I said.

Paul nodded. "She'll be more comfortable relaxing here after her long ride yesterday."

"What about Palace Guard?" Julie asked. "Is he going with us?"

I glanced at Larry, who smirked.

"Yes, I'm short and don't have any use for a window, so I'll ride in the middle," I said.

"I'm not taller than you; we can take turns," Julie said. "Let's go if everybody's ready."

On our way to the first resort, I asked, "When did you hear about Spike and Palace Guard?"

"Ages ago; it was not too long after Paul started working with Glenn. He overheard you talking to one of your men, and he asked Glenn about you."

"Actually, I asked Glenn if the doctors expected you to ever recover from your injuries after the explosion," Paul said.

Larry laughed. "No, she hasn't."

"Not funny," I growled.

Palace Guard grinned and nodded, and I blinked.

"Glenn set me straight and told me about the imaginary men," Paul said.

"Paul told me, except he said you and Glenn weren't well at all," Julie said.

"I did not," Paul said.

"Makes a better story." Julie chuckled.

"Why didn't you ever say anything?" I asked.

"Never came up," Paul said. "We're almost there."

When Paul slowed for a turn, Julie said, "It's definitely a resort that could pose for a stock picture, Gray Lady. The front of the property has classic split-rail fencing, and the entrance is landscaped with manicured grass and flowers with a backdrop of old magnolia trees for privacy, and there is a large, shallow pool with a bubbling fountain and lights in the water. I'll bet it's beautiful at night."

"Guard shack ahead," Julie said. "I've got this."

When Paul stopped, Julie lowered her window. "Hi, I sure hope you have air conditioning in your little building; it gets brutal hot out here by midmorning, doesn't it?"

"Yes, ma'am, it sure does. I heard they just put air conditioning in here last week."

"That is great; they must have had trouble keeping staff without air conditioning."

"That was the first thing Mama told me I should ask about when I interviewed, and I'm glad I did. Mama used to go to the farmers' market every Saturday and sell eggs, but she said she couldn't take the heat anymore. Now, she sells eggs to the ladies at her church."

"That's your mama I buy my eggs from? She was one of the first vendors to stop selling at the farmers' market; I thought then that was a really smart move. I have an appointment with Mary at the office. She supposed to be expecting me."

"Yes, ma'am. The office building is straight ahead."

As Paul pulled away, Julie raised her window.

"Who's Mary?" Paul asked.

"I have no clue, but did you catch how new the guard was? I was betting he didn't know either."

"Are you going to get a reminder to pick up your eggs at church?" Larry chuckled.

"Probably," Paul said. "I love to hear that woman work; she's everybody's favorite friend."

"You were awesome, Julie," I said. "I don't think all of us should troop into the office to see Mary or whoever is filling in for Mary today. Paul, if you can still pick up the audio, Julie could take in my jo."

"Perfect; tell her how your jo works."

I handed my jo to Julie. "Hold the pommel, so the three inset fake pearls that are in a line face you. The top one snaps a picture; the middle one takes a video and includes audio. The bottom one stops the recording. The picture and the video instantly load to a cloud, and Paul can hear and see what was just recorded."

"Y'all are spooky techies, aren't you?" Julie asked.

"It's Heather's work," I said.

"I can listen to the audio real time on my phone," Paul said. "I use my earbuds, so I don't miss anything, and I've never tried listening without them, but we can give it a try."

"Palace Guard must be going in with you, Julie. He's waiting outside your door," I said.

After Julie climbed out of the car, we heard her on Paul's phone. "Wave, honey, if you can hear me."

Paul waved.

"Good. I'll turn it off then back on when I find Mary. I like my new hiking stick."

We sat in silence.

"It's been almost ten minutes; do you suppose everything's okay?" Paul asked.

"Palace Guard would have come for help if anything was wrong," Larry said.

After a few more minutes of silence, Julie said, "Hi, I'm Julie; are you Mary?"

Paul exhaled in relief.

A woman chuckled, "No, I'm Brenda. I'm new here; Mary must work weekends because that's when we're really busy. How can I help you?"

"Really? I would have never guessed that you hadn't been here for quite a while. I didn't mean to eavesdrop, but you were very professional with the person on the phone. Of course, I couldn't hear what she was saying, but her tone was really angry until you calmed her down. You have a very soothing manner."

Brenda giggled. "Thank you; I'm a retired first grade teacher, and I'm definitely a professional when it comes to dealing with meltdowns."

"How long did you teach?"

"Twenty-five years; I'd still be teaching, but my knees gave out from being on my feet ten hours a day all those years. Here, I can give my knees a break when I sit at the desk or on the stool at the counter, and it's made a real difference for me. I enjoy being around people who are, for the most part, completely potty-trained."

Julie chuckled. "I was a teacher's aide at a kindergarten for three years during college, and I know exactly what you mean. My husband and I are looking for a nice resort that could be our vacation spot until he retires in two years, then we'd retire at our place."

"You don't look old enough to retire in two years," Brenda said, and I heard the smile in her voice.

"Thank you; it's the miracle of modern science."

"I know exactly what you're saying; when I tell people that I taught for twenty-five years, I hear the same thing. I tell them I started teaching when I was twelve." Brenda giggled, and Julie joined her.

I'm glad Spike's not here.

Brenda continued, "I have new brochures here, but I also have some of the old brochures that the resort plans to throw out. I'm not sure why because they are much more informative. The new ones are slick sales copy and have pretty pictures."

"The old ones are great; I see what you mean about sales copy on the new ones," Julie said. "I was never really interested in marketing. Do you suppose it would be all right if we drove around to see if the resort feels like us; does that make sense?"

"It makes complete sense to me. It's not allowed, but none of the big bosses are here, and the young man at the gate is newer than I am, so it's perfectly fine with me. Don't take any pictures, though, because that will definitely attract attention, and I'll have an irate mob storming the office. If anybody waves, be sure to wave back because that seems to be the thing to do here when you're a resident. Oh, here's a map too. It's for the residents because sometimes they get turned around and lost, which is why this building has a large flag. It's a landmark for those who don't read maps. These are their other landmarks: pool, bath house, laundry, and dumpsters."

"Gotcha. We won't linger; I just want to get a sense of the vibes, as we used to say." Julie chuckled.

Brenda snickered. "Groovy."

"It was nice to meet you; I enjoyed chatting with you, Brenda."

"You too, Julie. Come back any time, or call if you have any questions. I work Tuesday through Friday."

The building door closed, then Julie said, "That's a wrap."

When Julie opened the door, I slid over to the middle.

She climbed in and handed me my jo before she closed the door and handed Paul the map. "I see why the residents get turned around. The streets are not laid out in blocks at all. Paul, go to the laundry because it's the closest spot where we can turn around without being obvious, then we can come out the way we went in."

On our way to the laundry, Larry asked, "Do you get the life story of everyone you meet, Julie?"

"Doesn't everyone? I had to take a little extra time with her because of that call she was on. She needed time to shake off the irate resident who complained about the lines in the laundry for her favorite dryer, the crowded pool, her noisy neighbors, the neighbor who turned her in for parking her golf cart on their sidewalk, and the messes around the dumpster."

"I take it we're not retiring here," Paul said.

"Not at all; the residents sound like a bunch of spoiled brats."

"I'm glad you're going house hunting with us," Larry said. "We don't need cranky neighbors."

When we reached the next resort, Paul pulled into the driveway and parked. "I need to get out to look at this closer."

We all climbed out of the car.

"I can't really tell what I'm looking at because it looks like abandoned property to me," I said.

"Sweetie, that's exactly what it is. There are large, poured concrete slabs with rebar and plastic pipes sticking out of them; the areas without slabs are overgrown with weeds. It looks like the developers bulldozed down a large stand of trees then pushed away the debris into a large pile to clear the land. From the looks of where the weeds are, I'm guessing they didn't finish putting in all their slabs before they abandoned their project."

"They must have run out of money," Paul said.

"Maybe, but judging from all the hype on their website, maybe they took the money and ran," Julie said.

"They wouldn't be the first developers to run that type of scam," Larry said.

"Let's go to the next one," Paul said.

Before Paul reached the driveway, I asked, "Are we close?"

"We'll turn in about a hundred yards."

"Pull over; stop now." I had forgotten I was in the middle seat as I instinctively reached for the arm rest but clutched Julie's arm instead.

"Paul, pull over immediately." Julie used a command voice.

Paul slammed on the brakes and pulled over onto the shoulder.

"I need to get out." I gasped for air as I slid toward Palace Guard then to the door.

Palace Guard was waiting for me outside the car when I jerked open the door, and Larry jumped out at the same time I did.

"What's going on, sweetie?" Larry had pulled his pistol from its holster.

"Shh."

I crossed the small ditch with Palace Guard at my side, and Larry behind me. I stood very still, then I heard wave after wave of heart-breaking, soft sobs that drowned my soul, and I dropped to my knees. Larry immediately grabbed me up, and Palace Guard disappeared.

"What is it?"

I sobbed, and Larry held me in his arms and hummed one of my comforting fairy tunes, and I relaxed.

"I didn't know you knew any fairy tunes," I whispered.

He hugged me tighter then whispered, "I didn't either. What did you hear?"

"There is something horrible happening at that camp," I said quietly. "I heard sobs of complete despair."

Larry opened the back door, "Julie, ride up front with Paul. We'll wait in the backseat for Palace Guard."

When Palace Guard returned, Larry said, "He's back; we can leave now."

Paul asked, "Do we continue to the camp?"

"No," I said.

Palace Guard emphatically shook his head.

"Palace Guard agrees with Maggie. Let's head back."

Palace Guard held his small finger close to his mouth and his thumb near his ear.

"A phone?" Larry asked.

Palace Guard nodded then slid his fingers across the floor toward me then stood back after he touched my foot.

My phone buzzed a text and announced, "Text from Roxanne: I know you are close. Thanks for my phone. We are booby trapped. No rescue yet. Do not reply. Ever."

"Did you get Roxanne's phone to her?" Larry asked.

Palace Guard smiled.

"I don't know how you did it, Palace Guard, but well done," Paul said.

"What did you see?" Larry asked.

Palace Guard mimed flipping long hair then held up his hands and flashed his ten fingers seven times.

"At least seventy women and girls?" I shuddered.

He nodded as he created a small box in front of him.

"In a small space. Where is Roxanne?" Larry asked.

Palace Guard made a small circle with his right hand and moved it away from the box.

"Separate in an even smaller space. Is she alone?" I asked.

He nodded.

"She's alone, isn't she?" Julie asked.

"Yes, she is," I said.

Larry held me tight as Paul headed to our hotel.

When Paul parked in a visitor's spot, my phone buzzed another text and announced, "Text from Della: If you know where R. is, do not approach. Macy and I are on our way. Check in later."

Larry exhaled. "Della just saved me, sweetie. I was afraid I was going to have to force you into my truck to go back to Tennessee with me to keep you from rescuing Roxanne. This is the first time in my life that I've ever contemplated kidnapping anyone."

"Might as well start with the best, Larry; I would have helped you," Paul said.

"I would have sold tickets," Julie said.

Palace Guard rolled his eyes, and I giggled.

When we went inside, Lucy yawned and stretched then slowly slid off the sofa before she trotted to the back door.

After Larry, Lucy, and Spike went outside, Julie said, "I brought the fixings for sandwiches because the country boil sounded too heavy to me this morning. I need to pace myself for this evening."

While Julie and Paul made sandwiches, I asked, "How much time do we have before we should leave?"

"About an hour," Julie said. "I just realized that you wouldn't be able to see a clock clearly enough to tell time. Have you thought about getting a watch that would work for you?"

"I have, but nothing works for me. I don't want a talking watch, a men's watch, or a wristwatch, and I don't want to pay too much money."

Paul chuckled. "You want an inexpensive Gray Lady-sized pocket watch that you can flip open a cap and touch the face of the watch for the time."

"Exactly."

"I think you should talk to Heather," he said.

"That's brilliant," I said.

"Making sandwiches must bring out the best in you, honey," Julie said.

I pulled out my phone. "Send a text to Heather: I need a watch. I don't want one that talks, and I can't stand a bracelet on my arm."

My phone announced, "Reply from Heather: May take a while. Have you asked Palace Guard?"

"What time is it, Palace Guard?"

He held up one finger then moved it slightly to my right.

I cocked my head. "A little after one?"

He smiled and nodded.

"What if it was eleven o'clock?"

He held up ten fingers then closed his hands and held up one.

"That's easy; got it. I'll let Heather know because my eyesight still has a chance to improve."

I picked up my phone from the table where I had set it. "Send a text to Heather: Palace Guard will tell me. Thanks; I don't need a watch after all."

My phone announced, "Reply from Heather: Still a good idea when a light is unacceptable. You're my tester."

"That's exciting news," Julie said.

"I'll have it by Monday, if I know Heather; she loves a challenge," I said.

After we ate lunch, Julie asked, "What are our travel plans?"

"We want Lucy to go, so she can check the yard," Larry said. "We'll load up; do you want to meet us there or follow us?"

"We'll follow you," Paul said.

On the way, I said, "I kind of miss Julie's running commentary."

"I'll fill in for her. We just passed a house, and here's another one," Larry said. "How did I do?"

Spike gave Larry a thumbs up, and I blinked.

When we reached the house, Larry parked.

"What do you think?" I asked as he opened my door to help me.

"We're out in the country with only a few houses nearby. I don't know how crazy I am about semi-isolated, but the property is large enough that we could have our own running trail."

"I like that. Is the agent here?" I asked.

"She's on the front porch."

CHAPTER THIRTEEN

After Paul and Julie joined us, Julie walked with me and Palace Guard to the porch while Larry strode ahead of us with Paul-blob to talk to the agent. Lucy and Spike wandered to the back yard.

"Is it fenced?" I asked.

"The front isn't, but the back might be. That's critical for Lucy isn't it?" Julie asked.

"It really is; Spike usually goes out with her, but sometimes she likes to spend extra time on the porch by herself or lying in the sun to warm up her achy joints."

"I need to be more like Lucy," Julie said.

As we walked inside the house, I was grateful that Julie came along when Larry said, "Nice room; let's check the garage."

After they left, Julie said, "The living room has a bay window that overlooks the front yard and a woodburning fireplace that is old red brick; it's amazing that it escaped being painted white. The floors are wooden, and the house style is more farmhouse than modern and has rustic touches; for example, the mantel over the fireplace is distressed wood, and it's beautiful. The ceilings are tall, and there are two ceiling fans. It feels very homey to me."

After we checked the three bedrooms, the guest bath, and the master bathroom, we went to the kitchen.

"The kitchen is a country eat-in kitchen, but some may call it a great room because there is a living space large enough for a sofa and three or four overstuffed chairs. There's a bar between the living space and the kitchen, and the dining area could easily accommodate a large table. I'd call this a party room because twenty people could gather in here, enjoy food, and socialize without feeling crowded. There are more ceiling fans in here. We need to make sure there is a central air conditioning unit because the fans alone would not be enough."

"Is there a back door and a porch?" I asked.

"There is an actual back door not a slider; let's check the porch."

When we stepped outside, I listened to the birds and the squirrels. *No traffic noise.*

Julie said, "This is nice; the backyard is huge and is completely fenced by a chain link fence that looks very sturdy. The back porch is wide and goes from corner to corner of the house. More party possibilities."

"I'm not really a party host," I said.

"You may surprise yourself. You'll have Jennifer, Glenn, Ella, Moe, Kate, your mother, Sarge, Larry's parents, Paul, and me descending on you regularly. Larry's very outgoing and will invite his old classmates and new coworkers here for a cookout, and you'll take over as grill master. Tonya, Justin, and Martha will become regular visitors. You're actually more social than you realize."

As we strolled to the front of the house, Julie asked, "What did you like best, and what was not so great?"

"I loved the back porch, and Larry said the property was large enough to put in a running trail, which would be very convenient if I could run at home since I can't drive anywhere yet. I loved hearing the birds singing. The master bedroom is huge, but the walk-in closet seemed to be about the same size as the one at the hotel, which is a little small. Larry has more clothes than I do because of his uniforms, and they can't be crammed into a small space; I'm not really crazy about the bay window."

"Two more to look at tomorrow. I'll be interested in hearing what Larry has to say about the house."

When we joined Larry and Paul at the truck, a blob hurried past us.

"I'll lock up the house; won't be a second," Nell said.

"We told her we wouldn't leave until she was in her car. She's a little spooked by being out in the country because she said there have been some recent kidnappings around Atlanta, and she's worried the kidnappers might come here next," Paul said.

"Next?" I asked.

"There are several missing girls in Augusta, Georgia, but nowhere really close," Larry said.

Palace Guard followed Julie and me as we walked to the truck. Julie whispered, "Augusta is about an hour and a half away."

"I'm not going to mention the bay window because if I do, and Larry didn't notice it, he'd board it up."

"It is a beautiful view," Julie said. "You'll enjoy it when your sight improves."

I smiled. *Thank you for saying when not if.*

When we reached the truck, I said, "We'll see you at Martha's. Tonya wants us to come a little early, so we'll probably be there when you arrive."

"Martha sent Paul the address, and he claims it's easy to find. We've got Larry as backup, but I've never known Paul to get lost, only misdirected." Julie chuckled as she headed toward their rental car.

Lucy trotted behind Larry, and Spike strode along next to her as they headed toward the truck. After we were in the truck, Larry said, "It's three-thirty; what time are we supposed to be there?"

"Tonya asked me to be there at five, so we have a little time to relax before we go."

"I'd like to pick up a few things for breakfast tomorrow. Do you want to go along?"

"I wouldn't mind a few minutes to put up my feet before we leave, but if that's going to run you behind, I could go with you."

"The hotel is actually on the way to the grocery store, so I can drop you off. Lucy might like a break too."

After Larry parked, I climbed out of the truck and noticed a blob near the bushes across from our suite. *Am I seeing bad guys everywhere?*

Larry unlocked the suite door, and I went inside before he left for the store.

I sat on the sofa and kicked off my boots; Lucy flopped down on the floor next to me, and quickly dropped into a soft snore.

I picked up my phone and frowned. "Della said check in later. I thought she meant that she would check in later, but did she actually meant I should check in later? Do you suppose she meant when I was alone, I should check in with her?"

Palace Guard rolled his eyes and shook his head as he held his hands about three feet apart then moved them outward as far as his long arms allowed.

"What do you mean, that's a stretch? It's perfectly logical."

Palace Guard shook his head.

I one-eyed glared him then said to my phone, "Send a text to Della: Call."

My phone announced, "Call from Della."

"About time," she said. "Where'd honey boy go?"

I sneered at Palace Guard. "He went to the grocery store to pick up a few things for breakfast."

"He's a keeper. Now, tell me. Where's Roxanne?"

I told her about the camp and the intense feeling of despair I felt before we reached the driveway, then I told her about Palace Guard finding the seventy plus girls who were crammed into a tight space.

When I told her about Palace Guard getting Roxanne's phone to her, she chuckled. "That Palace Guard is a champ, isn't he? Did Roxanne text you?"

"She texted me right before you did. She knew I had something to do with her phone appearing and told me to stay away because they were boobytrapped. She also told me to never text her. I assume because her phone would be discovered if I did."

"Good to know. I won't either then."

"What about you and Macy? Are you really on your way?"

"Heavens, no. Macy still has no idea that Roxanne is even missing. I had a sudden feeling something was wrong and took a wild stab because Larry has been so nervous about leaving you there; I decided it was because he was certain you'd go looking for the kidnapped girls and wouldn't return for his remaining week of class, so he could protect you. If I was wrong, you would have immediately called to ask if I'd lost my mind in your sweet girl way. I'm not normally the feely kind of person, so maybe I have, but that's a discussion for another time. So, what do we do?"

"I really don't know because we don't know what Roxanne meant by booby-trapped."

"For our first step, we'll have to discover what the boobytrap is, so we can disarm it," Della said.

"Absolutely true, but how do we do that?"

"I come up with the ideas; you're the one that solves them." Della cackled. "A little FBI humor; I used it once on Kate right after I retired, and she threatened to fire me."

I giggled. "I'll bet she was mad that you were fireproof."

"You know it, sweet girl; now, about the issue at hand: give me a little time to think about it. What are your plans for this evening?"

"We're going to a barbecue at Martha's house to welcome Justin home. Paul and Julie are going too; I don't think anyone else will be there, but I don't know for sure."

"Text me when you have a few minutes to talk; I have a little something in mind that I could easily pull off if all the stars align."

After we hung up, I heard Larry's truck as it headed toward our suite. *I should have asked her if she had a drone.*

Larry came inside, stopped for a hug and a quick kiss then emptied his grocery sack of items and put them into the refrigerator.

"I'll feed Lucy, then we can go," Larry said.

While Lucy ate, I asked, "Do you know who is going to be there?"

"There may be a few folks there from the GBI office, but that's just a guess. If there are too many people for you, we can leave anytime."

"If there is a big crowd, Tonya and I might hide for a bit. She's not into large groups either."

"I'd forgotten; Justin told us his wife is shy."

"Justin says that because he understands how she feels and doesn't want to call attention to her hearing impairment. It's frustrating for her to have a conversation in a crowd because she hears all the background noise with her hearing aids; without them, she reads lips to get the gist of what someone is saying, but people forget to face her and speak clearly. Maybe her new hearing aids can be set to ignore background sounds."

Larry nodded. "That would be great for her, wouldn't it?"

After Lucy finished eating, she nosed the sliding glass door. Larry opened the door, and Lucy and Spike went outside.

"Spike is really good with Lucy, isn't he? It never occurred to me that he had a soft side," Larry said.

When Lucy was ready to come inside, Larry opened the door, and we all went to the truck. I surveyed the surrounding area, but I didn't see any lurking blobs.

While Spike helped Lucy into the truck, Larry helped me, and Palace Guard stood with his back to us as he scanned the parking lot.

"Palace Guard seems particularly vigilant. Did something happen while I was at the grocery store?" Larry whispered.

"Not that I know of."

"He must be on high alert because of the kidnapped girls and Roxanne; not that I blame him." Larry closed my door and hurried to his seat.

"What did you think about the house this morning?" I asked as we headed toward Martha's house.

"Paul and I had some concerns about the roof. According to the listing, it's thirty years old, and there were some spots on the ceiling that indicated old water damage. We'd definitely want an inspection of the roof, but I wondered about the condition of some of the other major systems like the electrical, air conditioning, and well because of the age of the house. The agent will tell the seller's agent the roof needs to be fixed and will suggest that the seller have the electrical, air conditioning inspected; she said we could list all of those things as contingencies in our offer, and before you say anything, I know we could afford to fix any problems, but I'm not sure we're ready to take on managing major repairs to a house. What did you think?"

"I loved hearing the birds and squirrels and being able to run when Palace Guard and I feel like it is awesome, but I worried about the small master closet."

"You're right; it was about the same size as what we have in the suite. I'm not sure that will work for us."

"We could use a closet from another room too, but that doesn't seem fair to any company that visits," I said.

"If we don't have any closet space for them, maybe they'll cut their visit short." Larry chuckled.

I giggled. "I dare you to say that to Jennifer and Ella."

Larry snorted. "I don't have a death wish."

Larry pulled into a driveway and parked. "Looks like Justin's already here. I'll ask Martha where she wants me to park after we go inside."

Before Larry opened his door, Lucy whined, so Spike and Lucy were the first ones out of the truck. When Larry opened my door, Lucy was waiting for me and wagging her tail in excitement. I hopped out with my jo and backpack, then she led me to Martha's front door. Tonya-blob threw open the front door and grabbed me into a hug then sat on the porch and rubbed Lucy's belly. I felt Kiki's tiny claws on my shoulder, and Tonya's imaginary dragon purred in my ear.

I giggled. "Y'all certainly know how to make your company feel welcome."

"Hey, Kev. I've got something to show you," Justin called from inside.

Lucy jumped up and went into the house with Larry and Palace Guard. Tonya looped her arm into mine, and we walked inside; Kiki stayed on my shoulder, and Palace Guard followed us.

When we went inside, I felt Kiki's talons push off my shoulder.

Tonya giggled. "You've been replaced by a tall, handsome man, Gray Lady. I think Kiki is enjoying the view from Palace Guard shoulder."

I peered at Tonya. "What color is your hair?"

"Mom calls it dark blond; I call it light brown."

"You're still a blob, but I'm going to imagine you with lightish hair."

Tonya squealed, and I cringed. "Oops, sorry, but I love it. Let's go into the kitchen, and you can see if you can imagine Mom with hair."

When we went into the kitchen, Martha said, "Hello, Maggie. I knew you were here when I heard Tonya squeal; Justin and Kevin went into the garage, and Lucy is with them. I got you a cup with a lid and straw; care for some iced tea?"

I smiled. "Sounds good."

Tonya nudged me with her elbow, and I shook my head.

She shrugged then opened the back door; I inhaled the tantalizing aroma of wood smoke.

"Something smells really good."

"Mom's been smoking a couple of racks of ribs in her smoker because that's Justin's favorite. My stomach has been grumbling since lunch. I think she uses hickory wood with ribs. Just wait; you'll love them. She puts only enough barbecue sauce on the ribs for the sugars to give the ribs what she calls a nice char; Mom's a barbecue aficionado. When Dad was alive, he used to tease her about needing catsup on his ribs. She would get really mad at him and threaten him with no dessert."

"Ouch," I said. "The ultimate punishment."

"No kidding; she's serious about her ribs. There will be a ton of food; just eat ribs, potato salad, and only one deviled egg, then you won't be too full for dessert."

"I'm glad you told me; I smelled pinto beans on the stove."

"She's a sly one; she'll put fresh rolls in the oven right after she brings in the ribs to rest."

While we sipped our sweet tea on the back porch, Tonya said, "Mom and I found the perfect house for Justin and me. I can't wait for him to see it. We have an appointment in the morning at nine. He doesn't know yet because Mom and I thought he'd like to take a breath before I rush him with news about a house. It's a block from here, so Mom and I can visit without driving, but we'll probably just pick up the phone now that my hearing aids make talking on the phone so easy for me. Mom said we'll get all our talking during the week, so Justin can have my full attention on weekends. I am definitely looking forward to that."

After she told me about the house in detail, she said, "My doctor recommended a speech therapist for me. I see her next week, and I'm excited about that too. With my new hearing aids, I've started to hear the different tones people use when they talk, and Mom said I've been mimicking them. Justin thinks the speech therapist will help me feel more comfortable around people. I certainly hope so because I've been feeling really guilty about holding Justin back in his career. He doesn't like to go to functions without me, but he knows how hard it has been for me to be in a group, so he's skipped most of the gatherings."

"That is really exciting news. I thought your voice had a new lilt in it. It's very refreshing, like bubbles."

Tonya giggled. "I've never been accused of being bubbly before; I think that's my new goal: I'll be bubbly."

I laughed. "A hairy, perky, bubbly blob."

Tonya snort-laughed. "Exactly."

Martha opened the back door. "What's so funny? Are you two up to some shenanigans again?"

"Yes, Mom," Tonya said.

"Okay, then; just let me know when I can jump in and help." Martha chuckled as she returned to the kitchen.

"What about your ribs? How are you doing?" I asked.

"Ugh; healing is slow, isn't it? My pulmonologist is a bully. He won't let me pretend I can't hear him when he tells me I have to take deeper breaths. He's even got Mom on his side because he told her and Justin that I have to keep up my breathing exercises because I am at risk for pneumonia. That's the only downside to Justin being home: he and Mom can tag-team nag me. The exercises don't seem to be helping lately, though, because I've been a little short of breath."

Lucy yipped then trotted to the back door.

"I think Paul and Julie are here," I said.

"Right on time," Tonya said.

As we went inside, Martha was greeting Paul and Julie at the front door. "Justin and Kevin are in the garage, Paul; I'll show you the door to the garage; the girls are in the backyard planning shenanigans, Julie. Do either of you care for some sweet tea? You can be polite and say no, but I already poured it. Oh, Gray Lady, I gave Kevin your coffee maker and he put it in his truck."

Tonya tugged on my shirt sleeve. "Let's go back outside. It won't be as noisy, and Mom will show Julie where we are after they chat a bit."

I nodded.

As we were settled in our chairs on the porch, I said, "That was a good move."

"Thanks. This gives Mom a chance to show off the house, and for Julie to be nicely appreciative. They can bond a little without feeling like they need to include us. Did you visit the first house Jennifer and Mom thought you might like?"

"We did. It had a huge yard, and the backyard was fenced; Larry said it would be easy to clear a running trail for me, but the master closet wasn't really big enough for our clothes and Larry's uniforms."

"That would be a showstopper for me," Tonya said.

"If it was all that was available, we could consider using the closets in the other bedrooms, but that wouldn't be ideal."

"If neither of the houses you look at tomorrow work for you, Mom and Nell are certain the right house will turn up soon. One of the features of my new hearing aids is to muffle background noises, like at a party. I forgot to turn that on earlier. If I can figure out how to do it, tonight will be a good test."

I leaned back in my chair and listened to nearby traffic, the neighbors' voices, and the rumble of trash trucks.

If we lived in town, I'd have to adjust to the noises.

Palace Guard joined us on the porch.

"Did you enjoy being tall like Palace Guard, girl?" Tonya cooed, and I heard Kiki's happy trill from Tonya's shoulder.

Martha and Julie came outside and hurried to the smoker. "It's time to bring the ribs inside to rest," Martha said as she slid a rack of ribs onto a large cookie sheet and handed it to Julie.

While Julie headed back to the house, Martha pulled out the second rack to carry inside; Tonya opened the back door for Julie.

"Thanks, Tonya; I was so focused on not dropping the ribs that I didn't even think about how I would manage the door." Julie chuckled as she went inside.

After Martha went in, Tonya returned to her seat.

"You're thinking about something. What?" she asked.

"Am I that transparent?"

"You are to Kiki; she told me."

"I was listening to the traffic and neighborhood noises. My apartment in Harperville was in a neighborhood and close to a bus stop. I'm certain it must have sounded something like this, but that's been a while ago. I don't know if I could get used to the noise."

"Your hearing is particularly acute, so I guess that's not a surprise. I heard a couple of women in Tennessee complain that the quiet there was eerie; I turned off my hearing aids, so I couldn't hear them."

I snickered. "I listened to chirping birds, chattering squirrels, and the occasional traffic sounds from the nearby road; I don't understand how anyone could call it quiet at all."

"You might adjust," Tonya said, "but maybe you're not a city gal anymore."

"That's actually what is keeping the small closet house in the running for me. The birds were noisy, there was no traffic noise to speak of, but most of all, the room for me to run was priceless."

"If it's an older house, it may need repairs, but I'll bet it's better built than the new houses now."

"I think Larry is worried that any major repairs would require outside help, and he's reluctant to have anyone there if I'm alone."

"That's an easy fix. I'll spend the day with you when the contractors are working, and don't tell me that's too much for me to do because it isn't. I can read and fix your lunch, and you can run in the morning then shoot the bad guys after lunch."

I nodded. "That would work, except I'm not telling Larry the bad guy part. He has absolutely no sense of humor these days."

"As long as you and I are considering contractors, maybe a contractor could look at what it would take to expand that master bedroom closet or put in a new one for uniforms."

"With the hanging bar too high for me to reach." I smiled.

I heard the door from the garage to the house close. "I think we're about to be invaded."

"I just got a call from Nell." Larry knelt next to my chair. "She told the seller's agent that we're looking at two more houses tomorrow to help put a little pressure on the urgency, and the seller contacted a roofer this afternoon to get an estimate next week. Our agent assured me that we'd have a firm commitment on the roof and the inspection results to review before she would consider submitting an offer, so I feel better about the house we saw today."

"That's great news," I said. "Tonya and I were thinking we could put in a second closet for your uniforms. Is the master bedroom large enough?"

"I think it might be," Larry said.

"I agree," Paul said. "A good contractor might be able to enlarge the existing closet too."

"I would really love being out in the country with the birds and wildlife, a fence for Lucy, and enough space for me to run," I said. "I'm interested in seeing what the two houses tomorrow have to offer."

"So am I, sweetie."

Martha opened the back door. "Are you folks ready to eat? Julie poured sweet tea for everyone while I set up our buffet on the counter. There is plenty of room for all of us to eat at the table."

As we filed inside, Larry said, "I'll fix your plate, sweetie."

"Start me off with ribs, potato salad, and a deviled egg, please," I said.

"You've been coached." Justin chuckled. "Same for you, honey?"

"Of course," Tonya said as the two of us strolled to the dining table.

"Now, if you sit at the far end, I can sit next to you, and Kevin can sit on the other side of you; Justin can sit next to me, and the rest of them are on their own, but I'll bet Julie sits next to Mom, and Paul sits next to Kevin." Tonya giggled.

"Makes sense to me; be sure to tell me how it all works out."

"Here's your seat. I grabbed your iced tea cup with the lid and switched it with the glass that was at your seat."

After we sat down, Tonya continued, "I'm sure there will be a long discussion between Mom and Julie, so you'll probably hear the details."

Before everyone sat down, Tonya whispered, "I'm turning off my hearing aids; I've used up my polite hearing time. Tap me if you want to say something, so I can see what you're saying."

I held up a thumb; Spike stood near the table across from us. When he held up two thumbs and grinned, Tonya giggled.

When Justin asked Tonya a question, and she didn't answer, I said quietly, "She turned off her hearing aids."

"I should have realized she would; thanks." Justin nudged her with his elbow. *I'll bet he did something to make her smile.*

After everyone had eaten, Martha said, "Julie and I will package the leftovers up for everyone, then we can have dessert."

Paul rose with his plate in his hand.

"Leave everything on the table; Martha and I will take care of the dishes," Julie said.

"Mom, how long until dessert?" Tonya asked.

"It won't take us five minutes to get these dishes in the dishwasher. Go relax on the porch, and we'll bring it to you."

Martha brought out our chocolate cake on dessert plates then returned with hers as everyone else followed her with their cake.

Larry, Justin, and Paul polished off their dessert and scraped their plates with their forks before they carried their dishes into the house.

After we finished our dessert, Martha and Julie collected our plates and took them inside.

I put my hand on Tonya's arm. When she turned to see what I had to say, I said, "Your arm feels hot; are you feeling okay?"

Tonya coughed. "I might be coming down with a cold, but I think I got a little overheated out here; maybe we should go inside."

"Is there somewhere I could make a private call?"

After we went inside, Tonya said, "Mom, Gray Lady and I are going into the office. I have to rest a bit," Tonya said.

"Of course, honey."

Martha knows Tonya had to turn off her hearing aids.

Palace Guard followed us to the office.

After Tonya closed the door, she said, "I'll put up my feet; I can't hear you, so you can talk, and I can relax."

I stood where she could see my face. "Can I get you anything?"

"I'm fine," Tonya mumbled as she sat on a soft recliner and flipped up the footrest then sighed and closed her eyes. "I need a power nap."

I said to my phone, "Call Della."

Della answered on the second ring. "Do you have a little time to talk?"

"Yes, Tonya and I are in the office. She turned off her hearing aids because she needed a break; she's napping."

"Put up your feet and relax; you probably need a little break from the group too. I think the catering company provides the food for a resort in your area, and that's our key."

CHAPTER FOURTEEN

"I don't have any information about the catering company delivering to a resort, but the camp I told you about is two miles outside of town," I said.

"Hopefully one of us can confirm the delivery before Monday, but I'm operating on the assumption right now that it's true, but I also need the location," Della said. "My partner in crime and I will be there Monday or Tuesday, depending on how soon we're positive about the catering company."

She must mean Macy; Della has always been careful in how much she says.

Della continued, "Your oldest friend is keenly interested in the catering company, but I'm not sure her team knows about the camp yet, so keep that close. My partner and I think we'll be better off with the quiet approach. I'll include your friend if it looks like she's about to stumble into a hornet's nest."

Kate's good and would never make a rookie mistake of going in without being informed about what she was walking into, and Della knows it. Della is keeping her in the dark for another reason, which explains why she didn't want to mention Macy. Is there someone on Kate's team that Della doesn't trust?

"Have you heard anything more from Roxanne?" Della asked.

"Nothing, and I don't know if that is good or bad."

"Neither do I, but I'm hoping it's because she's taking every precaution to avoid calling attention to herself. The one young man you called the tough guy was found dead behind a bar in Atlanta. The police recorded it as a robbery, but I have my doubts. I don't know where the other young man is. Rodney may have gone into hiding because he has disappeared. Everything is going too slow to suit me, but I can't rush in, especially if I'm going to accuse your old friend of doing exactly that." Della cackled.

"What about Walt?" I asked.

Della sighed. "Your old friend told me hands off when it came to Walt. When I pushed her to tell me why, she got ugly."

"That makes absolutely no sense to me."

"Doesn't to me either, sweet girl."

This may be one of Kate's typical distraction tricks. I frowned. "My old friend is devious enough to push us into investigating Walt because she said we shouldn't; she may be trying to divert us from...what?"

Della was silent for so long that I peered at my phone. *Have we been disconnected? I can't see well enough to tell.*

"You tossed me for a loop; your old friend is obviously not the only one who has a devious side. I'll ask my partner, and you talk to Paul to see what he thinks. What else do you have that's going to give me a raging headache?"

Walt said he had another woman waiting in the wings if Macy didn't work out; I've been assuming that was Roxanne, but what if it isn't? I don't think Della's in a   mood   to   hear that.

"I can't think of anything else."

"Neither can I. Hang onto honey boy for me. I'll check in with you sometime Monday." Della hung up.

Della's right: I do need to talk to Paul.

Before I left the office, my phone announced, "Text from Della: honeyboy2me"

I chuckled at the accidental text then closed the door behind me.

When Palace Guard and I stepped into the kitchen, there were no blobs. I opened the garage door and peered inside then closed it.

As he came in from the garage, Paul said, "Larry and Justin will be a while. Julie told us she and Martha were going to check out Martha's vegetable garden, so they'll be busy. I'm sure Lucy and Spike are with them. Where's Tonya?"

"She's napping in a comfortable chair in the office."

"Are you up for a stroll around the block? I'll check in with Larry."

"That sounds wonderful."

Paul opened the door to the garage. "Maggie and I are taking a walk around the block. We won't be long."

After he closed the door, he said, "I got a wave from Larry, so he heard me."

I grabbed my backpack on the way out, and Paul said, "I'll set the pace because I couldn't keep up with your pace."

"I'd rather run," I said.

"I wouldn't." Paul chuckled. "I was at the gas station before we came here, and I saw a truck with the catering company's logo on the side. It drove away before I finished refueling, but the guy next to me told me he'd never seen that catering truck before last month when the camp opened. I asked him if he knew how often they came to town, and he didn't, but the woman at the pump in front of me told us the catering company truck came every Monday and Wednesday, and occasionally on Fridays. She said her brother hired the local team that unloads the truck two or three times a week. When I asked why the driver didn't unload the truck, she told me it supposedly wasn't efficient for the driver to get out of the truck. The three of us had a good laugh over more money than brains."

"Wow. Did she know what kind of food was being delivered?"

"She said it was all junk food and cans of high-sodium food with questionable ingredients; she was disgusted that there was no fresh fruit, vegetables, or meat and added that they did ask her brother about finding a cook and a cook's helper for the camp. She's really proud of her brother and his business. She gave me his business card."

"Too bad I can't see. I'll pass that on to Della." I told Paul what Della had to say.

"She didn't identify her partner or your friend by name? She thinks someone's listening in. I wonder if it's her phone or yours," Paul said.

"What do you think? I don't want it to be mine," I said.

"Let me see what I can find for you in a disposable phone that we can use between us, then you can use your phone for everything else. Yours does the text to speech and vice versa, doesn't it?"

"Yes, and it announces the caller from my contacts."

I told him about Della and my suspicion that there was something she wasn't telling me about Kate or her team.

"My first thought is that Della thinks there is someone dirty on Kate's team."

"I thought the same thing. It's not like I can just ask Della or Kate."

"Interesting. Have you heard anything from Kate?"

"I hadn't thought about it, but I haven't heard from her in at least a month, if not more, which is unusual," I said.

"That goes along with our theory of someone crooked on her team, if we assume she's trying to insulate you. We do conjecture well, don't we?"

I giggled. "The best."

"One more block, and we'll be back at Martha's house. Do you want to take a second loop?" Paul asked.

"I wouldn't mind; I'd like to walk and think, and I find it difficult to think when a group is talking. I haven't learned the fine art of tuning people out yet."

When we rounded the second block, Palace Guard tapped my shoulder.

Paul said quietly, "Let's stop a minute and admire these roses. There's a young man on the opposite side of the street walking toward us. I saw him the first time around too, but he was walking the same way we were, just slower. I thought there was an older man with a cane following or walking with him, but the older man's pace was much faster, and he passed the guy and kept going. Get a nice video of him as he nears us. Is Palace Guard with us? Can he help you keep your jo trained on the guy?"

"Sure can; Palace Guard noticed him too."

"What do you have on you?" Paul asked.

"My knife inside my boot, my carry piece in my holster on my waist, a second pistol in my backpack, and of course, my jo. My best offense and defense, though, is Palace Guard. He guides my aim and lets me know when to hit the dirt."

"I've got my carry piece in my holster that is inside my waistband. You're better armed than I am. You and Palace Guard take the lead on this."

As I pretended to gaze at the roses, I held out my jo like a fancy dude's walking stick as I turned it under Palace Guard's guidance. When Palace Guard tapped my hand, I stopped the recording.

"That guy's got a moustache, and his hair's very dark, but I'm almost positive he's the smooth guy from the café. Wonder if he knows his buddy is dead," Paul said.

"Is that the same man from the track and the one near our hotel room?" I asked.

Palace Guard moved so that he was in front of me and nodded.

I shuddered. "Palace Guard said yes."

"I don't suppose you'd come stay with me and Julie," Paul said.

"I wish my suite had a second bedroom."

"We need to find something," Paul said. "I'll talk to Julie."

"It will only need to be for a week. Maybe a hotel with adjoining suites?" I asked.

"You'll want to keep your long-term suite, though, because short-term suites are much smaller and don't have the full kitchens that you have."

"See what Julie says because now it sounds more complex than it was in my head." I snickered. "We need to set up an expense account for you that is separate from your Coyle Detective Agency account. There are some expenses that aren't related to the Coyle Agency. I'll talk to my lawyer's assistant, Shantelle."

"Ask her about setting up a separate business. Can I be VP in charge of Operations?" Paul chuckled.

I rolled my eye. *I'm positive I'm improving.* "You got it."

"I don't want business cards," he said. "We're the Gray Lady Agency."

"If Shantelle sets up a business, I'll tell her that's our name; either that or Imaginary Agency; which do you prefer?"

"What about Plain Brown Wrapper Agency?" Paul chuckled.

I giggled. "That's my favorite."

"I've got it: Gray Flanagan Agency."

"I like that one too." I smiled. "Is there somewhere I can sit down and call Shantelle? Shall we let her be the tie breaker? She might not be there, but she'll get the message Monday morning."

"There's a bench at the bus stop on the corner," Paul said.

After I was relatively comfortable on the narrow board that pretended to be a bench, I turned the volume very low on my phone then said, "Call Shantelle." Paul-blob sat next to me, and Palace Guard stood where he could scan the area, but where I could see him.

"Hi, Gray Lady." Shantelle's voice dropped to a whisper. "What's our newest caper?"

Paul elbowed me, and Palace Guard grinned.

"We've decided to start up a business and thought a partnership was the best way for us to go."

"I'm taking notes, go ahead. You and Larry in a business partnership; I assume he's the silent partner because he has no clue that you're doing this."

I snorted. "You know me well; we have two choices for the name: Plain Brown Wrapper Agency or Gray Flanagan Agency."

"Gray Flanagan is perfect. I would have suggested Maggie Ewing Agency, but Gray Flanagan is you without being you: that's your plain gray wrapper." Shantelle chuckled. "It's fits because it's clandestine in plain sight. Can I be the Treasurer and Secretary?"

I glanced at Palace Guard, and he tilted his head toward Paul then nodded.

"If you would, that would be great," I said.

"I'll design the business cards tomorrow. I already have some ideas in mind. What's the source of our income? Services?"

"Exactly."

"I'll seed the business with half of the money from your monthly allowances that you haven't touched yet. I'm glad to see those funds put to use; I'm tired of making the bank rich. Do we have any employees?"

"One, for now: Paul Vargas. He's in charge of Operations."

"Got it. We'll put him on the payroll; I'll send him the forms. Is he full time or part time? We'll want him to have an expense account too, right?"

"He'll be part time for now, and yes, he'll need an expense account."

"As soon as I get the forms back from Paul, he can submit any expenses he has, and I'll pay them immediately, unless you want to approve each expense, which I know you don't; I'll put in a cap amount. You'll want to approve anything over the cap. Tell Paul to send me a text with his email, so I'll have his phone information. This is going to be fun, whatever it is." Shantelle giggled as she hung up.

I showed Paul my phone, and he sent Shantelle a text.

"You were right; she definitely knows you well." Paul chuckled as we strolled toward Martha's house. "Let me know when you tell Larry about the new business because I won't say anything to Julie until you do. Kate trained you to stay wary, and Spike taught you to cheat to win; I learned those lessons through misfortune and repeatedly making the same bad choices. Not many people are at our level of survival, Gray Lady."

"Paul, we can't move to a new hotel this next week because we know I'm being watched, and we don't want to tip off the bad guys that we think something is wrong. We need to maintain our blissful ignorance if we're going to save Roxanne."

"I thought Della was taking care of saving Roxanne," Paul said.

"I'm not so sure she is; she could be operating under Kate's orders to keep us out of the way. It bothers me that nothing's adding up. Why do we have to confirm the catering delivery for Della? That's her area of expertise; she could have checked in five minutes with her resources."

"Wonder if I could get a job unloading the catering truck. I've got the guy's card; I'll give him a call tomorrow."

"Won't Julie get suspicious if you disappear for several hours?"

"She won't be surprised because I do that regularly; she'll know I'm following up on something for you or Glenn."

"Another person that's dropped off the radar is Rodney. Della told me he must have gone into hiding, and I somehow translated that to a fact in my mind, but I don't know if it's important to care where Rodney is."

"We need to know what's important and what's not important, so we can shift to what's important. I know a tax attorney's admin in Atlanta who can check with a staff person at the catering office to see if Rodney's been there."

"I remembered something while I was talking to Della earlier, but I didn't mention it to her because she sounded overloaded."

"I'm not really sure I can imagine Della being overloaded. What was it?"

"Walt told Rodney that he had another woman in the wings that he was priming if Macy didn't work out. I've been assuming that was Roxanne because she's at the camp, but what if it was someone else?"

"You've had all this in your head, and it hasn't exploded?" Paul asked.

I giggled. "It feels like it's on the verge."

"We do know that young girls and Roxanne are at the camp against their will because Palace Guard saw them, and Roxanne sent you a text acknowledging that she got her phone. We also know that local folks unload the food delivery truck at the camp two or three times a week, and you are being followed by a shady character. Let's stick with what we know until we confirm any additional pieces to fit into our puzzle. What do we do about our shady character?"

"Palace Guard knows what he looks like, so I'm covered there. So far, all he has done is follow me."

Maybe I should keep him busy.

Palace Guard shook his head.

Paul stopped at Martha's driveway, and Palace Guard and I stopped with him.

"I know you, Gray Lady. What are you thinking?"

"There has to be a reason he's following me."

Palace Guard scowled as he crossed his arms.

"Right; what's your plan?"

"I don't know yet, but I'll let you know if I come up with anything."

"If I can't trust you to tell me, I'll have to follow him while he's following you, but I'd rather unload the truck to see what I can learn at the camp."

I wrinkled my nose. "Smells a little like blackmail to me."

"Whatever it takes: it's what we do in operations." Paul chuckled as he continued to the house.

Palace Guard grinned; I tossed my hair as I followed Paul inside.

When we went inside, I heard Larry and Justin talking in the garage while Martha and Julie rocked and talked on the back porch.

"Tonya must still be napping," I said.

"How about some sweet tea, Gray Lady? When we left on our walk, I thought I'd have to walk slower than I usually do, but I had to stretch out my stride to keep up with you. Both of us need to hydrate, or I do, so you have to drink some sweet tea too, or else I'll feel like an old man."

I giggled, and Larry came in from the garage. "What's funny?"

"It's one of those things that you had to be there." I rolled my eye, but no one noticed. "Paul and I took a walk around the block, and he said both of us needed to hydrate."

Larry furrowed his brow. "I don't get it, but a big glass of sweet tea sounds good."

Kiki dug her tiny claws into my shoulder and chirped a cry for help. "Is it Tonya?"

Palace Guard and I hurried to the office as Justin came in from the garage.

"Where's Tonya?" Justin asked.

"Maggie and um...just dashed off to the office. Something's wrong," Larry said.

Justin, Palace Guard, and I went in the office; Justin rushed to the recliner where Tonya had fallen asleep.

"Tonya, are you okay?" he shouted then said, "Maggie, get Mom. Tonya's burning up."

Palace Guard and I rushed to the back door. "Martha, Justin is worried that Tonya might have a high fever and wants you to check."

She hurried past me. "That's not good; the doctor said she's a prime candidate for pneumonia."

A few minutes later, Justin rushed out of the office. "I need to take her to the hospital right away."

"Slow down, Justin. I've called nine-one-one, and there is an ambulance on the way," Larry said. "I've already moved my truck out of your driveway."

"I'll move my truck. I'm riding with her," Justin said.

"Give me your keys, Justin, and I'll move it for you then park your truck at the hospital," Larry said.

"Martha can ride with me in the rental car," Julie said.

I ran two small towels under the cold water faucet, then Paul rung them out for me before I took the cool, wet towels to the office.

"Thank you, Gray Lady. These will help," Martha said.

"I hear sirens," I said. "Julie's going to take you to the hospital, Martha, and Paul or Larry will take Justin's truck and park it in the visitor's lot."

"Poor baby; this came on so fast," Martha said as Kiki cooed to Tonya. "Will you and Larry be sure to lock up the house, Maggie?"

I left the office before the ambulance pulled into the driveway, so I would be out of the way, then Palace Guard and I locked the doors to the garage and to the backyard while Lucy and Spike waited for us in the front yard.

After the ambulance left, Julie walked Martha to the rental car, then they left as Paul locked the front door.

Larry opened the back door of his truck for Lucy then put his arm around me as he helped me into the passenger's seat. "Paul's going to drive Justin's truck to the hospital. Julie wants to stay with Martha for a while, so Paul will either hang around or pick up Julie when she's ready to leave. Are you okay?"

"Not really. I'm upset that I didn't tell Justin that Tonya was napping before I left on the walk."

"Sweetie, you were gone a little over thirty minutes."

"Really? It seemed more like an hour; we walked around the block twice."

Larry chuckled. "Who set the pace?"

"Paul did. I told him I'd rather run, and he didn't quite say, 'too bad', but I think I can read his mind. Jessie would be proud of me."

When we were in our suite, I pulled off my boots.

"Can I get you a glass of wine? I think I'd like a beer while you tell me what you were not planning to tell me," Larry said.

"You're just fishing." I snorted.

"Not really, there is always something, so I thought it would be refreshing if we talked about whatever it is before next week when I hear something from the local GBI agency or the police."

My phone rang and announced, "Call from Paul."

When I answered, Larry poured wine into my covered cup then opened a beer.

"Are you at your suite?" Paul asked.

"Yes, Larry's pouring me a glass of wine; how's Tonya?"

"She's one sick girl. She's still in the emergency room, but the nurses are preparing to move her to intensive care. Justin's extremely worried, and so is Martha. Justin is going to stay at the hospital, but he wants Martha to go home because she would have to sleep in a chair in the visitors' lobby if she stayed. He promised he'd call her if there was any change at all. Martha reluctantly agreed after Julie said she'd stay with her. I'll call you tomorrow with an update. Feel free to call me if you get a feeling, and I'll check with Julie."

After we disconnected, I sipped my wine. "Thanks for the wine, honey. What were you all doing in the garage? Anything interesting?"

"Martha asked Justin to sort through all of the tools. Tonya's dad was a real handyman, and the tools haven't been touched in a while. Justin wants to keep all of them, so we'll clean and oil them then store them appropriately."

"Really? Can I help? I really miss cleaning the rental guns at the gun range and cleaning the tools would be similar, wouldn't it?"

"I'm sure Justin will welcome the help, and I can't think of anyone who could do a better job than you. I'll talk to him before I leave. Maybe that's something you could start on this week to help him out; I suspect he'll spend most of next week with Tonya at the hospital."

"I feel like I'd be helping Justin, thank you."

"What's our plan for tomorrow?"

"We have two houses to look at in the morning; I forgot to ask Paul if Julie could go with us. I'm not comfortable going through without her there to tell me what she sees."

"Call Paul back."

I picked up my phone. "Call Paul."

"Whatcha got, Gray Lady?" he asked when he answered.

"Do you suppose Julie can still go with us to look at the two houses in the morning?"

"You're so talented, those of us who know you often forget that you can't see. I'm sure she can carve out the time. We'll be there."

After we disconnected, I asked, "What makes you so smart, Mr. Sexy Pants?"

Larry unbuttoned my shirt. "I'm not sure."

He leaned over and kissed my throat. "Maybe this."

He slipped his hand into my shirt. "Or maybe this."

I smiled as he carried me to the bedroom.

***

While Larry and I sat on the patio with our first cups of coffee, my phone rang. "Call from Paul."

"Everything okay?" I asked when I answered.

"It was a rough night. Martha couldn't sleep, and Julie hovered. Julie said Martha finally fell asleep around three, probably from exhaustion. Julie cat-napped until she woke at five thirty, then she called me at six. I just dropped them off at the hospital. Have you two had breakfast?"

"Not yet. We're relaxing with our coffee."

"There wasn't even time for coffee this morning because Martha was so anxious to return to the hospital. Martha told me about a coffee shop that isn't far from your suite, but she called it a cute coffee shop with a lovely décor. After she told me about a diner that Justin loves, I decided maybe you and Larry would like to go to a diner too. Want to meet me there?"

Larry grinned, and I said, "We love diners."

"Good; you saved me from being obligated to report back about which flavored coffee I ordered."

After we hung up, Larry's phone buzzed a text. "Paul sent me the address."

"Spike, we're meeting Paul for breakfast."

Spike waved good-bye; Larry, Palace Guard, and I climbed into the truck. As we drove away from our suite, a man, who had his back to me, was bent over as he clipped a rose bush on the corner near our suite; I shook my head. *Why isn't that man a blob?*

"What's up, sweetie?"

"I thought I saw someone snipping back the rose bush on the corner. I didn't know who it was."

"It was probably the groundskeeper; the woman in the office told me about him when I picked up our key. She said he was new and was remarkably talented. I'm not sure why I had to know that. His name is Garrett, and he's a widower. I felt like I'd channeled my inner Gray Lady for a minute there." Larry chuckled.

I furrowed my brow. *Why wasn't Garrett a blob? Is my eyesight improving?*

On the way, Julie called me. "Paul just dropped us off, and Martha has checked in with Tonya's nurse. Tonya had a restful night; I'm glad somebody did. I asked Paul to talk to you about what Martha told me; you'll probably hear from him soon. I'm staying here with Martha; call me before you leave to see the houses because I'd like to go with you, and I think I've talked Martha into going too."

After we hung up, I said, "Does it sound to you that Julie is reluctant to leave Martha alone at the hospital? I have a feeling that something's up."

Larry peered at me. "I didn't get that impression at all, but I'm finally starting to learn to pay attention when you think something's not right."

When Larry parked at the diner, he said, "The parking lot's almost full, but Paul's rental is here. He's probably waiting inside for us."

As we walked to the diner, I inhaled deeply. "I want grits, eggs, fried potatoes, bacon, a grilled biscuit, gravy, a breakfast taco, and coffee."

Larry chuckled. "The diner aroma got me too. I'll have double your order."

After we went inside, Larry said, "The diner has tables not booths; that's different, isn't it? Paul has a table and a cup of coffee."

When we neared the table, Paul-blob said, "The menu doesn't have any fancy food, which is good as far as I'm concerned."

I sighed. *Why is Paul a blob? Shouldn't I see him too if my eyesight is improving?*

While Larry helped me with my chair, the server filled the two cups she had set on the table.

"The menu lists regular grits and cheese grits," Larry said. "Judging by the plates on the tables around us, the bacon order is generous, so I'll share mine. Scrambled egg, grits, and a grilled biscuit for you, sweetie?"

"Yes, and I'd like the cheese grits."

After we ordered, Paul said, "Julie told me Martha feels guilty about not paying attention to Tonya this week. Martha has a new friend that she met in Tennessee when she took Tonya to join Justin, and they have continued to text each other and talk on the phone regularly. Martha told Julie he's the nicest man she's met in ages, and he is coming here today to meet her for lunch."

"His name is Walt, isn't it?" I asked.

"Yes, except Martha calls him Wally. Martha asked Julie if it would be wrong of her to leave the hospital to meet with Wally. Martha said she didn't want to disappoint Wally because he has had so many people let him down in the past that she doesn't want him to think she's like other people. Julie said when they were sitting outside after dessert last night, Martha talked about Wally the entire time."

"I know Julie has something in mind. What does she want to do?" I asked.

Before Paul answered, our server brought our food.

"Eat first," Larry said.

"Smart man," Paul said.

I ate most of my food but gave half of my biscuit to Larry.

When the server came to clear our plates, Larry said, "I see one of the guys from the office at the counter. I'll be just a few minutes. Don't decide anything without me."

CHAPTER FIFTEEN

After Larry left with his coffee in-hand, Paul said, "We have to tell Larry about the Gray Flanagan Agency."

"Are you sure?"

Palace Guard scowled.

"Never mind; of course, you're right. What does Julie want to do?"

"I'll tell you both after we tell Larry about his new business."

"You operation types are good." I rolled my eye.

"Did you just roll your eye? I didn't think anyone could do that." Paul chuckled.

"I've been practicing, and no one's noticed; give yourself a raise." I giggled.

"I'm glad I talked to him," Larry said when he returned. "He's one of the senior guys; he'd heard about Tonya and wondered if Justin would be at work on Monday. I told him that Tonya's mom, her mom's best friend, and my wife, who is Tonya's best friend, are all here, so there are plenty of people who will be with Tonya while Justin's at work. I'll talk to Justin after we look at the houses, if you don't mind stopping by the hospital, sweetie."

"Not at all."

Paul cleared his throat, and I sighed.

"Remember when you were fishing yesterday? You were right. Paul has been digging up details about the catering company and has incurred some expenses that didn't seem right for Coyle Detective Agency to pay or for him to pay out of his pocket. Another business seemed like the best way to go."

Larry nodded. "Actually, I agree. Are you thinking a partnership?"

"Exactly, and you and I are the partners. I called Shantelle, and she's taking care of all the paperwork including putting Paul on the payroll as part time, so he can have an expense account. Paul is the Vice President of Operations."

"You did all of this in one short afternoon? Actually, you planned and executed all of this while you walked around the block, didn't you?" Larry shook his head. "What did Maggie leave out, Paul?"

Paul chuckled. "The name of the agency is Gray Flanagan Agency."

Larry snort-laughed. "That is absolutely perfect. It's Gray Lady plus a nod to her great-grandmother Marguerite. It's a hundred percent Maggie without identifying her."

Larry raised his eyebrows at Palace Guard. "Do you approve of all this?"

Palace Guard smiled and nodded.

"Do I have any papers to sign? Is Shantelle using our accumulated allowances for start-up funds?" Larry asked.

"She's using mine."

"Call her on Monday; I want to match your money that goes into the business, so I will be a fifty percent partner or however that works. Shantelle will know."

"I'll call the law office on our way back and leave her a message, so she'll have the information for the paperwork."

"My turn," Paul said. "Larry, Julie learned yesterday after dessert that Martha has a new friend that she met at the training center in Tennessee who has been paying her a lot of attention, and if that raises the hair on the back of your neck, it did mine too."

"Is it Rodney or Walt?" Larry growled.

"Walt is going by Wally now. Martha is supposed to meet him today at three for coffee, and she's torn between staying with Tonya and meeting Wally," Paul said.

"I'll fill you in on what we know as far as how they met, but they did meet in Tennessee at the beginning of the training course, so Walt may have seen you," I said.

"Right, and that's important," Paul said. "Julie wants to talk Martha into staying with Tonya by offering to meet with Wally herself. It's not likely that Martha will go for it, so Julie will insist that she goes with Martha. I don't want either one of them meeting with Wally without some protection nearby, but it needs to be someone Wally hasn't seen, which is me. My problem is that my hearing is pretty good, but not as good as it was. I'd have to sit at the closest possible table to eavesdrop."

"I can fill in for the hearing part," I said.

"We have to assume that Walt has seen you too, so that's a big no." Larry said.

"Actually, she can," Paul said. "Maggie's recognizable by her eye patch and jo. If she doesn't wear her eye patch or have her jo, she'll be practically invisible, especially if she wears a sunhat that will partially cover her eyes. Thanks to Palace Guard, she doesn't walk or act like she's visually impaired. If she and I go into the coffee shop together, we'll be just another table for two."

"What about Martha recognizing Maggie?" Larry asked.

"I think she'll be too distracted by Wally to look around, and I don't think she'll see me without the eye patch," I said. "Paul and I don't have to sit terribly close for me to hear them, even if they whisper, but Martha is so used to speaking loudly for Tonya, I don't think there will be much whispering. In fact, Julie can offer to drive Martha to the coffee shop and sit at a table by herself if Martha has qualms about what Wally might think."

"The idea's kind of growing on me. What's our purpose?" Larry asked.

"Julie's intent with her original idea of meeting with Wally without Martha was to find out how to get into the resort, but I squashed that idea," Paul said.

"We can rattle Wally if Martha mentions Rodney. Julie can tell Martha about her friend who met Rodney, but Rodney was not anything like Wally," I said. "Julie can tell a fascinating story that will be fresh in Martha's mind."

"Sounds good in theory," Larry said, "but how do we get Martha to mention Rodney?"

"That's Julie magic." I giggled. "If Paul asks Julie to spin the story so that Martha will mention Rodney to Wally, she'll do it, and Martha will be eager to repeat it."

Paul snorted. "You're right about Julie, the spinmeister."

The server approached our table with the coffee pot, and Paul said, "We're ready for the check. I'll take care of it."

The server carefully tore our check out of her pad then continued refilling cups at the tables around us.

"This goes on my expense account," Paul said.

As we filed out of the diner to the parking lot, Larry said, "We'll need to pick up Lucy and Spike; shall we meet you at the hospital, so we can all arrive at the first house at the same time?"

"Go ahead; I'll text Julie before I leave."

On our way to the hotel, I called our lawyer's office to leave a message for Shantelle.

After I hung up, Larry said, "Thank you for bringing me in on the ground floor; I loved taking part in the discussion."

"I thought you would be angry."

"This was different. I love the Gray Flanagan Agency; that was a brilliant idea, sweetie, to create a legal partnership to take care of Paul's expenses, so he didn't feel like you were offering charity by covering his out-of-pocket costs. You knew he wouldn't file for the expenses with the Coyle agency, didn't you? Do you think our business will grow? What about Paul and the Coyle Detective Agency? Are we robbing Glenn of his best investigator?"

"Jennifer has taken over the administration and business side of the Coyle Agency, and Ella is getting very involved in the investigations. Glenn's never been crazy about the administration because he'd prefer to investigate and research cases, and he's as bored as Paul is. Ella's trying to talk Moe into resigning from the department and joining her at the agency, and Jennifer thinks Moe is seriously considering it because he's become so senior that he rarely goes into the field, even to supervise."

"I didn't know that; Moe always said he'd resign when he got bumped up to a desk job. I can see where he would resign if that's where he is now, especially with Ella encouraging him."

"Wait here," Larry said when we reached the suite, "I'll tell Lucy and Spike we're ready to look at houses."

Lucy trotted out of our suite with Spike following her; Larry stayed behind to lock the door.

When the three of them were in the truck, we went to the hospital where Larry pulled into the hospital parking lot.

"I'll park next to Paul; Julie and Martha are waiting at the entrance."

I wonder if there's a way that Palace Guard and I could get into the camp. We need to know what the trip wire is or if this is a psychological way to keep their prisoners from trying to escape; Palace Guard and I could find out.

Palace Guard poked my shoulder; I realized what Larry had said.

I nodded. "Palace Guard and I are glad that Julie has Martha with her. Justin deserves some time with his wife without worrying that he's taking time away from her mother."

"Justin's a lot kinder than I am. I growled when anyone suggested I could leave you for a short spell when you were in the hospital." He shook his head. "After the library explosion, I visited you every day; I sat in the parking lot in my truck where I could see the window where your room was: nobody told me that was your room; I just knew. Moe caught me one time and told me I really had it bad, and I agreed with him."

I smiled and patted his arm. "I'm so glad you were there."

"I thought nobody knew except Moe, but looking back, Sarge did too."

"What are you going to do while we're all at the coffee shop?" I asked.

"I'll drop off you and Paul around the corner from the shop because Julie will have their rental car, then I'll park at the business next to the coffee shop and go browse."

"You can't come into the coffee shop, honey; you walk like a cop."

Larry grunted. "I hate it when you're right. Palace Guard will know where I am if you need me. I'll talk to Paul while we're looking at the house to let him know he's riding with us."

The first house of the day was on the outskirts of town. After we stopped in front of the house, Julie hurried to the truck. "Nell told us that the house is occupied, but the owners are moving next week. She told the owners that we would overlook the packed boxes; the house is unlocked, and we can go in because no one's home."

Martha hugged me when we joined her on the porch. "I was so excited that Julie suggested I help her describe the house to you. Justin needs a little private time with Tonya without me hovering. He starts his new job on Monday, and he's been worried that he would be abandoning Tonya. Tonya's nurse and Julie had a long talk with him; I don't know what they said, but he isn't quite as stressed now. I think they told him Tonya wouldn't want to have an impact on his new job, and he couldn't argue because he knows how angry Tonya and Kiki would be." Martha chuckled.

I giggled. "I wouldn't want those two mad at me either. How's Tonya?"

"She's doing much better; she may graduate from intensive care tomorrow, but her doctor is reluctant to turn her loose too quickly, so we'll see," Martha said as the three of us strolled to the house.

"This is a newer house than yesterday's, but it isn't modern-new. Does that make sense?" Julie asked as we went inside. "The walls have been freshly painted, so it looks bright and cheery. We're in the great room; there isn't an entryway or foyer, but a rug at the front door could catch most of the grass, leaves, and sand that people might track inside. The floors are beautiful; they're narrow planks and look like they were the original floor. The owners used area rugs; the rugs are rolled up and are against the wall. I like the idea of area rugs, but that's a personal preference."

"Lucy likes area rugs too." Lucy's head turned when I mentioned her name, and she wagged her tail; Spike grinned.

"I see that." Martha chuckled.

"Let's check the kitchen next," Julie said.

"Is there a fireplace in the living room?" I asked as Julie-blob led the way to the kitchen.

"There is, I'm sorry I didn't mention it to you; we'll cover it on our way to the bedrooms."

"The kitchen has a gas stove; don't you prefer gas, Gray Lady?"

I nodded.

"So do I," Martha said. "It has a fairly new dishwasher. Give me a dishwasher and a gas stove, and I'm set."

I miss cooking.

"It's an open kitchen and dining room. The kitchen has a breakfast nook near the window on the back of the house, and the dining area has plenty of room for an oversized dining table," Julie said. "You'll like this, Gray Lady: there is an actual door that goes out back. Let's see what we have."

When Julie opened the back door, Lucy dashed outside, and Spike followed her. We stepped outside, and Martha squealed; I covered my ears.

"I'm so sorry, Maggie," Martha said, "but this porch is beautiful: it's wide and has plenty of overhang to keep off any rain, except maybe during a hurricane."

"Are hurricanes something Maggie needs to worry about?" Julie asked.

"Not really; we're far enough inland that we won't get the brunt. We get high winds and heavy rain; we need to check this house for flood zone because that's important on whether it's a problem or not," Martha said. "I like the older houses because we know they've stood up through at least one hurricane. The new houses scare me; not that they aren't well-built, but they haven't been tested either."

"One thing that I noticed is that the property around the house has been cleared of trees; is that because of hurricanes, Martha?" Julie asked.

"It is, and I should have mentioned it. Did you see the generator on the side of the house? I wonder if it's wired as a whole-house generator."

"We'll ask the agent. The pantry is huge, Maggie," Julie said. "Except for fresh fruit and vegetables, you could easily get by with shopping only once a month."

"There's a farmers' market nearby that I like; you'll enjoy local, in-season fruits and vegetables," Martha said.

"How far are we from Larry's office?" Julie asked.

"No more than twenty minutes," Martha said. "It feels like we're in the country, doesn't it? There's a small town less than ten minutes away with a hardware store and a grocery store."

"Before we go back inside, I know you'll be interested in hearing that the backyard is much larger than the one at the first house, and it is completely fenced. Lucy is exploring the yard; I think it meets her approval," Julie said. "The fenced-in yard includes trees, which gives Lucy ready access to the squirrels that will keep her spry. Ready to inspect the bedrooms and bathrooms?"

After we were inside, Julie said, "Did I mention the small restroom between the kitchen and the dining room?"

"I love having a restroom that is convenient for guests," Martha said.

As Julie led the way to the hall, she said, "We'll have to weave our way past the boxes in the hallway; it's a little tight. I was right; here's the master bedroom. It's huge, Maggie." She stopped when she entered the bedroom. "Check out the walk-in closet."

"Wow," Martha said as she and I stood at the door.

I stepped inside while Julie continued, "There are a lot of shelves on the back wall, and there are two heights of bars for hanging clothes on each side. This beats the first house's master closet hands-down."

Martha disappeared then called out, "The master bath will be comfortable enough for the two of you to get ready in the morning at the same time. I love the step-in shower, and there's a separate soaking tub."

"Sounds perfect. The master bedroom gets a big plus," Julie said. "Let's go down the hall the other way."

"There are two bedrooms on the left," Martha said. "This first one has a queen-sized bed, and there's plenty of room for it, although most of the floor space is taken up by boxes, which we ignore, right? Every room has blinds; I like that."

"Two twin-sized beds in this next bedroom," Julie said. "I'll bet it was a kid's bedroom."

"I like this guest bathroom; it's across the hall from the two bedrooms; very convenient," Martha said. "It has a tub with a shower and two sinks. The vanity has enough counter space for two people to have their toiletries available."

"I'm not sure I realized this is a four bedroom house," Julie said. "This room looks like they use one of the bedrooms as an office. You have a perfect view of the back yard and trees from the windows, and I'm certain it won't be long until you can enjoy it, Maggie."

It was hard, but I forced myself to nod then smile. *I have a feeling my sight's not going to return.*

"Is there a garage?" Martha asked as we headed back past the boxes.

Julie snickered. "I was so entranced by the kitchen, I completely forgot to tell you and Maggie about the entryway I spotted that looks like it goes to the garage, but first, let's stop at the fireplace, and Maggie can feel the authenticity of the old brick."

"The mantle is wood; it looks like oak to me," Martha said

Palace Guard led me close enough to touch the brick, and I exhaled.

"Am I right?" Julie asked. "This brick was probably lightly sandblasted to clean it, but it has never been painted and the bricks are shades of red and brown. It's completely unique."

"It's very nice," Martha added.

"Tear yourself away from the bricks, Maggie, and I'll show you the garage," Julie said. "There's a small entryway from the garage to the house, and I'll bet there's a pantry there."

When we reached the small entryway, Martha said, "There's a small bench; they must have used this as a mud room. I'll bet they came through the garage as their family's main entrance to the house. Here's the utility room. There's a washer, dryer, farm sink, and a freezer in here. I love this house, Gray Lady. I can't wait to hear what Kevin thinks."

Julie opened the door to the garage. "They've loaded down the garage with boxes, so we won't go in there. Are we ready to find Larry and Paul?"

"I am," I said. "I'll need to convince Lucy to come inside."

When I called her, Lucy ambled to the house.

"We'll probably be back, Lucy. Let's find Larry to hear what he thinks." Julie said.

Lucy perked up and trotted inside. After we were on the front porch, Nell asked, "Don't you love it? The owners plan to rent the house until they can sell it, so that's another possibility for you. They just got confirmation yesterday that their moving van will be here at eight o'clock Tuesday morning."

Larry and Paul were waiting on the porch.

"We need to leave if we want to arrive at the other house on time, sweetie," Larry said. "We can talk in the truck."

When Larry turned from the driveway onto the road, a car was parked in the tall grass and weeds on the side of the road behind us. A blob was in the driver's seat, and as we turned away from it, the driver made a U-turn in the road and sped back toward town.

"There was a car on the side of the road when we pulled out of the driveway; it made a U-turn and went the other way," I said.

Palace Guard turned to look.

"I don't see anything in the rearview mirror," Larry said, "but I didn't notice the car when we turned onto the road from the driveway, either."

After a few minutes Larry asked, "What do you think about the house?"

"The house seems wonderful; the only downside I can think of is that I wonder if it's too much house for two," I said.

"That's a valid point, but if half of the people who have said they're going to visit show up half of the time they said they would, we definitely need the breathing space," Larry said.

I giggled. "You're right. What do you think?"

"The roof looked fine, but we'll still have the house inspected. The garage is a two-car garage, which means there's room for one car and some tools, but there's also a large carport where the owner apparently parks a truck and where he has a tractor, mower, and other yard equipment. Paul and I found a workshop that needs a little work to get it back into shape, so that would be a project for me. Did Lucy check out the backyard? What did she think?"

"She didn't want to leave. There are enough trees that it probably seemed like it was her private park."

Larry chuckled. "I like that it is fenced, but she still had plenty of room to roam. This next house will have to be pretty special to beat that one, as far as I'm concerned."

"There's another bonus. The owners plan to rent the house while they wait for it to sell, and Nell said their moving van will be here Tuesday morning," I said.

"Were you thinking we could rent it while we look for something else?" Larry asked.

"Not really; I was thinking we could rent it while all the paperwork to complete the sale lumbers through its paces."

Larry chuckled. "I love your way with words, and I agree with you, which makes me right two times today."

I giggled. "You are too much sometimes, Mr. Sexy Pants."

As we neared the third house, I asked, "Is there a small airport nearby? I just heard a plane, and there's another one."

"Not that I know of..." Larry exhaled. "Here's a sign that says there's a private airport one mile ahead."

My phone rang and announced, "Paul calling."

When I answered, Larry said, "Maggie heard the plane before we saw the sign. I'm looking for a place to turn around."

"Martha is on the phone with Nell, who asked if we'd like to meet at her office."

I nodded, and Larry said, "Yes, we'll follow you."

After we disconnected, Larry said, "Here we go; it's a rutted, overgrown driveway and might be a little bumpy."

He pulled in far enough for Paul to pull in behind us. After Paul backed out and headed to town, Larry followed him.

"Do you want to look at the house that we like again?" Larry asked.

Spike smacked the back of Larry's head, and I giggled.

"Ow. Okay, Spike; I'll give you that one because I deserved it."

When we neared town, Larry said, "Let me try again: do you want me to look at the house again?"

"Let's see what Nell has to say, but I would think we would like to have an inspector give us a report before we decide. Martha will probably be able to find a good inspector who might even be available next week."

Larry nodded. "I like that."

"I'd like to look at the house with just you because I went into sensory overload with both Julie and Martha explaining nonstop the details of each room; I think they were in competition. I didn't have much of a chance to get a feel for the house."

"Martha will probably want to get right to the hospital after they arrive at the office; we can ask the agent if we can go back to the house again this afternoon."

"You're the smartest man I know," I said.

"I am?" Larry peered at me.

"Absolutely."

"Well, then. Okay." Larry glanced in his mirror at Spike and sneered.

I rolled my eye, and Palace Guard poked my shoulder; when I turned to look at him, he rolled his eyes, and I coughed to keep from laughing.

"Are you okay, sweetie?" Larry's brow was furrowed.

"I'm fine; I just got a tickle."

"I just realized the only furniture that we have is our bed," Larry said. "We'll have to get a dining room table and chairs, a sofa and chairs, appliances, a grill for you, bar stools, guest beds, and who knows what else."

"That's why Jennifer planned to come here, so we'll be fine. You go to work, and we'll spend your hard-earned money," I said.

Larry chuckled. "You're welcome to it, but I know you and Shantelle have a pact not to touch it."

Paul pulled into the agent's parking lot and parked.

Larry pulled in next to the rental car. "Wait here a second. Paul is the only one who climbed out of the car; I'll see what he has to say."

I lowered my window and listened as Paul explained Martha and Julie wanted to get back to the hospital.

"We'll take it from here; thanks to everyone for the help," Larry said.

As Larry opened his door, Paul drove away.

"Did you hear?" Larry asked.

"Sure did; you called that one right."

After we arrived at the real estate office, Nell met us at the door. Larry explained we wanted to see the house again; she called the owner then said, "We can go now if you like. I'll follow you."

After Larry parked in the driveway at the house, we all climbed out.

"What do you want to do first, sweetie?"

"I'd like to start with the front yard, so I can listen and smell the air then go to the backyard."

"I'm with you."

A few minutes later, I said, "I didn't hear or smell anything that would put me off. Let's walk to the backyard."

On the way, a noisy hum startled me.

"The air conditioner just kicked in, sweetie."

"It surprised me because it suddenly started up, but now I know what it sounds like."

I smiled as I listened to the crunch of leaves under our feet; when we reached the backyard fence, Larry opened the gate then put his arm around my shoulders, and I put my arm around his waist.

"Nice breeze," I said. "Is there a river or a creek nearby?"

"There are several small lakes and creeks nearby. Do they smell bad?"

"No, I could smell the water and the vegetation that grows along the bank in the breeze. I'm ready to go inside. Can we go into the house by the garage door?"

"Sure can; our agent unlocked all the doors while we were in the front yard."

When we went through the garage, we followed the narrow path between the boxes and continued into the kitchen.

I paused. "Listen."

After a few minutes, Larry whispered, "I don't hear anything."

I giggled. "Isn't it great?"

While we walked from room to room, I told Larry what I remembered.

He chuckled. "You weren't even in the house that long; they must have been providing the commentary at double-speed."

"Yes, and double-volume."

I stopped in the master bedroom. "The living room feels homey; the bedroom feels safe. Does that make sense?"

"More than you realize, Maggie. The closet is also a safe room. If we had to take shelter because of a hurricane or tornado, the closet and the door are reinforced, so even if the roof is ripped off or collapses, we'd be fine, and there is plenty of room for all of us. The door has a bar that secures it from the inside, so if there was a home invasion, and I wasn't home, you and Lucy could go into the closet and be safe."

"That's really interesting. Does the house have hurricane shutters?"

Larry nodded. "They're on every window; they're the old-fashioned kind that stay up permanently and actually are an architectural feature to the house."

"Are there any other features you like?" I asked.

CHAPTER SIXTEEN

"There is a whole-house generator. I'll have to teach you how to start and stop it, in case I'm out of town and you need it, but you'll pick it up right away. We have a large propane tank for the stove, the water heater, and the generator. We may want to get a small, propane fireplace for the kitchen and dining area as an auxiliary for the heat pump and the fireplace. There's also a hook up for a smaller generator to power the kitchen appliances and the lights, but not the air conditioner. We may want to get a generator just in case. The well could be hooked up to solar, but it has a small generator hooked up to it. The pump is electric."

I smiled and hugged him. "It sounds like a great match for us. Are you ready to ask about getting an inspector here on Wednesday?"

"I'll talk to Nell right now."

After Larry went out the front door, I said, "I'm going to see if I can find the back door."

I headed in the direction of where I thought the door was; after Palace Guard tapped my shoulder, I stopped as he corrected my direction a few steps to the right then tapped again. He guided me to the door handle, and we went outside and relaxed on the wide porch.

"Thanks, that was fun," I said. "I don't think it will take me too long to learn my way around the house."

Palace Guard smiled.

When Larry returned, he said, "We're all set. Nell will have an inspector here on Wednesday, and the inspector will email you the full report on Thursday. I told her you would forward it to me."

"That's great news; if there's anything to find, I hope the inspector finds it."

"We'll wait for Nell while she locks up, then we can go back to our hotel and relax."

As we strolled to the truck, I said, "I'll call Jennifer tomorrow after you leave and give her a full report. What time do you plan to leave?"

"I originally thought I'd leave after lunch, but the weather forecast for tomorrow in the Georgia and Tennessee mountains is predicting a storm of high winds and heavy rain to hit in the late afternoon. I hate to leave early, but I'm not a fan of driving at night in a severe storm on mountain roads."

"If you leave right after breakfast, you'll be able to get there before four, right?"

Larry exhaled. "I guess that makes sense."

I hugged him, put my head on his chest to listen to his heartbeat, and sighed. "I love that you're always thinking; I appreciate that you checked the weather because I would have been frantic if you were driving in a bad storm."

He kissed the top of my head and whispered, "My sweet Maggie."

We held each other until he said, "Here comes Nell. She looks like she has something to say."

"Everything is locked up; the sellers want to know if you can use the washer and dryer because they just learned they can't move them. I guess they are a set, and the movers won't touch the washer because the sellers don't have the bolts to stabilize the drum. They could order the bolts, but they wouldn't get them before Tuesday."

"How frustrating for them," I said.

Larry added, "We don't have a washer and dryer."

"They were hoping you didn't. I'm sure you know how frazzled they are with all the little things that are popping up at the last minute."

Larry nodded. "Always happens."

"We can go now; thanks for staying until I locked up." Nell hurried to her car.

On our way to town, Larry said, "We'll get back to town just in time to pick up Paul for our afternoon coffee date. Text him and ask where he is. I'll bet he's at the hospital because Martha would have been too anxious to get back to take the time to drop him off at their hotel."

I picked up my phone. "Send a text to Paul. We are on our way. Where do we pick you up?"

He replied, "Hospital. I'm at the entrance."

Larry smiled. "Paul is as irritated by the constant chatter as you are."

When Larry glanced in his review mirror, Palace Guard and Spike raised their hands.

Larry chuckled. "I'm right there with you."

Paul held a tan sunhat in his hand. "Maggie, Julie loaned you her sunhat, and I have her sunglasses too."

I removed my eye patch and pulled up my hair into a high ponytail then put on the sunhat. "I think the sunhat's going to hold my hair in place."

"I think so, too," Paul said. "Here are Julie's sunglasses."

"You don't look like yourself at all without your eyepatch and your new short hair," Larry said. "Actually, Paul, you look like a tourist in that tropical shirt."

"I'm taking one for the team," Paul growled. "Julie bought this ugly shirt for me years ago because she said it would change my image and reputation as a tough guy; I've never even tried it on. I thought she'd thrown it away, but she packed it because she thought it would be a nice change from my work shirts. I've got a ball cap I don't like that an old friend gave to me as a joke. I'll wear it too."

"What's on it?" I asked.

"It's lime-green and says 'Florida Keys,'" Larry said. "Total tourist, Paul; well done."

"Thank you; I guess I should be grateful that Julie didn't buy me a suit and tie."

"I can't see you in a suit." I giggled.

Paul snorted, and Larry laughed.

"We're here," Larry said. "The coffee shop is around the corner. I'll lurk by my truck unless Palace Guard comes to get me."

As Paul and I climbed out of the truck, Larry added, "Palace Guard, there's a gun store across the street. I might be there."

"Do you want to take my arm?" Paul asked.

"No, Palace Guard guides me with taps on my shoulder, so I'm fine."

When we went into the coffee shop, Paul whispered, "They aren't here yet."

He spoke in a normal voice, "Where do you want to sit?"

I turned my head like I was scanning the tables then pretended to nibble on my thumbnail as I mumbled, "Close to the door is good."

I said, "I like to look out the window."

Palace Guard guided me to a table and to a chair that faced the window.

Paul chuckled as he sat next to me. "I enjoy the local color. It gives me ideas for my next novel."

"How's that going?" I asked as the server set menus on the table.

"How do you like your coffee?" she asked.

"Plain," I said.

Paul turned my menu then slid it to me. *It must have been upside down.*

"Do you all bake your pastries, or do you get them from the grocery store?" Paul asked.

I turned my head toward her like I was gauging her reaction to Paul's crass question.

The server snorted. "Order what you like, then you tell me."

"I can't decide," I said.

"You're always looking for something different: try the goat cheese brownie," Paul said. "I'll have an orange blossom scone and a French press coffee."

"Coming up," the server said.

Paul leaned close and whispered, "A man came in while we were ordering. He took a seat in the back and is facing the front door. Looks like our Walt."

I giggled. "You always say that."

Paul chuckled. "Have you seen Jim lately?"

Jim? Oh, J and M.

"Not since last week. What's Jim got into now?"

The server set our hot mugs and pastries on the table then left. Palace Guard guided my hand to the plate with the goat cheese brownie, and I pinched a small bite.

"Mmm, this is delicious. How's your scone?"

"Surprisingly good. I saw someone across the street that reminded me of him and wondered if you've heard anything."

Julie and Martha are here.

"Thank you for rearranging your schedule, Wally," Martha said. "This is my friend Julie that I told you about. She's my driver." Martha giggled.

"A pleasure to meet you, Julie. I got the impression that you were going to drop off Martha, but it's nice that you can join us," Wally said.

Wally is definitely Walt.

After they ordered, Julie said, "Please excuse me; I have a phone call to make."

She mumbled as she walked past us to go outside. "Giving them some alone time."

Paul's phone buzzed a text, and he read it. "Mom says the doctor is not pleased at all about her test results."

Wonder what his text really said.

"Sorry to hear that. Anything I can do?"

"She'll let us know."

I nodded then raised my hand to let Paul know I was listening to Martha as she talked to Wally.

"I heard the most interesting story before I left Tennessee. There was this man named Roger or Rocky, something like that. I understand he was a real gentleman, but I'm sure he couldn't be as nice as you are." Martha giggled. "Anyway, this Roger guy actually got access to the bank account of a sweet, naïve woman, and I understand he cleaned her out. The feds arrested him, of course, and I understand he's naming names and has documentation to back it all up."

Wally cleared his throat. "That wasn't around here, was it?"

"I thought it was in Atlanta, but someone else told me it was in Savannah, so I don't know. The people in Tennessee didn't seem to realize how big Georgia is. Atlanta is not a suburb of Savannah and vice versa." Martha chuckled then continued talking.

I whispered, "Julie can return to her table any time."

Paul sent a quick text. "I just realized I hadn't responded to Mom. I told her to take care of herself."

I nodded.

Paul put his hand on my arm and leaned close as he whispered, "I was watching for Julie, and our café guy strolled by the coffee shop. He stood at the window a while, but I guess he couldn't see inside because of the glare."

Martha continued, "My nephew is such a busybody; are all the law enforcement types so protective? He wanted to know if any of my friends or I had met a man lately, and I told him I had, but you weren't anything like that Roger character that he arrested."

Before Julie-blob joined them, Martha whispered, "Nobody's supposed to know that Roger or Rocky, whatever, had a partner or something like that; my nephew's wife's cousin told me they are closing in on the partner."

"You're very wise to stay safe," Wally said. "I'm glad we had a quick moment to meet; it was nice talking to you."

"Wally rose from his seat when Julie arrived at the table," Paul said. "I thought he was being old-school polite, but he nodded to her and is headed toward the door."

After the front door closed, Paul asked, "You heard everything, didn't you? It must have been good."

I snickered. "Definitely an understatement. I'll tell you and Larry after we leave."

When the server returned to refill our coffee, Paul said, "We'll take our check."

"Is everything okay? You weren't in there very long; what's going on?" Larry asked when we turned the corner.

"Everything is fine; all I know is that Wally suddenly walked out, but Gray Lady won't tell me what Martha said to Wally until Miss Persnickety could tell both of us at once," Paul said.

Larry chuckled. "Welcome to my world, Paul. We're lucky she's telling us at all; she normally would have run after him and tossed him to the ground then spiked his hand with her knife when he pulled a gun."

Paul chuckled.

"If you two are finished..." I tried for a haughty tone as I jerked off my sunhat and flipped my hair with my hand, exactly like Spike did, but I think I ruined the overall effect of my disdain when I giggled. "I'll tell you what Martha said."

Larry pressed his lips together then pinched his thumb and index finger together as he feigned a zipping motion.

I'll save my eyeroll for later.

Palace Guard motioned toward the truck, and Larry said, "Palace Guard's right. Let's talk in the truck."

Larry opened the back door for me, and Paul hopped into the front passenger's seat.

After Larry was in the truck, I said, "Martha must have fallen in love with Julie's story because it was a doozy the way Martha told it. Julie made a point to step outside; Julie said she wanted to give them privacy, but the longer Martha talked, the more I realized Julie left because she couldn't have held back laughing."

Larry cleared his throat.

"Okay, I'll skip all the good parts and jump to the summary. Martha told Wally that the feds had Rocky or Roger in custody; she said she couldn't remember what his name was. She said her nephew, who was on the fed team that nabbed Roger, asked her about Wally. She explained to him that Wally wasn't like Roger at all. The juicy part is next. Martha whispered that her nephew's wife's cousin said that nobody was supposed to know that Roger had a partner or something, and the feds were closing in on the partner."

"That has to be the most reliable source in the world: Martha's nephew's wife's cousin." Larry laughed.

Paul laughed along with Larry. "I gotta write that one down; I must be a lousy detective because I didn't know that. I'll put myself on report."

I sniffed. "Do you two want to hear this or not?"

"Sorry, sweetie; go ahead."

"At that point, Wally told Martha it was nice talking to her, and he almost knocked over his chair when he jumped up to get away from her."

"Are we going to be in trouble with Martha's nephew?" Paul asked.

"No, but we need to watch out for that cousin." Larry chuckled and wiped his eyes.

I glanced at Palace Guard, and he rolled his eyes.

I nodded. "I agree completely, thank you."

When Larry started the engine, Paul said, "I can ride with Julie and Martha now that Wally is out of the picture. Do you want to sit in the front seat, Maggie?"

Before I moved to the front seat, I handed Julie's sunglasses and sunhat to Paul.

"Thanks, Maggie; Julie would have sent me back; she loves that sunhat." Paul-blob closed the passenger's door after I was seated then hurried around the corner.

"I realized while I was in the coffee shop that I'll miss you the most of all, but I'll also miss having coffee every morning for a week," I said.

"I forgot to tell you that Martha gave me the coffeemaker that Jennifer ordered for you," Larry said. "It's still in the truck, but I'll check it to see if we need to get instant coffee or if it's fancier than what I was thinking."

"Instant coffee?" I shrugged. "I'll give it a try."

Larry parked near the store then read the side of the box. "I think this might work better for you than what I had in mind; would you like to go into the store and pick out your coffee?"

I shuddered. "You can shop faster without me."

Larry nodded then strode into the store while Palace Guard stood outside the truck and scanned the parking lot.

In a few minutes, Larry returned and grinned as he climbed in and dropped a shopping bag on the seat. "Success. I have medium roast coffee for you; I'll set it up then explain the operation to you and Palace Guard."

On the way to the hotel, I asked, "Where is my eye patch? My face doesn't feel right without it."

"It's on the console; when I stop at a light, I'll hand it to you."

When Larry pulled into our parking space, he said, "Sorry, sweetie. The traffic light trolls were against us; I didn't have one red light."

"We forgot to look like we were in a hurry, so the trolls could trick us and turn the light red."

"Are there really traffic light trolls?" Larry chuckled as he helped me out of the truck.

"Of course, there are; did you think I would make up something as serious as that?"

While Larry unlocked the door to our suite, I scanned our surroundings then frowned. *I don't see the man.*

"Is something bothering you?" Larry asked when we were inside.

Other than I couldn't see the man who isn't a blob?

"No, I'm trying to be extra cautious."

"I appreciate it, sweetie. Would you like hot tea or a glass of wine while we decide what we'd like to order?"

"Hot tea sounds good, but I'd like to make it myself on the new coffeemaker."

"Good idea; I'll set it up on the counter and put water in the reservoir; Palace Guard can keep an eye on the level of water and let you know when to ask Paul or Julie to refill it for you. It has an automatic shutoff, so you don't need to turn it off."

I dropped a teabag into my cup, then Larry explained where to put my cup and how to start it.

"Palace Guard, make sure she has her cup here and not off to the side because the water is very hot when it comes out of the machine."

After I pushed the button to turn on the coffeemaker, I asked, "How long will it take?"

"I'm not sure, but I don't think it will take too long; it will be harder for you to judge how long to leave your teabag in your cup."

"I won't hover then because there might be coffeemaker trolls."

Larry chuckled as his phone rang.

"It's Nell." He turned on the speaker before he answered.

"I heard back from my favorite home inspector, and he'll inspect your house on Wednesday at nine. I've cleared the day and time with the sellers, and that works for them. I usually advise my clients to attend the inspection because the inspector will explain his findings as he goes along. You'll still get a written report with pictures."

"I'd like for Paul and me to go," I said.

Larry nodded.

"Normally our inspector allows only his client, which is you, to accompany him, but I'll make sure he understands that you'll need Paul there," Nell said. "He'll pick up the key from me, and you can meet him at the house."

I smiled, and Larry said, "Thank you, we appreciate it."

After Larry hung up, he said, "It makes sense that the inspector would want only his client there, so he can speak freely."

"I'll call Paul."

When Paul answered, I said, "I have a nine o'clock appointment at the house with the inspector on Wednesday. He normally allows only his client to join him during his inspection, but Nell said she would explain that you'd be there too."

"Sounds smart to me; I'll plan to pick you up at eight thirty. Julie and I went to Martha's house, and Julie took the car to the hospital. Julie is hoping Martha will go out to dinner with her this evening then agree to go home. Julie's planning to come to our hotel after she drops off Martha tonight, but we'll see what works out. I feel behind on some of my research; I found a great burger joint near our hotel. I'm looking forward to eating a greasy burger while I dig into a few things that have been bothering me. When are you supposed to hear back from Della?"

"She said sometime on Monday."

"So, she wants us to stay away from the camp all weekend; do you think she and Kate have a rescue at the camp planned and don't want you in the middle of it?"

"Not really, but I can't put my finger on why I feel Della is working on an angle without Kate being involved," I said.

Larry snorted. "It's exactly what you would do."

"Enjoy your evening; let me know if you win this one, Larry." Paul chuckled as he hung up.

"Your tea is ready, but the water is super-hot; I don't think you should make tea because there's too many opportunities to get burned. I'll take out the teabag for you, then let's do a practice run of making a cup of coffee."

I brewed a cup of coffee while my tea cooled enough for me to drink.

"I'm glad that's over; I'm not crazy about you using the coffeemaker at all, though," Larry said. "I'm afraid you'll be burned."

"Let's set it aside; I can have morning coffee with Paul and Julie. It's only for five days; I can survive." I smiled.

"Ready to argue about something important?" Larry wiggled his eyebrows. "What do you want for supper?"

I giggled. "Paul's burger sounds like a great idea to me."

"Did to me too; I thought I saw something earlier." Larry flipped through the menus. "Got it. This might even be Paul's burger joint. They have fries and hush puppies."

"Yum; hush puppies for me," I said.

"I'll call in our order."

I lightly touched the outside of my cup with my fingertips, and it was hot. I waited a few minutes then picked up my cup by the handle before I set it on the table to cool while I fished out the tea bag with a spoon. *That was definitely harder than I expected.*

After he hung up his phone, Larry said, "The owner of the burger place answered the phone; she told me they're swamped on Saturdays, so she has taken over Saturday phone duty and has been surprised by the number of complaints about slow delivery time, which is why she added a note on the hotel menus to tell people delivery is especially slow because their business has grown. I told her I loved the notice; she laughed and said she'd never had anyone mention it before."

"What does the notice say?"

"Our business has grown, and we've hired more cheerful kitchen elves to grill your burgers, but only humans can get a driver's license. Please forgive our frazzled human drivers and write your congressman."

I giggled. "That's brilliant."

Larry smiled. "She asked me what I did, and we chatted a few minutes; she told me if I wanted to pick up our order and didn't mind waiting for twenty minutes after I showed up, I'd leave with burgers still hot from the grill and hush puppies straight out of the fryer, and she'd drop in a couple of desserts on the house. It sounded fine to me; want to ride along or would you rather stay here and relax?"

"I'd love to drink my tea with my feet up," I said.

Larry kissed me. "Sounds good to me; I wanted to see Justin before I left, but the time's getting away from me. I'll call him then pick up our burgers and be back in less than an hour."

After I finished my tea, I went to the back door. Lucy lifted her head to look at me then went back to sleep.

While I sat on the patio, I listened to the birds and squirrels and relaxed while Palace Guard stood next to me.

"I wonder what Della's doing."

I picked up my phone. "Send a text to Grandma D: Anything you need for me to do?"

A crow cawed three times; when another crow answered with the same call, the birds and squirrels became silent, then I heard the call of a hawk flying overhead as it established its territory.

When Spike came outside, he mimed spooning food into his mouth with a spoon.

"Is it time to feed Lucy already?"

He glowered at me.

I grumbled as I went inside, "It's not like I can see a clock or anything; you don't have to be grumpy about it."

I dished up Lucy's food under Spike's supervision then when he rolled his hand for the fourth time to indicate 'more', I put down the scoop. "If I feed her too much, she'll get sick."

Spike's shoulders slumped as he pointed at her bowl then the dog food bag and held up two fingers.

"Two scoops back into the bag," I said, and he nodded.

After I adjusted the amount of food in her bowl, I set it down for her.

She quickly ate then nosed the door, and the three of us went outside with her.

Lucy barked twice to see if any of her friends were outside too, but no dogs answered. She wandered the yard, and Spike followed her.

"The last time I talked to Della, she said, 'Hang onto honey boy for me.' I thought she meant Larry, so I didn't think much of it at the time, but does it mean something else, Palace Guard? I feel like she was saying more than she was saying and that just made me dizzy to say it."

Palace Guard shrugged.

"I'll bet I can figure it out before you do."

Palace Guard narrowed his eyes then disappeared.

"Well, I guess that means challenge accepted."

CHAPTER SEVENTEEN

P alace Guard returned to the patio and smiled then wiggled his fingers like he was typing on a keyboard.

"I haven't checked my computer in ages; is there something I'll find there?"

Palace Guard shrugged again then held out his hand, and I smacked it.

"At least you have an idea, which is more than I did, so I guess you win."

Spike raised his eyebrows and put his hand behind his ear then used his other hand to motion 'again.'

I giggled. "Palace Guard wins."

Spike and Palace Guard smacked a high five, and I turned toward the door, so they couldn't see my smile.

"I'm going inside to check my computer."

After I opened my laptop, I recited the words that Heather and I decided would make a great password then told my electronic assistant to open my email and find the most recent email from Della.

My electronic assistant said, "Email from Della. Subject is Honey Boy."

I squealed. "Double winner, Palace Guard. Here's honey boy."

I giggled as my electronic assistant tried to interpret double winner.

"Forward honey boy to Paul." I saved her from going into an electronic frenzy.

"Forwarding honey boy to Paul," the assistant said in her annoyingly cheerful voice.

I bit my lip. "Forward honey boy to Larry."

"Forwarding honey boy to Larry. Do you want to forward honey boy to Kate?"

"You're pushing it there." I logged off and closed the laptop. "I'll have plenty of time to read it tomorrow after Larry leaves."

I picked up my phone. "Send a text to Paul: Sent you an email. We can talk tomorrow."

"Reply from Paul: Will read it tomorrow."

"Oh, good; that must mean Julie isn't staying with Martha."

Palace Guard nodded.

When I heard Larry's truck turn the corner, I opened the front door as the man who was not a blob quickly strode across the parking lot and behind the building across from ours.

At least I haven't heard the café man. I frowned. *I don't know his name, but Della does; why hasn't she told me?*

"I'd complain about all these people that keep secrets, but I'm one of them," I grumbled as Larry came inside the suite.

"Yes, you are, sweetie; who is keeping secrets from you, and what secrets are you keeping from me?"

"Della knows what café man's name is, but she hasn't told me. I'm going to name him if I hear him again."

"Just don't challenge him and ask him what his name is," Larry chuckled.

I nodded. *Good idea; I hadn't thought of that.*

"Ready for your burger? Do you want sweet tea or a beer?" he asked.

"Sweet tea now; maybe a beer on the patio after supper for old times' sake." I took my seat at our small dining table.

While we ate, Larry explained what he'd learned in the first class and the topics they would cover in the second class. Palace Guard sat at the table with his full attention on Larry. When Larry told what was obviously an inside joke that only a chemist could appreciate, Palace Guard grinned and nodded.

Palace Guard is loving the course as much as Larry is.

I swiped at my greasy mouth with my napkin then said, "I was just thinking: wouldn't it be useful if Palace Guard was with you at the class next week?"

Larry and Palace Guard stared at me, and Spike strode to the table and narrowed his eyes; I took a long drink of my sweet tea in case there was food on my teeth.

"What do you think, Palace Guard?" Larry asked.

Palace Guard visibly exhaled then peered at me.

"Don't throw away the opportunity because you think you have to hover." *I wish I could glare or narrow my eye without looking like I have something in it.* "I'll have Paul, Spike, and Lucy. I'll be fine."

"What do you think, Spike?" Larry asked.

Spike assumed a boxer's stance then bounced on his toes and jabbed at the air as he mimed being in a fighter's ring.

Larry nodded. "Palace Guard was a tremendous help this week in the class, and I can see how useful he'd be for all of us in the class this next week. I could definitely use his expert knowledge while I'm learning in the field, but I understand Palace Guard's hesitancy because face it, sweetie, you have a knack for getting into trouble."

"Maybe so, but I can get into trouble whether you and Palace Guard hover or not." I took another bite of my burger.

Larry shook his head then chuckled. "Not your best argument, but I get your point."

Larry and Palace Guard exchanged glances, then Palace Guard nodded.

"Okay, but you have to let us know if you're in trouble," Larry said.

"I always do," I said.

Larry laughed, Palace Guard rolled his eyes, and Spike did his wacky dance.

"I do eventually," I growled. "Y'all are annoying."

The three of them high-fived, and I exhaled. *Didn't think I'd be able to pull that one off.*

"I'll talk to Paul after we're finished eating," Larry said.

"I think his phone might be off; he and Julie haven't had any time together because she's been so occupied with Martha."

"Good point; he deserves some family time. I know how important it is to me, sweetie," Larry said.

"I'll talk to him tomorrow morning," I said.

Larry nodded. "I haven't had a chance to complete Macy's online training that I started while I was still in Tennessee because we've been so busy this weekend; I wouldn't mind Palace Guard being with me while I go through the rest of it tomorrow afternoon."

Palace Guard's face brightened.

I'm glad I thought of it; both of them are happy.

After we ate, Larry said, "I'll toss our dirty clothes into the washer before we relax on the patio, so I can pack before we go to bed."

"I'll take Lucy outside, so I don't slow you down by trying to help."

Lucy, Palace Guard, Spike, and I went to the backyard. Palace Guard followed Lucy as she wandered around the yard, and Spike hovered.

"Spike, Palace Guard gives me more room. Could you back off a little?" I asked.

Spike grinned and shook his head.

I sighed. *Maybe I'm not as bright as I thought. It's going to be a long week.*

Larry joined me. "Here's your beer, sweetie."

After he handed me my beer, Larry clinked my bottle with his.

"Have you had any second thoughts?" he asked.

I smiled. "Not at all."

"You've got a busy week ahead too. I can't wait to hear about the house inspection," Larry said.

While we sipped our beer, we talked about the house, what we'd need to buy right away and items that we'd put on our wish list.

"I'm glad I'm starting at the regional office now; there have been rumors that the senior investigator will retire in six to twelve months, and I'll most likely be the last new investigator that he trains in the field. I'll learn things in the next six months that it would take years for me to learn on my own by trial and error."

I smiled as Larry talked about the equipment he would need to clear my walking path at the house, even though I didn't understand what any of it was.

I'll learn.

Larry went inside to move the clothes from the washer to the dryer; when he returned, he said, "If you and Paul work on a business plan this week, let me know," Larry said. "I'd be interested in reading what you decide."

"I've got a lot to learn too," I said. "Maybe we could get Glenn to help us."

"Good idea; you could use his as a template. Do you suppose Paul and Julie will eventually relocate here, or will you have your main office in Harperville?"

"I hadn't even thought about it; I'll ask Shantelle if it matters where the main office is located. I'm sure there is online training for new businesses that I can take, but right now, I don't have any idea where I should start."

We talked more about Gray Flanagan Detective Agency and what we thought we needed to do to become established.

I shooed away a mosquito, and Larry said, "You've finished half of your beer, I've finished mine, and the mosquitos are buzzing. Are you ready to go inside?"

He took my bottle from me before I rose, then Lucy rushed to join us as we went inside.

While Larry folded clothes and packed his few things, I sat on the bed.

"Why does one week feel like the four and a half months when you disappeared for GBI training?" I asked.

Larry chuckled. "You sure set me straight on that one."

I giggled. "Thank goodness you didn't take the hint when I slammed the door and told you to let yourself out."

"Hint? I was following you to talk to you in a rational manner, and you hit me in the nose when you slammed the door. You are not the subtle, hinting type, Maggie Ewing."

He sat on the bed with me and kissed me lightly then with increasing passion.

"I'll put my backpack in the living room," he mumbled as he nibbled my neck.

I woke while it was still dark and rolled toward the middle of the bed to snuggle with Larry. *Gone. I hope he hasn't been up all night.*

I tiptoed to the hallway then smelled coffee.

"Good morning, Naked Maggie. Palace Guard and I got up early and finished the online training. Take your shower and get dressed, and I'll have your coffee and more news for you."

"What news?" I asked.

"You have to get dressed because you're too irresistible for me to think of anything else but my naked wife."

"You're just saying that," I mumbled as I headed to the shower.

"Am not." He chuckled.

I quickly showered and dressed then hurried to join him.

"Sit at the table; I already poured your coffee. I can fry bacon while I talk."

"You are remarkably talented, Agent Ewing." I breathed in the aroma of freshly brewed coffee. "Ahhh."

"I'm glad Palace Guard and I went through the last bit of the online training because after we finished, I checked my email. You'll never guess what I found."

If Paul forwarded the honey boy email from Della to Larry, I'll faint then fire Paul. No, I won't fire him; I can't let him get off that easy.

"I give up." I held my breath while I held onto my cup with both hands.

"Our instructor for next week sent us a detailed outline of the class on Friday. Palace Guard and I reviewed it together, and there is nothing that we didn't already know, or Macy didn't cover when she took over last week's class. I am completely set for this next week. I was nervous about the class, but now I'm not."

I exhaled. "That is great news."

"Palace Guard and I decided there is no reason for him to go with me; both of us know all this material, so I wouldn't need his help, and he won't be missing anything."

I set down my cup. "That's a surprise."

"It is, isn't it? Palace Guard and I feel better that he'll be here, and Spike is glad he can continue to concentrate on his girl, Lucy."

Larry removed the bacon. "I'm making our version of breakfast burritos."

"Yum." I sipped on my coffee then smiled. *Spike won't have to hover after all.*

After Larry placed our burritos into the oven to warm and toast the tortillas, he said, "I checked the weather, and the forecast is still for severe storms this afternoon, so I'd still like to get an early start. I'll take a quick shower, then we can eat breakfast."

After breakfast, I said, "I just realized it's not actually a week because you'll be back on Friday."

"I like your attitude; you know I'll be packed and ready to go Thursday night."

Larry carried his things out to his truck then returned and opened the back door. Lucy trotted inside, and he rubbed her belly.

He lifted me off the floor in a hug, and I wrapped my arms around his neck. He set me down on my feet and kissed me then patted my bottom.

While I snuggled his chest, he said, "Loved you first, sweetie."

"Love you more, honey."

Larry sighed then released me and strode to the door.

"Do not." He closed the door before I could think of a snappy retort.

Palace Guard and Spike high-fived.

I sighed. "I miss him already; do you think we could go for a run, Palace Guard?"

Palace Guard glared at me then pointed to my laptop.

"That's right, I can listen to Della's email."

I set my laptop on the dining table then went through my login process. When I reached my email, I said, "Open honey boy email from Della."

"Email is open," my chipper electronic assistant said. "Document is password protected. Say or type the password."

"What password?"

"Say or type the password to open the document."

"Della didn't say anything about a password, did she?"

Palace Guard shook his head.

"Do you want to open the document? Say or type the password," the electronic assistant said.

"Log off," I said.

"Good-bye."

"Do you think Della was in a hurry and forgot to send it to me? I'll have to let Paul know I don't have the password."

I picked up my phone. "Send a text to Paul: I don't know the password for Della's document."

I put on my sweatshirt then took my phone out back with Lucy and Spike along. Lucy did her business while Spike waited on the patio with me. When Lucy joined us, she nosed the back door, then she and Spike went inside. I waited for Paul's reply until my toes were cold then hurried in.

I pulled off our bedspread from the bed and dragged it to the sofa then stretched out my legs before I tucked in the bedspread around me.

I leaned back and snuggled down and waited.

I was startled when Lucy's cold nose nudged my exposed upper arm.

"Thank you, Lucy. I think I fell asleep."

I picked up my phone. *Why did I not think of this before?*

"What time is it?"

My phone said, "The time is one sixteen, and the temperature is sixty-eight degrees Fahrenheit."

I stretched before I dragged the bedspread back to the bedroom and put it on the bed. After I returned to the kitchen, I opened the refrigerator and smiled. *Larry made me a blurry sandwich.*

I pulled out my lunch then put my plastic drinking cup in the sink; after I poured sweet tea into the cup, I put on the lid. *Not bad for a first time.*

I unwrapped my sandwich and smiled again. *My sandwich is cut into quarters. I'm spoiled.*

After I finished my lunch, I said, "Maybe Paul could take us to a track somewhere, and we could run while he watches."

Palace Guard nodded.

My phone announced, "Call from Larry."

"Hi, honey. How was your drive?"

I listened while Larry talked about the beautiful scenery, the terrible drivers, and the threatening weather.

"The clouds are starting to roll in here. We're all going to Bud's for a storm party. I understand his wife always cooks up a feast, and we might get sent home with leftovers."

I smiled. *That's definitely Lori for you.*

"If you want points with Bud's wife, her name is Lori. Tell her you loved her MeeMaw cake, and she'll send you home with extra food."

"She made the MeeMaw cake? I'll remember her name," he said then whispered, "Lori. Lori. Lori."

He cleared his throat. "How's your day?"

"I took a nap then ate lunch, which I absolutely loved; thank you for the tiny bite sandwiches."

Larry told me who had arrived as early as he did, and who was still on the road when he was interrupted by a large clap of thunder.

"Sounds like you need to head for Bud's apartment, if you don't want to get drenched. I love you, honey."

"I love you too, sweetie. I'll call you tomorrow."

I set my phone on the table and sighed after we hung up. *Five more days.*

My phone buzzed then announced, "Text from Paul: I am at ER with Julie. She has a kidney stone. ER doc says she can probably go home by dinner time."

"I was trying not to be anxious because we hadn't heard from Paul. I should have known something was wrong," I said.

While Lucy napped in the sun on the patio, Palace Guard helped me practice my knife-throwing accuracy.

"I wish I could shoot; I really need the practice because I feel totally rusty. I wonder if Paul could take me somewhere this week. I'll have to ask him."

Palace Guard nodded.

After I went inside, my phone announced, "Call from hotel office."

"I expected it to be Paul."

When I answered, a woman said, "Mrs. Ewing, we'll be bringing the rollaway bed that your husband ordered for your sister."

"My sister?"

"Oh dear, was it supposed to be a surprise? I'm so sorry. If you can forget that I blabbed who it was for, I'd appreciate it. Your rollaway bed will be there in ten minutes."

"You're fine; thank you," I said.

"Thank you, Mrs. Ewing."

"My sister? Is that Kate? Something's up if Kate's showing up here, but I have a feeling it won't be fun because she's all business except when she's off the clock." I chuckled. "I need to be ready to ambush her."

Spike grinned then went through his version of karate moves.

I applauded, and he bowed.

A few minutes later, I answered the knock at the door.

A woman-blob said, "Mrs. Ewing, I brought you the rollaway myself, so I could apologize again. I'll put the rollaway in the bedroom, but you and your company can move it where you like."

When I smiled, she exhaled then pushed the bed into the bedroom.

After she left, Lucy, Spike, Palace Guard, and I went to the bedroom. Lucy sniffed the bed, Spike narrowed his eyes with suspicion, and Palace Guard examined it.

"It unfolds, but I'm not going to do it now, in case we want to move it."

When we heard another knock at the door, we all hurried to our places: Lucy jumped up on the sofa, Palace Guard stood where he could give me the signal to strike, I took my ambush position, and Spike, our sentry, peeked out the window to confirm it was Kate.

Spike's eyes were wide when he turned away from the window, and he grinned as he put his hand on his hip and posed in his version of a sexy pose as he mimed brushing back long, flowing hair from his face.

"Heather?" I whispered. "Seriously?"

Spike walked his sexy Heather walk then nodded.

I opened the door. "Come on in, Heather."

"Did you get Larry's message that I'd be here? Is your vision clearing up? Can you see me?" Heather-blob asked as she came inside.

"I didn't get a message from Larry, but the hotel clerk told me my sister was coming to stay with me; I see a Heather-blob, so technically, I can see you. What's going on?"

My phone announced, "Text from Larry: Heather is going to stay with you this week. LYF&M."

I snickered. *Loved you first and more; he's really pushing it.*

"I guess I did get Larry's message."

"Where do I put my bag?" Heather asked.

"In the bedroom is fine; the hotel delivered a rollaway bed for you, and it's in there."

When Heather returned from the bedroom, she said, "Let's sit; I have sad news, but it isn't about Larry."

Lucy jumped off the sofa then flopped down on the floor near the soft chair; Spike sat on the floor next to Lucy in a perfect position to gaze at Heather, and Palace Guard stood at the front door.

Heather took my hand. "Maggie, Della and Macy were in Atlanta; we think they were investigating some type of illegal activity, but not in an official capacity; we don't know anything more than that. They must have had an informant because we have evidence they were in the main office of a conglomerate on the fourth floor; their informant must have been working both sides and turned them in to the bad guys, but we don't have any evidence to back that up yet."

"When was this?" I asked.

"According to the security camera across the street, Della and Macy entered the building at ten o'clock last night; the security camera in the stairwell shows they took the exit to the fourth floor fifteen minutes later. They were ambushed in the lobby of the building shortly after midnight. Della killed three of the ambushers before she was shot and died at the scene; Macy killed two others. There were more attackers; we don't know how many. They left Macy for dead and fled but left a trail of blood in the alley that led to a parking lot. Macy was in surgery for a long time; she's in the critical trauma unit, and the doctors are hopeful she will survive. Kate has a team looking into Della's death and the attack, so we'll know more later. Kate called Larry to see if he had any information because Macy is an instructor where Larry is training, but he didn't. Larry wanted to return here to tell you himself, so Kate asked me to call him. He told me you had to be told in person not through a phone call, so here I am."

Palace Guard and Spike looked as shocked as I felt.

"Della's dead?" I held tightly onto Heather's hand. *Please tell me I misunderstood.*

"I'm really sorry. Larry said you two were close friends."

The tears slipped down my cheek, then Heather held me while I sobbed.

When my tears slowed, Heather said, "I brought wine and snacks. I'm completely off the clock with no obligation to report to anyone, so when you're ready to make plans, I'm in."

After Heather put a tissue in my hand, I wiped away tears from my face then blew my nose.

Heather continued, "I do have additional information when you are ready to hear it."

I snuffled then exhaled. "I'm ready."

CHAPTER EIGHTEEN

"The building elevator security camera recorded Della and Macy taking the elevator to the fourth floor on Friday afternoon around two o'clock," Heather said. "They returned from the fourth floor to the lobby in the elevator a little after three. There is only one company on the fourth floor: a conglomerate."

I nodded. *The catering company.*

"There's something else, and no one knows this," Heather said. "Della asked me for a gadget that recorded like jo but is smaller, and I gave her a keychain with a small medallion on it. The hospital released her personal effects that she had with her to the FBI. Kate is sending Della's personal effects to you here, and before you ask, I think they will arrive tomorrow or Tuesday."

"How does the medallion work?"

"I took a short cut and essentially duplicated jo, except the communication comes to me while the jo sends communication to Paul."

That reminds me: I better let Larry know Heather is here.

I picked up my phone. "Send a text to Larry: Heather is here. Thank you. LYTTMAB."

"What on earth kind of code is that, Gray Lady?"

I snickered. "We are in the middle of a feud."

"Oh, of course," Heather said. "Will he understand what you said?"

"I hope not because that's the feud part," I snickered. "It means love you to the moon and back."

"How is that a feud? Never mind; tell me later. At Della's request, I put a switch on the medallion that she could press to send, so she could determine when to send what she had recorded. Can I get you something to drink? Do you have any sweet tea?"

"Sweet tea sounds good; there's some in the refrigerator."

When Heather walked to the refrigerator, Spike crowded her as she walked.

"Spike, give Heather some space, or you'll be banned to the backyard," I growled.

Spike glowered then stomped to the corner of the room near the dining table and faced the wall.

Palace Guard grinned, and I covered my mouth to keep from giggling.

When Heather handed me my cup with sweet tea, she asked, "Larry told me the real imaginary men would be here. Will I regret it if I ask what on earth is going on?"

"Probably. Spike put himself in time out."

"Of course. I haven't received anything from Della, so I'm hoping she was carrying the keychain with her, so we can capture whatever she recorded. There are no guarantees that she recorded anything, but I'm certain she must have." Heather sipped her sweet tea. "This is really good. What's our plan, boss?"

"I need to go running," I said.

Palace Guard shook his head.

"Heather can take us to a running track and watch our back."

"Are you arguing with Palace Guard?" Heather asked. "What did he say?"

"Well?" I asked.

Palace Guard disappeared then stood at the door in his running shirt, shorts, and shoes.

"We can go; I need to change, but I don't know where a running track might be."

"I'll check."

After I changed to my running shoes and shorts, and a T-shirt that felt like a running shirt, I joined Palace Guard at the door.

"You're out of timeout, Spike," Heather said. "Are you going too?"

Spike glanced at me, and I nodded.

When Lucy rose and trotted to the front door, Heather said, "If Lucy is going, then I assume Spike is too."

"You're right," I said. "He stays close to Lucy."

"Good. I found a track at the high school; we'll check that one first."

I climbed into the passenger's seat with my jo while Heather opened the back door of her car. Spike and Lucy then Palace Guard climbed into the backseat.

"Is everybody in?" she asked.

"Yep, you can close the door," I said.

Heather started her car. "I'm starting to get the hang of being around the real imaginary men."

After Heather parked, she said, "There is a bench outside the fence and trees and grass surrounding the track. No one is running on the track; that's good, right? If the gate is locked, there's a three-mile running trail not too far from here. I wouldn't have brought it up, but you'll have Palace Guard with you, won't you?"

"Yep; we'll have to try the running trail sometime too because that's more of a challenge for me than a track."

"I hadn't thought of how an uneven surface could be a challenge," Heather said. "I have a few things to learn about limited sight."

Palace Guard reached the gate first and opened it.

"Did Palace Guard open the gate? It's awesome watching the real imaginary men at work," Heather said.

"I have my phone; if someone shows up to run, you can text me, and we'll hear it."

"Do you run with your jo?" Heather asked.

"Always."

Palace Guard and I jogged to the track. We started off slow then increased our pace. I stretched out my legs to increase my stride and was soon running at my racing pace.

"Three laps," I said after we completed two at a full run.

Palace Guard increased his speed, and I stayed up with him. After we completed the third lap, we slowed to a fast walk then a slow walk to cool down on the fourth lap, and I used my jo as a walking stick because I had fatigued my arm muscles from carrying it.

When we reached the gate, Palace Guard and I high-fived.

"Did you just high-five Palace Guard?" Heather asked. "I held my breath on your third lap. You two were awesome."

She held up her hand; I smacked it and so did Palace Guard and Spike.

Heather stared at her hand. "I felt two distinct, light touches on my hand after you slapped it."

She narrowed her eyes and peered at me. "Was it my imagination or yours?"

I giggled while Palace Guard smiled, and Spike beamed.

As we strolled to the car, she said, "I need to see the real imaginary men."

On our way back to the hotel, Heather asked, "Who sees the imaginary men besides you?"

"Larry and young children do, and so does my friend Tonya, who has a tiny imaginary dragon. She's deaf, so we think Kiki stayed with her to protect her. Kate can see Spike, but not Palace Guard."

Heather chuckled. "I'll bet Kate is annoyed that she can't see Palace Guard too."

I smiled. "She is, but she was determined to see Spike; it was almost like she willed herself to see him."

"Tell me about your friend's tiny dragon."

"I can't see Kiki, but when she jumps on my shoulder, I feel her tiny talons, and she chirps and sings to me."

"Now, I'm jealous about Kiki too." Heather chuckled.

I told Heather about Kiki saving Tonya by torching Walt Dillard when he tried to kill Tonya.

"That must be totally awesome to have a fire-breathing dragon as a protector. I had completely forgotten about Shadow until you were telling me about Kiki. My first memory as a toddler was playing with my wolf. I was alone most of the time, but my wolf and I didn't mind. A babysitter asked me if I was talking to my shadow, and I said yes. Shadow stayed with me for a long time until I forgot about him after I started high school. Now I wonder if he's still around."

Palace Guard shrugged.

"We can't see him, but my theory is that you would have to see him before someone else could, and I just made that up."

Heather laughed. "I like it."

I furrowed my brow. *Gary Sloan sees the imaginary men as shadows.*

After we arrived at the hotel, Heather said, "I meant to tell you that while you were running, a man parked across the lot from me then stood next to his car for a while and stared while you ran. He wasn't casual about it at all, so he was either just a rude jerk or really bad at surveillance. I assume that Spike went to check him out because Lucy wandered toward the man. When she was close, he jumped into his car and left." Heather snorted. "I was raised by a wolf, so I don't understand why sweet Lucy would make anyone nervous."

"Good girl, Lucy." I rubbed her ears, then she rolled over for a belly rub, and Spike sat on the floor next to her.

"Spike is rubbing Lucy's belly, isn't he?"

After I changed from my running clothes to jeans and a T-shirt, I returned to the living room.

"This is a comfortable chair." Heather patted the cushion.

I sat on the sofa and put up my feet while Heather continued.

"The most interesting thing that happened, though, was another car pulled into the lot and parked at the far end away from the track. The man climbed out, stood next to the driver's door with his back to me, and watched the road, like he was waiting for someone. Now, he was good. I could tell he was keeping a close watch on the man in the car that was close to me because if there's one thing I know, it's undercover. The second man paid absolutely no attention to me or to the track, even though I know he was aware of you, Lucy, and me. Somebody that good at surveillance wouldn't have missed any detail, especially since his subject was riveted on you. When the first man left, the undercover man waited a while then made a big show of giving up by walking toward the road and scanning it then returning to his car before he left. I'm really sorry you weren't with me to enjoy the show. It was definitely well-executed."

"You didn't recognize the undercover man?" I asked.

Heather sighed. "I never saw his face, and he was wearing a nondescript ball cap, but I don't think I've worked with him because I didn't recognize his walk. I could tell he wasn't a young man, but he was in good physical shape and had the air of someone who was more comfortable working outside and not sitting at a desk."

I smiled. "You saw all that and watched me run too? That's awesome."

Heather-blob shrugged. "It's a survival skill that Shadow taught me. So, do I need to go to the grocery store to pick up some things to cook for our supper? Did you have anything planned?"

"Paul and I had planned to order meals from one of the local restaurants that delivers to the hotel, but he's with Julie at the ER; she has a kidney stone. I'll show you the menu, and you can decide what sounds good to you."

I picked up the menu from the dining table then handed it to Heather.

After I resumed my comfortable position on the sofa, Heather said, "This is torture; I may have to stay for two weeks, so we can try every restaurant."

I smiled. "When I was stressing over the amount of work Larry will have at home in addition to his fulltime job, Larry's dad suggested that I hire a cleaning service to clean every two weeks because I can't see well enough to clean and a personal chef to prepare weekly meals because Larry thinks it's unsafe for me to operate the stove or handle a knife unless I'm throwing it at an attacker. I'm supposed to have three personal chefs prepare meals this week, like an interview, so I can find one that I like. Martha, Tonya's mother, and Jennifer conducted phone interviews then picked the top three for a trial run; Martha will tell me tomorrow which days each one is scheduled. On Wednesday, I have an appointment at nine to meet with a home inspector. Larry and I found a house we liked before he left for Tennessee."

"You and Larry are an incredible team and always have been." Heather-blob shook her head. "Have you overdosed on seafood yet? What do you think about fried fish or crab cakes?"

"Both sound interesting, but I'm leaning toward crab cakes."

"I agree. I'll order crab cakes, fries, and a dessert for both of us. I don't think we'll have any leftovers, but if we do, we'll have them for a light lunch tomorrow."

After Heather ordered our food, my phone announced, "Call from Paul."

"How is Julie?" I asked.

"Finally doing better. We'll be leaving in the next hour or so, according to the ER nurse. Maggie, Larry called me and told me Heather will stay with you this week. I was very sorry to hear about Della. We'll all miss her, but I know the two of us were close. I still plan to take you to the house inspection on Wednesday. Julie is trying to decide whether she should continue to stay with Martha, but I'm encouraging her to let Martha have some personal space. I think Julie needs to rest, so I told her that Heather will fill in for her with the personal chef meals, and I'll still be Larry's stand-in. She told me she'd think about it; I wish I could convince her to take it easy; she's exhausted and needs recuperation time from the ordeal of the kidney stone."

"I can imagine how hard it would be to slow her down. I have to confirm how many we'll have for the interview meals tomorrow with Martha when we talk about the schedule, so she can discuss the number of people with the chefs. If you're available tomorrow, maybe you can brief Heather on where we are with the investigation of the camp."

"I need a little time to refocus on the camp, and I'll do that this evening after I get Julie back to the hotel. Martha encouraged Julie to get some rest because Tonya is doing fine; as far as the interview meals, I'll remind Julie that she helped with the house, so it would be a kind gesture if she bows out so your old friend Heather can help with the chef interviews."

"I'm impressed by your smooth negotiation skills; I can't see Julie turning down an opportunity to be nice."

"That's what I'm hoping," Paul said.

After we hung up, I said, "Paul wanted you to take Julie's place with the personal chef meals, but he's not certain what Julie's plans are for next week yet. Paul wants her to recuperate from the kidney stone. We'll either have three or four; Paul will remind Julie that the chefs will need a firm number by tomorrow. Paul will take me to the house inspection on Wednesday; the home inspector doesn't allow anyone except the home buyer to attend the inspection but agreed to allow Paul to fill in for Larry since Larry isn't available."

"I wouldn't have thought of a personal chef. Larry's dad is a genius because that's the perfect solution. I'm looking forward to this week."

When our food was delivered, Heather set the sack on the table then plated our food. "Maggie, I thought an order of crab cakes would be an appetizer not a complete meal that includes two crab cakes, fried shrimp, Cajun rice, and coleslaw. No wonder the kindhearted woman who took my phone order suggested we might not want fries; at least I had sense enough to listen to her. We definitely have plenty of food for our lunch tomorrow. I'll put half on our plates and wrap the rest. We have peach cobbler for dessert; I noticed all the restaurants listed peach pie or cobbler as their specialty." Heather chuckled. "We'll be peach connoisseurs by the end of the week. When Paul's available this next week, I have to run with you and Palace Guard because I want home churned peach ice cream with warm peach cobbler. I saw that on one of the menus. What do you want to drink? Sweet tea, wine, or beer?"

"Sweet tea then wine with my dessert."

"Perfect. I'll put the peach cobbler in the oven on low."

While we ate, I told Heather about Della and gumbo. When I told her that Della said I was smarter than she was, but she was sneakier, Heather laughed.

"That is so Della," she said.

I smiled and nodded.

When I told her what Macy said about meeting Della when Macy was the new instructor, Heather said, "That was their bond, wasn't it? That's why they instantly trusted each other; I'd wondered."

Larry called me. "It was one humdinger of a storm, but it's finally moved on, and we're down to light sprinkles; I sure am glad I left early and didn't get caught on the road. I have some research I'd like to do tonight in preparation for tomorrow's class. I'll leave for our apartment after we hang up. I'm supposed to tell you that Lori misses you, and she wants an invitation to our new house."

"She's welcome any time," I said.

"That's what I told her, and she said she had a suitcase large enough for three weeks of clothes. Was she kidding?"

"I hope not, but she probably was."

"What did you do today? No bad guys, right?"

The man watching me could have just been curious. I crossed my fingers. "No bad guys. Palace Guard and I ran on the high school track while Heather, Spike, and Lucy had our backs. It felt good to run."

"I'm really glad Heather's there. I know you're sick about Della."

"I am; have you heard any more about Macy?"

"Nothing new; one of the guys knows some people who work at the hospital and will see if he can find out anything. We're on a group text, so he'll let us know if he hears anything, no matter what time it is. I'm ready to dash to the apartment. I'll call you in the morning, sweetheart. I love you to the moon and back too, sweet Maggie." He hung up before I could reply.

"Dang it," I said. "He figured it out. Now I have to come up with something new."

"He figured out love you to the moon and back?" Heather asked. "We need to come up with something he'll never figure out."

"Exactly." I smiled.

"Let's bring that bed in here before dessert; then both of us will have a bed-room," Heather said.

After we pushed the rollaway into the living area, Heather unfolded it under the watchful eye of Spike.

When she laid on it, she said, "This is awful; I'd be more comfortable on the floor. I passed a big retail store on my way here; let's see if we can find a cot."

Lucy and Spike stayed at the hotel, but Palace Guard went with us. While we roamed the camping aisle, Palace Guard tapped my shoulder, and I glanced behind me as a blob stepped back into the other aisle.

"Let me know if he's a threat; should I warn Heather?"

Palace Guard shook his head as a man headed toward the aisle where the blob had gone.

Palace Guard pointed in the direction where the man followed the blob then held up his index finger to indicate "one."

Palace Guard knows it was the one other man I see besides Larry, him, and Spike.

"I agree."

"What are you agreeing with?" Heather asked.

"We need to look in bedding to see if there's a mattress we could add to the rollaway," I said.

Heather-blob nodded then led the way to the bedding aisle. "Feel this. It's two-inch foam and has a fluffy top. I think it might do."

I mashed the foam and nodded.

After we returned to the hotel, Heather unrolled the foam. "It's supposed to rest for two hours before I can try it out. Let's have dessert, wine, and snacks, then we'll tell Paul he has to go with us tomorrow while we walk around the track because I'll still be too stuffed to run."

Heather dished up the peach cobbler. "I made a mistake; I should have picked up ice cream at the store. We'll get some tomorrow."

We sat in the living room while we ate peach cobbler and sipped our wine. Heather told me another story about Shadow; in the middle of her story, her phone rang.

"It's Todd. Okay if I go outside to talk to him?" she asked.

"Absolutely."

Heather answered then said, "Hang on." She put her phone under her arm and carried her wine and peach cobbler with her as she maneuvered opening the back door without spilling her wine or losing any cobbler. Lucy slipped out in front of Heather.

"Impressive," I said, and Palace Guard and Spike nodded.

Spike headed toward the door before Heather closed it.

"No, Spike; Heather deserves some privacy."

He stormed to the corner and faced it with his arms crossed.

"Sorry, Spike."

Palace Guard rolled his eyes when Spike didn't budge from the corner.

When Heather came back inside, she said, "You're released from time out, Spike."

Spike turned and stared at her.

"Spike's staring at you, and so are we, Heather."

She giggled. "It was a guess. I heard you tell Spike he couldn't come outside with Lucy and me. I might not be able to see him, but I definitely know him."

Spike grinned then did his wacky dance.

"Spike is dancing," I said.

"His wacky dance?" Heather-blob bounced around the room in a jig and waved her arms.

When she laughed and collapsed on the soft chair, Spike, Palace Guard, and I applauded, and Spike laughed with her when she moved her blob-hand. Palace Guard pointed to Heather then waved the princess wave, and I laughed along with him.

"Tell us another story about Shadow, Heather," I said; Spike nodded as he and Lucy sat at her feet.

"I was five years old; my bedroom was on the second story of our house. Daddy had left his tall ladder near the house, and a burglar used it to break into our house through my open bedroom window one night. Shadow's growl rumbled in his throat, and it was a low, terrifying sound that you might hear in a dark cave. The intruder had one leg over the windowsill and in my room when Shadow lunged.

The man fell out of the window and onto the ground. He went to the hospital in an ambulance and handcuffs. The arresting officer was a woman, and I told her I wanted to be just like her. She stared at me then told me I'd be better because I had a fierce soul. At the time, I believed that she could see Shadow, but I learned later that the intruder told the police officers that he was attacked by a wild animal, and the police officer was shocked to see me alone in my room."

"What a great story," I said.

Spike and Palace Guard nodded.

"Spike and Palace Guard agree." I yawned.

"More stories tomorrow, but it will be your turn, Gray Lady. I'm exhausted from the drive to get here, but I'm glad I came because it's going to be a great week."

After I was in bed and had turned off my light, I picked up my phone. "Send a text to Larry: Love you while I'm sleeping."

When I woke, it was dark, but I was surprised that light came from my partially open bedroom door. *Is Heather already awake?*

I peeked around the corner, and Heather-blob said, "Good morning, Gray Lady. Lucy, Spike, and I went outside earlier, and I relaxed on the patio with a cup of coffee. I can't remember the last time I didn't grab a cup and dash out the door to work. I could get used to this cushy assignment of guarding Gray Lady. Bacon and eggs okay for you?"

"Yep; coffee first," I said.

I hurried to shower. While I dressed, my phone buzzed a text. "From Larry: 4 more days. LYF&M4e."

I giggled. "Reply to Larry: smooches."

When I joined Heather she said, "I know you usually let your coffee cool before you drink it, so I poured it while you showered. It's on the table at the same place that you ate dinner last night because I decided it was your seat."

"You're right on both counts."

While I sipped my coffee, Heather fried bacon. "Lucy showed me where her food was, so I fed her. I may have overfed her because she licked my hand. What's our plan for today?"

I told her what Della said the last time I talked to her, and the email she sent to me on Friday.

"Honey boy?" Heather cracked eggs.

"It was Della's nickname for Larry; she called me sweet girl."

"That's really fitting for you two as a couple, so when she told you on the phone to hold onto honey boy for her, you naturally assumed she meant Larry, which made the email puzzling, especially when you couldn't open it."

"That's exactly where I'm stuck. I forwarded the email to Paul, but Julie's kidney stone diverted his attention, so we haven't had a chance to discuss it." I sighed. "Normally, this is something Della and I would have tackled."

"It will take a while to adjust, won't it?" Heather asked.

"It will, but I'll do it. Della being gone reminded me of Parker. I'd forgotten how hard that was." I bit my lip.

"Larry used to worry that he was a rebound."

"He wasn't, and I think he has finally realized we were always partners when we worked together. It was completely different with Parker because even though he was my first crush, we never had that peer-of-equals relationship that Larry and I have always had. Does that make sense? I vaguely remember Larry on his first day as a police officer. He was working with Sarge. He told me not long ago that Sarge spoke sternly to him his first day because he kept staring at me."

Heather giggled. "I heard about that. Larry took a lot of ribbing about having a crush on someone who was three times smarter than he was because you were a librarian. I forgot to ask how you like your eggs, so you and I are having scrambled eggs the way I like them."

Heather put my plate in front of me and refilled our coffee then joined me at the table.

While we ate, Heather asked, "Did you brush your hair?"

"No, I couldn't figure out how to brush out the tangles, so I take out the tangles I can find with my fingers."

"How's your hearing?" she asked.

"My hearing is excellent."

She sipped her coffee. "Good; I can teach you how to brush out the tangles."

CHAPTER NINETEEN

After we ate, I gave my hairbrush to Heather.

"This is perfect. I'll take a small section of hair and repeatedly tug lightly with the brush through the section of your hair. You'll hear tangles at first then no tangles."

"Hear that?" she asked as she lightly tugged against tangles.

"Yes."

When she had cleared the tangle, she asked, "What do you hear now?"

"No noisy tangles; it's smooth."

"Exactly, now it's your turn."

I took small sections of hair, tugged lightly, and brushed through the tangles. "It was really easy; I should have asked you earlier."

"You are right, Gray Lady."

While I put away my brush, my phone announced, "Call from Nell."

"It's our real estate agent." I hurried to answer it.

"Maggie, do you have a little time today that you could come into the office? I have a few questions that I'd like to discuss with you, and I'm not good at taking notes while I'm on the phone. I don't have anything for Larry and you to sign yet, so don't worry about that."

"Sure, what time were you thinking?" I asked.

"It would be nice if you could come in this morning."

"This morning?"

Heather-blob held up her hands, then Spike held up ten fingers.

"How about ten o'clock?" I asked.

"Perfect; I'll see you then. Thank you for being so flexible."

After I hung up Heather said, "I thought I was being smart by not yelling out ten o'clock, but then I realized you couldn't have seen my fingers. You didn't, did you? Did Spike relay the message for me?"

"Sure did; how did you know it was Spike?" I asked.

"I don't know," she said. "I just knew. After we go to the real estate office, I'd like to go to the grocery store and pick up a few things. Do you have a cooler?"

"Yes, but I don't know if it's here."

"We can pick up a small one at the retail store, if I can't find yours. Evidently that store is addictive; I've been here two days, this will be my second trip to the store, and I'm planning for my next one. Have I found a new hobby?" She snickered.

On the way, Heather asked, "Do you think you'll need me with you while you talk to Nell? I could go to the store and pick up the cooler and some ice."

"That sounds good to me. I don't mind missing the noise and the crowded aisles of the large store."

"I'll look around to see if there's anything else we need while I'm there, so maybe I won't have to go back tomorrow."

When I walked into the office, Nell said, "Thank you for coming on short notice. Is Paul coming in or is he waiting in the parking lot? He's welcome to sit in because we're not discussing anything confidential."

I smiled. "A good friend of mine surprised me yesterday and is staying with me this week. Paul's taking a little time off to have some family time with Julie."

"That's wonderful. Come on into my office. Did you want to hold onto my arm?"

"Thank you."

Palace Guard rolled his eyes as Nell led me to her office.

"I'll be right back. I have my notes on the printer," Nell said after I sat in the visitor's chair.

After she left, I whispered, "It was easier to go with the flow since she asked."

Nell hurried into her office. "I'll send you my updated notes by email after we talk, so you can forward them to Kevin and your lawyer's assistant, Ms. Shantelle. I want to make sure I'm not missing anything on our contingencies first."

As she read through them, Palace Guard read over her shoulder. When he held up his hand, I asked, "Could you mark that last section with a star? I'd like to ask Shantelle if she has any concerns."

The office door opened and closed.

Nell continued, "Of course, and this is exactly why it was so helpful for you..."

"Nell? Are you in your office?" a man called out then walked into Nell's office.

Palace Guard tapped my shoulder then guided me as I shifted my jo toward the man then pressed the button to record.

"Excuse me just a second, Maggie." Nell rose from her desk and approached the man. "I wasn't expecting you so soon, Flint. Can you come back in a half hour?"

"I'm so sorry for barging in like this. I made better time than I expected and should have given you a quick call. I apologize for interrupting your meeting; I'll return in forty-five minutes."

After Flint left, I said, "My dad has an old friend named Flint. That's a fairly uncommon name, isn't it? My dad's friend is Flint Arrington."

"That was Flint Turner. I didn't expect him until later because his company is in Atlanta. He's the vice president of operations for the company that owns the exclusive campground not too far from town. Have you heard of it? His company has decided to sell the property, so Flint is here to take care of a few details that he calls loose ends before we put it on the market. Our target is to list it no later than Friday, so I can conduct a by-invitation-only open house on Saturday. I have some high-roller buyers that are interested; Flint is willing to allow them an early preview on Friday morning before I list it. I am very excited about this opportunity because that is a highly desirable piece of property and will sell quickly. Of course, this is all extremely confidential."

"I was never even here," I said.

"Thank you."

I stopped the recording.

We went over a few more things, then Nell said, "Thanks again for coming in to talk to me, even though you weren't here."

Nell is probably smiling, or maybe she winked. I nodded and smiled.

Palace Guard guided me out the door then to Heather's car. *Nell was so stressed, she forgot to lead me.*

"You and Palace Guard are slick." Heather opened the passenger's door for me.

After we were in the car, I glanced at Palace Guard, he nodded. "We know. Did you find what you wanted?"

"I found a sturdy cooler and did some browsing. I found some killer undercover outfits, but I'm not in narcotics anymore, so I wouldn't have any use for them."

Heather parked in the grocery parking lot in the shade. "Are you staying in the car? I'll leave the engine on, so you can turn up the air conditioner if it's too hot."

"If you don't need me, I'd rather stay in the car," I said.

Heather finished shopping, and while she unloaded her cart into the trunk, my phone announced, "Phone call from Nell."

When I answered, Nell said, "I just sent the email to you; I wanted you to know, so you could watch for it. Flint Turner asked me who the woman was in my office, and I was surprised that he'd heard of the Gray Lady; he asked me if you were investigating anything in particular here, and I explained your husband was with the GBI, and you were still recuperating from your severe injuries. He acts charming, but he's a suspicious man; I told him real estate was not your field at all, so he wouldn't think I was talking to a client about the campground behind his back. He wants me to take some pictures of the main office building this afternoon. He made it very clear that none of the other buildings are ready yet, so I was absolutely not to approach any of them. I don't have to like my clients, but there's something slimy about him. Did you notice? Get back to me if Kevin has any questions."

I sighed after Nell hung up.

Heather hopped into the driver's seat. "Do we have any other stops we need to make?"

"Nothing for me."

"I need to think of something that I have to buy tomorrow, so we can go back to my favorite store. I found peach ice cream at the grocery store, so we're set for dessert this evening."

When Heather turned at the hotel, the man was trimming the edges around the sidewalk to the office.

"That's the groundskeeper, right? He looks so familiar to me," Heather said.

"He should; I'm positive he's the man that was following the first guy at the track."

Heather asked, "Do you know him?"

"Let's go inside."

When we were inside, I sat on the sofa, and Heather put away the groceries then asked, "Do you want any sweet tea or hot tea?"

"Sweet tea because I'm close to hyperventilating."

"In that case, I'll have sweet tea too."

Heather handed me my cup with sweet tea then sat across from me. "Go, and start with the punch line."

"You and Larry," I muttered. "While I was in Nell's office, Macy's ex-husband came in..."

Heather interrupted me. "Okay, I apologize; give me the full Gray Lady version."

"Macy told me her ex-husband, Flint Turner, was a Vice President of Operation for the conglomerate that owns the catering company, and he came into Nell's office while I was there. After he left, Nell told me the conglomerate owned the campground, and Flint was there to get the camp ready to sell. Nell is supposed to hold an open house for the elite, she called them high rollers, this weekend. Unfortunately, after I left, Nell gave Flint Turner as much information about me as she gave me about him, so I've lost any advantage I might have had by being an unknown."

"That stinks," Heather said, "but it sounds like you weren't really surprised."

"No, I wasn't; I don't think Nell has many filters. Moving on to the campground: Roxanne and a number of high school aged girls are being held prisoner there, except Roxanne is isolated from the girls. Palace Guard saw them and gave Roxanne her phone. She sent me a text because she knew I was close when she got her phone and warned me not to text her, so I haven't. That's the Flint Turner part."

"Wow. There's more? I need a beer, but it's not even time for lunch yet."

"I wouldn't mind taking a break. Can we go outside?"

"Good idea. What do you have in mind?"

"I'd like to take a stroll around the grounds. I need to talk to the groundskeeper."

"Okay, but you have to tell me why."

"Remember the skilled undercover person at the track?"

"Of course."

I sat on the sofa. "All people are blobs to me except for Larry, Palace Guard, Spike, and one other person: my dad, Gary Sloan. I didn't know that until I saw him at the training center in Tennessee. I was surprised that the groundskeeper wasn't a blob, but I never really got a good look at him, and that was no accident. I'm a little annoyed at myself for not recognizing Gary immediately."

"So, Gary is either guarding you or tailing the guy who is following you."

"Right; I'd like to know why."

As we headed out the front door with the scowling Palace Guard walking alongside me, Heather said, "Will I get in trouble for this?"

"Only by association."

When I strolled to the groundskeeper as he spread mulch around the flowers, he shook his head and sighed.

I smiled and pretended to admire the flowers. "I need to talk to you."

He continued to spread the mulch. "I'll be there in ten minutes to fix that back gate for you."

I returned to my suite with Heather at my side, and Palace Guard close behind me.

When we were inside, Heather said, "He wasn't happy at all that you walked right up to him."

"That's too bad, but I need to know what's going on. I'll be on the patio."

"Does that mean I'm not invited?" Heather's voice was cold.

"Exactly, but do you suppose you could switch jo from Paul to you?"

Heather snorted. "I should have realized you wouldn't have left me out. It will take me less than a minute."

I sat at the patio table while I waited for Gary. Gary came in through the gate then stood close to the table as he continued to scan the area.

He rubbed his hand across his face. "I've always seen a shadow around you, but lately I see a..."

He cleared his throat. "Would you and Heather meet me for lunch at eleven thirty? There's a café near here that you would like," he said.

I nodded.

He pulled a card out of his pocket. "Here's the address." He strode toward the gate then paused. "I'm looking forward to talking to you, Maggie. You're always full of surprises, but maybe I can help you this time before anyone shoots at you."

I stopped recording; when I went inside, Heather said, "It sounds like you didn't surprise him as much as I thought. He knew it was only a matter of time, didn't he? Where are we going to lunch?"

I handed her the card.

"This sounds good; I'll check the menu online for you."

After Heather read the menu, she asked, "What would work for you?"

"The fish bites appetizer sounds perfect for me."

"I'll order the scallops appetizer and a side of hush puppies, and we can share the hush puppies."

"If you'll pick up the check, my new company will reimburse you. This is a perfect business expense."

"You can tell me about your new company on the way home from the restaurant; I can't tell you how excited I am to have a ringside seat because I know Gary Sloan's reputation: he's going to pump you for your information, but I'll bet you come away with more than he does."

I snorted. "It won't be easy because he won't underestimate me."

When we went into the restaurant, Heather asked, "Where do you want to sit?"

"Gary's already here; he'll be at the most strategic seat here. When you see him, lead the way."

Heather turned to look back at the door. "You saw him when we came in, didn't you?"

"You got it."

When Gary waved, Heather said, "Ah, there he is."

I took the back of her arm, and we strolled to the table. Gary narrowed his eyes at me, but I ignored him.

After we ordered, Gary asked, "Whatcha got, Maggie?"

"Not much; like you said, no one's shot at me, but what do you need?"

Gary laughed. "This is like talking to my younger self, except you're more experienced than I was at your age. Fine, we'll do an information exchange."

"You first, Gary."

"That guy that's following you is only tracking where you are and what you're doing. His orders are absolutely no harm."

"When I saw you following him, I knew how convenient he was for you, but I still don't know why you have been keeping track of me unless you expect someone you want to approach me."

Gary growled, "Are you saying I'd use my own daughter as bait?"

I rolled my eye, and Palace Guard nodded and smiled.

"Yes, I am; I think you want the big dog, not any of the small fish, and you need me to draw him out because you don't know who he is."

Heather snickered.

"I have a menagerie, don't I?" I asked.

"I was going to say zoo." Gary chuckled. "So, what do you have for me?"

Palace Guard narrowed his eyes then pointed to the door.

"It was nice seeing you, Gary." I rose, and Palace Guard and I strode outside; Heather rushed out behind us.

"Are we leaving?"

"Yes."

"What was that all about?" Heather asked after we were in the car.

"How fast can you get back to the hotel?"

"Hang on, sister."

She floored it and skillfully maneuvered through the traffic. Palace Guard's face paled. *She must have run a red light.*

When she stopped in front of my suite, all three of us jumped out of the car and raced to the front door. When I opened it, Spike grinned and pointed to Lucy. Lucy had soaked the ripped piece of jeans fabric that she chewed on while she held it lovingly between her paws, and there were dog treats scattered around her.

"Good girl, Lucy," I said as Heather hurried to the back door.

"No wonder Spike gave Lucy her entire box of dog treats. How many were there, Spike?" Heather asked.

Spike held up three fingers.

"Three," I said.

"Was Lucy injured in any way?" Heather asked, and Spike shook his head.

"No," I said.

"Don't go out back, Maggie. I want to take some photos, and I think I can get some nice samples of DNA. Did Lucy bite all three?"

Spike grinned and nodded.

"Yes."

"You are awesome, Lucy," Heather said.

Heather returned with a black bag then went to the back.

I sat on the sofa and relaxed.

"I don't mind waiting, but I wish I could spy on Heather and watch."

Spike grinned then disappeared.

"I shouldn't have said anything," I grumbled. "He took that as carte blanche."

Spike reappeared then mimed Heather's process of photographing from different angles and taking close shots of the blood in the grass then shifting to collecting samples of blood before she spoke into a recording device.

Palace Guard and I laughed when Spike put a hand on his hip then shifted his weight while he pouted then held an imaginary microphone close to his mouth.

When Heather came inside, she said, "I'll warm up our leftovers. Are you starving, Gray Lady? I am."

While we ate, she said, "I want to call Larry and tell him what happened. I need to turn over all this evidence I've collected to GBI. Spike, did they have a key?"

Spike nodded.

"Yes; are you surprised?" I asked.

"Not at all; it goes with what you thought: Gary was stalling to keep us at the restaurant, so the team of thugs could what? What do you have here that Gary wants?"

"I have a few documents saved on my computer, but nothing of consequence. Gary might not have known that Della's document is password-protected if that's what he was after."

"We need to figure out the password. Let's do that tonight. I don't think anyone expected your suite to be guarded by a highly-trained attack dog. Gary must have expected his henchmen to slip in, copy the file from your laptop, and slip out undetected. Lucy is just like you: she seems like such a sweet, easy-going girl until she's riled up. Well done, Spike and Lucy." Heather said.

Spike bowed and threw kisses to his adoring imaginary fans.

"Spike said thank you," I said.

Heather snorted. "He did not; he's taking his well-deserved accolades."

I giggled.

After we finished eating, Heather put the few dishes we used into the dishwasher. "Text Larry and tell him we need to talk after his last class."

"Why can't you text him?" I growled.

"If I do, he'll panic because he didn't hear from you."

"I hate it when you're logical."

I spoke to my phone, "Send a text to Larry: Heather and I need to consult with you this evening. What time can you call me?"

"Reply from Larry: Seven."

"Ready to tackle the password?" I asked.

"What emails have you received from Della or Macy in the past week?"

I turned on my laptop. "Nothing from Macy; she was focused on getting everyone through the last week of the basic chemistry class, so they could pass the test, and only the honey boy email from Della."

"Let's look at that email again."

I turned on my laptop then turned it toward Heather's seat at the table. "You can read it."

Heather sat and read the screen then sat back and exhaled. "There's nothing here. I could try some combinations of her email address, yours, and the words she used in the email, but none of that makes sense because Della was too savvy to put even a scrambled password in the same email after she went to the trouble of restricting who could read the attachment in the first place. I see why you were stuck. I'm not sure why she didn't send the password in a separate email unless she didn't have a chance."

"Text," I said. "I thought it was an accidental pocket text because it came right after she told me to hang onto honey boy for her."

I pulled out my phone and handed it to Heather.

"The text from Della says, 'honeyboy2me'. Is that your accidental text?" Heather chuckled. "What are your initials, Gray Lady?"

"M.S.," I said automatically. "No, my initials are M.E." I smiled. "This is exactly something Della would do because neither one of us would forget it, and she knew it would make me laugh when I figured it out."

"Give it a try," Heather said.

"It's easier if you type it then tell me what Della's document says."

I listened to the taps on the keyboard, then Heather said, "This first page is a list of the backers of the catering conglomerate. The list is long and includes top politicians and all types of celebrities. These might not be backers," Heather scrolled to the next page. "This may be a customer list. What do you think? This goes to Kate?"

"What else do we have?"

"A copy of a tax form. The auditors on Kate's team will drool all over this because Della included a copy of an accountant's initial report that highlights the irregularities in accounting and what the standard accepted practice is, and here's the final report that essentially says there is nothing to see here." Heather chuckled. "Have you heard that saying before? It means to look the other way. Did you send this to Larry?"

I frowned. "I did, right after I got it, but I didn't send him the honey boy text because I didn't realize they were related. Larry hasn't said anything about the email, and neither have I, but both of us have been busy. I'll mention it to him when he calls and tell him we're sending it to Kate then text him the password, so he can read it too."

CHAPTER TWENTY

"There is a lot more evidence here, including real estate deals that look really shady to me," Heather said. "Most of the real estate contracts are signed by Flint Turner. This is a gold mine, isn't it?"

I grinned. "It's glorious; I can only imagine how long this is going to keep Kate busy and out of my hair."

Palace Guard frowned, and I wrinkled my nose at him.

"Why would Gary need to steal this? Couldn't he have just asked nicely?" I asked.

"I'll keep reading; there must be something...this is not good."

"What is it? What did you find?"

"Ten or so contracts on the conglomerate form for several hundred thousand dollars each for Coyle Detective Agency to provide investigative services, and the contracts are signed by Kate Coyle. This is awful: that amount of money would not be for investigative services; it looks like a payoff. We need a copy of Kate's signature. How do we do that?" Heather asked.

"Paul can handle it. I'll talk to him." I picked up my phone. "Call Paul."

Paul answered. "Please state your emergency."

Heather and I giggled.

"No emergency. How's Julie?" I asked.

"She's doing much better. I'm going to drop her off at the hospital after we eat this evening, so she can keep Martha company. Tonya is out of intensive care and claims her hearing aids itch too much right now. I think Tonya is brilliant. So, why did you really call?"

"I need a copy of Kate's signature, preferably several copies on different dates."

"Okay; that's easy. How fast?"

"Tonight would be okay."

"On it." Paul hung up.

"That was impressive. You and Paul have a great trust relationship, don't you?"

"Paul said it's because we both have the same dark side."

"Wow," Heather said. "That means that neither one of you can get away with anything because the other one will bust you."

"It's very annoying sometimes," I said.

I strolled to the window. "I'm going to watch for Gary and yell at him for frightening my dog. Do we have a broom or mop that I can wave in a threatening manner?"

"Put me down as officially advising you against such an ill-conceived idea, but I'll record it if you like, and if you run low on words, I'll be happy to take over with some juicy street words that Sarge never allowed me to use in the office. I'm sure housekeeping has a nice mop that I could borrow for you."

"You can't do that." I rolled my eye.

"Watch me," Heather said. "Oh wait, you can't."

I laughed. "That was a joke worthy of Tonya. She always tells me, 'See you before you see me.'"

Heather laughed. "Tonya sounds awesome."

"She really is."

Heather's phone buzzed a text. "The courier is ready to meet me in front of the post office. Do you want to go with me? It won't take long."

"I'll stay here," I said.

"Are you sure?" Heather asked. "Does that growly look on your face mean you think I'm hovering as badly as Julie? Fine, I'll go, and you stay."

After Heather left, I peered out the window but didn't see Gary.

"I want to know whether Gary is working today, but I can't see much from this window."

Palace Guard shook his head then disappeared. When Palace Guard reappeared, he nodded his head.

"Show me where he is." I headed to the front door.

Palace Guard scowled.

"If he sees me outside, maybe he'll tell me what's going on. I could sit on the bench outside the playground."

Palace Guard's scowl changed to a frown.

I turned my head away. *If he doesn't see me gloat, it doesn't count.*

After we went outside, Palace Guard guided me to the bench. While I sat, I enjoyed the warm rays of the sun and the songs from the birds in the surrounding trees.

Palace Guard tapped on my shoulder, and I turned in the direction he pointed then watched Gary push a wheelbarrow full of mulch toward me.

He stopped at the bench. "You make it dang hard for me to keep you safe, Maggie. Lucy terrified three of the toughest guys I know." He sighed. "I would have given you your laptop back. It's not safe for you to have the documents Della and Macy copied last week."

"Why not?"

"There's a cartel that would kill for those documents, and I'm not exaggerating; they may not realize yet that you have them, so you need to get rid of them. I'd tell you to give them to me, but I've lost my creds with you. Call Kate and turn them over to her."

I nodded as I rose. "Thanks for the advice."

Palace Guard and I returned to the apartment.

"If I want to go somewhere without Gary following me, I'll have to be sneaky like Della. Of course, that's it."

I picked up my phone. "Call Nell."

When Nell answered, I said, "I realized that you felt a little nervous about going alone to take the pictures at the campground this afternoon. Heather and I are available, and truthfully, I'm bored with Larry still in Tennessee; we'd enjoy the drive in the country with you, and we can wait in the car while you take pictures or walk around with you, whichever makes you comfortable."

"You're right; Flint told me the gate will be locked and gave me a key, so I have been anxious because I don't think anybody will be there to help me if I fall or come across a snake. Thank you; if you can be at my office at three, we'll leave from here."

When Heather returned, she said, "I have Della's key chain and a few other things that I'll examine after I listen to the recording. I thought I had my earbuds that fit the key chain, but I don't; I'll have to pick up a set of earbuds at the electronics store."

"We're invited to go with Nell to take pictures at the campground; we'll meet her at her office at three. I noticed she seemed nervous about it when she talked about it this morning, so I called her and offered to go along."

"Both of us? What's up your sleeve, Gray Lady?"

"We'll be sneaky like Della and visit the campground with a legitimate excuse to see and hear whatever we can."

My phone announced, "Call from Martha."

After I answered, Martha said, "Before you ask, Tonya's feeling great; we're hoping the doctor will release her today, but it may be tomorrow. One of the chefs will come to your hotel on Tuesday, Thursday, and Friday at four in the afternoon, so plan on eating around six. The first chef will prepare chicken fried chicken and gravy to show off her rustic style; at least that's what she called it. I told the chef to plan on three people because Julie admitted to me that her doctor put her on a low fat, low protein diet for a while."

"I don't see how you do it all, but thank you," I said.

"You're welcome; I've enjoyed getting to know you. Tonya wants you and Heather to come to our house for dinner on Wednesday. I'll check in with you tomorrow."

After I hung up, I said, "Martha told the chefs to plan for three people for the interview meals because Julie is on a restricted diet."

"I'm glad that's decided. If we leave for Nell's office in fifteen minutes, we'll arrive early and won't add to Nell's anxiety, then we can stop at the electronics store on our way back."

When we went into the real estate building, Heather said, "I'm Maggie's friend, Heather. What's wrong, Ms. Nell?"

Nell sniffled. "I'm so sorry; the stress is just getting me down."

"Shall I drive?" Heather asked. "I'm a well-trained, safe driver; Kevin and I were coworkers before he accepted the GBI position."

"It certainly is comforting to have a police officer with us, Heather, and I think it's a great idea for you to drive while I pull myself together. Here's the address, or would you rather I gave you directions?" Nell asked.

"I'll just pop that address into my phone, and my gps will take us right there," Heather said.

When we reached Nell's car, Heather opened the back door for me, and Palace Guard and I climbed into the backseat; Nell sat in the passenger's seat.

On the way, Nell said, "It was just about the last straw, Maggie. The sellers of your house called me; they want to take the house off the market and rent it. It's up to you because we have a contract; do you want to discuss it with Kevin?"

"I'm so sorry, Nell. I love that house; did they say why?"

"It's been in the wife's family for ages, and she doesn't want to let go. She decided she'd rather rent it, and her husband relented; evidently this is something they've been discussing for quite a while."

"That might work; how long do they expect to rent it?"

"Her husband has a five-year contract, so at least five years. The advantage for you is that you could move in as early as this weekend. The disadvantage is that five years from now you could be looking at houses again."

"I'll talk to Kevin," I said.

"The driveway is coming up on the left, Heather," Nell said.

"Thanks; it's really hidden, isn't it?"

"I've never been good with keys and locks; I'm a magician when it comes to lockboxes, but locks themselves befuddle me. Isn't that strange for a real estate agent?" Nell chuckled.

"Not really; it all depends on your familiarity. I'm not sure I could manage a lockbox," Heather said. "Do you want to give me the key, and I'll unlock the gate?"

"I would appreciate it," Nell said. "It was really oily when Flint gave it to me, but I scrubbed it with soap and warm water. Why do people oil a key like that?"

"Sometimes people think it's what they're supposed to do when a lock is new." Heather grabbed her backpack as she climbed out of the car.

While Heather unlocked the gate then rolled it back, Nell said, "The oily key surprised me because it was a sticky oily, like peanut butter; I would have left sticky fingerprints everywhere."

"I would have done exactly what you did; I couldn't deal with sticky fingers either." I shuddered appropriately. *I wonder if Nell knows what a brilliant move that was.*

Heather climbed back into the driver's seat. "Here's your key, Nell."

Heather drove very slowly; Palace Guard narrowed his eyes and carefully scanned both sides of the driveway. When we reached the main building, Heather pulled into the parking lot then turned the car around and parked in the driveway. "I thought you'd rather not have your car in the promotion photos," she said. "We'll stay here by the car unless there's anything I can do to help."

"I'll take a few shots of the front of the building, then I'd like for you to help me inside," Nell said. "Too bad the spotlights across the front aren't on; it would be a far better photo with more light on the porch, so it doesn't look so dim."

Nell climbed out of the car then Heather whispered, "Take some videos of the trucks then put some gps trackers on every vehicle you can find along the side of the building." Heather reached back and handed me a small plastic bag.

After Heather joined Nell, I climbed out of the car and stretched, then Palace Guard and I strolled to the side of the building. Palace Guard pointed to back bumpers, wheel wells, and front bumpers as I strolled along toward the back. I held onto my jo as I leaned down to place a gps at each location that Palace Guard pointed to along the way. *Seven trucks and panel vans.*

Palace Guard strode toward the back of the house then disappeared around the corner. When he returned, he held up one hand.

"Five more trucks?" I whispered, and he nodded.

"Can I slip around the corner and put trackers on all of them?"

Palace Guard disappeared then returned. He shook his head then curled his fingers and put them on his thumb to make a circle. When he brought his hand up to his eye, I whispered, "Security cameras?"

He nodded; we headed back to the car.

I frowned. "Do you think I could disable them?"

Palace Guard grinned and nodded.

"Let's do it then."

I grabbed my backpack, and Palace Guard guided me to a side door. When I reached for the door handle, he shook his head and pointed up. *I feel like such a rookie. Of course, the door is alarmed.*

I peered at the alarm. *It's old and would be simple for me to disarm if I were taller.*

Palace Guard looked around, then pointed to a ladder on top of a truck. I climbed up on the truck then onto the roof and removed all the straps before I pushed the ladder off the top of the truck. I cringed as I waited for the ladder to crash to the ground. When I didn't hear anything, I peered over the side, and the ladder was on the ground. *Of course, Palace Guard caught it then set it down.*

I wrapped up two of the straps then stuffed them into my backpack. *Never know when a set of good quality ratchet straps will come in handy.*

After I climbed down, the ladder was in place near the alarm, and Palace Guard smirked.

I climbed up the ladder and disabled the alarm. When we went inside the building, Palace Guard led me to a panel.

Palace Guard guided my hand as I flipped the circuit breakers that he selected, then we left. After I reset the alarm on the door, we took down the ladder then put it on the ground next to the truck.

We hurried to the back, and I put gps trackers on the vehicles then returned to the car.

"We got back first," I whispered, and Palace Guard and I smacked a high five.

When Nell and Heather came out of the front of the main building, Nell said, "Thank you for your help, Heather. You really have a photographer's eye. Have you thought about photography as a career? You're a natural."

Heather giggled. "I do love taking pictures, but I could never be a professional."

When Heather opened the back door for me, I passed the empty plastic sack to her.

"A dozen?" she whispered. "What did you do? Go around back?"

I bit my lip and climbed into the backseat as Heather muttered, "I can't wait to hear this story."

After we returned to her office, Nell said, "I cannot tell you how much I appreciate your help, Heather. Let me know if you change your mind about photography because I have contacts. I'll be interested in hearing what Kevin thinks about the sellers' request, Maggie. I'll cancel the home inspection; I cannot tell you how bad I feel about this terrible turn of events."

"It will all work out," I said.

On the way home, Heather said, "Tell me where the dozen gps trackers are."

"Long answer or short?"

"Definitely long."

I told Heather about the seven vehicles along the side of the building, five trucks in the back, the security cameras, the alarm, the ladder, the circuit panel, and placing the gps trackers on all the vehicles.

"You did all that while Nell and I were inside? I feel like such a slacker."

"Actually, I couldn't have done any of it without you because you kept Nell occupied. What do you plan to do with your copy of the gate key?"

"I'm not surprised you caught that. I don't know; it just seemed important."

Heather pulled into a small parking lot. "There's an electronics store in this strip mall. I'll be right back."

When she returned, Heather waved a small sack. "I have my earbuds."

After Heather parked at the hotel, Palace Guard and I headed to our suite while Heather locked her car. I went inside, and Palace Guard followed me but left the door partially ajar because Heather was close behind him.

"Heather," Gary said.

I stopped near the door to listen.

"I don't have any reason to talk to you, Gary." Heather put her hand on the doorknob.

"I know, but I need you to tell Maggie something for me."

Heather snorted. "Tell her yourself."

"I can't do that. She doesn't trust me, and I'm afraid she'd shoot me on sight."

"I fail to see the downside of that." Heather stepped inside then turned to face Gary before she closed the door. "You know she's blind, right? But she wouldn't miss," Heather growled as she slammed the door.

"You heard?" she asked. "I couldn't believe the audacity..." Heather exhaled. "He was annoying me."

"Does it seem to you like he really does have something to tell me?"

"I don't know; he's very insistent, isn't he?" Heather went to the window to peer outside. "He's gone."

Spike shook his head and pointed to the backyard.

I rolled my eye. *Gary's sitting at the patio table.*

"Stay close to the back door and listen, Heather."

Heather headed toward the back door. "What are you..." She snorted. "He must have run to the backyard."

Palace Guard stayed close to me as I neared the patio table.

"Get to the point, Gary, or I'll cut your lying throat." I sat at the table across from him and dropped my left hand to my thigh, so I could easily reach my knife.

"I know you will, Maggie, but this is important for you to know since I blew any chance of helping you. The documents you have from Della implicate Kate's involvement in a shady deal. The point of putting suspicion on Kate is to divert the entire investigation into proving that Kate is innocent. The problem is that the lead on the team who will be investigating Kate is also the man who planted the phony evidence and is the head of the human trafficking ring; you are a real threat to him."

"Who is it?"

"His name is Fletcher Turnage, but he's used another name for years."

"Flint Turner," I said, and he nodded.

"You know him?" Gary asked.

"I know of him, and I know his voice because he came into the real estate office while I was in there."

"That wasn't an accident." Gary exhaled.

"I don't think so, either. Anything else you wanted to say to me?" I rose from my chair.

"I don't suppose you'd let me be included in your plans."

"Not hardly."

Palace Guard and I went inside, and I quietly closed the door then locked it with a satisfyingly loud click.

"Did you hear that?" I asked.

"All of it. I'm going to listen to what Della recorded."

While Heather listened, Paul called me.

"Glenn and I have identified all of the board members with the exception of the chairman of the board. The name Flint Turner keeps popping up, but Glenn says that is a false trail, so we're still looking."

"I'm not so sure it's a false trail," I said.

"He's Kate's number two man and has been for a few years, Maggie."

"Gary told me Flint Turner's real name is Fletcher Turnage."

"You talked to Gary?" Paul asked.

"It's a long story."

"Did you shoot him?"

"He told Heather he was afraid I would, and she told him she failed to see the downside."

Paul guffawed. "I almost feel sorry for Gary, but at least his peace offering may help us out. Glenn and I will dig into Fletcher Turnage."

After Paul hung up, Heather said, "We need to look at all of the honey boy documents carefully. Della said Kate's signature was forged on all of the contracts that were supposed to prove that Kate had accepted money to look the other way, and while a simple investigation would discover that very quickly, Flint Turner would drag out the entire investigation and divert all the resources from the racketeering, drug, and human trafficking teams to the team that was working to clear Kate. Della included documents that proved that Fletcher Turnage is Flint Turner and is also the leader of a long-standing cartel that has shifted to human trafficking in addition to their established money laundering, extortion, racketeering, and monopoly on drug channels."

Heather picked up the menus. "We need burgers and sweet tea. I'll order a cheeseburger then pick it up, so we can share it and still have room for ice cream after we talk to Larry."

After we ate our cheeseburger, Larry called. "I'm ready to listen."

I told him about the sellers deciding they didn't want to sell the house after all and asking us to release them from the contract. "They are offering us the opportunity to rent it. What do you think?"

"I like the house with the plans that we had for it; I doubt if the current owners share our vision, so we'd never see the changes that we considered. I don't mind releasing them from the contract, but if we're going to rent, let's find something that's right for us."

"I agree, honey. We have our long-term suite, and it's comfortable for us. We don't have to be in a rush."

"What else?"

"I forwarded an email to you that Della sent to me. I'm sure you haven't had a chance to look at it, but the attached document is password protected. I can give you the password, but Della left a recording that Heather recovered tonight."

"I'll send you a transcript of the recording in the morning," Heather said, "but you need the transcript as a guide when you read the documents."

Heather elbowed me.

"Three men had a key to our suite, but Lucy and Spike chased them off. Lucy bit all three of them, and Heather gathered the evidence."

"I'd like to turn over the evidence photos and blood samples that I collected to the local GBI office and hoped that you could coordinate that for me," Heather said.

"I'll let you know who will be contacting you first thing in the morning. How did they get a key?"

"That's a great question; we're not sure, but we think they got it from the maintenance shed," Heather said. "I'm sure that will be where the investigator will start."

"What's the password?" Larry asked.

"I'll text it to you," I said. "The only other thing we have is that the chefs will be preparing meals on Tuesday, Thursday, and Friday this week, so Paul will fill in for you on Tuesday and Thursday, then you'll have a chef meal on Friday. How was your first day?"

"Not nearly as rough as last week." Larry chuckled. "I still have some research to do this evening; the class is informative but still challenging."

"Right up your alley, Agent Ewing," I said. "I'll send you the password."

"Wait for my transcript, though," Heather said. "It will put some of the documents in perspective."

After we hung up, Heather said, "Not bad, Gray Lady, but we'll still be in trouble later because of everything we left out. Send Nell a text, and I'll dish up a little ice cream."

I sent the password to Larry and texted Nell that we wanted to continue looking for another house.

Larry replied, "Thanks. I know there is more."

"Are we in pre-trouble?" Heather giggled.

"Do we want to read the rest of the documents?" I took another bite of ice cream.

Nell replied to my text, "Understood. I'll search for new listings tomorrow."

"I don't think we'll find anything that Della didn't mention, but there may be some details about the camp that might help us; it's up to you."

I nodded. "I'm glad we went with Nell because we have reference points."

"Are we going to turn over what we found to..." Heather sighed. "I was going to say Kate, but we would be instantly alerting Flint Turner, wouldn't we? I don't know anyone at the Savannah GBI office, does Larry?"

Heather's phone rang. "I don't recognize this number; do you suppose Larry had someone at his new office on speed dial? I'll answer with the speaker on."

"Detective Kaminski? My name is Adam Wagner; I'm the crime scene investigator at the GBI office in Statesboro. Agent Ewing gave me your name and number and told me you had some evidence for me. Could you and Mrs. Ewing come to our office in the morning when it's convenient for you?"

I nodded, and Heather replied, "Thank you; we'll see you in the morning."

After Heather hung up, I said, "I'll listen while you read."

"Perfect, I'll start us where we left off because I didn't see anything about the camp in what we've covered so far."

I listened while Heather read.

"Stop a second," I said. "What was that about the supply chain in the memo?"

Heather read aloud. "The distribution channel is drying up because the intermediaries are syphoning a high percentage of the product to their own customers. We will shut down our offending distributors before the end of this month and open a direct selling channel at the first of next month to boost our profit."

"What does that mean?" I asked.

"This actually makes sense to me because there has been a marked increase in murders of gang leaders over the past month or so. The assumption has been that there is an ongoing turf war, but it sounds like the cartel is sending a message to its intermediaries."

"It fits, doesn't it?"

CHAPTER TWENTY-ONE

"There's really a lot here," Heather said. "We'll go to the GBI office right after breakfast because I have a feeling Agent Wagner will be a receptive audience to all our theories."

"That's different for me," I said. "I'm not used to anyone believing what I know before I uncover all the facts."

Heather snorted. "Only because you don't share your theories until the bad guy is dead."

My phone announced a text. "From Roxanne. NOW."

Heather peered at my phone. "It's in all caps. What does it mean?"

"We need dark clothes." I rushed to the bedroom with Palace Guard and Heather following me. "After Palace Guard gave Roxanne her phone, she sent me a text that said, 'No rescue yet.' We need to go now."

"Palace Guard, grab a dark long-sleeved T-shirt for Maggie and her darkest pair of jeans. I'll change too."

I changed then hurried to the living room.

"You're wearing a black T-shirt; perfect. What's our plan?" Heather asked.

"We'll drive most of the way there and hide the car in a field or trees then go through the woods to approach the campground."

"I think I spotted the perfect place when we went to the campground with Nell," Heather said.

I continued, "Palace Guard can check to see if the gate is open and if there are any bad guys around." I glanced at Palace Guard, and he nodded. "Our first priority is to release Roxanne, then get all the girls out."

"How will we get them out?" Heather asked.

"The best way would be for them to all jump into the back of a truck, then you could drive them out. Roxanne and I could cover your back." I picked up my backpack. "I can't think of anything else I need to take. Are you set?"

"I'll take my backpack, and I have a pistol I can give to Roxanne; better yet, she could drive, and I'll stay," Heather said.

On the way to the campground, Heather grumbled, "How are we going to convince all those girls to hurry quietly to a truck and be closed up again? Why can't I stay back and shoot with you?"

"I don't have a firm plan yet; maybe Roxanne can convince them. We'll have to figure that out. I'm not sure Roxanne knows the roads well enough to drive to town. We'll have to play that by ear too."

"Now I remember why you have always scared Larry so badly; you've just said the most terrifying words I've ever heard in my entire life: play it by ear. My perfect place to ditch the car is just ahead."

Heather slowed the car then turned. "Hang on."

I clutched the armrests as the car lurched and rocked on the rough ground and shivered when the high weeds scratched along the sides of the car.

Heather parked, then we quietly exited the car and eased the doors closed. "Let's get into the trees; we have a little cloud cover, but there's enough moonlight to make me nervous."

Palace Guard guided me into the trees then disappeared; I turned off my phone.

"Palace Guard is going to scope out the campground," I whispered. "Do you think you could get us a little closer? He'll find me."

Heather stepped in front of me. "My left arm on your right side."

I put my fingertips on her arm, and we quietly treaded through the woods.

When Palace Guard reappeared, I whispered, "Stop. Palace Guard is here."

Palace Guard held up eight fingers.

"Eight men?" I whispered, and he nodded.

"Can we avoid them and get to Roxanne?" I asked, and he nodded again.

"He said yes, follow me," I said.

Palace Guard led us in our silent hike to the campground. When we reached a wire fence, Heather whispered, "I have wire cutters; can I cut it?"

Palace Guard nodded, so I nodded.

I heard the quiet snip, snip as Heather cut the wire.

We waited, and I listened to the shouts of men from the front of the main building. When Palace Guard moved his arm to indicate a forward motion, I copied him for Heather to see, then he led us away from the shouts and the bright spotlights.

After we reached the side door, Palace Guard held up eight fingers again then pointed to the main building. He led us away from the front in the pale moonlight; when we rounded the corner, Heather poked my back.

I nodded. *All the vehicles that were back here are gone.*

Palace Guard continued toward a small, cinderblock structure that reminded me of a bath house at a rustic campground.

"Roxanne?" I mouthed, and Palace Guard nodded, so I did too.

He led us around to the back then pointed to a door that appeared to be a storage closet. Heather quickly picked the lock then gasped at the sight of the blob who was curled in a fetal position in a corner.

"She's been badly beaten," Heather whispered.

Roxanne. I quietly whistled a song as I knelt next to her.

"Gray Lady," she whispered. "Help me up; let's get the girls."

Heather lifted Roxanne as I continued to whistle.

Heather whispered, "I'll take you to a safe place to wait for us while we get the girls."

Roxanne gasped for breath with her first few steps then slowed her breathing.

Heather led Roxanne away from the terrifying lockup; Palace Guard and I followed them until Palace Guard diverted me in the opposite direction; we stopped in front of a large steel storage building.

Heather slipped up behind us. "Roxanne won't leave the property without the girls. She showed me a truck that has a clear path to the exit; she's hiding close to it. She wants us to transport the girls and her in the truck; would that work?"

Palace Guard disappeared. When he returned, he nodded then mimed driving and pointed to Heather.

"Palace Guard said the keys are in the truck, and it's clear to drive it out, but you will have to drive it."

"I can't leave you alone; Roxanne has to drive the truck," Heather whispered then exhaled. "She'd be determined enough to do it, but I don't know if she's strong enough."

Palace Guard shook his head.

"Palace Guard said she isn't; if you drive, Roxanne can ride in the back with the girls."

"I hate this; I hate this," Heather muttered. "Larry should be here too."

Palace Guard and I nodded our agreement.

"I'll hand you my two pistols before I get into the driver's seat." Heather picked the lock then opened the door. "The girls are huddled in the far corner. Time for a fairy tune, Gray Lady."

While I stood near the door and softly whistled, Heather cooed as she slowly approached the corner. "Time to go home, sweet girls." Her voice had a soft lilt that reminded me of Mother.

She quietly sang along with my tune, "We'll all sneak out together; as quiet as we can be. Not a word, not a whisper, and soon we will be free. No one will ever see us or hear us slip away; the soft night will hide us, and away we soon will be."

The girls followed Heather as she quietly repeated her soft song and led them to the truck. I followed them and hummed. When Heather reached the truck, Palace Guard quietly opened the door, and the group slipped inside. "Hold on to each other," Heather whispered. "I'll be driving, and I might have to drive fast over bumpy roads; away we soon will be."

"Away we soon will be," Roxanne whispered.

Palace Guard quietly closed the door, and Heather handed me her two pistols then raced around to start the truck.

Palace Guard guided me close to the main building. Men shouted when the roar of the truck's engine filled the night.

"Hey, stop!" One blob shouted as he ran toward the truck. Heather swerved to hit him, and he cursed as he fell in his rush to get out of the path of the truck.

Two blobs ran down the driveway after the truck while five blobs ran to the other trucks.

"Keys are gone," a man shouted. "Somebody get the keys."

"Get them yourself," someone else shouted.

Palace Guard tapped my arm and guided me to the fence then through the woods to Heather's car.

I listened to the beautiful wail of sirens. "Heather called for backup," I whispered; Palace Guard nodded.

I shivered. "I'm freezing, and I don't care."

Palace Guard shook his head.

The flashing lights on the cruisers raced past us on the road, then I smiled at the shouts coming from the campground. *Not one shot fired.*

When a car pulled into the grass behind Heather's car, I dropped down into the grass. The car headlights went off, then Paul whispered, "Maggie?"

I rose and brushed myself off. "Right here," I said.

He hurried to me. "Is your phone off? I tried to call you. Heather sent me to pick you up. She said she would be a while at the police station and thought you might like a ride home."

"I turned it off when we parked. Did Heather call Larry?"

"I don't know if she's had time; she called me right after she called nine-one-one."

"I think I'll leave my phone off until I'm home."

"Turn it on, Maggie. You just terrorized a gang of thugs; you can deal with a phone call."

Palace Guard poked my back and grinned.

I turned on my phone; it announced, "Text from Larry: You better be at home hiding under the bed. Call me."

Paul laughed. "Good news travels fast, but bad news is faster."

"Thanks for picking me up," I said as Paul parked at the hotel in front of my suite.

"I'll wait until you're inside, then I'll pick up Heather and bring her here. We can get her car tomorrow," Paul said.

After Palace Guard and I were inside, I hurried to the bedroom and put on my sweatshirt then called Larry.

"Are you at home?" he asked. "You wouldn't believe the story I heard."

"The story about Heather rescuing Roxanne and kidnapped girls then stealing a truck?"

"That's the one except she wasn't alone. I didn't think it was you because I heard that not one shot was fired. Are you slipping, sweetie?"

"You're not leaving me much wiggle room," I said.

Larry chuckled. "I should be mad, but I also heard that Roxanne texted you to rescue her and the girls immediately."

"That's one part I can confirm."

"I know you were there because Roxanne claimed she and the girls were calmed by a song that wasn't like anything else she'd ever heard before. You whistled one of your fairy songs, didn't you, sweetie? I know that's the only way the girls could have been moved from where they'd been imprisoned to the truck so quickly and quietly."

Larry's voice softened. "Heather called me while she waited for the ambulances to take Roxanne and the girls to the hospital to be examined and fed. She was terrified because she had to leave you, even though she knew Palace Guard was with you. I love you, sweetheart; four more days then I can yell at you because it's much more satisfying than yelling on the phone." Larry chuckled, then hung up before I could say anything.

When Heather arrived, I opened the door and hugged her.

"You aren't mad at me for calling Larry?" she asked.

"Of course not. He told me he'd yell at me in four days. Best news ever," I said.

Heather giggled. "Wine or beer?"

"I don't care; you pick. I put your two pistols on the counter."

"Do you have a second weapon as a back-up? Keep one of my pistols, if you like because I have my concealed and a pistol in my backpack."

"Did you feel naked without your second concealed pistol?"

While Heather opened a bottle of wine, she said, "Moe called the GBI office and tried to bribe one of the guys into taking a picture of me with my empty holster, and the agent refused. That's one advantage of having a history as an undercover cop; I dress up fancy, and Moe's just another cop. I've worked with two of the men here at the GBI office. They knew your reputation, which is another reason I called Larry. I wanted him to hear our version, but I got the distinct impression it wasn't news to him."

"How's Roxanne?"

"Her spirits are surprisingly good; she's very resilient. Her body however, is a mess of bruises and broken bones. The hospital called in a therapist for the girls right away. The girls came from different towns and states, so they didn't know each other before they were kidnapped. The therapist told me they looked after each other, which she found amazing, and would have only a few scars with a little follow up and extra support."

"Palace Guard saw more kidnapped girls at the campground than what we found; do you think your gps trackers will help?" I asked.

"I'm positive they will; I gave Adam Wagner the tracking information, but he wasn't surprised that I had twelve gps trackers or that you put a tracker on the vehicles. Della's honey boy document will be a huge help in finding others too."

We took our wine to the patio and relaxed while Lucy wandered the backyard, and Spike gazed at Heather.

"Don't stare, Spike. I got plenty of that at the police station," Heather said.

Spike pouted then joined Lucy in the yard but continued glancing at Heather.

"I think I'm finally relaxing," I said. "Sure was a good plan, wasn't it?"

Heather snort-laughed. "I thought I was going to have a heart attack when you said play it by ear, but when I had to leave you, I was certain Larry would never speak to me again, and I knew I'd never forgive myself because I left you to be slaughtered. What did you and Palace Guard do? Just walk away while they fought among themselves?"

"Sure; I figured I'd let them work it out without my interference. Thanks for sending Paul to pick me up; it turned cold fast." I yawned.

"Bedtime, Gray Lady."

We went inside; I climbed under the covers and closed my eye.

After I dressed the next morning, I heard the shower running, Heather humming our fairy song from last night, and the coffeemaker gurgling in the kitchen.

I sat at the kitchen table and waited for the coffee. Lucy whined, and I grabbed my sweatshirt, then Spike and I took her outside.

When Palace Guard joined us, I asked, "Is the sun coming up?"

Palace Guard's smile was weak as he nodded.

"I'm kind of sad I can't smell or hear the sunrise," I said, "but no one else can either, can they?"

Palace Guard rolled his eyes then mimed drinking from a cup with two hands.

"You're right; I really do need coffee." We went inside, and Heather had poured my cup.

"What's on the agenda for today, Gray Lady? We're having dinner with Paul here tonight, and I'm looking forward to that. Paul's going to take me to pick up my car after we have breakfast. Anything special you want to do? I think I need to go shopping for a warm sweatshirt. It was chilly last night."

I sipped my coffee. "I wouldn't mind keeping a sweatshirt in my backpack."

"Good; it's settled. What about breakfast? I feel like making an omelet."

I nodded and listened to Heather while she talked and put together an omelet.

My phone rang and announced, "Call from Tonya."

I squealed as I answered, and Heather chuckled.

"Homey, home, home," Tonya said. "You and Heather are coming to Mom's for dinner tomorrow night, right? I need to know because I'm no longer in the hospital: I'm home."

Tonya chattered, and Heather refilled my coffee cup.

"Breakfast is ready," Heather said.

"Mine is too," Tonya said. "See you tomorrow before you see me."

Tonya giggled as she hung up.

"Tonya feels better," I said.

"Talk about good spirits; she's completely bounced back, hasn't she? Do you want any salsa? I ended up making a breadless burrito."

"Sounds good to me."

While we ate breakfast, my phone buzzed a text. "From Larry: Three. Told you first."

Heather chuckled. "He's really entertaining himself, isn't he?"

I smirked. "Send a reply to Larry: Three. Three. Three. Told you more."

Heather laughed. "He really left himself open for that one, didn't he? You two are a trip."

Heather's phone rang. "It's Paul."

"I'm listening." Heather strolled to the back door and went outside. When she returned, she said, "Paul will pick me up in ten minutes; he wants you to call him."

I called Paul.

"Hi, Chief. I may have found our first real client for the Gray Flanagan Agency. The client is in Savannah, and I'm meeting her at her office this afternoon at one o'clock. Julie thinks we should open an office in Savannah, so we won't conflict with the Coyle Detective Agency. What do you think?"

"I think it has possibilities. What about your work with Glenn?"

"He and I have already discussed it, and we'll still collaborate. I'd like to think about hiring staff, so I offered Heather a job in operations, and she didn't immediately turn me down. I know you told me operations is up to me, but I'd like for you to help me with interviewing and selecting staff."

"I think that's a great idea; I'm not as great with hands-off as I thought."

"No kidding. If we have an office here, we'll need an office manager, but first things first: I'm starting to develop contacts and line up work for us. I'll let you know how this afternoon goes."

After I hung up, Heather asked, "Did he tell you? What do you think?"

"I think Paul plans to put you in charge of the stealing trucks division. I'm wondering if you're overqualified."

"Steal one truck, and they never forget." She giggled.

"What about Todd?"

"He's a wonderful, dedicated man, but we have completely different ideas on how our two different career paths can coexist. He isn't content to remain teaching at a successful school system in a small town; he wants to live in a big city and make a difference in a failing school system. I have to be an investigator and ferret out bad guys. He's afraid I'd put his most promising students in jail, and I'm certain he's right."

"It's up to you. As a private investigator, you won't be able to arrest anyone; you'd have to hand them off to the Moes of this world."

"Even Chief Detective Moe Ross is getting tired of it, but you're right: I wouldn't have any control over whether a bad guy is arrested. Paul told me to take my time because it's a big decision. His parting shot was that you were the chief. I think I could sign up half the Harperville Police Department on that alone; we'd never have a staffing problem. I'll talk to Larry sometime to get his take; he's levelheaded and won't pull any punches."

Before Paul picked up Heather, Nell called me. "Hi, Gray Lady. I have some paperwork that needs to be signed: you know, on the contract for the house. Could you be here around ten or a little earlier? I have honey buns; I know they are your favorite."

"Sure. I think Paul or Heather could drop me off."

"That's nice; I'm looking forward to meeting your friend, Heather."

After we hung up, I frowned. *How many red flags can be thrown in one short phone conversation?*

"Everything okay? You look funny."

"Nell has paperwork for me to sign. I assume it's the release of the contract, but it was a really odd conversation. I don't think this is a scam or anything, but I'll ask her to email me a copy while I'm there, and I'll forward it to Shantelle then call her to make sure it's okay for me to sign it."

"Sounds like the best way to go. Paul's going to be here in ten minutes; Paul and I can drop you off at Nell's office, then I'll pick you up."

"Perfect. I know this is a little far-fetched, but do you happen to have a left-handed holster I could use for the pistol you loaned me?"

"I may; give me a second to look in my equipment bag."

After I put on my sweatshirt, Heather said, "Ah-ha! Found it."

She handed it to me. "It's an outside holster, so you'll need to wear a belt."

I hurried to my closet, and Palace Guard followed me then guided me to a belt; I put on the belt and returned to the living room.

"That's perfect; I'll help you with the holster."

After my holster was in place, I slipped the pistol into the holster then out again.

"It's perfect for the holster," Heather said.

"Paul's here," I said.

After Paul parked in front of Nell's office, he asked, "Shall we wait for you?"

"No, it's supposed to be just paperwork, but I don't know how long I'll be. Heather's going to pick me up when she returns to town."

"Okay, Chief. Call me if you need me."

I sighed. *Why has Paul decided to call me Chief?*

After Paul drove away, I noticed the sign on the door. Palace Guard motioned around the building. "We're supposed to go around back?"

Palace Guard nodded then disappeared around the corner.

When he returned, he held up two fingers.

"Two men?"

He nodded then held up both hands as he pointed his index fingers and held his thumbs up.

"Both armed?"

He nodded again.

"An ambush. Glad I'm not taking just a knife to a gunfight. You'll position me in the best place to shoot both; I'll listen for the pebble, and you'll let me know when to dive down, right?"

Palace Guard scowled, but he nodded.

I removed my sweatshirt and dropped it next to the building after we were off the sidewalk. As we slowly stepped to the back of the building, I paused then frowned. *Did something move across the street to my right?* I turned on the record button on my jo and tried to will my eye to focus, but I didn't see anything.

When I neared the alley, I paused again while Palace Guard disappeared.

I peered to my right. *Nothing there.*

Palace Guard returned and guided me forward, and we moved quickly.

As I rounded the corner, I dropped my jo while it was still recording then put my left hand on the butt of Heather's pistol; Palace Guard positioned me on the far right side of the alley, so I wouldn't be too close to the building.

The man who ran the track when I did said, "Hey, Gray Lady. Haven't seen you in a while. Some of my friends were arrested last night. Did you have anything to do with that?" *He is close to the real estate office.*

"I don't know. What were they doing?" I put my right hand near my waist.

"Don't be coy," Flint Turner said. "Talk's over."

Flint Turner is standing a little to the right of the middle of the alley.

"Right, boss."

Palace Guard tossed a pebble to the left, and I pulled out my pistol and fired a split-second before the guy did; Palace Guard dived to the left, and I dived to the pea gravel in the alley alongside him then pulled and fired my pistol with my right hand straight ahead at the point where I heard him toss the second pebble. I heard the ring of a second shot over my head from the alley in front of me and a third shot from behind me after I dived. Shards of shattered brick hit my face. Palace

Guard tapped our 'run' signal, and I leapt to my feet and ran with Palace Guard as we zig-zagged to the front; I snatched up my jo and sweatshirt as we dashed past them.

When I reached the front of the real estate office, the sound of sirens ripped through the air, and the first cruisers raced to the alley while the second cruiser stopped near me.

A blob rushed to me. "Mrs. Ewing, Gray Lady, are you okay? Detective Kaminski called me and told me you were under fire at the real estate office. I'm Adam Wagner from the GBI office. You have cuts on your face. We'll have the paramedics check you as soon as they arrive."

A car slid to a stop; Heather-blob jumped out of the passenger's seat, and Paul-blob jumped out of the driver's seat.

"Your face is cut, Chief," Paul growled.

I rolled my eye. "They're superficial; I'm fine."

"All we need to do is wash your face, and you'll be as pretty as ever, Chief," Heather said.

Palace Guard smirked, and I stuck up my nose into the air.

Agent Wagner came close to me and spoke quietly. "Nell was bound and blindfolded in her office. She said she tried to warn you. Why don't you let Detective Kaminski take you home and care for your wounds. We'll take your statement later."

Heather put her arm protectively around me, then she and Paul walked me to Paul's car.

On the way back to the hotel, I growled, "Paul, why do you insist on calling me Chief? I'm not a chief of police, and I hope I never am."

"I was afraid you'd fire me if I called you Mrs. Ewing, so I tried Boss, but it didn't fit. I never had a boss that I could tolerate for long, but my favorite chief of police had a strong sense of integrity and a streak of orneriness; just like you," Paul said.

"I like to call you Chief because Paul does," Heather added, "and because it gets on your nerves."

Paul laughed, and Palace Guard grinned.

"It wasn't funny."

"Was too." Heather giggled.

I tried to hold it in, but Paul's laughter and Heather's giggle were catching, and I giggled too.

When Paul parked in front of the suite, Heather, Palace Guard, and I went inside.

"Call Larry," I said.

"I already heard," Larry said when he answered. "In fact, when GBI called, the instructor stopped the class, and we all listened to the report. You destroyed a major cartel when you took down Flint Turner. Three more days, sweetheart." He hung up.

I frowned. *Who called him first?*

CHAPTER TWENTY-TWO

Three Days Later

"Okay, Chief, I'm on board. I gave two weeks' notice, and I'll be working for you and Paul." Heather hugged me. "Don't do anything for two weeks because it's my job to steal the trucks."

After Heather left, I sat on the patio and waited for Larry.

I wasn't surprised when Gary joined me at the patio table. "I knew that was you behind me when I heard the third shot, Gary."

"I thought I could help you; instead, I had the pleasure of witnessing your remarkable skills. Your shadow reminded me of a Buckingham Guard. How is that possible?"

"I don't know, Gary, but thanks for having my back."

Gary swaggered to the gate then saluted Palace Guard. Palace Guard returned the salute, and I rolled my eye as Gary left.

I exhaled. "When will Larry be here?"

Palace Guard held up two fingers.

I moaned. "Two hours?"

Palace Guard smirked and shook his head.

"Two minutes?" I squealed and jumped up and ran to the front door.

Larry swept me up in his arms when I opened the door then kicked the door closed behind him.

He gently kissed me at first then with increasingly intense passion before he set me on my feet. While he unbuttoned my shirt, I unbuckled his belt; he exhaled then whispered, "I'll yell at you tomorrow."

ABOUT THE AUTHOR

Judith A. Barrett is an award-winning author of mystery, crime, and survival science fiction novels with action, adventure, and a touch of supernatural to spark the reader's imagination. Her unusual main characters are brilliant, talented, and down-to-earth folks who solve difficult problems and stop killers. Her novels are based in small towns and rural areas in south Georgia and north Florida with sojourns to other southern US states.

Judith lives in rural Georgia on a small farm with her husband and two dogs. When she's not busy writing, Judith is still busy working on the farm, hiking with her husband and dogs, or watching the beautiful sunsets from her porch.

Website   www.judithabarrett.com
Barrett Book Shop www.BarrettBookShop.com

Subscribe to the eNewsletter via her website!
Let's keep in touch!

ACKNOWLEDGEMENTS

Huge thanks to my husband for being the best business partner in the world by letting me run with the ball and sweetly guiding me back when I'm off track.

Thanks to my family and friends for their support, and to my beta readers and fierce editor.

Thank you for reading. *You keep reading; I'll keep writing!*

What to read next?
COUNTED IN BLOOD, BOOK 7
MAGGIE SLOAN THRILLER

Has Maggie finally met her match? A serial killer leaves a grisly message for Maggie: she's next.

Maggie and her Gray Flanagan Agency staff, Paul and Heather, have their first case: investigate the grisly murders of young women. When the team doubles-down to find the killer, Maggie gets too close, and the killer sends her a clear message: it's time for Maggie to die.

Subscribe: to the newsletter!

Look for the Subscribe button on www.judithabarrett.com

ALSO BY JUDITH A. BARRETT
Maggie Sloan Thriller Series
Grid Down Survival Series
Riley Malloy Thriller Series
Donut Lady Cozy Mystery Series

Judith A. Barrett writes Series of Books for you: Mystery/Thrillers, Sci Fi Survival Thriller, and Cozy Mystery ... Stories with a Twist!

You keep reading; I'll keep writing! ~ Judith